MORE BLOOD

BASED ON CHARACTERS AND CONCEPTS BY WARREN MURPHY AND RICHARD SAPIR

Edited by Donna Courtois and Devin Murphy

This is a work of fiction. All the characters and events portrayed in this book are fictional, and any resemblance to real people or real incidents is purely coincidental.

The use of characters and ideas from the intellectual property of Warren Murphy has been authorized for this book by Warren Murphy.

MORE BLOOD: A SINANJU ANTHOLOGY

Published in 2014 by Destroyer Books/Warren Murphy Media

ISBN-13: 978-0-9906566-5-4
ISBN-10: 0990656659

Requests for reproduction or interviews should be directed to
DestroyerBooks@gmail.com

Front cover art by Gerald Welch

Dedicated to the family of loyal Destroyer readers, who, after half a century, just keep coming back and not getting tired of these little tales of ours.

— Warren Murphy and Richard Sapir

CONTENTS

FOREWORD

Warren Murphy

His name was Remo and more than 50 years ago we had written the first episode in his life story, but as most young writers will tell you, it isn't always easy to get published. In the case of Dick Sapir and me, it was hard, damned hard — eight years hard before we saw the light of publishing day.

But eventually that day arrived, and along came an eventual swarm of books: fifty, a hundred, a hundred and fifty, movie, TV, comics, short stories. And we roll on.

Dick Sapir died a long time ago, but the *Destroyer* keeps going, cheered on by a resolute gang of fans who looked beyond the senseless covers to find the legends and stories within, then refused to let Remo Williams die or to let me do the honorable thing, declare myself old and useless, go out of business, and retire to the dog track.

No, instead these readers kept buying books and demanding more, and thus here we are — sixty million copies later, with a new spinoff series, with e-publishing, with a new movie in the works, with new worldwide rights sold to bring back all 150 of the Remo Williams adventures in every corner of the world.

Ten years ago, I thought to honor these fan-folk who'd been with us for so long by doing an anthology of reader-written stories called New Blood, which eventually helped give a lot of young writers a leg up on crafting their own stuff.

But that was a decade ago, and time marches on. Now we have new young readers, and since there's nothing wrong with sequels, you

i

hold in your hands the second love letter from the *Destroyer* creators to the people who've kept us in business. You are all — well, mostly all — loved. Some are merely tolerated.

Welcome to Remo's world. Welcome to the world of <u>More Blood</u>.

— Warren Murphy

And what am I? Chopped liver?

Let me warn all of you who have befouled your hands by picking up this gross malevolence that the immoral fat drunken scribbler insists is a book.

Know this: he has gotten everything wrong. Every fact, every statement, every nuance is untrue — either a lie or an idiocy.

Someday I will write the true stories of the Master of Sinanju and his useless stupid manservant, and I will not rely on the services of some useless sot to help me. You who read this and those who write these excrescences should be ashamed of yourselves. If you ever meet me, do yourself a favor and cross the street.

And never expect a nickel in royalties from this po-faced poseur. He is a thief as well as an imbecile.

I remain,

Chiun.

Master of Sinanju.

SUN SOURCE: JAGUARMEN OF MEXICO

C.E. Martin

Chapter One: The Hundredth Master

THE MASTER OF SINANJU was dead. No, wait, that wasn't right. Now *he* was the Master of Sinanju.

Yui stood slowly, releasing the hand of his dead father as a cold chill raced up his spine and his stomach began to knot up. He was now the Master — responsible not just for the House, but for the entire village of Sinanju.

Fear was something Yui had never known before — not in his entire life. Raised by the ninety-ninth Master of the preeminent House of Assassins in the entire world — a House whose origins were thousands of years old — he could not once remember being afraid. Not even during all the training he had endured the past 26 years of his life.

But now, Yui was afraid. His stomach churned and he felt the weight of the world pressing down on him. This was so much more than he had ever expected. He was no longer just responsible for the life growing in his wife's stomach — now he was responsible for every man, woman and child in the village of Sinanju. He was responsible for traditions that went back thousands of years.

He felt like he was going to throw up.

Yui took a deep, cleansing breath and steadied his nerves. He forced the oxygen from the air into his body, charging his system with strength. He was a Master of Sinanju. Something more than human, capable of feats no other human — save for another Master of Sinanju — could dare attempt. A killer of killers, a Master of mind and body and even the very laws of nature.

He could do this.

1

Yui walked out of the Masters' House and looked out over the assembled crowd of villagers. The look on his face told them all they needed to know. Several women began to wail.

The villagers knelt in front of the Masters' House and began to pray. As Yui looked upon them, he noticed that not one would look him in the eye now. In fact, as he stepped down from the stairs leading from the door of the Masters' House, he saw that many scurried out of the way, heads bowed, bodies tense with fear.

They feared *him* now.

They did not know that Yui was struggling with his own fears. Mostly, the fear of the responsibility that now fell upon him as the new Master of Sinanju. But that same title now made the villagers fear him. Not that a Master would ever harm a villager. That was forbidden. But living under the rule of someone who could end your life with the flick of a wrist, or the gentlest of touches tended to scare anyone.

Masters of Sinanju were, when all was said and done, harbingers of death. It was a profession that had fed the village for thousands of years. Master assassins from the tiny village of Sinanju had worked their deadly magic around the world through all of history.

But, growing up, Yui had not been a terrifying personification of death. He had been the favorite son of the village — adored by all. He had regaled his peers with feats of strength and agility learned through his training in the ancient sun source of martial arts — Sinanju. Every villager had looked upon him with kindness, had welcomed him with wide smiles when they saw him. They had adored him.

And now, because of a title, they feared him.

Yui walked past the assembled crowd, ignoring the whispers from the elders who worried about what would become of Sinanju now that Yui's father was dead. Sinanju had no resources of its own. The poor fishing village on the West Korean Bay was a barren, cold place. Even the waters were mostly devoid of life. But the village had endured — fed by the gold brought back by generation after generation of Master assassins.

Worse still, the villagers knew that Yui was not yet a full Master. His training was incomplete. Where tradition normally held that a Master unable to train his son could rely on his own father to complete the next generation's training, Yui's own grandfather was also no more. Master Pong had passed just five years earlier after a long retirement.

For Yui to complete his training now, he would have to consult the ancient scrolls. It was not unheard of, but it did not reassure the villagers.

Yui was about to step into his mother-in-law's home, to tell his young wife the news, when a villager stepped up quietly behind him.

Yui turned slowly in place to face her. "Yes, Onna?" He had recognized her step, her breathing and even the beat of her heart as she approached. As a Master of Sinanju, heir to generations of training that had made him and his ancestors more than human, he was aware of his surroundings at all times.

Onna, his tutor in all things scholarly, bowed deeply to Yui. It was a strange thing, as the woman was several years his senior and it had always been he who bowed to her — at the beginning and end of his non-Sinanju lessons. "There is a stranger, Master."

Yui was surprised. The passing of his father would be news that would spread like wildfire throughout the land, but surely no one outside the village could yet know. "Who?"

"A white man. Dressed in all black. He waits just outside the village."

A white man? Yui knew this could mean only one thing — employment. None dared come to Sinanju unless it was to deliver goods, trade, or to hire a Master. Given that the visitor was a white man, it had to be the last.

Yui sighed. While he wished to see his wife and find comfort in the company of the only family he now had left in the world, he knew that his responsibility to the village came first.

"Please inform my wife that Master Ik has passed," Yui said, again fighting the urge to bow to his elder as he had so many times before.

"Yes, Master," Onna replied, bowing deeply.

Yui gave a slight bow in return, and then walked around his former tutor. He wound his way through the village, over the damp, muddy streets, not caring that the wet soil clung to his soft shoes. His father was dead, and could for once not lecture him to do better. To let his shoes be dirty was both an act of rebellion and a way for Yui to mourn.

The stranger was indeed a white man. He reeked of beef and potatoes and the many other western foods so rare in this part of the world. And, as Onna had said, he was dressed all in black — pants, leather riding boots, and a long wool coat. His face was hidden by the hood of a long, black cloak that reached nearly to the ground.

3

When the stranger saw Yui approach, he bowed deeply.

"*Ahn-hyung ha shib nee-ka!*" the man intoned in terrible Korean.

Yui stood calmly, his hands at his sides. He was surprised when the stranger stood, his cloak falling down off his head.

A head taller than Yui, the newcomer was old — very old. What little hair remained on his head was gray and silver, like the short beard on his face. Brown eyes twinkled under bushy gray eyebrows.

"Uh...*Buenos Días?*" the stranger said in equally bad Spanish.

"I speak English," Yui at last said calmly.

"Blessed Virgin, Mother o' God!" the old man replied, sighing heavily. "'Tis the first time I've been to this part o' ta world." His accent was thick — one Yui had never heard before.

The old man reached under his robes and pulled out a rolled up parchment. "I come seekin' ta Master of Sinanju, in ta name of his Grace, Pope Pius the Ninth, Sovereign of — "

"Yes, yes, priest," Yui said, noticing the white collar around the visitor's neck for the first time. "What do you want?"

The priest hesitated for a moment, and then broke into a wide smile. "I've come ta see yer Master, young man. Ta Church wishes ta hire ta House o' Sinanju."

Chapter Two: The Order of Schott

It HAD BEEN A LONG ROAD to Sinanju for Father James Murphy. Born to an Irish farmer with aspirations of becoming a distiller of spirits, young James had been sent to Catholic school when he was very young. Long before the blight had struck his beloved Ireland and famine had driven so many of his countrymen to leave, James's family had been able to send him to university. There, his father hoped he would learn enough to help turn the family farm into a distillery and make them all rich.

Instead, James had chosen the priesthood. At first, his father had been very cross with James, but having a priest in the family might mean a blessing for the family farm. Or perhaps it was a sign the Lord did not want the Murphy family making whiskey after all.

James had been successful in the Church, becoming a teacher at the very school he had attended as a youth. He excelled in his studies and soon found himself a professor. In short order, he joined the Order of the Jesuits and devoted himself not just to God but also to learning.

Then James had joined an even higher order — the Order of Schott.

A collective of Jesuit scientists, the Order of Schott was tasked with following in the footsteps of Gaspar Schott, a Jesuit who had devoted his life to studying knowledge gathered from around the world. The Order collected and reviewed vast amounts of knowledge gathered from libraries and churches in both the Old and New Worlds. And Father Murphy — Professor Murphy — had become something of an expert on the study of knowledge.

In his sixty-sixth year of life, Father Murphy was summoned to the Holy City. There he met a Cardinal, an adviser of his Eminence, Pope Pius. Father Murphy had been recommended by the Order as one of their finest thinkers, and the Church needed him to think on something of great importance.

In the New World, in a land called Mexico, a series of gruesome murders had been taking place on church grounds. Once he had examined the reports of these incidents, Father Murphy came to a conclusion: the reports of supernatural beings attacking churches were untrue. That was a just a smokescreen obscuring something larger. But someone was removing the Church's leaders in the region — assassinating them, slowly, one by one.

It was the word *assassination* that had piqued the interest of the Cardinal.

Father Murphy was taken deep into the Vatican, into a vault containing the most precious secrets the Church had accumulated in its almost two millennia of existence. It was here that Father Murphy was made privy to the existence of the House of Sinanju — the most feared assassins in all the world — and tasked with determining if they were responsible.

After much study, Father Murphy offered his opinion that Sinanju was not to blame — but that they might be able to help. For if the greatest assassins in all of history were not to blame, surely they would be able to stop those who were.

That got him put on a boat headed for Korea — tasked with hiring a Master.

Chapter Three: Contractual Obligations

Yui WAS TROUBLED to hear what his wife was saying.

"I — we — will be fine without you. The village is your family now — you must provide for us all and accept this contract."

"But the baby will be here soon," Yui said, rubbing his wife's stomach.

She slapped his hand away. "You are the Master now, Yui. That is more important than being this child's father. Would you have your own child be one of the first to return to the sea?"

Yui shook his head from side to side. It was a tale all Masters had told their students. How, in leaner times, when there was no food, babies of the village had to be returned to the sea, for otherwise they would starve. It had not happened in many generations, but Yui did not want to be the first Master to return to those days. And that meant accepting contracts.

Yui's father had not been lucky, as Masters went. Despite a longer reign than most, Master Ik, as well as his father before him, Master Pong, had reigned over the House during an era when the kingdoms of the world were falling before waves of angry peasants. Work for the House was not as plentiful as it had been in the time of Yui's great-grandfather. The treasures accumulated over the centuries were beginning to run low.

Yui smiled at his wife. "As always, you are wiser than your years, my wife. I will see what this priest has to say and make my decision. But I will not leave Sinanju until my Master has been properly buried."

"Of course not, husband. You would never wish to dishonor the House."

Yui kissed his wife's stomach, then her forehead, then left the small hut. He made his way purposefully through the village to the guest hut the priest had been taken to. When he entered the priest was seated on a tatami mat on the floor, reading by candlelight.

"Will yer Master be seein' me now?" Father Murphy asked, starting to rise.

Yui held out a hand, motioning for the priest to stay put. He crossed the small room and sat before the priest on another mat. "Tell me what your Church wishes of Sinanju, and the Master will think on it."

7

Negotiation was something Yui's grandfather had taught him well, before he had passed away. The young Master was not about to let the old priest know someone as young and inexperienced as he was now Master. That might lower the price the Church was willing to offer for Sinanju's service.

"Of course," Father Murphy said, closing his Bible. He once again picked up his parchment, unrolling it to check his notes. "An what's yer name, young man?"

"I am Yui."

"I couldn't help but notice yer village seems gripped with a feelin' o' despair. Is everyt'ing all right?"

Yui was surprised at this. He had been careful to lead the Priest directly to these guest accommodations and gave Onna strict orders that he was to be kept secluded. Some of the village women must have been whispering outside the door. Gossip was the one thing, besides Master assassins, that Sinanju could produce in abundance.

"There has been a death in the village."

"Oh, my deepest condolences," Murphy said, kissing the crucifix hanging around his neck, then making the sign of the cross. "Was it someone close ta yer Master?"

"The whole village is close to the Master," Yui said, getting annoyed. This priest was asking far too many questions. "Tell me of the task at hand, priest — I have other duties to perform."

"Certainly," Murphy said. He looked at his notes again, then pulled a small bag from a pocket under his wool coat. He set the small bag on the table and the coins within it clinked together.

"His Grace, Pius ta Ninth requests dat ta Master o' Sinanju protect ta Church's clergy in ta New World."

"New World? There is only one world, priest, and we are both sitting on it."

Murphy smiled. "Ta land across ta sea — to ta east. We call it ta New World."

Yui frowned. He knew of the lands across the ocean — they were not new. He had learned of them from the scrolls he had studied since he was a child. The scrolls that told the history of the House of Sinanju, written by its Masters, and containing every bit of knowledge they had learned in their travels abroad.

8

"Sinanju is a house of assassins, priest. Who does your Church wish killed?"

"Ah, well," Murphy said, embarrassed. "We don' exactly know tha', just yet."

Yui's eyes narrowed to thin slits. His patience was wearing thin.

Father Murphy held up a hand. "You see, someone is killing me brutters an' sisters, but we have no idea who t'at might be."

"Does the Church not have soldiers?" Yui asked.

"They haven't been able ta stop ta killins."

Seeing Yui was quietly listening, watching him carefully, Father Murphy continued.

"Survivors tell a story o' half-man, half-jaguar creatures tat have killed priests and nuns and even ta little ones in our orphanages."

"Little ones? Children?" Yui asked, surprised.

"Aye. Ta soldiers patrol but never arrive in time, I'm afraid. Ta Jaguar-men are always long gone by ta time word of ta attacks gets out."

"Why turn to Sinanju?"

"Ah, well," Murphy said, reaching under his coat. He pulled out a small flask and took a quick drink. "I believe t'at these attacks are assassinations."

Yui bristled. In the eyes of Sinanju, the only true assassinations were carried out by Masters. Everything else was just the work of sloppy amateurs.

"His Eminence would like ta hire yer Master ta accompany me ta Mexico, where I believe I can uncover who or what's behind ta murders."

"And Sinanju will do the rest?"

"Aye."

Yui considered. Travel to the faraway lands across the sea would take considerable time. His child would be born any day now. "What does the Church offer?"

"Well, fer one, gold," Father Murphy said, pouring out the small bag of coins. Each was a gold coin — a Spanish Doubloon.

"And a pardon, for ta House, for ta unfortunate misunderstandin' with his eminence, Pope Calixtus ta Third."

Yui looked at the gold then the priest. He knew full well what Murphy meant. Over the centuries, the House had worked for and against the Church. Pope Calixtus had been a contract taken by a Master just a few centuries before, when the Church angered Spain.

"I must go now — there are funeral arrangements to be made. The negotiations will begin tomorrow evening."

"Aye…Master Yui," Father Murphy said, smiling.

Yui frowned. The old priest was smarter than he looked. But he would not give in so easily. "That is not the village Master's name," he said, rising.

"Oh?" Murphy said, confused. "My pardons…may I ask who is ta Master?"

"You will find out tomorrow," Yui said, leaving the hut.

Chapter Four: The Journey East

AFTER THE FUNERAL of Master Ik, Yui had met the priest in his new home — the Masters' home. Yui's young wife had served the men tea, as was Sinanju tradition.

Father Murphy had offered his sincere appreciation for Yui's welcoming, and had blessed the young Master's unborn baby. Then they had settled down to negotiate.

The old Priest had been surprisingly easy to barter with. Yui's requests, even for rice to accompany him to the New World so he did not have to eat barbarian food, had been met. Murphy proved to be an affable and kindly man, who reminded Yui of his own grandfather.

Once negotiations were complete, the priest had said his goodbyes and headed back to his ship.

The following morning, with his meager possessions packed in a rolled up blanket fastened around each end with strong silk cord, Yui bid his wife and his home goodbye. It was time to go to work.

The young Master followed the coast, working his way down to the cold beach below. Several hundred yards out in the water, a sleek, two-masted sailing ship sat at anchor. On the beach, there was a small rowboat, and the priest, Murphy.

"Good mornin' to ya, Master Yui," Murphy smiled.

"I am Master Hwa," the Master of Sinanju declared. He had thought on it for many hours, all through the funeral of his father, the negotiations with Murphy and his final night in Sinanju. Many a Master had signified a great change in life by taking a new name. Master Nonga, Master To-un, even The Fly — who had forsworn any traditional name in order to spread fear into the hearts of Sinanju's enemies.

It was not an uncommon tradition in Sinanju. And he, Master Hwa, had been through a great deal of change. Once a favored son of the village, he was now its Master — feared by all and relied upon for sustenance. The happy, carefree days of his youth were over. His life as Yui had ended.

He was Master Hwa.

"Very well, Master Hwa," Murphy said, waving a hand to the small boat. "Shall we be on our way?"

Hwa regarded the boat carefully, surprised at how small it was. There was barely room for two men. He walked to the boat, a slight leap carrying him from the wet sand. He landed as light as a feather in the rear of the boat — not even a ripple emanating from around the small craft.

Father Murphy pulled off his long cloak and tossed it in, revealing the black cassock he wore, and bare feet. The priest rolled up his pants legs and waded out to the boat, pushing it off the sand, then climbed in quickly. Once seated, facing Hwa, he grabbed an oar and used it to turn the boat around.

Hwa was surprised the old man had the strength to do so. He looked so old and frail.

Once they were facing the right direction, the priest dipped both oars into the water and sent the tiny boat out into the bay, toward the anchored sailing ship. As they approached, Hwa could see a small crew scurrying around on the deck, working the rigging and preparing the ship to get underway.

"Your ship is on fire, priest," Hwa said, pointing.

Father Murphy looked back over his shoulder and smiled. A thick column of black smoke was rising from twin smoke stacks set amidships.

"She's a steamship," the priest explained. "Fastest schooner t'is side o ta Pacific, I'm told."

Hwa studied the ship closely. Unlike most sailing vessels he had seen, this one had two enormous structures on either side — from which extended large paddle wheels. It reminded him of the drawings of water mills he had seen in the books Onna had him read for his studies.

"What is a steamship?" Hwa asked.

"Ta ship burns coal, ta turn water ta steam — hot air," Murphy explained, rowing. "Ta steam's released, turnin' ta paddles on ta sides — propellin' ta ship troo ta water."

Hwa was confused. "What of the sails?"

"Oh, she uses sails as well. But t'ere isn't always a wind ta be had."

They finally pulled alongside the ship, and two lines were lowered over the side. Father Murphy hooked one to the bow of the rowboat, so Hwa did the same at the stern. Then the priest went scurrying up the large net hanging on the side of the vessel. For an old man, he was quite fit.

Father Murphy stepped over the railing onto the deck of the *Silver*

Sapphire and saw several of the crew standing there, mouths open, eyes wide as they looked to his left. Turning his head, Father Murphy was surprised to see Master Hwa standing there quietly.

"So this is why we came to this god-forsaken country?" a woman's voice rang out.

All eyes, including Master Hwa's, turned to the rear deck of the ship. Leaning against a rail, looking down at them, was a woman. With a dark complexion and long, flowing black hair, she wore a loose-sleeved white shirt, with a wide scarlet silk sash around her middle. The handles of two pistols jutted out of the sash. A matching silk scarf was tied on her head, holding her thick hair in place, out of her eyes. Coarse black wool pants were tucked into tall cracked brown leather riding boots.

"Have what you came for, priest?" the woman asked.

"Aye, Captain Blackman. May I present Master Hwa, o' ta House o' Sinanju."

Captain Blackman sized up the newcomer to her vessel. Hwa was a typical, small Asian, dressed in a loose black shirt that hung slightly below his waist. Loose black pants billowed out above his knees, but were wrapped tightly against his lower legs. He wore soft, slipper-like black shoes on his feet. His black hair was cropped very short, and he had a very young face.

Captain Blackman took a step, and sat on the banister of the stairs leading down from the stern deck. She slid quickly down the railing, landing lightly, and then walked over to the priest and young Master.

"Captain Jacqueline Blackman," she said, extending a hand to Hwa.

Hwa looked at the woman's long, thin fingers, her tan, weathered face, and the open neck of her loose shirt. She was nearly as tall as Father Murphy, and had mischievous brown eyes.

"This is a woman's boat?" Hwa said in surprise, turning to Father Murphy.

The old priest turned red, embarrassed for a moment, and not sure what to say. There was a collective gasp from the assembled crew as well.

"Oh, I'm a woman all right," Captain Blackman said, smiling. Her right hand suddenly snaked out, long, black-lacquered nails lunging below Master Hwa's waist.

But they grabbed only air. Hwa had suddenly shifted to his left — his movement so fast no one could see it. He was just suddenly in another place.

Captain Blackman stood with her mouth open, a sarcastic, taunting remark on her tongue. But with nothing in her hand to squeeze but air, she gulped like a fish out of water and remained silent.

"Please show me to my quarters, woman," Master Hwa said. "And see that I am not disturbed."

* * *

The Master of Sinanju was not pleased. Despite the many stories told to him by his father and grandfather, he was not prepared for the long journey across the Pacific Ocean. Three weeks aboard the small, twin-masted steamship was wearing on his patience.

The rolling of the deck as the ship moved through the sea did not bother Hwa. He had mastered his balance as a child. Nor did the cramped quarters of his cabin bother him. It was a welcome respite from the stench of the dirty crew, and the horrible foods they sweated from their pores. True, some of the crew had been inquisitive and dared to enter his quarters, but Hwa had dealt with them by demonstrating to the barbarians what a pressure point was. None bothered him now.

What bothered young Hwa was the inactivity. He was able to meditate and train in his cabin, perfecting those techniques handed down by his father and forefathers in the scrolls he had memorized, but it was not enough. Hwa wanted to be doing something more. It was nearly as bad as the waiting he had experienced by his dying father's bedside.

And then there was the Captain.

Jacqueline Blackman seemed quite insistent on annoying Hwa. The round-eye hussy had come to his quarters many times, making small talk, offering the Master some of the horrible rum she always seemed to have on her breath. She had talked incessantly about the father she had inherited the *Silver Sapphire* from, about the ship's former life as a blockade runner taking contraband weapons to something called the Confederacy just a year prior, and about her cravings.

As the son of the Master of Sinanju, young Yui had his pick of the daughters of Sinanju. Marrying a future Master was a great honor. And while some Masters had arranged the marriages of their sons, Master Ik had no interest in the matter — other than insisting that Yui be married and produce a child before he became Master.

Thus, Yui had taken his time to know all the daughters of Sinanju — perhaps in ways his father might not have approved, but which fell just

14

short of dishonoring them. In the end, he settled on just one, and vowed to be loyal to her in exchange for a healthy son. A contract she had undoubtedly either completed by now, by granting him a son, or that she had failed — by granting him a daughter.

Unfortunately, Captain "Jack" as she preferred to be called, had gotten the idea of attempting to complete such a contract with Hwa herself.

It was to be expected. Most women seemed to find themselves drawn to the majesty of a Master of Sinanju. As a single man, Yui had benefited greatly from this attraction. But as a married Master, he found the drunken advances of the large-chested, round-eyed barbarian to be annoying at best.

Each visit to Master Hwa's cabin, Captain Jack seemed to be missing another button on her loose shirt — under which she apparently wore no undergarments.

"So, Master Hwa," Captain Jack said, reeking of rum on her latest visit. "How old are you? I like my men young, you know."

"Old enough to not be tempted by your feeble attempts at seduction," Hwa responded. He sat on a tatami mat on the floor of the small cabin, eyes closed as he meditated.

"Is this more to your liking?" Jack asked, ripping open her shirt and exposing her large breasts.

"Your udders will undoubtedly provide much milk for many mouths when you finally find a man foolish enough to marry you," Hwa said.

Captain Jack frowned and stormed out of Hwa's cabin, yelling at her crew to get back to work. None dared to look at her and she swept by. Growing up on ships her father captained, Jack had proven her worth as a sailor and a fighter.

Between his meditations and the visits from the rum-soaked temptress, Hwa found himself exploring the small ship. As much as he would not admit it aloud, he found the mechanical steam engine below deck fascinating.

Halfway through their voyage, Father Murphy caught him staring at the engine, attempting to deduce how it worked.

"Steam is ta future," Father Murphy said. "It'll make our world a much smaller place."

"But how does it work?" Master Hwa asked.

The steam engine was below deck, amidships, in what had once been a cargo hold. Now it was a hot, steam-filled room, lit by the orange glow of the furnace two crewmen shoveled coal into.

"Ta fire heats ta water — turns it ta steam," Father Murphy explained. "Hot air rises — it expands."

"Yes, I know of heated air," Hwa said, remembering the first time he had ridden a thermal layer in the air, diving off the cliffs of nearby Mount Paekustan as his grandfather watched.

"Ta expansion o' ta' air is turned ta motion — turnin' ta paddles on ta sides o' ta ship."

"That is the engine?" Hwa asked, pointing.

"No, t'at's ta boiler — where ta water's heated. It's under tremendous pressure — very dangerous."

"How?"

"If ta boiler were heated too much, it'd explode — tearing ta ship apart. Or, if ta boiler were suddenly punctured, it'd cause ta whole thing ta rupture…an destroy ta ship."

"Then why have it on board?" Hwa asked. These westerners and their devices were so foolish. Even a child knew not to play with fire.

"It allows us ta continue sailin' — wit'out ta wind."

Hwa considered. There had been no wind for two days now, but the small steamship had continued on, plowing through the waves, emitting the foul black stench from its smokestack, burning up coal he thought would be better used for cooking.

"What happens when you run out of coal, and there is no wind?" Hwa asked.

Father Murphy rubbed his chin. "I reckon we'd have ta pray for a little help."

Chapter Five: The New World

FATHER MURPHY WAS GLAD to be on solid ground once more. The old priest had spent his entire life on land. Aside from a few trips across the English Channel, the ocean journey from Korea to the Americas was the most time he'd ever spent at sea.

"Welcome to Acapulco, gentlemen!" Captain Jack said as she stepped onto the dock beside her ship.

Father Murphy and Master Hwa followed her quietly down the gangplank from the *Silver Sapphire.*

"If your men'd have our cargo ready within ta hour," Father Murphy said, "I'll see about a wagon an horses ta continue our journey."

"Within the hour?" Jack laughed. She drained the last bit of rum from a bottle she'd carried off the ship, and then threw it into the water. "We've been cooped up on that ship for nearly three weeks. The first order of business is a pub for the men, and a nice long bath for me."

She smiled wolfishly at Hwa. "Care to join me, Mister Hwa?"

"It is Master Hwa, and no, I do not wish to wallow in your filth."

"Captain," Father Murphy said sternly. "Ta Church has paid ye handsomely for yer service. T'would be greatly appreciated if ye could continue ta honor ta terms o' t'at contract."

"Fine, fine," Jack said, raising an arm and sniffing her own armpit. She made a face. "I'll just smell like a pig a few hours more, I suppose."

Father Murphy scowled and walked past the Captain, along the creaky boards of the dock. He had nearly reached the shore when he realized Master Hwa was quietly walking beside him. The small Korean made no sound at all on the old warped wood.

"I can handle t'is, Master," Father Murphy said. "I'll be back in just a wee bit."

"I would rather see more of this land you call Mexico."

"Don't fancy a few more hours with our lovely Cap'n?"

"A few more seconds would be unbearable," Hwa scowled.

The two men all in black made their way into the thriving port of Acapulco, occasionally seeing French soldiers making their way through the dirty streets.

"Those men reek of cheese and wine," Hwa said as they walked past a pair of soldiers.

Father Murphy sighed in relief when the soldiers continued past, apparently oblivious to the comment.

"His majesty Maximilian ta First is a Frenchman himself," Murphy said. "T'ose are his countrymen here ta help keep ta peace."

"Soldiers do not keep peace," Hwa said. "They make war, killing indiscriminately with their boomsticks."

"Still, even though we be representatives of ta Church, would be better if ye were a wee bit more polite to our hosts here, Master."

"I am Sinanju — I fear no man."

"Well, I be Irish, and while I don't fear no man either, I'd rather not have ta fight if I can avoid it."

"You would fight if you had to?" Hwa asked surprised.

"Ta good Lord made us Irishmen good at two things," Murphy said, pulling his small flask from a coat pocket. "Drinkin' and fightin'. Who am I to argue with ta Creator?"

He took a long drink from the flask, then tucked it away. "But I'd rather not have ta use me God-given talents."

"As you wish, priest."

Eventually, they found a stable, where Murphy negotiated a fair price for a large buckboard wagon and two horses.

"You are familiar with these beasts?" Hwa asked as Murphy checked the horses' teeth.

"Aye. I grew up on a farm — we only had ta one horse, but he was a fine animal an' a good friend."

Hwa raised an eyebrow in surprise. "In Sinanju, we rely on ourselves for needs."

"I rely on our Lord for my needs," Father Murphy countered, making the sign of the cross. "But His creatures often lend a hand."

"Horses do not have hands," Hwa said, climbing into the wagon.

Murphy and the young Master made their way slowly back through the town to the docks, where the crew were busy unloading several large steamer trunks from the forward hold of the steamship. They carried the trunks to the end of the dock, piling them up on the ground.

"Easy wit' t'at trunk, lads!" Murphy exclaimed as one trunk was dumped heavily on the dock.

"I did not order that much rice," Master Hwa said, stepping down from the wagon. "One trunk will be sufficient."

Father Murphy pointed to a crate beside the growing pile of trunks. "T'at's yer rice, Master Hwa. T'ese trunks're mine."

"I did not think priests owned anything."

"Well, technically, tay belong to ta Church."

"And what is in them?" Hwa asked as the priest struggled to carry a trunk to the back of the wagon.

"Scientific equipment," Murphy answered. Suddenly the trunk was much lighter. Hwa had lent a hand, placing the trunk in the back of the wagon, one-handed, with no apparent effort.

"I don't believe there's anyt'ing supernatural 'bout these attacks. I plan ta discover exactly who's behind 'em t'rough scientific study o' ta crime scenes."

"Crime scenes?"

"T'is ta field o' forensic science," Father Murphy explained. "All o' ta murders are crimes, an' whoever committed 'em left behind evidence — clues we can use ta determine who t'ey were."

Hwa continued to load the priest's trunks into the wagon — three large steamer trunks that he lifted easily with one hand, much to the astonishment of the sailors nearby.

"Well, gentlemen," Captain Blackman said, walking up behind Hwa. "It seems we are about to part ways."

"We'll send word when we're ready ta return," Father Murphy said, climbing up into the wagon. "Until t'en, try and keep yer crew out o' trouble, Cap'n."

"Don't worry, Father. We'll be waiting when you're ready. The Church has promised me far too much money to run out on you. Just take your time — this looks like a nice place for a vacation."

Chapter Six: Wagons East

After checking with the local church in Acapulco, Father Murphy and Master Hwa set out for the most recent church to be attacked by the mysterious Jaguarmen, their wagon loaded with supplies. The journey was a long one, over dusty trails that wound through the hills and valleys of the country.

For most of the journey, the two men sat in silence, regarding the countryside. Father Murphy quietly read his Bible, which he held in one hand and the reins to their two horses in the other. Hwa meditated and reflected on his lessons, or studied the maps of the region the priest had brought along.

By the night of the third day, Father Murphy decided to try and speak to his young companion.

"Master Hwa, ye shoulda been a monk," Murphy said as he struck a small piece of curved steel against a piece of flint.

"Monks take a vow of poverty — and that would not feed my village."

Murphy laughed. "So tis true — Masters o' Sinanju kill ta feed their people?"

"You find that humorous, priest?"

"Only t'at ta old books're right."

"What old books?"

"Back in ta Vatican — ta Holy City."

"I am familiar with it. My forefathers have written of it many times. Tell me of these books that speak of Sinanju."

Murphy leaned in and blew on the small pile of kindling he had just showered with sparks, trying to get it to light. "Ta Church has many records, taken from aroun' ta world. Everywhere ta Church has been t'ey write down about ta people an' places o' ta world."

"Sinanju does the same. Each Master adds to the Sacred Scrolls — imparting knowledge for the following generation."

Murphy raked the flint across the steel again, emitting more sparks. "I've spent many an hour studyin' ta books o' ta Church. But I'd never heard o' Sinanju 'til a coupla months ago."

20

"Once, Sinanju was known throughout the civilized world, and feared by all."

Murphy frowned at the small bundle of dry grass and wood shavings he had so far been unable to light. "I suppose t'at bit o' trouble wit' his Eminence Calixtus changed ta Church's opinion o' yer village."

Hwa nodded and stepped forward. He crouched beside the priest. "Yes. Many others have been angered by the glory of Sinanju and tried to erase its name from history."

Hwa took a stick from the ground beside Murphy. "May I?"

The priest nodded, and Hwa began to rub the stick between his thumb and forefinger. His fingers moved quickly, almost a blur. Smoke began to rise from the wood, then a flame leapt up from it. Hwa dropped the stick on the small pile of grass, which also ignited.

"But the sun source can never remain hidden long."

Father Murphy grinned and began adding small sticks to the growing flames. Soon, he had the beginnings of a campfire.

"Tay say ta victors write history," Father Murphy said, settling onto a blanket he'd placed beside the campfire.

"As Sinanju will always be victorious, that will not be a problem."

* * *

After five long days across the arid wilderness of Mexico, Murphy and Hwa at last reached their destination — the Cathedral de Coatlu, the church of the town of Coatlu.

A small town, barely more than a village, roughly halfway between Acapulco and the capital, Mexico City, Coatlu was a quiet place. Few locals were visible when the duo arrived.

The wagon clattered along the wide dirt street through town, directly to the church. When they pulled up in front of it, both men noticed the doors to the adobe and brick building stood open.

"It appears abandoned," Hwa announced.

"Aye — I was told in Acapulco t'at ta church was abandoned after ta jaguars attacked."

"Then the clues you seek should remain undisturbed," Hwa said, jumping down from the wagon. He landed lightly, only the faintest puff of dust rising from the ground. Unlike Murphy, his black pants and shoes remained clean — with no dust clinging to them. The priest had been wondering at this their entire journey. His own Jesuit cassock, pants, and boots accumulated a thick layer of dust each day that could only be partially brushed off.

Father Murphy eased himself down then rummaged around in a trunk in the back of the wagon. From it, he collected an old black leather bag, similar to those used by physicians.

The priest led the way through the wooden doors of the church, Hwa silently following him.

Inside, bright light streamed down from three large holes in the ceiling. The many wooden pews were in disarray, knocked over, with several broken. Dark stains were scattered all about on the floor.

"It is blood," Master Hwa announced when Murphy bent to examine one stain. "Human blood."

"You're sure?"

"I have smelled it before."

Murphy frowned and pulled a large magnifying glass from the leather bag as he moved to an overturned pew. He looked through the thick lens carefully. Deep scratches were in the back of the wood, as though made by some horrible creature.

While the priest examined the strange claw marks, Hwa walked slowly around the church. In just moments he found something — a small stone lodged in the wall of the building.

"What've ye got?" Murphy said, walking over as Hwa poked at the stone projectile carefully.

It was a small stone object, barely two inches long, flat in the middle, with both ends tapering down, almost to points, like two cones back-to-back. The small stone was lodged firmly into the wall, nearly one-third of its length embedded in the thick adobe.

"A projectile of some kind."

Father Murphy tried to pull the small stone free, but could not budge it. He began rummaging in his bag for a tool, but Hwa simply reached up and pulled the stone free. He handed it to the priest, who examined it under his magnifying glass.

"Now where d'ya suppose t'is came from?"

Hwa pointed up. "Above."

Murphy dropped the stone into his bag and stared up at the ceiling. He walked around, trying to get a better vantage. As he stepped, he heard a crunching sound beneath his boot, as though he'd stepped on glass.

Kneeling, the priest found a piece of black obsidian.

"Very interestin'," he said, holding it up to the light.

"The timbers of the roof were broken from above," Hwa said, pointing up. Sure enough, Murphy was able to see that all the broken timbers pointed down, into the church.

The priest moved around, looking at the ground below the holes. The wood floor of the church was badly splintered in each spot, as though something very heavy had fallen. But whatever had fallen was long gone.

"This does not look supernatural," Hwa said.

"No, it doesn't," Father Murphy agreed.

He walked outside quickly, pulling a map from the wagon. He placed it atop a trunk in the back, unrolling it. Master Hwa was barely tall enough to see the map.

"Each o' t'ese spots I've marked're churches t'at've been attacked — wit' ta dates they were hit."

"It forms a circle."

"Aye, I noticed t'at too. All 'round Mexico City. Whoever t'ey are, t'ey haven't ventured inta tha capital — probably 'cause of all ta soldiers."

"What are these marks?" Hwa asked, pointing to small crosses on the map.

"Churches t'at haven't been attacked...yet."

Hwa studied the map intently for a moment. "The next attack will be here," he said, pointing to a church northeast of the capital.

"T'at's at least ten days ride from here!" Father Murphy exclaimed.

"I think they will be attacked tonight, if they have not already."

"How canya be so sure? T'ese attacks're random."

"No. They only appear to be random. Great effort has gone to placing them so they appear so."

"How canya tell?"

"The Mongols did this. Long ago, before your church. Along the Great Wall in what you call China."

"Learn t'at from yer scrolls?"

"Of course," Hwa said. He pointed to another church, much, much closer. "I believe this will be the attack after next."

"T'at's only two days from here."

"Enough time for us to set a trap."

"We've got ta warn ta Church in San Adele!"

"No. If we warn them, whoever is responsible will know we have deduced their pattern. We must wait."

"T'at's barbaric!" Father Murphy said, his face paling. "We can't just let t'ose people die!"

"People die every day. It is a natural part of life. They may already be dead. But the ones here," Hwa said, thumping the map, "They yet live. Should we not move to help them?"

Murphy examined the map again. "T'ere's no way anyone could get from San Adele ta Los Alvarez so quickly."

"Look at your dates, priest," Hwa said. "Many of the attacks are too far apart to be possible — yet they did happen."

Murphy rubbed his beard. "T'at's ta main reason ta Church was willin' ta believe 'twas ta work o' ta supernatural."

"Men often claim something is magical when they cannot explain it," Hwa countered.

Father Murphy raised an eyebrow in surprise. "Why, Master Hwa — ya sound like a scientist."

Chapter Seven: In God's House

LIKE SO MANY OTHER TOWNS in Mexico, Los Alvarez was just a gathering of a few buildings near a small church built by the Spanish nearly fifty years earlier. Serving the farmers in the region, the Church provided a symbol of God's presence on earth, and reminded the locals that there was only one true way to salvation.

The Church had only a single priest assigned to it, who lived in a small room at the back of the church.

On a moonless night, the door to that room swung slowly inward. A dark figure crept in, past the door, glowing eyes searching about the room. They settled on a cot, upon which a figure slept.

The stranger charged forward, his wool-wrapped feet silent on the wooden floor, his long club, studded with bits of black obsidian raised above his head. Powerful arms, just visible beneath the jaguar pelt he wore like a cape, swept the club down.

The impact was so great that the cot broke in two. The pillows and blankets heaped upon it, in the shape of a sleeping man, deformed under the blow only for a moment. The Jaguar-headed attacker stood still, bewildered by the empty cot.

Three large crashes sounded in the main hall of the church — followed by war screams. Sliding down ropes that hung down through three new holes in the roof of the church, six Jaguar-headed men descended into the building. They began to swing their obsidian clubs, smashing into pews, splintering the wood. One wielded a different kind of club — the end tipped with a metal claw he used to rake along the walls of the church and the back of the toppled pews.

Less than a hundred yards away, Father Murphy had his eye pressed against the wall of the small building he had sat in all night. Built of adobe, with wooden timbers holding up a thatched roof, the small building served as a shop of sorts for the town. Goods were stacked around the building, while the owner slept in a small room in the back.

"Master Hwa! They're here!" Father Murphy said, turning away from the peephole he'd made in the wall. But the Master of Sinanju was no longer on his mat. He too had heard the commotion from the church.

It had taken Hwa only seconds to sprint silently down the street to the church. He had flung the massive door open and swept inside before the strange Jaguar-headed men destroying the church could even register the sound of the rusty hinges opening. When they did turn toward the door, they saw nothing but the darkness outside.

Each of the men wore a jaguar pelt like a cape, partially covering their bare arms. A thick, quilted cotton tunic covered their bodies, hanging halfway down their naked legs, and circled by a leather belt. Wrappings of wool and leather covered their feet. And each had the head of a jaguar.

Hwa regarded the men quietly from the shadows he hid in. He watched as one crossed to the open door of the church, the others standing still, confused.

Just as the Jaguarman reached out to grab the door and close it, Hwa struck.

Moving so fast he was nearly invisible, the Master of Sinanju darted from one shadow to the next, passing behind the Jaguarman. As he moved, he drove the tips of his right index and middle fingers into the back of his target's head, just below the base of the skull.

Like a cobra striking, his hand flicked out and back as he passed, a loud cracking noise sounding.

Like a melon, the halves of the Jaguarman's head fell apart, tumbling off his shoulders. From his new hiding place, Hwa instantly saw that they were not the halves of a head, but the halves of a mask.

Each of these attackers were human — all wearing a form-fitting mask made of carved wood, painted black like a jaguar. Where the jaguar's eyes should have been, holes allowed the men to see out. Wooden snouts extended past their mouths and noses, completing the illusion.

The man Hwa struck whirled around, his pale face showing great surprise.

"What?" the Jaguarman gasped, his free hand reaching up to his head. His mask was gone.

Hwa stepped from the shadows now, slowly, so he could be seen.

The five men facing him recoiled, startled by his appearance. The unmasked attacker spun to his left to look at Hwa. As soon as he saw him, he started to raise his club.

The obsidian-studded war club moved only an inch before the signals from its wielder's brain stopped directing muscles to lift it. They stopped because Hwa had again snaked his hand out and back, faster than the deadliest snake, and with sufficient force to collapse the man's forehead. He fell to the floor of the church.

The remaining Jaguarmen screamed loudly and charged forward.

***

Father Murphy knew that the Master of Sinanju had been hired to eliminate whatever this threat was to the Church in Mexico. But the priest had to see for himself. He had crept quietly out of the small shop and was moving down the dusty street as the sounds of battle continued from the House of God.

The priest circled the church, avoiding the partially-open front door. He crept around to the back door that led into the priest's quarters — Father Dominguez, whom Murphy had persuaded to hide on a nearby farm for the night.

He was almost to the door when it was flung violently open and a figure bolted out.

Even with virtually no light in the sky, Father Murphy could see the jaguar-shape of the running man's head and the flapping cape of animal hide tied around his neck. Then the runner was past him — sprinting away as fast as he could.

Father Murphy scowled and gave chase.

***

Only one Jaguarman remained standing now. His compatriots were scattered about the wrecked interior of the church, arms and legs bent at impossible angles, their heads rotated around like an owl's. All had been killed swiftly, without the small Asian man in black ever having appeared to touch them.

The last Jaguar, fearing for his life, tried to flee. He leapt atop a barrel-sized boulder in the middle of the church that was tied to the end of a large rope that led up and out, through a hole in the roof.

The Jaguarman looked up and opened his mouth, attempting to scream.

His head bent back at an impossible angle, the sound dying in his throat as all the vertebrae in his neck exploded. He fell off the boulder, dead fingers releasing the rope.

As one, the three anchor-like boulders rose swiftly up into the air, vanishing through the holes in the ceiling. Hwa briefly considered riding one up, as the Jaguarman had intended on doing.

Instead, the Master dashed out the front of the door and leapt. He rocketed upwards, far higher than any normal man should have been able to, and landed lightly on the roof, ready to dispatch more of the Jaguar-masked men.

But the rooftop was empty.

Hwa looked around, puzzled. Not even the boulders and their long ropes were to be seen. They had vanished into thin air.

A noise caught his attention and Hwa crossed the rooftop in the beat of a heart. Looking down, he saw the priest, Father Murphy, rolling around on the ground with another Jaguarman.

Hwa leapt down lightly from the roof, just as the Jaguarman rose to his feet. The old priest was considerably slower than the strangely-garbed man he'd tackled. He was barely up on one knee when the Jaguar pulled a small, obsidian-bladed knife from his belt.

The blade swept through the air, slashing at the priest, then stopped inches from his face. A sickening, crunching noise sounded, and the blade rotated around in place then flashed away into the darkness.

The Jaguarman staggered backwards, away from Father Murphy, his arm torn off just below the elbow. Blood spurted from the stump and the masked man dropped to his knees.

Hwa's hand flashed forward and the mask on the man split and fell away.

"He's a man!" Murphy gasped, still trying to catch his breath as he rose to his feet.

The unmasked Jaguarman's eyes rolled up in his head and he pitched forward onto his face in the dirt. The blood spurting from his arm stopped — as did his heart.

Hwa held out a hand to Murphy, to help the old man up.

"T'ank you, my son," Father Murphy said, reaching for the hand.

Suddenly it wasn't there. Instead it slammed into the priest's chest and propelled him backwards, through the air, several feet.

As he was thrown back, Father Murphy saw Master Hwa spin in place and snatch at the air. He held something in his hand, looking at it for a moment. Then he looked up, into the pitch-black night sky, and threw the small object.

Several seconds passed, then the sound of something striking the ground could be heard. It sounded heavy.

"What was tat?" Murphy gasped, standing up. His chest burned where Hwa had pushed him, but no ribs seemed broken.

The young Korean reached down to the ground and dug in the dirt with his fingers. He then offered what he had freed from the soil to the priest. In the darkness it was hard to make out, but Murphy recognized it immediately — a stone projectile like the one they had found lodged in the last church. Had he not been shoved aside, the small stone would have struck Murphy.

"Come," Hwa said, and walked away. He kept looking up at the sky as he walked. Murphy glanced up as well, but could see nothing but darkness.

Hwa finally stopped, not far from the abandoned church. At his feet lay a body.

Like the others, this Jaguarman wore a quilted tunic and jaguar-skin cape. But instead of a carved, form-fitting Jaguar mask, the man had a strange contrivance on his face, consisting of two long tubes over each eye, held in place by a leather harness-like mask. The ends of each tube were covered with dark lenses.

"Another one from ta church?" Murphy asked.

"No. From there," Hwa answered pointing up.

Murphy looked up into the dark sky. "Heaven?"

"I do not think so."

"T'en where?"

Hwa considered what he had seen with his Sinanju trained eyes. Clearly, the western priest had not seen it. And Hwa had no idea of what it could be. He did not recall any such thing from the scrolls he had studied since he was a child.

"I do not know."

Murphy frowned — he could tell the young Master was being evasive. He turned to the corpse and pulled the bizarre headpiece from the dead man. He held the contraption to his own eyes and let out a whistle.

"Saints be praised!" Murphy exclaimed. He handed the harness to

Hwa. "It lets you see in ta dark!"

Hwa took the weird headpiece and looked through a tube. Sure enough, the world was revealed in a purplish haze several degrees lighter than the night around them. But nowhere near as well as Hwa himself could see.

"An interesting toy," Hwa said, handing the headdress back to Murphy.

"T'ere's definitely more ta t'ese men t'an meets ta eye. I can't wait ta examine 'em come first light..."

Chapter Eight: Into the Circle

As THE MORNING SUN rose, Father Murphy was busy examining the bodies of all eight Jaguarmen, laid out in a neat row behind the church. Each appeared to be of European ancestry — light-skinned and several with blue eyes.

"Most interestin'," Murphy said as he examined the corpse that had fallen from the sky. He was particularly interested in the man's fingernails, from beneath which he scraped a black substance.

"It is coal," Hwa declared.

"Coal? How canya know t'at?"

"I smell it on him — he reeks of it the same as the men on the woman's sailing ship."

"Holy Mary, Mother of Christ!" Father Dominguez exclaimed, making the sign of the cross. He had just rounded the corner of the small church and saw the bodies laid out in a neat row.

Father Murphy tapped the coal dust into a small glass vial then rose from where he had been kneeling.

"Father Dominguez! An' a good mornin' to ya."

"Father! What have you done?" Dominguez exclaimed. A dark-skinned man, Dominguez had been born and raised in Mexico, and considered himself one of the people. He crossed himself again.

"T'ese are ta men t'at've been attackin' our brutters and sisters," Murphy said. "T'ey — "

"Are Jaguar warriors!" Dominguez gasped. His face was pale and he was shaking visibly.

"Jaguar warriors?" Murphy repeated. "Ya know t'ese men?"

"No, not these particular men," Dominguez said, stepping forward slowly. He knelt by one body — the first Hwa had killed in the church. "But I know the legends."

Hwa was interested now. "What legends?"

"Before the Spanish came, this land was ruled by the Aztecs — a fierce and mighty people who controlled all of what we know now as Mexico and beyond. They worshiped many false gods, including Tezcatlipoca — the god of the night sky. Their culture believed in human sacrifice and slavery."

"These are the Aztecs?" Hwa asked.

"No, these are the *cuāuhocēlōtl* — the Jaguar Warriors. They gathered slaves for sacrifice throughout the land, taking them back to their temples where their hearts were torn out and sacrificed to *Tezcatlipoca* or *Quetzalcoatl*."

"Where are these Aztecs now?"

"Gone," Father Murphy said. "Ta Spanish wiped 'em out more'n a hundert years ago."

Dominguez crossed himself. "You must get these bodies out of here — away from town! Immediately! The villagers must not see them!"

"No," Hwa said. "We should mount their heads on spears around the town as a lesson to others not to stand against the Church."

Dominguez and Murphy looked with horror at the young Master.

"Sinanju has done this for centuries," Hwa explained. "It will make your enemies fear and respect you."

"Sinanju?" Father Dominguez said, looking to Father Murphy. "Who is this man?"

"A consultant, employed by ta Church ta assist me in my investigation," Murphy explained.

"All hail the Glory of the mighty Emperor, Pious the Benevolent!" Master Hwa said, bowing deeply.

"Emperor?" Father Dominguez was truly baffled now.

Father Murphy shot Hwa an angry look, then took the younger priest by the arm and turned him around. "Come along, Father — tell me more about t'ese Jaguar men. Brutter Hwa will give t'ese men a proper Christian burial, won't ya?"

"As you wish, priest."

* * *

Several hours later, with the sun high overhead and the bodies of the Jaguarmen removed from town, Father Murphy and Master Hwa sat around a campfire cooking their midday meal.

Murphy rolled one of the small stone projectiles between his fingertips, studying it. "It's a bullet."

"Yes, I know," Hwa said, stirring the rice in his pot. It was comforting to have the food in this savage land — even if it was Japanese rice.

"But t'ere's no powder on it — no sign o' burnin'. How could it have been fired by a rifle?"

"Perhaps the Chinese have devised a new method for cowardly striking down enemies from afar," Hwa sniffed.

Murphy put the bullet aside and looked at his map again. "T'ere must be more of 'em. T'ey couldn't have made it all ta way here by horseback. T'ere aren't even any horses around."

"Correct — they did not ride on horses," Master Hwa declared. He sipped at a spoonful of rice. "I searched for tracks in the area — there were none."

"Well then how did t'ey get here?" Father Murphy asked. He checked his own small pot — the bubbling stew of potatoes and meat was done as well. He put down the map and began scooping out stew onto his plate.

Master Hwa wrinkled up his nose at the smell of the thick stew. Pouring his own rice into a wooden bowl, he moved upwind, circling the campfire before settling down to eat.

"Your enemy moves through the air," Hwa said at last.

"T'rough ta air? Are ya tryin' ta say t'ey fly?"

"No," Hwa said after chewing a mouthful of rice. "They travel on ships in the sky."

"Airships?" Father Murphy asked, surprised. He'd seen balloons in his lifetime — even models of huge airships the French were trying to develop. But that was in Europe — a world away. Nothing like that existed in the Americas.

"If that is what you call them," Hwa said, taking another bite. He remembered the stories from his own grandfather, Master Pong, who had seen great balls of heated air lifting men into the sky in France. Balloons, he had called them. A foolish invention of the west. Men should keep their feet on the ground.

Father Murphy considered this for several moments, gulping down his stew. The warm meal filled his stomach and made him feel better. It also cleared his head.

"T'ose men didn't look French," he said at last.

"No, they did not smell of cheese and wine."

"What did they smell like?"

Hwa considered for a moment. "They smelled no different from the other men in this land."

Father Murphy took another bite. "Ya really can smell what a man has eaten?"

"Yes," Hwa answered. "Just as you smell the difference between the rabbit in your soup and the cow you have been eating for many years. Each has a particular odor caused by their diet."

Hwa was done now. He did not require much rice, for his Sinanju-honed body was far more efficient than that of the old priest gobbling down his vile concoction of meat and potatoes. "May I see your map?"

Murphy nodded and passed the map over to the young Master.

Hwa studied it intently for several moments, and then pointed to a spot on the map with his fingernail. "Here is where we will find these heart-takers."

Murphy set down his bowl of stew and studied the map.

"Cholula? What makes ya t'ink t'ey're hidin' t'ere?"

"A bird does not range far from its nest," Hwa said. "It travels out in all directions, seeking prey, but always returns to its home."

Murphy studied the map intently, and saw that the town of Cholula was indeed at the center of the large ring of attacks of the past six months.

"T'at's tree days ride from here," the priest said.

Hwa rose and kicked at the fire, his foot snapping out and back in a blur. A gust of wind thrown up by the kick caused the flames to flare briefly, then die out. "We should start now."

Chapter Nine: Into the Nest

After another long, dusty ride in their buckboard wagon, Father Murphy and Master Hwa finally reached their destination — the city of Cholula. Following a long and winding road up to the top of the hill the city was named for, they stopped at a large Spanish church, San Gabriel.

While they waited patiently to see the bishop, a monk from the adjoining monastery walked them through the building.

"The church and monastery were founded in 1529," the monk explained in Spanish as Murphy and Hwa looked at the rich tapestries and ornate trappings of the main chapel. A short man, he wore a brown robe with a coarse rope tied around his middle.

"What have ya heard of t'ese attacks on our churches?" Father Murphy asked the monk. Even speaking Spanish, the priest's Irish accent showed.

"Ah," the short monk, Javier, said. "Not much news of the atrocities reaches us here."

"What do you know of the Aztecs?" Hwa asked, changing the subject. His Spanish was perfect, much to the surprise of Father Murphy.

Javier seemed visibly relieved for the change in topic. "Very much, brother. In fact San Gabriel is built on the ruins of a heathen temple. The very hill we are on was purported to be built by the Aztecs. In their language, *Cholula* means hill."

"Brothers!" a new voice called out. Father Murphy turned to see a bishop wearing crisp clean clothes approaching. With fair skin and dark hair, the Bishop had a thin mustache, above even thinner lips. His hawk-like nose and high cheekbones gave him a sinister look.

"Bishop Salazar," Father Murphy said bowing.

Salazar handed over a folded packet of papers. "I have examined your letters from Rome, brother. You are more than welcome to stay here as long as you need before continuing your journey."

"Thank you, Bishop," Father Murphy said, folding the papers and tucking them into a pocket of his dusty black cassock. "But I believe we will actually remain here until our investigation is complete."

"Oh? Do you not wish to travel to all the churches that have been struck thus far?"

"We have seen enough," Hwa said.

"Who is this?" Salazar asked, turning and extending a hand to Hwa.

"Allow me to introduce M — " Murphy started to say.

"I am H'si T'ang, servant of Rome," Hwa said, bowing. "I am here to assist Father Murphy in his study."

Murphy seemed taken aback at Hwa's duplicity. "Uh, yes. H'si journeyed with me here all the way from the Far East."

"Are you a Jesuit also?"

"No," Hwa responded.

"He is my student," Murphy said quickly. "In the forensic sciences." It was not completely a lie. Father Murphy gathered that Sinanju cared little for the after effects of death, only in causing them. He was, in effect, teaching the young Master something his House had probably never studied.

"Welcome to Mexico!" Salazar said. "But tell me, Father, why do you feel you can solve this puzzle from our humble church and monastery?"

"It is at the center of the attacks," Hwa said.

"We believe San Gabriel may be attacked next," Murphy hurriedly countered.

"Nonsense," Salazar laughed. "We are too close to the capital. All of Emperor Maximilian's troops are a sure deterrent to any violence here. Unless these disguised devils want to join their heathen brethren in Hell, eh?"

Salazar laughed loudly — his raspy cackling echoing in the chapel.

"Come, come — you must be tired after your long journey," Salazar finally said when his laughter died out. "Brother Javier, please show our guests to their quarters in the monastery."

"Yes, your grace," Javier said, bowing deeply. He then turned to Murphy and Hwa. "Please, this way, brothers."

Murphy and Hwa fell into step behind the monk. Once they were outside, headed for the nearby monastery, Hwa dropped his voice to a whisper.

"Tread carefully, priest," he said in Korean. "We have found the nest."

"What?" Father Murphy responded back in Korean. "Here? This is a

House of God." He was willing to believe the Jaguarmen could be from the area — but to imply they lived in the church? It was blasphemous.

"You are wrong, Master of Sinanju," Father Murphy continued. "These are my brutters and sisters — not killers."

"We shall see."

* * *

Several hours after nightfall, Father Murphy rose from his bed. Tucking his leather shoes into the back pockets of his trousers, he crept to the door of his room. He had been thinking about Hwa's words for many hours, and those of the bishop.

Something made Hwa believe San Gabriel was more than what it seemed. But he hadn't thought so before they arrived. Something in the church, or something the monk or the bishop had said must have aroused the young master's suspicions.

But what was it?

It had taken Murphy hours of replaying the brief visit in his mind. Finally he had hit upon it. Bishop Salazar knew that some of the Jaguarmen were dead.

That was clearly impossible. Only Murphy, Hwa and Father Dominguez knew that. And despite the speed with which gossip spread in the Church, the distances were too great. Dominguez could not have gotten word here so quickly.

That left only one possible conclusion.

Murphy refused to accept this. Bishop Salazar was a man of God — entrusted with not only the church and the monastery of San Gabriel but of the entire surrounding Diocese.

So Father Murphy decided to investigate.

Barefooted, he crept out of his small accommodations in the Franciscan monastery. He tiptoed through the wooden halls, easing past doors, and finally walked into the courtyard atop the hill upon which San Gabriel had been built.

"You make too much noise, priest," Hwa whispered in Murphy's ear. The old Irishman nearly jumped out of his skin.

"What're ya doin'?" Murphy exclaimed as loudly as he could in a whisper.

"The same as you — searching for the rest of the vipers."

"Ya can't go killin' me brutters and sisters on suspicions, Master Hwa!"

"I know this. But I will prove to you I am right."

Master Hwa then began walking toward the main chapel. Murphy looked around nervously and followed him.

Once past the main entrance, the two men entered the great hall of the chapel. Hwa was as silent as a gentle breeze, while Murphy's bare feet slapped against the marble-tiled floor.

Hwa finally stopped before the great altar itself.

"Well?" Murphy asked. "Now what've ya got in mind?"

Hwa said nothing and instead reached out and pushed against the altar.

The huge slab of marble — at least three feet thick, and topped with an elaborate wooden podium from which the priests led services — must have weighed several tons. But at Hwa's light touch, it rumbled and moved back quickly, the splintering sound of wood and breaking metal clearly audible in the chapel.

"No!" Murphy hissed. "What're ya do — " The protest died in his throat as cool air swept up over him, from a large, man-sized rectangle cut in the floor beneath the altar. It was a passage, with rough-hewn stairs leading down.

"The air by the altar was cooler than the rest of the church," Hwa said. "It is a common mistake made by those attempting to hide their treachery with secret tunnels."

Hwa turned and started down the passage.

"Wait!" Murphy said, touching his sleeve. The old man had studied a great many manuscripts and journals in the Vatican. He knew that old catacombs and tunnels were often guarded by the same mechanical devices he had heard Hwa breaking when he forced the altar back.

"The enemy is below," Hwa said. "If we hurry, we can catch them before they leave to kill more of your Pope's followers."

"Hang on," Murphy said. He pulled the leather headband and its darkness-seeing lenses from the pocket of his wool jacket. "There could be traps."

"Sinanju does not worry about traps."

"Well, I'm Irish, not Sinanju. T'ey worry me."

Murphy put the goggles on, then pulled a small metal flask from another pocket of his coat. He took a long drink, and then tucked it away. Pulling his shoes from his back pockets, he slipped them on and quickly tied them.

"Are you ready now, priest?"

"Lead ta way," Father Murphy said.

Chapter Ten: A Secret Revealed

THE PASSAGE LEADING DOWN into the hill of Cholula, beneath the San Gabriel church, was lined with stone blocks and the occasional wall niche for a torch. Even with the strange night-seeing glasses Murphy had taken from the dead Jaguarman, the passage was almost unnavigable in its inky darkness.

After what Murphy guessed was a good one hundred feet, the passage began to brighten — dim, flickering light coming from below.

Hwa and Murphy slowed their descent, eventually coming to a large chamber lit with torches. The walls were lined with racks and shelves, on which sat supply crates, and the costume and gear of the Jaguarmen — most of them. Murphy did a quick count and guessed that there were at least two dozen of the fifty-odd uniforms missing. Minus the eight already killed by Master Hwa, that meant sixteen more men were out terrorizing the countryside.

Hwa walked slowly around the chamber, looking intently at the floor. He finally knelt and began to brush away dirt.

"Find somet'in'?" Murphy asked, coming over. A wooden panel was visible. Hwa grabbed it and ripped it free, dislodging the dirt covering the rest of it. It was the lid of a coffin. It had been covering a large wooden crate in which lay three badly-decomposed bodies.

Father Murphy recognized the brown robes of Franciscan monks on the bodies.

"May ta Lord forgive me for my vengeful t'oughts," Murphy said, crossing himself.

"These are your people, priest. The others are imposters."

"Murderers."

Hwa stood, walking once more around the chamber. He stopped by a wall and pressed one of the many stones in it. A huge section of the rough-cut stone wall swung back, revealing a horizontal passage.

"This way," Hwa said.

Murphy nodded and followed Hwa into the passage. This one was slightly wider and appeared more modern. After several hundred feet, Murphy realized the passage was not level, but at a very slight decline.

Stone walls gave way to earthen ones — held up every few feet by timber supports, as if the passage were a mining tunnel.

The sound of voices began to echo faintly in the distance.

The two men finally emerged into a massive chamber, far larger than the whole church of San Gabriel. At least four hundred feet across, the vast pit in the earth was round and lined with rock and dirt — a natural opening. Overhead, stars twinkled in a night sky.

But it was what sat in the middle of the chamber that astounded Murphy.

It was huge — at least three hundred feet long. A massive, fifty foot-high tube, rounded at both ends, and painted a dark color that matched the night sky. Beneath the vessel, something resembling a boat was suspended — one end marked with windows, the other with a large blade. It was like a riverboat suspended from the vessel floating in the air.

It was the airship Hwa had claimed to see. But it was of a design that Father Murphy had never before seen.

Stretching across the huge chamber the airship sat in was a large metal and wooden bridge, at least fifty feet wide. At first, Murphy thought it was flooring, but a quick glance down revealed that the huge chamber had no bottom — it extended down into the earth an indeterminate amount, its depths lost in darkness.

"A sinkhole," Murphy whispered.

Hwa tugged on the priest's arm, pulling him behind a large stack of crates on the bridge, near where they had emerged from the passage leading from San Gabriel.

"We have arrived in time," Hwa said.

Sure enough, the Jaguarmen were still in the chamber, bustling about the strange airship, both on it and beneath it. They appeared to be getting the strange vessel ready to get underway.

"How does it work?" Hwa whispered.

"Ta airship?" Murphy asked. "I'm not sure. I've read some're filled with a flammable gas — hydrogen."

Hwa looked blankly at Murphy. "Flammable? Hydrogen? Speak English, priest."

"It burns — the gas burns, like oil. It is lighter than the air around us, thereby providing lift..."

The priest's explanation was cut short by the sound of someone running. A Jaguarman charged out of the tunnel they had just come from. He ran loudly across the metal and wood bridge spanning the gaping maw of the pit.

"Sir Henry! Sir Henry!" Brother Javier shouted. Only the faux Franciscan was no longer wearing the brown robes of his disguise. He was dressed in a full Jaguar costume, clutching a thin tube, about three feet long, in one hand.

The Jaguarmen under the airship parted and Bishop Salazar walked out to meet Javier.

"What is it? Are they dead?" he barked.

Javier dropped to one knee, bowing. "No, Sir Henry — they were not even in their quarters. We cannot find them anywhere."

"Dammit!" the man called Sir Henry swore. "They must be snooping around the monastery."

"Sir Henry?" Father Murphy whispered, looking at Hwa, who shrugged impassively. "T'at man is no Spaniard."

"I think they found the passage!" Javier loudly exclaimed. "The altar was pushed back, and will not close. They tore up the graves of the monks."

"So, they are here?" Salazar turned to the men around him. "Spread out — search the upper levels!"

Father Murphy glanced up, and for the first time noticed that at ground level, around the massive sinkhole, buildings had been built to hide the secret lair from passers-by at street level.

"Master Hwa, I believe — " Father Murphy said, turning to his companion. Only Hwa was no longer there.

Murphy glanced back at the bridge, underneath the airship. The half-dozen men there were turning to leave when a black blur sprang into their midst. It was Hwa.

The young master lashed out with his hands and feet — moving so quickly Murphy's brain didn't register what he was doing until after it was over. The Jaguarmen began to topple, one after another, like dominoes.

Sir Henry, as Javier had called him, recoiled in terror as his men were dispatched with quick strokes from the small Asian. He turned and sprinted away, headed for one of the many ropes dangling from the airship.

The sound of something hitting metal — many somethings —

erupted from the bridge. Hwa dashed to his right, and glanced up. On the deck around the airship's long undercarriage structure, two Jaguarmen were pointing long tubes at him. One end of the tubes was connected to flexible hoses that came down out of the airship. The other ends, open and facing Hwa, were disgorging projectiles — the same stone projectiles they had found earlier. The Master of Sinanju spun and twisted, moving away from the stone bullets with ease. Many seemed to pass through him as though he were not solid.

Hwa plucked two stone bullets from the air. With a flick of his wrists, he sent them back at the two men. Each collapsed to the deck, the stone bullets lodged deep between their eyes.

Sir Henry reached a rope, the bottom end tied to a large boulder. Immediately, the rope was pulled upwards — hauled up by one of three large reels on the airship. Boulder and the Jaguarman aboard it were rapidly reeled in.

Hwa spun in place, hand snaking out, and grabbed at a small dart in the air, catching it between his thumb and forefinger. He glanced at it, then at the Jaguarman, Javier, who had fired it at Hwa's back from a thin blowgun.

Father Murphy tackled the Jaguarman, knocking him to the rough floor of the bridge.

"Go! Don't let him get away!" Murphy yelled.

Hwa nodded and vanished — racing away to another rope. Faster than Salazar, he shot upwards — but not because the rope was being reeled in. Hwa was climbing it like a spider, but far more swiftly.

But as fast as the Master of Sinanju was, the Jaguarmen were able to stop his ascent. One quickly drew a long stiletto knife and slashed at the rope, sending Hwa plummeting thirty feet, back down to the bridge.

The Jaguarman named Javier had recovered from being knocked down and was trading punches with Murphy near the tunnel leading into the airship cavern. Despite his age, the Irishman managed to land several good jabs on the Jaguarman's head, dancing about in place, hands held in front of him in a bare-knuckle boxer's stance.

But as Hwa's feet touched lightly down on the decking of the bridge, Javier whipped a stiletto from his belt. "Enough!"

Father Murphy dodged the first slash of the weapon — his guard dropping. He then took a solid strike to the face from Javier's free hand.

The old priest felt his knees buckle and down he went. Javier lunged with his thin blade.

Hwa's hands suddenly appeared, moving quickly along the length of the blade, as though he were vigorously rubbing them together to stay warm. Metal splintered and shattered, and the dagger's blade broken into several dozen pieces that dropped through the grate-like floor of the bridge and vanished from sight.

Hwa shifted slightly on one foot and his hand lanced out and back, Javier's sternum exploding in his chest, bone fragments ripping through his body like shrapnel.

The Jaguarman fell to the floor of the bridge, dead.

The airship was moving now. A great roar came from it as its steam engine lurched to speed. The huge propeller at the end of the ship began to turn and the air-filled vessel began to rise.

"They're getting away!" Murphy exclaimed, rising to his feet.

Suddenly, the old man jumped in front of Hwa, surprising the young Master. He grunted and Hwa caught him to keep him from falling. When he turned Murphy around, Hwa saw a thin dart sticking out of the priest's chest.

Hwa plucked the dart out, then eased the old man to the deck of the bridge.

"No — don't worry about me," Murphy declared. "Don't let 'em get away…"

The old priest was gasping for air now, his lips turning blue. The poison from the dart was rapidly working its way through his system.

Hwa looked back and forth between the priest and the rising airship. Then he was gone.

In the gondola of the airship, Sir Henry was feverishly working levers hanging down from the ceiling. Suddenly, the airship lurched, the bow dipping down. Their ascent had stopped.

"More steam!" Sir Henry screamed into a tube to the left of the airship's huge steering wheel. He watched as gauges showed the increase of hot air being pumped into the lifting bladder of the airship. Like a hot air balloon, this allowed the airship to adjust its vertical height without venting any of the precious hydrogen in the fore and aft bladders.

But despite that extra hot air increasing the airship's buoyancy with every passing second, the vessel would rise no more.

Sir Henry raced to the door of the airship's bridge and threw it open.

Far below, he saw Master of Sinanju, streaking back and forth on the bridge over the sinkhole, grasping at the long mooring lines dangling down from the blimp. Pausing at each one only long enough to tie it to the bridge, the Master moved quickly, from one line to another.

Hwa had four of the lines secured when he felt the pressure wave of another dart slicing through the air at him. He batted it away with one hand, and grabbed another mooring line with the other. He quickly looped the line through the grating of the bridge, securing it with a tight knot. Another dart passed through the air toward him — but Hwa was no longer standing there.

Above, on the deck around the airship's gondola, Sir Henry and two other Jaguarmen were firing darts from their blowguns as fast as they could, plucking the darts from pouches on their belts.

Again and again, they fired their slivers of poison-tipped death. But Hwa ignored the darts, which seemed to pass harmlessly through him. He was busy tying down the mooring lines.

The bridge shuddered as the airship's buoyancy increased and it struggled to rise. One of the Jaguarmen screamed and pitched off the side of the airship — vanishing into the dark maw of the sinkhole. The airship was beginning to dip forward, its nose held firmly in place, but the tail unfettered.

Sir Henry clawed his way back into the control room even as Hwa raced back to Father Murphy's side.

Kneeling beside the priest on the side of the bridge, Hwa worked a nerve cluster in the small of Murphy's back. "Why did you do that, old man?"

"A boy needs his father," Murphy gasped.

Hwa frowned and glanced back at the airship. He saw that the last Jaguarmen had stopped shooting darts from their blowguns and were now desperately trying to cut at the mooring lines that held them in place — their thin stilettos sawing away at the ropes, which began to part, one after another.

Hwa stopped purging the poison from Murphy's body — an ancient Sinanju technique he had learned early in his training. He began rummaging in the priest's pockets, eventually locating his small fire-making kit. Hwa popped open the small metal tin, plucking out the piece of steel and flint and dropping the rest.

He stood and snapped out both his arms, releasing the two pieces at supersonic speeds. They sliced through the air, seemingly moving parallel to one another. Then they punctured the thin, cloth skin of the airship, just above the front of the gondola.

But the flint and steel were not moving parallel to each other. Hwa had thrown them so that their paths crossed just inside the airship. Steel crashed into flint, shattering it, and producing a spray of sparks.

Flames shot out of the small holes the flint and steel had made entering the airship. The holes ripped and tore as geysers of flame erupted out. The whole air ship shuddered as flame swept through it from front to back. The cloth sides of the huge craft split, and the flames spread along the craft's length. The entire ship, a blazing length of fire, began to drop.

The burning wreckage struck the center of the bridge, each end continuing on, as the middle was momentarily supported by the platform. Then an explosion erupted from the crumpled, burning gondola. The boiler of its steam engine had just ruptured.

Bridge and gondola were blown apart and the airship separated into two immense, burning halves that fell, along with a great section of the bridge's middle, into the deep sinkhole.

Hwa turned back to Murphy, and once more began to work the old man's nerves. Murphy felt his lungs contract and fill with air, his heart to race. He felt strange — invigorated by the deep, deep breathing his body was being forced to do. It was unlike anything the old priest had ever experienced before.

After several seconds, Murphy felt himself rolled onto his side. His body spasmed and he began to cough up bile. The numbness in his limbs was fading.

"I guess we'll never know who t'ey were," Murphy coughed, slowly sitting up.

Hwa walked to the body of the false-monk Javier and pried his dead hand open. He lifted out the handle of the bladeless stiletto he had destroyed moments earlier.

"Priest!" Hwa asked, walking back to Murphy. "How do you know my wife is pregnant with a boy?"

"She carries her baby low, Master o' Sinanju. Everyone knows t'at means a boy."

The young Master handed the broken knife to Murphy, frowning.

"I know of this symbol from the Scrolls of Sinanju," Hwa said. "Once they served your Church."

Murphy's vision was still a little blurry, but he was finally able to make out the symbol. He inhaled deeply in surprise. The pommel of the thin stiletto bore a symbol that had not been seen in Europe for over five hundred years. Not since Pope Clement the Fifth had disbanded the group.

The knife belonged to a Knight Templar.

ABOUT THE AUTHOR:

C.E. Martin has served his local Midwestern community for two decades in criminal justice. A Desert Storm-era USAF veteran, he served four years in uniform before returning home to Indiana. A long-time fan of pulp fiction and men's adventure, C.E. was first inspired to write by the *Destroyer* series, of which he has been a long-time fan. When not blogging or authoring the latest in his own *Stone Soldiers* military thriller series, C.E. can be found watching B-movies with his kids or battling virtual Communists on X-Box.

REMO AND CHIUN

Scott Driscoll

RECRUITMENT DRIVE

Elizabeth Sloane

Chapter One

Conrad MacCleary walked out of Smith's office. As he let the door close behind him, he deflated slightly. When Smith had recruited him all those years ago, he had argued for an enforcement arm. He knew then that CURE would need to kill — it was the nature of what they did. But making someone not exist?

First things first, he thought as he rubbed the bridge of his nose. He had to track down the soldier from Vietnam — the one who had done the impossible.

MacCleary walked down the stairwell to his quarters in Folcroft. He closed the door behind him and picked up the phone. He dialed a single number and waited while the phone rang.

CURE had several departments, all staffed with people who thought they worked for other government agencies. The work was divided up so no one person or department would ever put the pieces together, but with all their agents and data crunchers, someone would be able to find the man he was looking for.

The line picked up.

"This is MacCleary," he said, without waiting for the person on the other end.

"Yes sir, what can I do for you?"

"I need someone found. Vietnam Vet. The CIA should have a write-up on a mission he completed over there involving five dead Congs and some files."

"That shouldn't be too hard to find. Forty-eight hours at the longest."

The nameless voice started to ramble off some unintelligible jargon about how he would go about finding it.

"I don't need the details," MacCleary said. "Just the file."

He hung up the phone. He would find his soldier. Conn just hoped he was still everything he had been.

* * *

It only took thirty-two hours for the men with the computers to track down the soldier MacCleary was looking for.

The ringing phone woke him from a sound sleep. He got up and rubbed his eyes. The phone continued shrieking. Finally, he picked up the receiver.

MacCleary growled into the phone, "What?"

There was a beat of silence on the other end, followed by a slightly timid voice, "Mr. MacCleary, sir?"

MacCleary sighed and in a calmer voice said, "I take it you have news for me?"

"Yes, sir," the voice said, more confidently this time. "We found him; I'm sending the full report up to you."

"Give me the important stuff now."

The unnamed worker on the other end rattled off a few details, "Remo Williams, Newark PD, Vietnam Veteran..."

Conn listened while he started to dress. He had gotten used to doing it one-handed, but it meant holding the phone up with his shoulder. He knocked an empty bottle off his nightstand and cursed silently. It hit the ground and rolled under his bed. He'd deal with that later.

He missed Willams' age and most of his service record, not that he needed to know more than he already did.

"...You know about that mission. Orphan, raised in a Catholic orphanage. Real parents are unknown. I can probably find that with more digging."

"No, it doesn't matter. Hold on." MacCleary put the receiver down and finished pulling the shirt over his head.

He picked the phone back up, "Wife, kids, any of that?"

"No, he's the only one registered at his address. Anything else?

"That's enough for now. The rest is in the file?" He asked.

"Yes sir. Can I do anything else for you?" The voice asked, eager to be useful to the top brass.

MacCleary hung up without responding. He had never felt a need to make friends with any of the others who worked for CURE. He didn't see why he should start now.

He picked the hook that took the place of his left hand and strapped it to his empty left wrist. He took a cigarette out of the pack on his bedside table and put it in his mouth. He picked up the lighter and flicked it on, lighting the tobacco.

MacCleary inhaled deeply, enjoying the sharp, acrid flavor.

A minute later there was a knock on his door. Folcroft wasn't that big; the internal couriers could get from one side to the other relatively quickly.

MacCleary opened his door and took the file from the kid on the other side. He closed the door and sat down at his desk. He put the file down and rested the cigarette in the ashtray. He opened to the first page of the file and started reading.

"All right, Remo Williams," he said to no one, "Let's see if you're the man we need."

An hour and three cigarettes later, Conn MacCleary knew what he had known when he walked out of Smith's office — this was their man. Now it was just a matter of making him disappear.

Chapter Two

THE NEXT DAY, CONN MACCLEARY exited the gates of Folcroft before dawn. He had gone to Smith to requisition the car when he had handed over Remo Williams' file.

Smith had given him approval with a nod of his head and then waved MacCleary out of his office.

His car was an utterly unremarkable Impala, which had been one of the most purchased cars of 1971. No one in Newark would notice him, especially not a beat cop named Remo Williams.

The drive down from Rye, New York took less than an hour. He pulled to a stop across the street from the police station just as the sun was rising. He lit a cigarette and waited for the man to come.

Years in the CIA had taught Conn how to track someone without being noticed. Step one was to visualize his target. He knew where Williams lived, but he wanted to watch him work. See what kind of man this Remo had become.

MacCleary didn't have long to wait. Williams had drawn the early shift that week; he walked into the precinct just after dawn.

While he waited, MacCleary watched his surroundings. There was very little going on at this hour. The criminals had scurried back to their holes with the sunrise, and it was still too early for the regular folk to be out and about. The only people out at this hour were cops…and spies.

An hour later Remo Williams walked out of the precinct in his uniform and got into a patrol car. MacCleary put out his cigarette, turned over the engine of the Impala, and waited a moment. The patrol car pulled away from the curb and MacCleary followed.

He stayed three car lengths back. When the patrol car stopped for Williams to talk to someone or to chase off some loitering kids he turned the corner and watched from a distance.

MacCleary watched Williams stop near a school to bust some dope dealer in a purple Cadillac with whitewall tires. MacCleary shook his head. He loved his country, and he was watching it destroy itself.

This was the reason CURE needed an enforcement arm. Not just to take down small-time scumbags, but to get their bosses and the crooked politicians and judges who lined their pockets with dirty money.

MacCleary followed him back to the precinct. He watched as Williams walked the pusher into the station in handcuffs.

How long until this one's out?, he thought ruefully.

It didn't matter — not really. Getting one dealer off the street wouldn't stop the flow. Even if this one stayed in jail, there would be another one to take his place by sundown. That was how it worked.

MacCleary didn't bother to wait around for Williams to finish his paperwork and go back out. He would follow the unsuspecting cop again tomorrow. In the meantime, he wanted to see where, and how, Remo lived.

* * *

The apartment was small, but enough for a bachelor living alone. MacCleary put a glove on his good hand and went up the fire escape. He went in through the window. The lock on it was cheap, and he was able to open the window without breaking it.

The apartment was surprisingly tidy. He would have expected a bachelor cop to have cardboard takeout boxes overflowing in the trash and clothes spread over the floor of the bedroom.

There was none of that. There weren't a lot of clothes in the closet, but they were hung neatly. The trash looked like it had been taken out that morning. The linoleum floor in the kitchen was dusty, but otherwise clean.

MacCleary continued to peruse the apartment's contents. There were very few personal items. He had no photographs of friends or family. Not that that was surprising for someone raised by the nuns.

This looks like a place I could live, Conn thought. Of course, if his quarters at Folcroft were any indication, he wasn't nearly as neat.

MacCleary left the same way he came in. No one noticed him.

Chapter Three

Maccleary drove to the small motel he would be staying in while he assessed his target. The place was run by a middle-aged woman and her husband. It was one of those places where public officials went for activities they'd rather the press didn't get wind of.

CURE paid the couple handsomely for information and to keep a room open for their operatives, should one ever be needed.

He walked into the front office. The wife — Susan, if he remembered correctly — was working the desk. She gave Conn a once-over, and offered a small smile that was part curiosity — no doubt the motel had very few one-handed guests — and part invitation. He briefly wondered how many customers had taken advantage of that invitation.

"Room thirteen," he said, not returning the smile.

The woman was good; she didn't betray any knowledge she might have had that the room was special. But the smile did leave her face. Not that MacCleary had any intention of taking her up on her invitation. He had work to do.

* * *

MacCleary only brought a small bag. It contained a change of clothes, and a back-up weapon, which he left in the car. He kept his primary weapon on his person at all times.

He had made it clear to the woman at the desk that there was to be no maid service until he checked out.

After he was settled in at the motel, he went out to find a payphone. He wouldn't use the phone in the room. CURE had bugged the entire motel years before. He didn't need some data collector back at Folcroft listening in to his conversations with Smith.

He found a suitable payphone two blocks away to the side of a gas station. He checked to make sure no one was around, and dialed the familiar number.

In an office at Folcroft Sanitarium in Rye, New York a phone rang. A lemon-faced man in a gray suit picked up the receiver.

"Smith." He answered.

"Smitty, I've made contact."

Smith pinched the bridge of his nose and sighed. "MacCleary, you know better. Use the code."

"You know, Smitty, I can just imagine you sitting at your desk, in a gray suit, eating prune yogurt. Am I close?" MacCleary said, suppressing a laugh.

Smith looked down at his lunch, which was prune yogurt. "Is he what you remembered?"

"Hard to tell after just a few hours. I'll watch him again tomorrow."

"You will make a decision tomorrow. I expect to hear from you."

MacCleary wanted more time, but knew he didn't have it. "You'll hear from me."

"Conn," Smith said, addressing his friend.

"Yes, Smitty?"

"Be sure." With that Smith hung up the phone.

MacCleary stepped out of the booth and pulled the cigarette pack out of the pocket of his chinos. He pulled a stick out with his teeth and put the pack away.

Exhaling smoke, he gazed skyward. One more day — one more day to decide if this was the man whose life they should destroy.

"Goddamn us," he said, words slurring around the cigarette.

MacCleary took his time walking back to the motel. All he would do was sit anyway. He stopped at a small diner first. He ordered a hamburger, rare.

He returned to the motel and sat on the bed, planning out his day tomorrow. He wouldn't drink that night.

Chapter Four

THE NEXT MORNING WAS an early one, earlier than the day before. He would follow Williams from his apartment that day.

MacCleary pulled up in front of the apartment building where Remo Williams lived. The officer had yet to leave for work, but it should be soon, based on the time.

Sure enough, Remo came out of the building a few minutes later. He got into his car, an older model that still ran well. Like his apartment, it was clean and well cared for. He pulled onto the street and drove away. Conn put out his cigarette and followed.

Williams pulled into the station lot and walked into the precinct. This time, MacCleary waited a few minutes and followed his target inside.

It was early and the shift was changing, so there weren't many people in the building. A dozen cops sat at desks finishing up or starting paperwork. A few criminals sat handcuffed to chairs waiting to be processed.

MacCleary looked around. He didn't see Williams.

Must be changing, he thought.

Not that it really mattered. MacCleary had no intention of talking to the man. He looked around. No one had approached him. They were all busy, or trying to look busy.

The secretary at the desk finally looked up and saw the blue-eyed man who had entered several minutes before.

"Can I help you, sir?" she asked.

MacCleary turned to look at her. She was young, petite, and blonde. She was pretty, but too young.

"I think you can." MacCleary said, formulating an idea. "I'm Conrad Smith, with the Times. I'd like to speak to your Captain."

"Yes, sir. I'll tell him you're here. He always cooperates with the press." The young secretary ran off to get her captain.

MacCleary shook his head. It was sad, the way the police jumped every time a reporter came sniffing around. It was these people's jobs to stop crime. Yet they cowered in fear of what the press would say about them. Pathetic, really.

The captain came out of his office and greeted the false reporter, never even asking to see identification. As they walked away, the secretary finally noticed the hook where his left hand should have been. It unnerved her slightly, but by the end of the day she had forgotten all about it.

The captain let the door close behind him and motioned the man to take a seat. He took his own seat behind his desk and watched the man take a tape recorder out of his jacket pocket.

MacCleary put the recorder on the desk and asked, "Do you mind if I record this conversation?"

"Of course not," the captain readily agreed.

He looked at the reporter's left hand or, more specifically, the hook where the hand should have been. He didn't know why, but seeing it sitting there, in the man's lap, made him nervous.

"Who would you say your best officer is?" MacCleary asked.

The captain was startled out of his reverie. "What?"

MacCleary repeated, "Who is your best officer? The guy who brings in the most criminals?"

"Suspects." The captain corrected him; he was used to being politically correct with reporters. "Best would be Williams. Remo Williams."

MacCleary nodded, a slight smile forming. He was right about the man at least.

He asked a few more formulaic questions about crime statistics versus the number of people arrested. The captain was happy to oblige. He rambled about how crime was down (not true), how busts were up (misleading), and how the drug problem was abating (again not true).

MacCleary listened, pretending to be interested in what the captain was telling him. He asked a few more questions about Williams' record, and declared the interview successful.

As MacCleary left, a smile graced his hard features. The captain breathed a sigh of relief. He was happy to be rid of the reporter. He didn't like them anyway, but this one reminded him of a predator.

MacCleary walked to his Impala and turned the engine over. He waited while the Williams and the other cop came out and got into their patrol car. He followed them to the scene.

The police car rolled up on a fight in progress. Remo and his partner left their car to go break it up.

From MacCleary's vantage point across the street, the altercation looked like a fight between two dealers. They were both big men, though one obviously had the upper hand. He had the other in a headlock and was punching him in the stomach.

MacCleary shook his head. That was poor technique. But what more could he expect from some half-witted pushers?

Remo identified himself as a cop. The one dealer dropped the other and charged him. Remo stepped aside. The dealer stopped and turned, ready to attack.

The pusher took a wild swing, and Remo easily ducked the punch. He used the opening to punch his attacker in the gut. As the dealer staggered back, Remo kicked out his knee and grabbed his arm. As the dealer dropped, Remo twisted his arm behind his back and cuffed one hand. He grabbed the other arm and finished cuffing him.

Remo Williams looked around. As he read the dealer his rights, his partner already had the unconscious dealer cuffed and was calling in for an ambulance.

Crude, MacCleary thought, but efficient.

He rolled up his window and drove away. He had enough. He had made his decision.

Chapter Five

MACCLEARY FOUND A GAS station with a payphone, different from the one he had used the day before. He put a dime into the phone and dialed.

The phone picked up.

"It's him," MacCleary said.

"Come back. We'll discuss the next steps."

The line disconnected and MacCleary hung up. He walked to his car and drove back to the motel.

He picked up his bag and returned the key to the person at the front desk. It was a man this time — probably Susan's husband.

As he drove out of Newark, MacCleary's mind raced.

Someone who doesn't exist, he thought.

There were two ways for someone not to exist: either never be born, or die. The first was out. Williams was in the system: he was an orphan, a veteran, and a cop. They could erase him from those systems. MacCleary was confident that CURE had people who could do that. But people might still remember Remo.

No, he thought. Remo Williams has to die.

Now it was just a matter of figuring out how. They could fake his death. A body that looked enough like Williams could be procured. It might take time, but it was possible. If not, they could always do plastic surgery. CURE had done that before.

But there was the small matter of altering the body's fingerprints. New dental records could be placed in William's file — that would be easy — but fingerprints were problematic.

MacCleary sighed. That would take too long, and they didn't have enough time. They were going to have to actually kill the man.

MacCleary had made men disappear. He had faked deaths, but it wasn't easy, and in a case like this there would have to be no doubt that the man was dead. His death would need witnesses, and CURE would need a way to get the body.

He thought about it more, and by the time he had crossed into New York MacCleary knew what he was going to have to do, and he hated it.

* * *

Exactly four minutes and seventeen seconds after MacCleary had parked his car he was walking into Smith's office.

"MacCleary, that was fast." Smith said

"You sonofabitch! You knew exactly what I was going to have to do when you read his file." MacCleary was seething, and he didn't bother to hide it.

"Conn, sit down. We both knew what we were getting into when we signed up for this."

"No, you signed me up, remember?" MacCleary slammed his hands down on Smith's desk.

"Conn, sit down," Smith said in an infuriatingly calm voice.

MacCleary walked over to the couch by the wall and sat.

"You killed men for the CIA. You've set men up for CURE. Why is this different?" Smith inquired, concerned by his friend's outburst.

"Those people deserved it. They were criminals. Williams is innocent, as innocent as anyone can be these days. He was a good soldier and he's a good cop."

Smith sighed, "You know this is the only way. He cannot exist. That is our directive."

MacCleary leaned his head back and ran his good hand over his face and through his hair. He sighed and looked back at Smith, who, as usual, was calm.

"You'll take care of it?" Smith asked.

"Who else?" was MacCleary's deadpan reply.

Smith did not reply; the statement was not really a question. They both knew MacCleary was the only one who would — who could — do it. The job was to be an absolute secret.

MacCleary stood up, "I'll go back day after tomorrow. It may take a couple days, but get a judge lined up, and make sure the governor knows not to step in on this one."

Smith nodded and offered him a piece of paper, "I've begun looking into possible trainers. I have generated a list for you to review. Please do so and give me you thoughts before you begin drinking."

"Yeah, sure," was the reply he got, as MacCleary took the paper and left his office.

Chapter Six

RETURNING TO HIS quarters, MacCleary put the list on his desk and went over to his cabinet. He took out a bottle and picked up his glass from the bedside table. He plunked them both down on the desk.

First things first, he thought as he opened the whiskey and poured himself a glass.

MacCleary drank the contents down in one gulp and poured another. This time he sipped it. When the glass was empty again he finally turned to the list Smith had given him.

The choices were solid. Weapons training, spycraft; it was all there. MacCleary crossed out the name of the man Smith had recommended for strategy. He'd do that. He worked his way down to the bottom of the list, marking his choices.

The last one was martial arts. There were three names listed, he crossed out all of them. They would need something special for this. He knew just the man — but first they needed Williams.

MacCleary finished the bottle of whiskey, took a shower, and went to bed.

* * *

The morning came quickly. MacCleary groaned, because he knew it was time to see Smith again.

Conn walked into the room, across the office, and put the list on Smith's desk.

"There you go, Smitty. I've made my choices."

"I'll take them under advisement." Smith said as he looked at the marked up paper.

"No you won't, you'll use the people I approved. That's why you gave me the list." MacCleary smiled a self-satisfied smirk.

Smith did not respond; his friend was right. He trusted his judgment in this matter.

As MacCleary turned to leave Smith called out, "This last one, for martial arts, you crossed out everyone on my list."

"Mine's better," Conn replied.

"Sinanju. What is that?"

"North Korea. Look it up in that super computer of yours, and then get me clearance to go."

With that MacCleary left the office to get good and drunk. He needed a few drinks before he had to go back to Newark and ruin a good man's life.

Chapter Seven

THE NEXT DAY, CONN MacCleary returned to Newark. He decided to spend the day watching Williams again. He felt that if he was going to destroy this man, then he should know more about him, something more personal than what was in his file.

Remo Williams was good at his job. That much MacCleary knew. He also smoked, ate like crap, and drank. He was just like every other red-blooded American. That was what made it all worse.

On the outside, there was nothing that made Williams special. It was all on the inside. And so Conn watched and waited to find out what that was.

It was easy to figure out what made some men tick. He and Smith did it for love of country — they were patriots. So much so that they were willing to violate the Constitution to protect the land they loved.

Remo Williams was a harder man to figure out. He had turned down the CIA, and had no interest in a career in the military. He had just wanted to go back to Newark and be a cop. That was what he had told MacCleary in the jungles of Vietnam, after he had achieved the impossible.

Finally MacCleary gave up and returned to the motel he had stayed at before. Room thirteen was, of course, vacant. He collapsed on the bed and scratched absently at his temple with his hook.

He was practiced enough that he wouldn't cut himself, no matter how little attention he paid his actions. He thought about how to frame a man for a murder he didn't commit.

It'll have to be brutal, enough so that everyone calls for his head.

Now it was just a matter of figuring out the victim. He didn't want to hurt anyone innocent, at least not any more than necessary. Kids were entirely out of the question. He would not kill a kid.

That left one option. He smiled at the thought. At least he could do something to clean up the streets while he was there.

* * *

MacCleary went out just before midnight. He was confident that was when most of the scumbags and lowlifes would be out.

He drove through the slums with his lights off. He stopped occasionally to watch a fight or a drug deal. He drove by the bars and restaurants, watching drunks stagger out into the night.

He had his pick of criminals. Any one of them would do really, but the choices all left him cold. MacCleary didn't know why, but he was looking for something specific. Had anyone asked what that was, he wouldn't have been able to answer. So he kept looking.

He drove most of the night, but still wasn't sure. It was close to three a.m. when he stopped at a stop sign in front of a school. A scene in the parking lot caught his attention.

Perfect, MacCleary thought, watching.

There, by the same school as before, the drug dealer with the Cadillac.

Yes, he thought. The same whitewall tires, the same purple paint.

He watched as the dealer, the same one Williams had busted a few days before, handed something in a bag to a teenager. It was perfect. They had history, and this asshole had a pattern. Now he just needed the evidence.

MacCleary went back to the motel to change. Black Chinos, black turtleneck, and a glove for his right hand. Being invisible — as invisible as possible for a man with a hook — was important here.

He drove to Williams' apartment and parked a block past the building. He had checked. Williams had the night off. He was at a bar, welcoming a rookie to the force. If he was back before dawn MacCleary would be surprised.

MacCleary made his way up the fire escape and through the bedroom window again. It was dark, but he didn't turn on a light. He could see just fine in the dark.

He made his way around the room, looking for the shine of metal. There it was, on the dresser across the room.

Sloppy, Williams, leaving your badge at home.

He picked it up off the desk and left the way he came in.

* * *

CURE could have counterfeited a badge. But it would have taken time, and it would have been missing something.

This badge belonged to Remo Williams. It had his fingerprints on it. There were smudges from greasy fingers. There were scratches from use that no amount of polishing would ever take away. It was better to use this one.

Chapter Eight

MACCLEARY WENT BACK TO THE motel to shower and sleep. The frame-up would wait until tomorrow.

He walked into the room and lay down on the bed. He removed the hook from his wrist and threw it aside. He decided the shower could wait until he had slept.

The bed wasn't comfortable, but he didn't wake up until noon. He took a shower and dressed. He had to look around before he found his hook. It had landed on the floor beside the bed when he had thrown it the night before. He strapped it on and sat on the bed contemplating what he had to do.

MacCleary knew he should find a payphone and check in with Smith. He just didn't feel like it.

Smitty can wait, he decided, before leaving the room to find something to eat.

He wouldn't drink until he got back to Folcroft.

***

MacCleary hadn't gone back to the hotel after he had gone to breakfast. He had found a gas station and bought another pack of cigarettes. He hadn't touched them yet, but he had a feeling he'd need them.

After that, he found a coffee shop that wasn't infested with hippies, and drank more coffee than was probably healthy, waiting for the sun to set.

When it was finally dark, he drove the long way around the city to the school where the pusher would eventually be. He parked his car on the other side of the school and walked around to the parking lot.

MacCleary hid in the shadows, confident that no one would see him, and waited.

Two hours later, the dealer pulled his Cadillac into the parking lot of the school.

Showtime, he thought, walking over to the car.

He allowed the dealer to see him. He must have thought Conn was a buyer because he got out of his car and walked towards him.

MacCleary walked right up to him and before the dealer could even blink MacCleary jabbed his fingernails into the dealer's throat. The man crumbled and MacCleary caught him with his hooked arm.

This was going to have to look like a beating, so he gave him one. He slammed his fist into the scumbag's face, breaking his nose. A second punch broke his jaw and cheekbone. Then he slammed his fist into the pusher's gut, breaking a rib, then again, this time he got two ribs.

He laid the body down, picked up an arm, and slammed his foot into it, shattering the elbow. Kneeling down by the body, Conn used the flat of his hand to crack the sternum. He did it again, sending a rib into the right lung, then another rib into the heart, which soon stopped beating entirely. He did it wrong, so that bruises would form.

MacCleary took the badge out of his pants pocket and put it in the hand of the dead pusher. He stood and turned to walk away, then thought better of it. Conn turned back and gave the dealer a swift kick in the head, fracturing the skull.

With that, he walked back to his car, drove three blocks to a supermarket, found a payphone, and called the Newark police.

"I'd like to report a murder in the parking lot of St. Mary's Catholic School." He hung up before the dispatcher could ask any questions.

MacCleary waited until he could hear sirens. He got into his car and drove to Remo Williams' apartment. He at least owed it to Remo to look him in the eyes, even if he didn't know it.

Chapter Nine

HIS NAME WAS REMO and he was confused. At that moment, he was face down on the floor of his living room, being handcuffed.

The officer who handcuffed him read him his rights. "You have the right to remain silent. Anything you say can and will be used against you in a court of law. You have the right…"

He knew all this. He had read these rights to plenty of criminals during his tenure as a Newark cop. And yet here he was, having them read to him like one of the men he had arrested.

The police had busted down his door just after dawn. He had been getting ready to go in to the station when the police, some of them men he had worked with, had tackled him to the ground and cuffed him.

Remo Williams had no idea what he had done, but he had no intention of talking to anybody until his union rep and lawyer showed up.

The burly cop who tackled him first lifted him up and planted him on his feet. Another cop grabbed him by the shoulder and marched him out. They went down the stairs and out the front, right into a throng of reporters and photographers.

* * *

MacCleary had waited across the street from Williams' apartment, chain smoking and waiting for the police to arrive. Just before dawn, a dozen police cars and a van rolled up. Dozens of policemen streamed into the apartment building.

He got out of the car and waited until they brought Williams out. He lit another cigarette and watched.

Williams didn't fight as they brought him out. MacCleary had to give him credit for how calm he was. He didn't struggle; he didn't scream; he didn't even protest.

He probably thinks this is all a misunderstanding, MacCleary thought, a pang of guilt stabbing him in the heart.

This wouldn't be cleared up. There would only be a trial with perfect, unimpeachable evidence, followed by a sham sentencing, and a quick rejection of any appeals. Then there would be the execution. And if all went well, Remo Williams would awaken with CURE.

After the police drove Williams away, Conn dropped his cigarette and stubbed it out with his shoe. He got into the car and drove to the nearest payphone.

He put the call into Smith. "It's done."

There was silence on the other end. Finally, Smith responded. "Good. By the way, you've been cleared for travel. I hope this Sinanju is as good as you say."

"It's better," MacCleary responded, then hung up.

Epilogue

FOUR MONTHS later, Conrad MacCleary waited outside a cell on death row. He waited for a call to the guards that would allow him to see a particular prisoner.

Dressed as a monk, he was there, ostensibly, to give last rites to a condemned man. In reality, he was there to save this man. A man he had gotten put in this place.

He waited. Finally, the call came in, and the guard opened the door.

"Thank you, my son," he said in a gravely voice as he entered the cell.

There, sitting on the bed, was Remo Williams. The man he had framed. Remo finally looked up, and MacCleary began his recitation.

❧

ABOUT THE AUTHOR:

Elizabeth Sloane is a long time *Destroyer* fan, ever since her dad gave her the first book in junior high. As a Scorpio, she enjoys being mysterious, but is very bad at it — which is why she became a Classicist instead of a spy.

HAPPY BIRTHDAY, REMO

Chris Ivanovich Ragaisis

REMO WILLIAMS WAS in a mood. Not a snit, not on the snot, and definitely not being bitchy. Just a mood. *And Chiun could cram it*, he thought.

Chiun and Remo were the two deadliest assassins on the planet. Chiun was the Master Emeritus of Sinanju — the original martial art. Sinanju was the sun source of the martial arts. All others — karate, kung fu, ninjutsu, were but shadows cast by Sinanju. All were simply outlines that showed only a fragment of the original. Sinanju was the only one which defined what a martial art could and should be. And Remo was his student.

Student, Remo thought, *was a strange word for it*. After all, Remo was the current Reigning Master of Sinanju. And though Remo's lessons had started decades before, and Remo had since succeeded Chiun as Reigning Master, Remo was still the student, and he knew he always would be.

During that time, the relationship between them — teacher and student — had evolved. One of respect and love had grown. Chiun and Remo became like father and son. Of course, frustration was also a part of the relationship — the frustration that only comes from dealing with family.

And their first conversation earlier that morning hadn't started out well.

"Remo!" Chiun called out from the kitchen of their currently rented house. "Why are you loafing about? The sun has risen and the day invites you!"

There was a sound of Remo banging about before he emerged into the kitchen.

"Why are you carping on me already this morning?" Remo responded.

"I do not carp. I remind. I instruct. I guide you as you stumble from the path of proper behavior."

"And what path have I strayed from now?"

"You haven't started the rice for breakfast."

"Rice? That's it? You're screeching about dippy rice?"

Remo looked aggravated, Chiun thought. Even more aggravated than usual, since 'aggravated' was one of Remo's defining characteristics. But he was white, so maybe it meant something else. The white mind was often difficult to understand. *If only Remo had the perfection to be Korean.*

"Why would you not prepare rice for your father as is good and right?"

"Chiun," Remo asked, "Do you know what day today is?"

"Sunday. And what has that to do with cooking rice? Is it rice-free Sunday? I think not."

"But what particular Sunday?"

"What difference does it make? Sunday is Sunday. Rice is late…"

"It's October 13th, Chiun. Sunday, October 13th."

"Yes," Chiun agreed. "I see you agree it is Sunday. Why do you not start the rice and we can discuss your strange belief of not honoring your father with Sunday rice."

"Blow it out your wazoo, Chiun." Remo retorted. "It's October 13th. My birthday. Well, maybe."

Chiun shook his head. "You do not know your birthday, Remo. You were a foundling, and raised by the carpenter cult's virginal acolytes. You could choose any day to celebrate falling from the womb. Or none. Both are equally valid and equally unimportant compared to the rice which remains unprepared."

"Bulldooky, Chiun. Yeah, I don't know my actual birthday. Not even the year. But the nuns at St. Theresa's orphanage told me to use my saint's day, October 13th, and so I've always stuck with it."

Chiun rolled his eyes. More white insanity, and deeply ingrained by the tainted upbringing of religious zealots. He knew there was no logical way to explain this to Remo. Remo tended to get touchy when his childhood beliefs were brought up.

"Remo," Chiun asked, "Are you on the rag?"

"I can't be on the rag, Chiun."

"Then why are you on the snot? Snot. Rag. Heh, heh."

71

Chiun chuckled at his own joke. Remo did not.

"Blow it out your mother's wazoo, Chiun."

"If you're going mope and be insulting, Remo, do it elsewhere. If you're having a problem with this particular Sunday, maybe you'd best take it up with those who attached that day to you rather than your frail, aging father."

"Frail my ass, Chiun. You could tear down this house without breaking a sweat."

"Sweating is for Chinese. It suits them as they toil in the earth — a task for which they are well suited. Masters of Sinanju never sweat."

"Bulldooky."

And Remo left, slamming the front door behind him hard enough the knob broke clear of the door and shot across the hall into the kitchen, falling neatly in the sink.

* * *

Remo shuffled down a trash-littered street in Newark, New Jersey. His old stomping grounds. Right in front of St. Theresa's Orphanage.

Remo wasn't exactly clear what led him here, but here he was. Or maybe he did know what led him here. After all, this town made him what he was. No, he corrected himself. Chiun made him who he was. But that wasn't right, either. How could Chiun train him if there wasn't the basis — the clay — to work with?

And, for Remo, Newark was that clay. He was raised here as a child by the nuns. He had gone to school here. He had been an honest cop here — before he was framed for a murder he didn't commit, so he could be recruited into an organization which didn't exist, to be trained by Chiun to be a perfect killing machine, and used by this organization to defend the Constitution by working outside it — breaking and twisting that Constitution — so it would still hold up, and so the country he loved could still be protected by it, rather than have the country devolve into either chaos or a totalitarian police state.

Geez, thought Remo. *No wonder I'm a mess. My entire life is nothing but contradictions. And there seems to be no point.*

This neighborhood even looked like that clay. The scenery was gray, lumpy, and full of potential. And not bright, clean potential. It was the kind that comes from the destruction of something that didn't turn out as planned, and was thrown back into the pot waiting for a better artist to come along.

Remo walked up to the site where St. Theresa's Orphanage used to be. Now it was an empty lot with a tattered chain link fence around the burnt-out ruins of the building. Even Remo's childhood had crumbled and collapsed. It used to be that "upstairs" forbade him to come back here. After all, someone might recognize him. As the enforcement arm of a secret government agency operating outside the law, anyone who recognized him would need to be eliminated to preserve that secrecy. And Remo would have to perform that elimination. Killing a bad guy was one thing. Killing a childhood buddy, or a cop he used to work with, was something else entirely. So Remo had always avoided the area.

But anybody who would have remembered him was long gone. The neighborhood had changed from fairly bad when he was a kid to just plain miserable. It used to be that growing up here would make you tough and streetwise. Now it just made you hard, with a twisted view of what you owed others, what the world owed you, and how to survive.

Remo's trained senses heard the elevated heartbeat before he saw anyone. And the smell of sweat and aerosol gave him a clue as to what was happening.

He casually strolled around to the backside of one of the larger burnt and broken walls of the ex-orphanage and spied a young teen with a tattered backpack full of spray cans getting started on a section of wall. He'd slipped through one of the spaces where the chain link fence pulled away and snuck in to do a bit of tagging.

Remo silently moved behind the kid.

"What's up, champ?" Remo queried.

The youth spun with a high-pitched shriek and Remo reached up quickly to block the startled young man from spraying him in the face.

Remo's hand held the arm in a grip of stone. Not so tightly the boy hurt, but enough that no matter what he tried, the tagger couldn't break free.

"What you want, mister?" the kid asked as he struggled and kicked.

"I just want to know why you're defacing a treasured childhood memory," was Remo's response.

"What you talking 'bout? This ain't no memory. It's a hunk of bricks and I'm practicing."

Remo looked at the boy. He was an African-American in his early- to mid-teens, skinny, short, and wearing clothes that looked well-used. A typical neighborhood kid.

"What's your name?"

"Stanley," the boy responded. "What's it to you?" And the boy straightened up and tried to look tough.

Remo flipped the thumb and index finger of the hand holding the boy's arm, and Stanley found himself pirouetting in place and then flat on his rump on the hard ground.

"It just wasn't what I expected. Not in this neighborhood. The name's not tough, doesn't sound like an obvious nickname, and it's an actual name, not just a bunch of letters tossed together."

"My mom gave me that name. Don't you say nothing against my mom." Stanley actually looked offended.

"Don't worry, Stanley. I wouldn't think of it. But why the name Stanley?"

"My mom thought a good name would help me to get out of here and get a good job. She's always telling me I need to get out. So she named me after that famous explorer — Stanley Livingstone. So that's me. Stanley Livingstone Harris."

Remo smiled, "You know those are two different people, right? Livingstone was a missionary who got lost in Africa. Stanley was the guy who found him. At least that's what I remember from an old movie."

"Yeah," sighed Stanley, "But don't tell my mom."

"I won't breathe a word. But back to my original question, why are you defacing this wall?"

Stanley stood up straight. "Defacing? It's just an old wall. What is it to you?"

"This is where I grew up. This was my home."

Stanley laughed. "Home? Nobody lives here. Nobody's lived here for longer than anyone can remember. My mom says it's always been like this."

"I lived here."

"Then you old, man."

"Can't argue with that. Although there are some who would say I'm just a kid."

Stanley turned, picked up the spray can and started in again with broad strokes.

"Stanley, didn't you hear what I said? This was my home."

"Look, man, nobody lives here now. And I gotta practice."

"Practice what? You're spray painting a wall. On top of other spray paint."

"I gotta practice my art. You don't get good if you don't practice. And I hear there are people paying real dollars these days for good art. Now how about letting me go?"

"No chance, Stanley. This was my home, and I don't want it defaced." Remo reached down, picked up one of the spray cans and with a quick compression of both hands rendered the can inoperable by simply mashing the top down and folding the can over on its seam. The can didn't explode and now took up about a quarter of the space it did earlier.

"Come on, man!" Stanley complained. That was my red. How can I do this without my red?"

"How about finding another place?"

"There is no other place. Gangs in the neighborhood got everything pretty much sewed up. This here is no-man's land. If you can sneak through a couple neighborhoods, you can come here and not be bothered most of the time. Now how about it?"

Remo thought for a moment. *Yes, this was his home. But it wasn't now.* He'd lived too many places — some for longer than others — to have a home. 'Home' was a strange and precious concept to Remo. Maybe it was because he didn't have one. But he did have Chiun, Sinanju, and all the history that brought. *Damn, more contradictions.*

"I'm not in a good mood today, Stanley. Why not give it a rest for one day. Just for me?"

As Remo uttered those words a dozen men, ranging from teens to men in their mid-twenties, approached the chain link fence. Remo could tell all were carrying weapons from the way they walked and carried themselves. Three, he noticed, were carrying guns. The others most likely had knives, chains, or other bludgeons.

"Hey, asshole, watchoo doin' in our neighborhood?"

As Remo looked them over, Stanley grabbed him by the sleeve. "Shit. It's the Kings. Dammit. I took a long detour to keep out of their way."

Remo looked the gang over. "Isn't it past bedtime for your and your dippy club? Go home and leave honest folks alone." Remo knew it wouldn't work. But that didn't bother him. He was in a mood, after all.

"Check out the crazy idiot!" one of the gang called. "Big man. Maybe he got big money he like to contribute to the Kings?"

This was spoken by a gang member with a scraggly, untrimmed beard and mustache. He had a fairly big and beefy build, and Remo assumed he was the oldest. His heartbeat wasn't elevated, so he was still calm. And he had a gun. It was likely that he was the one in charge.

But Remo knew from training and experience he wasn't the one to watch out for. It would be one of the mid-level members. Someone with something to prove; someone who was more prone to excitement.

"How about it, asshole? Care to make a donation?" another thug said, cracking his knuckles. Tall and thin, the man was wearing rings on all of his fingers. He looked like a basketball player. Too bad he put more effort into roughing up people in the neighborhood instead of practicing his jumper.

Remo knew the first attack would come from the latest speaker. Heart rate high, carrying a gun, and telegraphing an attack so obvious Ray Charles could have seen it.

"Wanna see my art, Stanley?" Remo said over his shoulder.

Remo hooked a flattened aluminum beer can lying on the ground with the toe of his left shoe and gave it an upward flick. The can almost levitated straight up. Then Remo pulled back and kicked the edge of the can. The can rocketed forward with an audible whistle and shot over the fence and off into the distance.

Big Beard chuckled, "You kickin' shit at us? That's it, man. You just disrespected the Kings. It's all on you now."

Two of the gang pulled guns. They were widely separated on the other side of the fence. One was the member Remo pegged for the initial attack. The other, a sphere of a man weighing around 280 pounds gave Remo a cold smile that said he'd done this before and would be happy to do it again.

Just as both were about to pull the triggers on their weapons, a high-pitched whistle started to wail behind the gang members, growing steadily louder. As they turned to see the source, they witnessed a flattened beer can spinning towards them. The can Remo had kicked earlier had boomeranged back and was heading directly at the skinny gunman. With a whistle that turned to a shriek, the can imbedded itself in his forehead. He dropped like a rock, stone dead.

Confusion reigned for a moment as the members split up. A few ran, but several didn't. Those remaining were making their way into the lot with murder in their eyes. Remo felt it. He wasn't worried for himself. This wasn't anything to him. But there was Stanley to worry about. Sure, he was trying to deface the home of Remo's childhood, but he seemed like a decent kid.

"Art," Remo explained to Stanley as he picked up a handful of gravel, "Is in the eye of the beholder. So we target the eyes."

Remo balanced a pebble on the tips of each of four fingers. He casually flicked each pebble off of each fingertip. Each sped like a rifle crack and pegged an individual gang member in the eye. And each member dropped. None were dead, but each would need medical care if they hoped to see again. Some screamed, some fainted. But all of the gang stopped where they were.

"It's my birthday," explained Remo to the gang members. They looked up uncomprehendingly. Remo walked up to the man he assumed to be the leader.

"You in charge of these dipshits?" he said, lifting the man by the ear. *Just like the nuns did to us when we acted up*, thought Remo.

"Listen," Remo said. But nobody was listening.

"Listen!" Remo shouted as he twisted Scraggly Beard's ear. When the leader yelped in pain, everybody got quiet.

Remo continued in a tone of voice he remembered the nuns using when they felt they were imparting the most vital of lessons.

"It's my birthday. Well, not exactly. I don't know when that is. But it's my *name* day. St. Remo's Day. So I'm in a mood. It's a bad mood. But it's also a charitable mood, since that's what I was taught here. So I'll give you a choice. You can all get out of here, or you can end up like doofus over there, killed by a piece of street trash."

Remo smirked at the Chiun-like joke and nobody else got it. *Very Chiun-like*, he thought.

There was no argument. The gang dragged those who could not walk back through the holes in the fence and were gone within a couple of minutes.

Remo turned to Stanley. The boy looked terrified. And amazed. And stunned.

"How'd you do all that?" Stanley whispered.

"Practice." was Remo's reply. "As you said, you need to practice your art. I get what you're trying to do, Stanley. But this is where I was raised.

The nuns who brought me up were my only family, and they raised me to respect my home. Although it's not much of a home now."

"Behind you!" Stanley shouted and pointed past Remo's shoulder.

The rotund gang member with the killer's smile was back, and drawing a bead on Remo from behind.

Remo picked up the spray paint can he'd compressed earlier and threw it. The can traveled in a straight line and wedged itself into the gang member's open mouth. He then took one more pebble and flicked it so it traveled at supersonic speed directly into the can.

High-speed pebble met super compressed aerosol can. The resulting explosion was red. Red spray paint. Red blood. And a headless body dropped to the ground.

Remo stood there and thought. He thought of home. He thought of art. He thought of practice. He thought of where he came from and where he might go. He stood still and thought for minutes on end.

"Mister, can I go?" Stanley was looking very uncomfortable.

"Sure thing, kid." Remo said without turning around to look at the boy.

"Wait." Remo stopped Stanley as he was picking up his backpack. "Go ahead and practice here if you want. Even though I grew up here and it helped define who I am today, it isn't all I am today. No place does that. It's something only I can do for myself. The same goes for you. You're not hurting anyone here, so go ahead. And good luck to you. I hope to see your art some day."

And Remo didn't look back as he went and picked up the two dead bodies to remove them from the area that was his childhood home.

Some day, people would say Stanley was a good artist and a good kid and would go far. And they'd trace it back to a painting he did on the old St. Theresa's orphanage ruined wall. It featured nuns helping children around the world and was titled *St. Remo's Day*.

Remo never saw it.

Later still, Stanley would learn the song that this strange man was whistling, this man who tried to save a burnt and crumbled brick wall from spray paint. The tune was "Whistle While You Work."

* * *

Back at the rented house, Chiun waited, sitting on his tatami mat in the center of the floor in the living room. No furniture was to be found, but a large-screen plasma TV was mounted to one wall. The TV was off and Chiun sat, meditated, and waited. He knew his adopted son would return eventually. He hoped this quest would have settled whatever issues caused him to leave the previous day.

Remo entered through the patched front door and noticed that it was repaired. Chiun must have called in workmen.

"Thanks for getting the door fixed, Chiun," was the first thing out of Remo's mouth.

"You sound better than when you left yesterday. You left a pale piece of a pig's ear and returned a Master of Sinanju. What brought on this glorious transformation?"

"*You* made me a Master of Sinanju, Chiun. But I was thinking a lot about what made me what I am and where I came from and how to link all of that together with where I'm going. I'm still confused, but the old neighborhood doesn't hold the interest for me it previously did."

Chiun barked, "Good! Now will you make me rice?"

Remo glared. "Didn't you hear what I said, Chiun? I'm working out some deep feelings and all you can think about is rice? Geez! Why did I come back?"

"Feelings come and go, Remo. With you even more so than others. But there are things that are constant. Your training. Your breathing. Sinanju. And the need to eat. We concentrate on those and let the other things work themselves out. But I'm glad to know you are more centered. It does not speak well of a Master who isn't."

"I'm centered, Chiun. For now."

"And I have a birthday present for you, to celebrate another year your feet have trodden the soil of this barbaric nation."

Chiun produced a package wrapped in white paper with a red ribbon perfectly bisecting both sides of the box.

Remo used his one long fingernail to cut the ribbon and opened the box. Excitedly he removed the interior wrappings to find an elaborate kimono of the "to be worn for dignitaries of Persia" variety, a blank scroll, ink, and a quill pen.

"I'm not going to wear any dippy robe, Chiun." Remo said with an air of finality.

Chiun's eyes softened. "My son," he said quietly, "you are a Master of Sinanju. No one can make you do anything you do not want to do."

Remo looked up, slightly startled, and started to smile.

"But you do have obligations to the house. No matter what else you decide."

Remo sighed, nodded, and took the box to his room. He removed the robe and hung it in the closet. After spreading a mat in the center of the floor, Remo knelt, and removed the other items from the box. He laid out the scroll, weighted the ends to keep it from rolling up, and dipped the pen into the ink.

Then, with his best penmanship as taught by the nuns at St. Theresa's, he started to write.

His name was Remo...

ABOUT THE AUTHOR:

Chris Ivanovich Ragaisis is a former Soviet Threat Analyst turned professional magician, and erstwhile banjo player. He's been a hero pulp addict for over four decades, and was introduced to the adventures of Remo and Chuin with the debut of the movie "Remo Williams: The Adventure Begins." Becoming an instant fan, he eagerly devoured every *Destroyer* item he could find. More than once. Occasionally literally. This is his first piece of published fiction. This biography could be his second.

ASSASSIN EIGHT

Bruce James Rae

HIS NAME WAS REMO and he was number eight on the list. The first seven assassins had been easy to catch, but Remo was impossibly elusive.

Killing is easy. Any sociopath with a gun and access to an unsuspecting victim can kill. Getting away with murder, however, is not so easy. Witnesses, forensic evidence and motive can all provide clues to lead an investigator to catch a killer.

A professional assassin could obscure the motive behind his crime, but a successful assassination was always more difficult than casual murder. Targets were often under protection from bodyguards or security services. Access to a high-profile target was usually restricted to public locations during a very short window of time and in places where surveillance, human and electronic, was close to omnipresent. Although movies and shows and novels were populated with any number of assassins and professional killers, there simply were not many out there.

Special Agent Charlie Grove looked at the list of assassins he had brought to justice. Seven names — a remarkable accomplishment for his career. He could have been happy with that list. He should have been happy with that list. But now, knowing that there was an assassin named Remo, he couldn't be satisfied until he captured number eight.

Charlie Grove had started out as an analyst, collating data and examining patterns of evidence. With almost no effort, he had been able to identify a small-time mob enforcer and have him brought in. Charlie found that he had a knack for identifying killers. After his promotion to agent, he had proved to be adept at catching them, too.

Looking at a surveillance video of a busy street, Charlie noticed subtle clues that would lead him to pick out an assassin from the rest of the crowd.

Patterns of motion — a purposeful stride or a head turned away from a camera — were enough for him to identify a suspect. Others who saw the same footage might not see it, but, to Charlie, the smallest, most insignificant detail was often enough to separate a suspect from an innocent civilian.

Seven hired killers and professional assassins were no longer at large because of Charlie Grove.

Assassin number eight had been a surprise.

Charlie had thought his career would end after number seven. However, when the seventh assassin was caught, an anonymous source had sent him information about a man named Remo. No one could even confirm the existence of this mystery man, but the more Charlie looked into the patterns of evidence, the more he came to realize that Remo was real. Pushing back his retirement, Charlie knew that he could not stop until he caught Remo.

"Dinner's ready, Charlie. Wash your hands and come downstairs," called Charlie's mom.

Maybe catching Remo could wait. The smell of his mother's delicious chicken Parmesan was enough for twelve-year-old Charlie Grove to shut off his computer. After dinner, he would return to Assassin Hunter, his favorite video game. If he could beat the game by catching Remo, then he might be eligible to collect the million-dollar prize offered by the game's publisher — a small startup named Friend Simulations.

ABOUT THE AUTHOR:

A man of many talents (and many stories), Bruce Rae's other story, "Signature," appears on page 206 — along with a longer biography.

WELCOME TO THE FUTURE

John E. Bailor

THE MASTER OF SINANJU sat silently, centered on the tatami mat which itself was centered in the spacious hotel room, giving him a perfect view of the flatscreen television. Rad Rex looked resplendent in his bright orange shirt. The top three buttons were casually unbuttoned, revealing the thick — if graying — hair at the top his chest, as well as a thick gold chain with an orange-colored trinket hanging just below Rad Rex's throat. He was driving an expensive sportsmobile, but Chiun was more interested in the gold chain.

Rad Rex sped along a back road with the radio tuned to an advertisement expounding the virtues of Orange's latest and greatest MyPhone. *Bah*, the Master thought. *What was the big deal about a phone named with a number and a letter?*

The advertisement repeated their annoying mantra, "Welcome to the Future," that Chiun heard and saw everywhere. The constant hawking of gadgets in *As the Planet Revolves* had become almost as intrusive as the chatter of the blathering idiots who broke these great stories into segments of no more than seven minutes each.

Chiun was pleased he had chosen his chrysanthemum pink kimono today and not one that contained any orange dye. He must protest the ubiquitousness of this round fruit. He would make a point to tweet about these tasteless intrusions into his daily dramas — but not until today's episode ended, of course.

* * *

Chiun's annoyance was interrupted by a crisp knock at the hotel room's door, which he patiently ignored the first three times. When the knock came a fourth time, he gracefully swept up from the mat and lightly padded over to the door. Who would be so insolent as to interrupt his enjoyment of the beautiful dramas? And just as Rad Rex was pulled over by a policeman for Oogling while driving! It couldn't be Remo. He had been trained better and would have entered quietly — at least as quietly as a pale piece of pig's ear could plod through a room. Chiun had not ordered room service, so it must be Smith. Chiun muttered in Korean and opened the door.

Harold W. Smith stood still and erect in his gray suit. His green striped tie sat so tightly against the pressed white shirt's top that it constricted the fool's airway. *How could this man secretly rule a nation when he did not even allow himself to breathe properly?* His battered briefcase was grasped tightly in his hand. The observant Chiun noticed all of this, as well as the sweat on Smith's brow and around his collar. While Chiun wasn't affected by the dry, triple-digit heat of the Las Vegas summer, Smith obviously was. Chiun opened the door wide and bowed. "Oh magnificent Emperor, what brings you to your humble servant who would gladly have crossed your great country at your slightest whim?"

The man outside the doorway glanced sharply up and down the hallway, quickly entered the room, and closed the door behind him. Bowing stiffly he asked, "Master Chiun. Is Remo here?" and looked around the room.

"He is completing the important mission you assigned him, O Emperor."

The white appeared anxious, and shifted his weight. "I see. Then he's not back yet."

Chiun stood graciously, waiting for the idiot to get to the point or, better yet, leave. Perhaps Chiun could hasten this process?

"Most generous Emperor, tell me how I may serve you so you may hurry back to the many important tasks only you can perform."

He cleared his throat then replied, "Chiun, would you give Remo a message for me?"

Chiun bowed again, hoping the moron would soon be gone. In only eight minutes *As the Planet Revolves* would end and Chiun would have to wait until Monday to see what he had missed. "I am, as ever, your humble servant."

As Chiun rose out of the bow his employer said, "Very well." In a blur of motion Chiun never thought possible, Smith swung his arm in an arc. Only then did Chiun see the sharp edge jutting from the bottom of

Smith's briefcase. The blade sliced through Chiun's pink kimono and deeply into the parchment-thin skin of his abdomen.

Chiun shrieked and pressed his hand against his split skin, not to stop the blood from pouring out, but to keep his internal organs in place. He began to step forward, but fell. He turned mid-fall so he would land on his back, which would help to keep his insides inside. Chiun realized something else on the blade, and whispered "Poison."

Chiun's attacker sneered down at him. "Thanks for everything, Chiun. I'll look forward to seeing Remo after he gets my message." He turned and exited the room, leaving Chiun to die a painful death.

* * *

His name was Remo and he was in Las Vegas to meet the Prophet Jimmy MacCleary. After being raised by nuns in a Catholic orphanage, Remo was very willing to deliver justice to those who used religion as a front for their personal agendas. Prophet Jimmy performed dozens of civil ceremonies to unite same sex couples. Remo was perfectly fine with that. But that wasn't what brought Remo out west.

Remo approached the velvet rope that, along with one blonde and one redhead, guarded the entrance to the Hazy nightclub at Melody. The girls were giving the overweight man at the front of the line a hard time. The three exotic women with him were getting impatient as the man impotently tried to enter the club.

Remo heard the man say, "Dammit, Ah'm Billy Bush an' ah paid $20,000 fa' a table. Ah was tol' ta be here at nine. I was here bafor nine. Now it's afta nine-thirty and ya still haven't let me in. Ah wanna talk to ya' boss."

The blonde looked down at a clipboard in her hand and frowned. "I told you I'd let you know when your table is ready."

The man's face became beet red. "Ya've let everyone else in, dammit." He was ready to say something else when Remo lightly put a hand on one shoulder of Billy Bush's expensive suit.

Remo didn't feel out of place in his black tee and matching chinos. "Allow me." The exotic beauties weren't subtle about the glances they gave Remo as he brushed past them. Reaching the rope, Remo smiled first at the redhead, then at the blonde. "Evening, ladies."

The girls seemed torn between distaste at his choice of attire and wanting to have his babies. The blonde adjusted the front of her top so it exposed more of her ample chest than was legal to do publicly in most states. "I can't let you enter dressed like that. Come with me so I can get you out of those."

The redhead slid over and bumped the blonde aside with her firm bottom. "Not this time!" The blonde hit the wall chest first and bounced back. Red smashed her clipboard over the blonde's head then raked her nails across the girl's face.

Slaps gave way to pushing and pushing to fists and high-heeled kicks as the fight over Remo intensified. When the fight moved away from the entrance, Remo opened the rope. "Your table is ready."

Billy Bush led his entourage inside, looking confused. "Uh, which table's mayhn?"

Remo closed the rope behind him, ducking out of the way of the fighting attendants. He motioned vaguely toward far wall. "Back there."

Billy Bush peered into the club but couldn't tell which table was his. He turned back to ask the man in black to escort him to the table, but he was no longer there.

* * *

The walls and floor seemed to thump in time to the dance music's bass. Remo's ears tuned out the music, allowing him to hear the clubbers as they tried to impress their dates or tell their friends to avoid "whales." His eyes quickly adjusted to compensate for the colored lights aimed at the stage and the darkness engulfing the tables along the outer edges. He quickly scanned the main floor's crowd before making his way upstairs.

Remo passed through the crowded second floor, finding gaps where none existed. The rope across the stairway to the next level held a dangling sign marked "PRIVATE." Remo floated over the rope and found what he was looking for on the top floor.

The Prophet Jimmy and his Apostles must have reserved the entire floor for themselves. They were seated along the far side of several tables that had been pushed together. The Prophet was the smallest of the group. The Apostles were all big men, even compared to Remo. Thirteen-to-one odds. The house of Jimmy was about to lose. Remo concealed himself in the shadows along the outer wall until the wait staff left the party to themselves. Remo didn't want witnesses.

He ignored the stink of sweaty bodies as he centered his breathing and approached the center table. It took a few moments until he was noticed. One of the Apostles jumped up and pointed, "Who the hell are you?"

Remo grabbed the Apostle's wrist and spun clockwise. The man sailed over the table, across the room and into the far wall. His flight ended with an impact loud enough to be heard over the bass. The Apostle crumpled to the floor, his neck bent at an impossible angle.

The Prophet stood. "You damned heathen, you can't waltz right in here and kill my Apostles. Who the hell do you think you are, boy?"

Knowing the man's dislike of homosexuals, he replied, "Remo Fey." He looked from one end of the group to the other then settled his gaze back on Prophet Jimmy. "Maybe you can see the future. Looks like you knew this was your last supper."

The remark lost on the group, the Prophet motioned to three of the Apostles to his left. They circled behind Remo. The Prophet stared at him. "Before my men set your soul free so you can burn in hell, tell me why you're here."

"You've joined a lot of couples in the BLT community — "

The Prophet interrupted, "BLT community?" His face screwed up in thought for a moment and then he smiled widely. "I get it! Bi-Lesbo-Tranny!" His face dropped as he realized something. "What about the fags?"

Remo sensed the men behind him shifting, preparing to strike. Unconcerned he answered, "Don't worry. We'll get to them soon enough. Excuse me a moment." Remo turned to face the men behind him. Although he appeared to back away, he actually moved closer, centering himself within the group.

The Apostle on the left was a dark-skinned man with long, dirty dreadlocks. He wore a tan jacket over an orange shirt, unbuttoned far enough to show off the thick gold chain around his neck. "You picked da wrong potty ta crash, mon."

What happened next occurred so quickly that the spectators didn't realize Remo had moved until they noticed the three attacking Apostles were now stacked atop the first of their assembly to die. Remo now held a gold chain. "My partner will love this." He pushed the chain into the front pocket of his chinos.

The Prophet seemed to make a mental connection. "Fey, huhn? You and your partner queers?"

"It came to my boss's attention that it isn't long after you join members of the community in wedlock that they're found dead in their homes. Apparently robbery victims. You use the information they provide to rob and kill them."

"It's God's will to purge the earth of those people. Like what God did, just without the brimstone and fire."

Thinking back to someone he knew long ago, Remo's eyes were burning and black. "You're a disgrace to the name MacCleary," he hissed.

"What's that you said, boy?"

"Never mind that. But if we're discussing God's will, have you heard about the eleventh commandment?"

"No, son. My Bible only has ten." The Prophet motioned again and the rest of the Apostles now spread themselves around the room.

"Thou shalt not get away with it."

There were more Apostles on Remo's left, so he started there. Remo approached the tallest Apostle, who stood at his full height of six-foot-five. Remo stepped back, as if reconsidering. The tall Apostle never saw Remo's right hand shoot forward like a spear, he only felt the impact against his solar plexus and a horrible pain in his chest. His eyes rolled up into his head and he fell to the floor as his heart lost track of its natural rhythm and gave up trying to remember it.

The next Apostle he approached pulled out a switchblade and warned, "Chu gonna die esta noche."

Remo smiled. "My partner has told me for years I need to learn foreign languages. I'm really trying. How's this? *Su madre es mi puta.*"

The Apostle lunged. His dark eyes seemed confused when he saw the switchblade sticking out of his own chest. That was six.

Remo had already spent enough time in Vegas, and was ready to leave as soon as possible. Maybe he'd celebrate with some duck. And a big glass of water.

Fingertips, ball of foot, side of hand. Seven, eight, nine. The Prophet pulled out a semi-automatic. Weave, gunshot, ten collapsed behind where Remo had just been. Remo ducked and weaved until the gunfire stopped. Surely someone downstairs would have heard the gunfire and the police would be on their way. The Prophet looked down and reached inside his suit jacket for a fresh clip. When he looked back up he paused, shocked to see the last two of his Apostles had gone down in the brief moment he had looked away.

Remo took the gun and clip away from the Prophet. He slid the bullets out of the clip one at a time, then tossed the empty clip aside. Not knowing how the manufacturer suggested field stripping the gun, Remo casually pulled the slide until it snapped off in his hands, then he tossed the stock and slide to opposite corners of the room.

The Prophet walked across the room to his fallen chosen ones and, unable to see the future, asked, "Now what?"

"The police will find you here with twelve dead bodies and lock you up. You asked about homosexuals." Remo smiled, "I'm sure you'll meet some in prison." Remo gently tapped his index finger against Prophet Jimmy's forehead. He fell, his head landing facedown in the lap of one of his former Apostles.

* * *

Remo whistled contentedly and entered the hotel. He and Chiun could catch the next available flight back east. He stopped outside the door to their suite. He heard the canned laugh-track of some inane sitcom. Chiun didn't watch sitcoms. Remo listened intently but could not hear Chiun's breathing. He hoped that maybe his ears hadn't fully adjusted from the loud club music, but he knew better. Remo didn't waste time with the key card. He grasped the door handle and effortlessly pushed the door through the inside frame.

Remo saw Chiun on the floor, motionless, lying completely still — in a pool of his own blood.

* * *

The energetic man sat behind his Luna Office Desk with the custom-colored modesty panel. Not because of humility, but because he liked the statement it made. His agent walked in and stood before him. "Welcome back, Doctor Smith. How did everything go?"

The agent loosened the Dartmouth tie and unbuttoned the starched collar. "More straightforward than projected, Mr. Hobby. The target has been eliminated," he said, looking down at his hands. "I find I am eager to disengage myself from this disguise. Smith is so uptight that being him elevates my blood pressure."

"You'd need a heart to have high blood pressure, yeah?" The man laughed heartily at his own joke. "Perhaps your next persona will be more to your liking," he said and slid some photos across the desk along with a new MyPad. "There are some video and audio files here for you to study. I can't emphasize how critical your success is. Your only hope will be to take your target by surprise."

"As you asserted last time. Your instructions were followed and there were no deviations to plan." The agent picked up the photos and studied the young man in a black uniform, holding some kind of machine pistol. "What is this weapon? I cannot identify it."

"Don't worry. Specs are in there," he pointed to the MyPad. "I have had one custom made for you. You'll find it in your office."

"When do I depart?"

"I have put some plans into motion. The simulations I've run indicate they will bring our next target to us. We leave in five hours."

The agent turned to go. His boss spoke quickly, "The Oriental. You saw him die, yeah?"

The voice that replied was cold, mechanical. "It was not prudent to delay egress. No one could have survived that wound. Or the poison."

* * *

Remo rushed over and placed his head on Chiun's chest. Chiun's hand was pressed tightly to his abdomen. There was no heartbeat. No breath. Remo noticed a faint scent of bitter almond. Poison. That explained why Chiun's was the only body Remo had found in the room. If it hadn't been for the poison, surely Chiun would have taken out his attacker.

Remo stood, rotating his wrists absently. If it weren't for the complete control he had over his body, he would have cried. Would this be Remo's future? Sacrificing decades of his life to save America — but would it all end for him like this someday?

How could anyone catch Chiun with his defenses down? As soon as they made a telltale giveaway of their intention, Chiun would have seen and reacted. No one moved as fast as Chiun. Except Remo. Now, only Remo. Whoever did this would pay.

He heard a faint sound, a light breeze through reeds.

"Chiun?"

Remo kneeled down and looked into the Master's eyes. The hazel eyes, normally clear, were now cloudy. Remo leaned close. "Chiun, what happened?"

He faintly heard one word before the Master's eyes closed and his breathing stopped: "*Smith.*"

* * *

Remo knew he couldn't take Chiun to a regular hospital. He needed to get him to Folcroft, and soon. But when Remo had asked Chiun what happened he'd said, "Smith." Did he mean Smith had somehow done this? Or was he telling Remo to call Smith for help? Right now it didn't matter. He needed to contact Smith. He'd figure out what happened later. He opened the MyPhone application and held his finger on the number one.

*　*　*

"The almond scent you noticed is indicative of cyanide," the lemony voice said. "Whoever chose this toxin must know how important breathing is to Masters of Sinanju."

The key-lime walls of Chiun's room at Folcroft weren't having the calming effect they were meant to. Smitty's vitals didn't indicate that he was hiding anything from Remo, but, then again, Chiun had been surprised by whoever had attacked him. Was Smith subtly admitting his role in this? Remo would find out for sure, but for now, he needed Smith's help. "What do you mean?"

"Cyanide is versatile. It can be introduced orally, inhaled, or absorbed through contact with the skin. But, more importantly, it stops red blood cells from using oxygen. Chiun cannot use Sinanju if his body cannot use oxygen. Remo, it is possible for Chiun to suffocate even though he is breathing. If by some miracle he survives, his brain may be irreparably damaged."

"Can you do anything for him?"

"We've administered the antidote kit, stitched him up and replaced the blood he lost, but he doesn't seem to be responding. But I'll order one of the doctors to establish a transfusion and keep it running. If we cycle in good blood and force out the poisoned blood, Chiun may receive sufficient oxygen to recover." He lifted one of Chiun's eyelids and studied the pupil. "We may still have time." Without another word, Smith hurried from the room.

Moments later, Chiun rolled to his side and vomited violently into the bedpan. When he finished, Remo handed him a cup of lukewarm water. Chiun drank it down quickly, then another. He spoke weakly at first, but became stronger as he continued. "The blood I was given is not Korean." He noticed the coolness against his backside and realized it was exposed. "And this gown is disgraceful. Where is my kimono?"

"Chiun, I was afraid I'd lost you."

Chiun handed the bedpan to Remo. "Dispose of this."

"That reminds me, I have something for you, Little Father." Remo reached into a pocket and held out the gold chain he'd picked up in Las Vegas.

Chiun's eyes seemed to clear at the sight of the gold and the chain quickly disappeared into his gown. "This is unusually thoughtful of you, Remo. I must rest now, but I will keep this safe until we return to Sinanju." Chiun rolled onto his back. Before he began to snore loudly he warned, "Do not trust Smith."

* * *

After Remo had found Smith and told him the transfusion wouldn't be necessary, he'd followed Smith to his office.

Remo paced the office while Smith busied himself on his computer. "I am defining parameters to determine who or what could have done this to Chiun. It may take some time. Any information you can provide about the scene of the attack may prove beneficial."

"He was alone. On his back, near the door, holding his guts in. The rooms weren't disturbed. Nothing out of place. No signs of struggle." Remo leaned onto Smith's desk and stared directly into his eyes. "I thought he was dead. Then he took in a shallow breath and I asked him what happened. Do you know what he said?"

Smith sat back, returning Remo's gaze. "How would I know that, Remo?"

Remo continued to stare intently at his employer. "He said 'Smith.'"

Placing his index fingers together like a tent, Smith raised the fingers to his lips. "Interesting." He shot forward and typed furiously on the touch keyboard.

Remo sat and exhaled loudly. He hadn't realized he'd been holding his breath while he waited for Smith's response. There was no way Smith had anything to do with what had happened to Chiun. The man was cold and emotionless, but even he would have had a reaction if he'd tried to kill Chiun.

Remo didn't know how long he'd sat there before he heard Smith say, "Remo."

He walked to Smith's desk. "You have something?"

"About Master Chiun, no. But I do have an assignment for you while he recovers."

"Yeah, ok. I probably should do something instead of just waiting around here. What do you need me to do?"

Remo flew to Mexico City then on to Tuxtla Gutiérrez, arriving in Chiapas in the mid-afternoon. He reached the outskirts of the Lacandón jungle after four-and-a-half hours of driving. Night had fallen and Remo sensed a thunderstorm approaching. Sliding out of the Jeep, he walked to the edge of the jungle and took a quick look at the tan-colored, rutted road. With the rain coming soon, that road would be a challenge, even for the four-wheel drive Jeep. Remo took the keys and left the Jeep.

The Lacandón jungle was dark, impossibly dark, but Remo's eyes quickly adapted and he confidently hiked forward in silence, not disturbing the occasional snake or jaguar. He had walked deep into the jungle, paralleling the path Smith specified in his directions. The path was well-used and the grass no longer grew there. Once the storm came, it would become a muddy stream. Remo moved easily through the underbrush, keeping the path in sight. He didn't feel the heat or humidity.

Thunder roared and lightning flashed as the storm clouds released their natural fury. The heavy rain rushed through the thick leaves overhead, drenching Remo's tan tee, sand-colored chinos and new loafers. Like the heat and humidity, the rain didn't slow him. He'd come prepared with everything he'd need: his MyPhone — fortunately, in a waterproof case — and a canteen filled with bottled water from the States.

Some hacker had made the mistake of trying to access Smith's computers. Smith traced the convoluted path to the location where the attack originated. Remo didn't really care about this assignment. Smith had already stopped the threat from Rye, but he sent Remo to terminate the connection once and for all.

Remo hoped it wasn't some pimply-faced kid. That would be a game-changer. He'd cross that bridge if he came to it. In the meantime, the mission got Remo away from Folcroft and kept his mind off Chiun.

Only a few more klicks to go. This wasn't the first time Remo had been here. *When was the last time?* Late nineties. Ninety-five, ninety-six. Yeah. Nineteen ninety-six. Almost twenty years ago. Remo thought back to his and Chiun's fight with Gordons. *It had killed Assumpta and eventually would have killed —*

His train of thought was interrupted when he noticed the steady pounding of the rain against the jungle canopy had been joined by the repetitive sounds of sloshing followed by a sucking noise. It reminded Remo of the sounds made by his unit in Vietnam, when their boots stepped in and out of muddy, jungle puddles. Someone was on the path Remo had not taken, and was headed his way. Remo stopped and focused his vision on the source of the footsteps. The sloshing stopped and was replaced by the sound of someone pushing through the leafy underbrush. Lightning flashed and silhouetted a figure in black as it stepped into Remo's path. The stranger raised the barrel of a BFG, pointing it directly at Remo, and walked toward him.

***

Remo asked, "What are you doing here, Stone?"

Winston Smith replied coldly, "I was ordered to kill you."

Remo said, "Disengage."

"Disengage," the gun replied and shut down.

"What the…" Winston asked as he reached for the side-mounted button to reactivate the gun.

Remo didn't give him the chance. He grasped the barrel of the Hellfire. Its shoulder strap snapped cleanly in two as Remo yanked. He bent the barrel backward and tossed the now-harmless weapon aside. "I thought that gun was one-of-a-kind. How'd you get another one?"

Winston didn't answer.

"Lodestones." Remo raised two balled fists, held them before Stone's chest, and began to circle him, aware of his footing on the wet grass and leaves.

Not mirroring Remo, Winston entered an aggressive fighting stance, saw an opening and struck. Remo dodged, bringing down his hands. "Okay, junior, we'll do this your way."

Remo struck out with an open-hand jab. Winston deflected the blow with a well-timed block. Even though Remo hadn't meant it as a killing blow, most people wouldn't have been fast enough to block the thrust.

Stone, however, wasn't like most people. He was Remo's son, and had begun training in Sinanju under the tutelage of Remo's own father, Sunny Joe Roam. But what the hell was Stone doing here? Had Smith sent him to kill Remo? Or maybe to be killed by Remo? He remembered Chiun's warning not to trust Smith. And now Chiun was in Smith's care, two thousand miles away at Folcroft.

While Remo's attention was divided between the jungle and the sanitarium, Winston landed a closed-fist strike to Remo's left bicep. Remo's arm fell to his side, useless, as he saw Winston's heel coming right for his face.

* * *

Harold W. Smith rubbed his bloodshot eyes and swiveled his chair so he could look out over the Long Island Sound. He'd been looking at his monitor all day and his weary eyes could barely focus on the distant sights outside of the sanitarium, out in the world he'd defended for…how many decades had it been?

When he had started at Folcroft, he'd built the Folcroft Four — computers much more powerful and smaller than their contemporary counterparts that filled entire rooms. He pulled out his MyPhone 5 and rigidly dragged a finger across the screen. He looked at the handful of icons on his home screen, each representing an application, which was a computer program. *How things have changed*, he thought. *Any of these programs would have crashed an earlier computer or taken far too long to process.*

He turned the small phone around in his hands, impressed with the foresight leaders of companies like Orange and MecroSoft must have. Envisioning hardware like this and knowing there would be no shortage of companies providing software that would quickly push these amazing devices to their limits, creating the demand for the next generation of hardware.

Smith looked across the sound again, pocketed his MyPhone and turned back to his computer.

An idea struck him, and he pulled up stock performance comparisons. MecroSoft shares continued to trade in the low-to-mid thirties. Orange stock, however, had recently climbed to over five hundred dollars a share. The consensus among analysts was the Orange shares were overpriced and, when the company ran out of new product and innovation, would plunge to four dollars a share.

It was getting late and there was still the matter of Chiun. Smith created a new subroutine and launched it with priority processing. If all went well, he wouldn't be gone long. Hopefully the results would be waiting when he returned. Smith stood, his knees cracking loudly. He walked once around his office to get the circulation flowing through his legs, which had fallen asleep.

Leaving his office, Smith stopped along the way to pick up the supplies he needed to take care of Chiun. Smith continued on and reached a nondescript corridor. He stepped as quietly as he could until he reached Chiun's room. He looked through the door's window. Chiun's color had returned and, from the sound of his loud snoring, he seemed to be sleeping deeply. Smith opened the door to Chiun's room and entered as softly as possible, hoping not to wake him.

* * *

The pain Remo felt before his left arm stopped responding brought his attention back to the present. Winston's heel closed on Remo's face, but Remo easily dodged the kick. Winston pulled his leg back before Remo could break it, but slipped and fell. Yet somehow he was back on his feet before Remo could reach him.

Remo's arm throbbed with each beat of his heart.

Stone continued the offensive. Remo defended himself from the blows and kicks, but it was difficult with only one good arm. Stone was just too quick. But his attacks were not those of Sinanju. They reminded Remo of military training. Training a Navy SEAL would receive. Whoever was impersonating his son either didn't know he had Sinanju training, or wasn't able to perform the moves. The latter was more likely, since he would need years to learn proper breathing and the most basic skills.

Breathing. Remo focused his hearing. He heard only one heartbeat and only one set of lungs expanding and contracting — his own. Remo knew he once again faced an inhuman opponent in this jungle. Time to gain the offensive. Remo noticed the pain in his left arm. Feeling was returning to it, but he dodged and ducked carefully, to protect the arm from further harm.

Remo took a deep breath and relaxed. His opponent continued attacking in a blur of speed, but Remo analyzed each movement, easily avoided each blow. Now Remo noticed a pattern, as if the impostor were performing a *kata*. Remo determined the best opening between strikes and timed his move perfectly. Remo's attack was countered and he felt a vise grip around his throat.

Remo was lifted off the ground with one hand. Stone's white teeth smiled at Remo through the black and olive camouflage face paint. Winston held a tiny plastic fire extinguisher in his free hand and hooked it onto one of Remo's belt loops. "I am going to extinguish you," he said as the hand around Remo's throat constricted.

* * *

Once Remo realized he was fighting a machine, he also recognized the obvious opening was a trap. Remo's throat pressed back against his attacker's grip, allowing Remo to speak and, more importantly, breathe. "You couldn't even kill an old man. There's no way you can kill me."

Winston's face registered surprise. Remo reached out with his right arm, twisted the wrist of the arm holding him, and pulled. The arm came loose and Remo landed lightly on his feet. Stone's impostor turned away from Remo's good arm, which moved in a blur. It struck the machine's chest and continued forward. An instant later Remo withdrew his arm. It wasn't a heart he held in his hand, but a mass of electronics. He didn't care what they were; only what they did. He yanked them free. Rain poured into the machine's chest cavity. Sparks flew. The circuitry shorted out, and the machine, off-balance, fell forward into the mud.

Remo tossed the plastic extinguisher onto the impostor's remains. "That's the biz, sweetheart."

* * *

Remo followed his internal compass and ticked off the remaining klicks until he smelled diesel fumes and heard the two-stroke motor of a generator. He followed the sound until he reached a large and brightly-lit tent. He stopped, expanding his senses, before entering the enemy's lair. He only sensed one person inside, but were there more machines? He didn't hear anything to indicate there were any, but wanted to be sure.

He stepped to one side of the tent's entrance and remained outside of the perimeter of light surrounding it. He picked up a fallen tree branch and tossed it past the tent's entrance. It hit a tree on the other side of the tent with such force that it sounded like a gunshot.

A bald, very recognizable head peeked out of the tent and looked in the direction of the sound. Seeing nothing, the bald head was followed by a lithe body clad in a black mock-turtleneck and faded blue jeans. The man stepped out boldly. He walked quickly around the tent, his worn sneakers squeaking across the wet foliage. Remo took the opportunity to let himself inside.

Remo looked around the tent. The generator wasn't here to power just lights. Along the far side of the tent was a table holding a laptop connected to two huge monitors. A MyPad sat on the metal chair that had been quickly pushed back from the table. Remo picked up the MyPad and saw a game of chess was in progress.

He turned at the sound of someone pushing aside the tent flap and entering. The man stopped momentarily when he saw Remo, but quickly recovered and strode over, hand extended. He introduced himself, unnecessarily, "Steve Hobby. Welcome to the future."

Remo ignored the hand, mentally playing out the remainder of the chess game. Hobby stepped over and looked at the electronic game board. "Do you play?"

Remo thought back to how he had defeated a Nazi war criminal from an apparently hopeless position, using an unexpected attack with the white queen. The game just wasn't the same without physical pieces to move.

"It's been a while," he answered, and handed the MyPad to its inventor.

Hobby asked enthusiastically, "How long did it take you to realize you were fighting a robot with artificial intelligence?"

Remo looked into the younger man's fanatical eyes. He answered without answering, "There was no heartbeat and it didn't breathe."

Hobby looked around the tent nervously then smiled widely, "But it was pretty damn good for a prototype, yeah? I'm going to call it the MyBot!"

"Why did you send that gizmo to kill us?"

Hobby beamed as he replied, "When my spiderbots accidentally came across your database and discovered the United States government made payments in gold to the House of Sinanju, I saw an opportunity. If I eliminated the Masters, MyBots could take their place and Orange would make a killing. A killing, yeah?" He laughed at a joke that was funny only to himself. He continued, "I knew it was possible because the MyBot wouldn't project its attack. It would strike without warning. Leaving you and your master unprepared." He leaned closer to Remo and said, "The most dangerous man is the one who does not appear dangerous."

"I've heard that before." Remo grabbed the black turtleneck in his hand and made a fist, careful not to rip the shirt, and pulling out a patch of chest hairs in the process. "I broke your little toy and now I'm going to put you out of business. Permanently."

Hobby smiled his natural, charismatic smile. "Unlike Sinanju, my business will continue with or without me." He saw the deep-set black eyes and felt as though he were looking into a living death's head. He swiped furiously at the MyPad. "No. Look here," he said pointing at the display. Our stock price is at an all-time high, thanks to my recent marketing campaign. MecroSuck can't touch us. I had thought about buying them once, yeah? But then realized we look so much better because they make themselves look so bad." Hobby laughed again, giddy, but nervous. "I can be invaluable to you. How about a merger?"

Remo took the MyPad from Hobby's sweaty hands and curled his fingers around it. The device crumbled to plastic and silicone bits. Remo opened his hand, spilling the debris onto the jungle floor, when his MyPhone unexpectedly rang. He took the phone out of his chinos' front pocket and glanced at the screen. "It's my boss. I should take this. Give me a minute." He released Hobby and answered the call, "Remo."

Hobby was shocked. Not that the phone had reception. His set-up here included its own mini-cell tower that had a range not permitted by the FCC. No.

He was shocked that Remo had not changed the ringtone from its default setting.

Remo ended the call. "Change in plans. You're coming back with me."

"Yeah?"

"Yeah."

* * *

Chiun paced his room at Folcroft, the case of water bottles Smith had brought him empty. When he heard Smith and Remo approaching, he leapt into the bed and pulled the sheet up to his neck and feigned sleep.

Smith opened the door to the room and allowed Remo to enter first. Remo walked to the bed silently.

Chiun sat up quickly. "What is with all this noise? Disturbing an old man who needs his rest to recover from a fatal wound."

"You're not fooling anyone, Chiun. We didn't wake you."

Chiun pretended to notice Smith for the first time. "Emperor Smith, your presence here is not necessary. Your servant does not wish to take you away from your important duties. You need not linger here."

"I'm glad you survived, Master Chiun. That wound and the cyanide would have killed anyone else."

"That is why you trust Sinanju to protect your empire, O Great One. Only Sinanju can eliminate all who threaten the Eagle Throne."

In Korean he continued, "The one who attacked me has been

dispatched?"

"Terminated," Remo answered in English.

"Thank you, Remo, for bringing Mr. Hobby to Folcroft. Now that CURE is Orange's majority shareholder, we don't want anything to happen to its most valuable asset."

Remo asked, "Why did you decide to buy Orange? I could have just killed Hobby and left him in the jungle. No one would have found him there."

"I couldn't take the chance their contingency plans would allow anyone else to learn about Sinanju." Smith's lips stretched back in what must have been a smile. "And my financial analysis of Orange indicates the dividends we'll receive from our investment can keep CURE funded in the event of future governmental shutdowns."

If Smith was the grandmaster, did that make Remo a pawn? A pawn to be sacrificed at Smith's whim?

No. Smith may have taken away his life as Remo Williams and created the Destroyer, but Remo was the Reigning Master of Sinanju, and he would determine his own fate.

"Let me know if you need anything. I'm going to see if Mr. Hobby is comfortable in his new, *ahem*, office."

Smith turned to go. Remo placed a hand on his arm. "Not so fast, Smith. We need to discuss our contract."

Smith's face changed and Remo easily recognized this expression. A frown. Behind him, he couldn't see the look of pride on Chiun's face.

ABOUT THE AUTHOR:

John E. Bailor is a full-time loan officer and part-time writer living in Harrisburg, Pennsylvania. Bailor's first professionally-published work was a short story in DESTROYER WORLD: NEW BLOOD. Still a big fan of Warren Murphy and the *Destroyer* series, he was pleased to contribute to MORE BLOOD. You can learn more about him at www.JohnEBailor.com.

KISSING COUSINS

Ralph L. Angelo, Jr.

Prologue

THE OLD MAN SLOWLY STEPPED OUT OF THE DARKNESS and walked into the scant illumination the grimy streetlight offered, then faded back into the darkness until he walked back into the next lights' glow. He was as much clad in dirt as he was in the ratty, threadbare old jacket he wore. He stopped in front of the corner deli that was already closed for the night. At the curb was a row of garbage cans. Slowly, after looking both ways to make sure he was not being watched, he lifted the first garbage can lid and began to rummage around in the trash. He removed a half-eaten sandwich. He smiled as if he just found a brick of gold, and placed it in a plastic shopping bag he had in his left hand. He covered the first garbage can and silently moved on to the next.

A sound assailed the old man's ears. Just a slight scratching and one he would normally ignore.

But the hairs on the back of his neck rose slightly in warning, and after spending many years on the streets, he knew which warnings to ignore and which to heed. He moved his head quickly from side to side listening and trying to part the darkness. His rheumy eyes squinted while trying to discern what was out there.

To his left and across the street he heard a cat hiss. An instant later it ran across his path. The old man smiled and shook his head. "Just a cat," he muttered through a mostly-toothless mouth.

He opened the next garbage can, and then the next. Scavenging through them he removed odds and ends he considered edible. A half-empty soda bottle, some fruit that wasn't quite rotten. All of them went into his shopping bag.

The old man shuffled his feet and began making his way down the block when something in the alleyway between stores caught his eye. It was a small thing, just a glint of light on something metallic. But whatever it was it was behind another row of garbage cans.

He turned and walked toward whatever was gleaming in the darkness. When he arrived at the pails, he bent over searching for the shiny object that had caught his eye. Shoving cans aside as quietly as possible, the old man pulled free what appeared to be a metal plate. It was shiny and bright. But it was like no plate the old man had ever seen. It bulged on both sides, almost like it was two metal plates welded together. The old man flipped it over and looked at it quizzically. "How you s'posed ta eat outta this thing?" he murmured.

With a shrug, he tossed it aside and went to open another garbage can when he noticed something else. It was a shame, really. If he had just kept his head inside the garbage can he would have lived.

But his usually slow and foggy mind realized that he never heard the plate hit the ground. It was metal it should have made some kind of sound when he tossed it away, shouldn't it?

The old man turned around, more curious than afraid. But his eyes widened in shock at what he saw. Behind him were an Asian man and a woman, dressed in all black. The woman was small and compact, five feet tall at most. She was quite stunning, though her most interesting feature was her impossibly long black hair. She stood impassively holding the pie plate he had just thrown away in her left hand. In her right she held a long, thin katana. Her companion was rail thin, and a bit taller than the woman, around five foot eight. He carried a sword that matched hers.

The old man slowly backed away from them both, his hands held up before his face. "A-ah don't want no trouble. Just lemme go an' I'll be on mah way," he pleaded.

The male looked at the female and smiled. It was an evil thing to see. Both turned back to the old man and advanced on him, their twin drawn blades held high, glistening brightly in the moonlight.

Chapter One

His name was remo and he was angry. Remo didn't like punks, especially ones who thought that because they bought a gun they were now the toughest guys on the block. Remo didn't need a gun anymore, since becoming a master of Sinanju, and he had nothing against them. They were a tool, like a steak knife or a hammer. But the punk Remo was dangling by his left ankle off the roof of the Smith Haven Mall in central Long Island had thought that pulling that gun on Remo made him one scary dude. He thought that gun made him the master of every situation. He kept thinking that, until he pulled the gun from the waistband of his pants and pointed it at Remo.

But then something funny happened. G-Badzz — "with two Z's," he had told Remo — suddenly couldn't feel the gun in his hand. In fact, he couldn't feel his hand either, or his arm. When he instinctively looked at his arm he began to scream. "Whatchu do to me? Whatchu do to me?"

The arm of G-Badzz — whose real name was Gordon Badalowski — now hung limply at his side. It looked like a boneless sack of flesh. The gun lay at his feet, but it was in pieces — completely dismantled by the crazy white dude in the black t-shirt who held him above his head by one arm, smiling like a lunatic. *Maybe this guy's crazy?* thought Gordon. That could be. The dude definitely had crazy-man strength. *And what the hell was with that smile? Maybe he's a retard? It could be retard strength? Maybe I should talk to this crazy cracker?*

"Yo crazy cracker, whatchu doin' ta me? Let me go an' I won't be killin' yo punk ass."

"Ritz or Saltines?" the crazy cracker said, still smiling.

"W-what? Whatchu say?" G-Badzz shook his head in disbelief.

"You said something about crackers, and I asked you if you liked Ritz or Saltines."

"Y-you, w-wait, what?" G-Badzz stammered, "Crazy white foo', I gon' be bustin' a cap in yo ass, if yo don't let me down, and I mean now."

The skinny man continued to smile, and then said, "Okay, Skippy let's cut to the chase. My name's Remo, and I have to ask you a question: what did you think you were doing when you punched that old woman in the face and ran away? I really don't understand what that was about."

"W-wha?"

Remo reached up with his free hand and touched G-Badzz just below his collarbone. The pain was so excruciating that G-Badzz thought he would pass out.

"Whachu want, crazy white dude?" Gee began again.

"First, I want to know your name. Second, I want to know why you keep calling me a 'crazy white dude' when your skin is whiter than mine. Third, I want to know why you punched that sweet old woman in the mall. You can answer the last one first, Skippy."

"Yo man, I ain't tellin' you— "

The crazy white dude touched that spot below his collarbone again and then everything went black for G-Badzz.

When he came to, G-Badzz was hanging over the edge of the mall roof by his left ankle, suspended there by the crazy white dude.

"Now as I was saying, Skippy— "

"G-Badzz! M-my name's G-Badzz!" Gordon Badalowski screamed.

"Uh, right. Just so I understand, you were born with that name?"

"Hell no, you crazy white dude, but it's what I go by now. It's my street cred."

"Okay, Skippy. Whatever you say. Let's go back to the nice old lady you slugged while she was window-shopping inside. You wanna tell me what that's all about?"

"I-it's a game."

The crazy dude who called himself Remo narrowed his eyes as if he didn't understand what G-Badzz was telling him, "Let me get this straight, G-String. You beat up a seventy-five-year-old woman for a game? What kind of game is this? And what do you get when you 'win'?"

The crazy white dude shook G-Badzz while he spoke, like he weighed nothing, and Gee watched as his baseball cap, which, up until now, had been perched sideways on his head covering his tightly-cut red hair dropped off and sailed to the ground fifty feet below him. Gee swallowed hard.

"A-ain't no prize dude, ain't no prize!" Gee spat out, "I-it ain't that kinda game. Donchu watch TV none? Is a game all over da place. Lotsa kids're doin' it, man."

"Really? Because I thought every game had a prize at the end. Like a

Cracker-Jack box. There's always a prize at the bottom. They used to be worth getting a long time ago. They used to have some interesting stuff in there. Now I hear it's all junk. Anyway, let me ask you something else — since we're talking about Cracker-Jacks, I'm starting to feel a little hungry. Is there an organic market around her anywhere? I need to pick up some rice, but not the junk they sell in the regular supermarket. Oh, by the way to answer your question, no, I don't watch TV. My father is always hogging it. I'm not really that interested."

"Wha'-what?" G-Badzz asked in disbelief, "Rice? Yo wants rice?"

Crazy white dude Remo shook him once more, "Answer the question D-bag, and I'll tell you what prize you won. See, in this game you actually win something, but you have to play along first so tell me where I can get some rice. Preferably brown rice."

"Round da corner, round da corner, dere's a big organic, snooty rich people place dat sells dat stuff you want. Now howzabout my prize? What I win? You gonna put me down? Jus don' drop me man, please don' drop me."

The crazy white dude named Remo furrowed his brow and said, "Let me ask you one more question, Heebee G-bee. You said something about rich people a moment ago, and it almost sounded like you didn't like them because they had money. At least that's the feeling I got out of that comment. Are you poor? Did you have a hard life?"

"Hell no! My 'rents, they be part o' the problem. They be the one percenters that be holdin' me down. They had plenty o' smack. But they ain't sharin' it wit' me. They be tryin' ta take my street cred away, an' it be all about da cred."

Crazy white dude Remo shook his head and said, "I have no idea what you just said, but let me guess — your parents wanted you to go to college and get a degree, maybe take over the family business, but you decided that you wanted to walk around malls punching old ladies and maybe dealing drugs to get by — instead of living the life your parents wanted you to have? I bet you even were part of that whole suckupy Wall Street thing that went on in Manhattan a while back, weren't you? Am I close?"

G-Badzz shook his head, and it hurt. The blood was all rushing to his head by now and he was starting to wonder just how long this crazy cracker could hold him like that by one arm.

"Yeah crazy man, you right 'bout all of it. I got no idea how you know this shit but you right. Look man, all I did was play a game. It called da 'knockout game,' dat all. It funny seein' da fools go down."

That was when G-Badzz (AKA Gordon Badalowski) had the serious notion he should have shut up while he was ahead. The reason? The crazy white dude named Remo stopped smiling.

"You're right, Cheez-whiz. It *is* funny seeing the fools go down." With that, Remo opened his hand and walked away.

G-Badzz, with two Z's, born Gordon Badalowski, began screaming immediately, but the last thought he had before his skull impacted with the pavement fifty feet below was that he could have sworn the crazy white dude named Remo said "That's the biz, sweetheart."

Remo walked to the other side of the roof and stepped over; bouncing up against the wall he touched it lightly with his fingertips and toes over and over until he stepped to the pavement a second later. If anyone had been watching, they would have sworn he had just spider-crawled down its side.

They would only have been partly right. People were running and screaming away from the spot G-Badzz had landed. Remo walked in the opposite direction when he heard the word 'Jumper' and smiled. He began to whistle one of his favorite songs, "Whistle While You Work."

Chapter Two

An hour later, Remo entered his hotel room, carrying a bag of groceries. "Hey Loo-Ceee, I'm ho-ome," he called, tapping the door with his foot. To the naked eye it would have looked like he barely touched the door, but it shut with a solid snap, like it was shot out of a cannon.

"Hey! Where are you Little Father?"

"I am here, my most ungrateful of sons," a squeaky voice replied from around the corner of the suite, where the TV was located. Remo followed the sounds emanating from the TV, which sounded like a discordant screeching, to find an old man sitting cross-legged on a rattan mat, wearing a golden kimono emblazoned with dragons, who promptly hushed him. "Now be quiet, the great Cheeta Ching is on the television. I must bask in her beauty once more."

"Really? You're back to her again? No more 'Madam Googoo'?"

"Bah. Madam Googoo could have secured Sinanju's future by bearing the fruit of my loins and giving me a son, an heir I could be proud of. A child that would not embarrass me at every turn, unlike a certain worthless pale piece of a pig's ear who cannot straighten his elbow."

Remo sighed, "Okay, Little Father, what is it this time?"

"I want you to take me to see Cheeta Ching on Broadway. She is playing the lead role in 'Hello Dolly.' It is a limited engagement."

"It'll be even more limited after she plays her first show," Remo muttered.

"I heard that. Cheeta Ching is the flower of Korea. She is an international treasure."

"Yeah, she's a treasure all right — one that should have stayed buried."

"You are a bad person, Remo Williams. I gave you the best years of my life, the very best years and this is how you repay me? Cheeta Ching will love me like Rose loved Jack in 'Titanic.'"

Then the old man stood up and stretched his arms out to his sides while closing his eyes and smiling contentedly.

"Really, Chiun? *Titanic*? You do know the ship sunk, right? Hey! What if Cheeta Ching had been on the *Titanic*? Then she could have been an international treasure, buried at sea. Come to think of it, she was probably in her thirties when that boat sunk, so she could have been on it. What do you think, Little Father?"

The old man, Chiun, pouted as if mortally wounded. He dropped his arms to his sides and walked into the rear bedroom of the suite they shared. "I think I will die an unhappy man because of my ungrateful son."

Chiun placed the back of his right hand to his forehead and lay down upon a grass mat he had placed next to the queen-sized bed in that room. "My time is at an end. I ask for only one thing from my ungrateful lout of a son before I pass into the great beyond to stand side by side with the great Masters who stood before me, and yet, my only son refuses my wishes. Woe is me. Woe is me. I am sorry, Cheeta Ching, but it is not to be. Our love will never be consummated, all because of my ungrateful child, for whom I sacrificed everything."

Remo sighed while he unpacked the bag of groceries. He knew that when Chiun got this way there was no end to it, so he might as well let him have his way.

"All right, Little Father, when is the show? I'll ask Smitty to get us a couple of tickets."

Instantly Chiun was standing at his side. "You do your father proud, Remo. No matter what the mad emperor Smith has said about you, I know better."

Remo looked at him through slit eyes and nodded, "Uhh, right."

"Oh, the mad emperor Smith called looking for you; he said it was very urgent."

"And what? You just decide to tell me this now?"

"Cheeta Ching was singing, I could not interrupt such beauty for the mad emperor."

"Where's my phone?"

The aged little man stared at the TV with a smile on his face. One would think he was simple in the brain for such a look. But then they would not realize Cheeta Ching's face was once again being displayed with information about ordering tickets to her Broadway show at the bottom of the screen.

Remo shook his head in mock disgust. "Little Father, my phone?"

Chiun waved his hand silently toward the window without turning his head. Remo grumbled and stepped toward the balcony. Remo looked down towards the pool and saw his phone sitting at the bottom. Remo knew immediately that it was indeed *his* phone because he could see it as clearly as if it were in his palm. It was just one of the abilities that being the reigning Master of Sinanju gave him. Chiun was also a Master of Sinanju, who had trained Remo to be his successor.

But Remo and Chiun were more than just masters of a mysterious martial art. They were assassins, in a long line of assassins who, for thousands of years, had had worked for the richest kingdoms in the world. The proceeds were not used for personal gain, but rather to feed a small village in Korea — the village of Sinanju.

Though their bond had deepened over the years, training Remo was not something Chiun had initially done out of love; Remo had been trained in Sinanju because Chiun had been paid by the United States Government to do so. The U.S. wanted a weapon — one that could be forged and used against those enemies that the Constitution would not allow them to touch under regular circumstances. So a candidate was needed. One who had no ties to anyone else. An orphan with a sense of justice. A young cop in Newark, NJ was chosen. Framed for a murder he didn't commit and executed, Remo awoke as a man with no past and no future. A dead man who could not be traced, used by an organization that did not exist. An organization named 'CURE.' Only one other person knew of CURE's existence — Harold W. Smith, a lemon-faced and bespectacled patriot who ran CURE out of Folcroft Sanitarium on the banks of the Hudson River in Rye, NY. The same Harold W. Smith who was now knocking impatiently at Remo's hotel room door.

Remo opened the door and smiled.

"Smitty! Glad you could make it. Welcome to the party. Can I get you anything? Some brown rice, or maybe some fish? I'm not sure what other kinds we have today, but I'm sure there's plenty of 'carp' to go around — right, Chiun?"

The elder master of Sinanju stared at Remo with disgust then turned toward Smith with a smile. "Emperor Smith, what a surprise! It is so good to see the august personage of the great and mighty Emperor of the young land called America. Have you come to your senses yet? Do you wish for your humble servants to kill the pretender on the throne and install you as king, as you so clearly deserve?"

Smith's dour countenance did not change. "No, Master Chiun. As always, the President is the nation's leader, not me. If you'll excuse me, I need to speak to Remo alone for a moment."

Chiun bowed graciously and exited the kitchenette of the suite, removing himself to the bedroom, whispering in Korean to Remo, "The lunatic Smith grows more unstable every day. We should leave this land of chicken farmers and go to the Middle East. Perhaps Persia is looking for an assassin? They always paid well."

"So you've told me repeatedly, Little Father." Remo glared at him until he left the room and shut the bedroom door. He turned to Smith.

"What is it, Smitty? Why'd you come all the way out here to see us?"

"If you had answered your phone, I wouldn't have had to come out here," Smith replied tersely. "There is a mission for you."

"Who needs to be killed this time?"

"There's more to this than just killing someone, Remo. It involves national security, and something that is now in the wrong hands."

"What? Spy work again?" Remo shifted his legs uncomfortably, "You know I hate spy work, Smitty. You want someone taken out, aim me at the target and they're as good as dead. But all the espionage stuff..."

Smith said nothing for a few seconds before continuing. "An experimental prototype was stolen from a lab in New Jersey. A security camera caught these two holding it some hours later, after they had killed a neighborhood homeless man." Smith handed Remo several grainy black and white photos of two black-clad Asians hacking an old man to pieces.

"What'd they steal?" Remo asked.

"This."

Smith handed him another photo. The picture looked like a flying saucer from a 1950's science fiction film.

"You're kidding me, right? A flying saucer? These two ninja wannabes stole a miniature flying saucer? And this is what you call a national security threat?"

Smith sighed. "It is not a toy, Remo. This is the holy grail of modern science. It is a working magnetic repulsion flight system. This is the first step in man leaving Earth and exploring the stars. This is the only working prototype. Even worse, the scientists involved have all been murdered, and I believe it is these two who are responsible. In any event they now hold the device. I need you to recover it."

"What about Frick and Frack?"

"They are Chinese spies known as the 'Kissing cousins.' I've tracked them to Nevada, where I have to assume they are meeting a contact from China and handing off the device."

Remo stared at the photos with a furrowed brow. "Chinese spies who use Japanese swords to kill on American soil. Aren't there any secure borders anywhere anymore?"

"I never said they were Chinese, Remo. The Chinese employ them now, but their past remains a mystery. We believe they are both Japanese and may actually be cousins, hence their nickname. They sell their swords to the highest bidder, usually."

"Usually," Remo repeated.

"Yes. This time it's different, I'm afraid. The Chinese employed them directly to obtain that flying saucer. I need you to get it back and to clean up any loose ends."

Remo stood. "No sweat, Smitty. When do I leave?"

"Immediately. Here are tickets for you both." Smith got up to leave after handing Remo the tickets, but turned back to ask, "What are you doing on Long Island anyway? I had no mission for you here."

Remo shrugged. "You know how it goes. I wanted a change of scenery, to see the sights…and I had a few things to, uh, knock out while I was here."

"Knock out? You had something to do with that knockout game thug who jumped off the roof of the local mall, didn't you? Forget it. I don't want to know. Just deal with this — this is important."

"I thought we weren't doing any more work for the current whack-job-in-chief?"

"We're not, Remo — not unless we have to. He didn't call me on this. I doubt that man knows what part of the phone is supposed to go to his ear and what part he's supposed to dial. We're doing this for America. Someone still has to."

Smith closed the door behind him. Immediately Chiun reappeared, the first of his dozen lacquered steamer trunks in hand. "Pack quickly; we can be out of this land of the mad before the sun falls. The lunatic Emperor Smith will not even realize we are gone."

Remo sighed, "Why are we leaving this time, Little Father?"

"Do you pay no attention to my teachings of ancient Sinanju? Smith the mad would place you in contention with the 'cousins who would kiss.'

It is a thousand-year-old prophecy of death for the ugly master who would face them."

"Wait; let me get this straight, you're afraid of a couple of katana wielding Japanese hit men? Since when? And when did I become the 'ugly master'?"

"It is obvious you are the ugly master. Your face is not a Korean face. You have not the perfect symmetry of jaw and eye. None of the beautiful cheekbone structure only a Korean possesses. Your skin is pale and sallow. You are an American, and thus the ugly master." Chiun smiled to himself and began to cackle while he began to pack his trunk enthusiastically.

"Okay, Little Father. You continue to pack for your trip to Persia or wherever the heck you're going. I'm going to hop a flight to Vegas to see about these two killers."

Chiun turned to look at Remo, standing up from his packing, "You would not heed your father's advice and run from the prophecy that would spell your doom?"

"Chiun, how many of these prophecies have we had to deal with in all the years we've been together? It seems like there's a new prophecy every week; and they all seem to deal with me being killed or dismembered or something like that. Now this is the lamest one I've heard yet. Two katana-wielding punks are supposed to scare me? I'm sorry, Little Father, but Remo's going to Reno. Are you coming?"

"It is Las Vegas we must travel to, ugly master. Las Vegas."

"Wherever…"

Chapter Three

A FEW HOURS LATER, REMO AND CHIUN left their motel room on the outskirts of Las Vegas behind and began pulling out of the lot to drive toward the Grand Canyon.

Before Remo even left the lot, a young girl with long brown hair was flagging their car down.

"What the heck is this?" Remo exclaimed.

"It is a mad woman! Run her over and be done with it. She is part of the prophecy, sent by the demons to becloud your weak, degenerate, sex-filled American mind."

Remo looked at Chiun and shook his head. "Believe me, Little Father, you managed to somehow take all the fun out of sex for me years ago, and this kid looks like she can't be any more than fourteen or fifteen. She's probably lost." He pulled up next to the girl and rolled the window down, "What's up, kid? You lost or something?"

The girl looked at him with pleading eyes, "Please mister, m-my tour bus pulled outta here and left me behind when we left the diner. Are you goin' to the canyon? Can you give me a lift?"

"Sure, kid, hop in."

Chiun hissed in Korean, "She is devil spawn. Also nincompoop, at fourteen in the village of Sinanju she would have had at least three children already."

"Yeah I know Little Father, and they probably all would have looked like Cheeta Ching." Just the thought made Remo shudder.

"Wow, aren't you guys hot in here? It's like a hundred an' ten out there, an' you don't have the A/C on. How come?"

"If you want the A/C, you got it." Remo reached over and fiddled with the A/C controls, not quite sure how to turn them on. Since Remo had become Sinanju, his grasp on the mechanical had slowly faded, for some reason he did not quite understand.

"Wait, I'll get it," the girl offered. She reached over from the back seat and turned the A/C on, then slid back and plopped back into the rear seat of the sedan. "Who are you guys anyway? An' how come you're not sweating? You know you can roll the window up now that the A/C's on, right? Were you driving with the A/C off and the windows up?"

"We weren't hot kid. We don't get hot," Remo replied calmly, which was true. Through Sinanju Remo and Chiun were able to regulate their body temperatures so that they were never hot — or cold, for that matter.

Chiun spoke to Remo in Korean. "Let me kill her. I will throw her body out the door and you will not even have to slow down. The coyotes and other vermin-eaters will dispose of the carcass. She is obviously a demon in human form, sent to kill the ugly master."

"I thought the inbred ninjas were sent to kill the ugly master?"

"Details, details. Because you did not listen to me we will miss Cheeta Ching's first Broadway performance tonight. I will not forget that."

"And probably her last," Remo muttered.

"I can hear you, ugly master."

The young girl leaned forward between the front seat backs "What's your names? What language are you two talking? Do you like Judson Beeper?"

Remo sighed in exasperation. He briefly wondered what happened to the days when he used to kill bad guys and hang out with hot chicks.

"Are you guys gonna answer me? Guy-eyes? My name's Sally by the way. What's yours?"

"My Name's Remo, kid. His names Kvetch, because that's all he does — kvetch, kvetch, kvetch."

"Oh. Okay, what's a kvetch?"

Remo rolled his eyes.

Chiun repeated "Demon-child."

"What do you guys do for work?"

"We're bank tellers. Here for a convention."

"Really, Mr. Remo? You don't look like bank tellers."

"Sometimes I feel like the janitor — always taking out someone else's trash."

"Yes, but then you would be the ugly janitor," Chiun cackled. "Ugly janitor, hee hee hee."

Chiun turned toward the back seat, "Devil child, what have your masters sent you here to do? Befuddle the ugly master?"

"All righty, Chiun, enough, leave the kid alone. I'm sure she's scared enough as it is without having to deal with a crazy man in a kimono."

"It's okay, Mr. Remo. I like him. He reminds me of a crazy man around the corner who always forgets his meds. He talks just like him."

"What did I tell you, my son? She is a demon in child form," Chiun continued in Korean.

"She seems pretty sensible to me."

"I will keep an eye on her to protect your unworthy life." Chiun slowly turned his head toward the young teenager in the back seat and kept one eye staring at her as Remo drove.

Sally watched the old man for a few minutes, then frowned, stuck her tongue out at him, and turned to stare out the window, watching the scenery go by. The ride was quiet until an hour later the girl reached over the seat again and turned the radio, and immediately hunted down a local station playing her crush, Judson Beeper.

"Oh don't you just lo-o-ove him? He's so sweet, an' cute too! I love how he does his hair, don't you? Have you two ever seen him in concert? I have. Five times this year."

Then she began to sing along with the incessant noise emanating from the radio.

Almost as one, both men reached for the radio, but Remo was a hair quicker. He jammed his hand in through the front of it, and yanked it free of the dash with a screech of breaking plastic and bending metal. Even as he did this with his right hand he was pushing the window down button with his left. In one smooth flawless motion he tore the radio free of the dash and hurled it out the window like a missile. It disappeared high above the desert. Remo rolled the window back up and began whistling contentedly before the girl could speak.

"A demon-child…" Chiun repeated once more.

* * *

Remo pulled the rental car into one of the many parking lots along the Grand Canyon, nearest the tour buses.

"Thanks for the ride, Mr. Remo. You too, Mr. Kvetch." The girl hopped out of the back seat and ran toward a bus parked nearby.

Chiun wagged a bony finger at the departing girl, "I tell you my son, that child is a devil-spawn."

The two men exited the rental car. "You go left, I'll go right," Remo said, "and if you find them, call me on your cell phone."

"I do not have it. I left it in the hotel on the island of Long."

Remo stopped, looked heavenward, turned around and began to ask

115

'why,' then stopped himself. "Fine, if you find them, just don't kill them in front of anyone. I don't care if you tear their heads off and throw them over a cliff, as long as no one sees it. Got it?"

"As you wish, Ugly Master," Chiun said, still smiling. He bowed, turned, and disappeared into the milling crowd.

Remo turned, shook his head, and walked to the right. His Sinanju-sharpened eyes scanned every face he saw, instantly remembering the faces from the grainy photographs Smith had shown him.

Remo moved toward the railing overlooking the Grand Canyon. He looked down as far as possible and then he began searching left to right.

"This is getting ridiculous," he muttered. *But*, he thought to himself, *Smitty said this was going to be the right time and the right place.*

Remo effortlessly hopped up to the top of the railing that stopped sightseers from going over the edge to the canyon floor far below, and began to look around.

Guards immediately ran toward him blowing whistles. Tourists screamed and ran away from him, shielding their children's eyes. The guards and park police continued blowing whistles and shouting at him to get down.

Remo ignored them, as he craned his neck in one direction and then the other.

"C'mon where are they?"

One of the guards lunged for Remo's legs. Remo ignored him completely and stepped over his reaching hands.

Again the guard tried; again he missed without seeing Remo step over his arms.

"What the hell?" the guard grunted as he reached again and missed a third time.

Now two of the park security guards were trying to tackle Remo's legs as he slowly walked along the top of the railing. They each continued to miss, while Remo continued to scan back and forth along the railing.

Finally, about a half-mile from his position, something caught his eye.

"Hello, sweetheart," Remo said aloud, starting to run along the two-inch-wide railing, accelerating quickly before disappearing down the railing into the distance. The guards looked at each other and didn't know what to make of what they had just seen.

Remo hopped off the railing directly in front of the female assassin

116

from the photograph.

"Hello, sweetheart, I think you've got something of mine. Actually, it belongs to my Uncle Sam. If you give it back, I'll make this easy on both of us."

The young Japanese woman fumed at the sight of Remo, and immediately kicked at Remo's midsection. Remo merely stepped around her kick, tapping her on the side of the neck with two fingers as he passed. She dropped to the ground, paralyzed.

"Now, as I was saying, you have something that belongs to my Uncle Sam. Where is it?"

The woman looked at him and hissed, "American dog, I do not know what you have done to me or how you have done it, but you will die at my feet, and I will savor every one of your last breaths."

Remo looked at her and furrowed his brow, and then after a few seconds asked, "Hey lady, do you think I'm ugly?"

"Wh-what?" she asked.

"Ugly, do you think I'm ugly? Just do me a favor and answer the question."

"You are not...unpleasant, I suppose." The woman answered incredulously.

"That's good to know. Now where's that item you and the other bozo stole from that lab in Jersey? Actually...where *is* the other bozo?"

"Bozo?" she hissed. "What is a 'Bozo'?"

"A clown, sweetheart, a clown. Sorta like you and your cousin."

Remo stepped right without looking. A katana blade sliced through the spot where his head had been only a second earlier.

"Forget it, sweetheart. I think he found us."

Remo turned while bending at the knees, ducking below the second swing of the blade.

"Hey, bozo, how'd you get that sword in here? They have rules against that sort of thing, you know."

"I kill you for what you did to Mai-Li."

"Just wait a minute, and tell me, where's the package you took from Jersey?"

"The package has been delivered, ugly American."

"Okay, now we're getting somewhere. What's your name, bozo?"

The sword-wielding assassin screwed his face up and said "What is this 'Bozo'?"

"Look it up, fruit loops."

Remo ducked under the next swing of the blade, then snapped his right foot out in a blur, knocking the male assassin's leg out from under him so quickly that he did not realize he was on the ground until Remo was standing over him, and standing on the man's hand.

"As I said, what's your name, bozo?"

"I call myself Johnny Thunder."

Remo guffawed immediately. "Really? You're not embarrassed by that? Wasn't there a line of toy cars with that name?"

The man growled beneath him and tried to kick Remo, who easily avoided the kick.

"No, wait. The cars were called 'Johnny Lightning.' That was it. Now, who has the pie plate?" Remo growled.

"I'll never tell, Gaijin."

Remo stepped back and off the assassin's hand. 'Johnny Thunder' climbed to his feet, never removing his eyes from Remo. He brought his sword up and charged at Remo screaming. Remo stepped to the inside of the blade and almost imperceptibly flicked the back of his right hand out, striking the blade. The sword exploded into hundreds of tiny fragments, most of which embedded themselves into Johnny Thunder's face and chest.

Johnny Thunder looked down in disbelief; he was bleeding from countless tiny wounds.

"Wha-what are you?" he whispered.

Remo smiled, "I'm a Master of Sinanju," was his reply. "Now where's the pie plate?"

The blood ran from Johnny Thunder's face. He locked eyes with his cousin, Mai-Li, still lying on the ground and unable to move.

A gunshot rang out. Remo ducked slightly and the bullet sailed over his head. Again and again a gun fired and again and again Remo moved imperceptibly. Each time, the bullets missed their target.

"This is getting annoying," Remo muttered.

Johnny Thunder backed away toward his cousin. "Mai-Li, we must escape. Did you not hear? He is a Master of Sinanju."

"H-he did something to me, Johnny. I cannot move."

Bullets continued to fly around Remo. He continued to look for the angle of trajectory and finally found the shooter crouched behind a small bathroom facility.

"You two wait here. I have to go talk to someone."

Remo snapped his first two fingers out on his right hand, hitting Johnny Thunder on the forehead. He crumpled to the ground. "Good doggies. Stay."

Remo hopped up and over a small fence and ran toward the bathroom facility from which the shots were originating. Remo turned a corner and stopped short.

"Don't make another move. I don't know how you managed to avoid those bullets, but, at this range, I can't miss," Sally growled.

Remo grinned. "Hey short stuff, what's up? Decided to come clean, huh?"

"Oh yeah, like you knew I wasn't a fourteen-year-old kid."

She kept the gun aimed steadily at Remo with her right hand, and placed a cigarette in her mouth with her left. She flicked a cheap lighter and after inhaling a few times stuffed the lighter back in her pocket.

"So what are you, kid? Some kind of sleeper agent?" Remo asked.

The girl had a backpack on. Remo knew she wasn't wearing it when he dropped her off.

"Let me guess, that's our pie plate?"

"Not yours. It belongs to my government."

She took a long drag on the cigarette, staring at him through slit eyes.

"Hand over the bag, kid, and I'll go easy on you."

"You idiot," she spat, "I'm thirty-four years old. I'm short and thin and had massive amounts of plastic surgery to look this way. But it works pretty good, doesn't it?"

"Coulda fooled me." Remo replied with a grin, "But you didn't."

"What?"

"Lady, you smelled of cigarettes and booze, probably from two nights ago judging by what's seeping out of your pores. We both knew you weren't a kid. Now I'm starting to lose my patience. Hand me the backpack and I'll kill you quickly."

"You'll...kill me?"

"You heard it here first, cupcake."

Sally began firing at Remo's chest. But then the gun was out of her hands and crushed to metal fragments before she could blink. Remo grabbed her by the collar and lifted her off the ground like a feather.

She began to scream for help, but Remo tapped her on the side of the neck, freezing her vocal chords. She tried to run, but Remo hit another nerve cluster and froze her in place. Tossing her up on his shoulders, as if he was giving her a ride, he made his way back to where he had left the cousins. Chiun was there, waiting for him.

Smiling, Remo propped Sally up against the railing.

"Finally found me, Little Father? Took you long enough."

"I never lost you, loud and insufferable one. You made so much noise that a deaf Chinese monk could have found you."

"Kvetch, kvetch, kvetch. What should we do with these three now?"

"You are the 'ugly master.' You tell me."

Remo bent down and dragged Johnny Thunder to his feet, placing his immobile body next to Sally. Next, he reached down for Mai-Li, but, with a surge of adrenaline, she leapt to her feet and ran past Remo.

But Chiun was there, and Mai-Li was not entirely recovered from Remo's nerve cluster strike. She stumbled awkwardly, tripped, and fell into Chiun, entangling herself with him and carrying him along with her over the railing toward the depths of the Grand Canyon so far below.

"Chiun!" Remo shouted.

His hand shot out and caught the golden kimono by the sleeve before Chiun was out of reach. Remo hauled him over the upper railing effortlessly.

Then, with a flick of his fingers he sent Johnny Thunder and Sally over the railing to meet their companion below.

"I think that ties things up nicely," Remo said, slapping his hands together. He was grinning wildly as they got back into their rental car, and continued to grin as they drove away, passing the dozen police cruisers heading toward the entrance of the park.

"Why are you smiling, dimwitted one? Did one of the ninjas strike your head?" Chiun asked.

"I was just thinking — "

"Something you should avoid at all times."

"Yeah, sure, anyway, like I said, I was just thinking — "

Again Chiun interrupted, "See? You are repeating yourself. You must be brain damaged."

"Okay, fine. Anyway, I'm not the one who almost died there. You were. Does that mean *you're* the ugly master?"

"Drive me to the airport, ungrateful one. Cheeta Ching awaits."

And Remo did just that, smiling all the way.

ABOUT THE AUTHOR:

Ralph L. Angelo Jr. is the author of The Cagliostro Chronicles, books 1 and 2, Torahg the Warrior, Sword of Vengeance, and Redemption of the Sorcerer, the Crystalon Saga, books 1 and 2, as well as the non-fiction Help! They're All Out to Get Me! The Motorcyclist's Guide to Surviving the Everyday World. Ralph has been a *Destroyer* fan since junior high school when he read Created, the Destroyer, and then every *Destroyer* novel he could get his hands on. To add a story to the legendary lore of the greatest series ever written has been a lifelong dream, and is an honor Ralph won't soon forget!

THE ROADS NOT TAKEN

Brad Mengel

HIS NAME WAS REMO and he had nearly finished patrol. The Vietnamese jungle was dense, but he glided through it silently. His hands gripped the M-16 the US Marines had issued him, alert for signs of danger.

He'd been in Vietnam for a while now, and he knew how things worked. His conscious mind began to wander as his warrior's instincts told him that he was alone. His hitch in the Marines was due to finish in two months and he planned to go back the Newark Police department, marry Katherine Gilhooly, have two kids — a boy and a girl — and get old and fat behind a desk.

Remo forced himself to focus on his environment. He'd seen too many of his fellow soldiers killed because they were distracted, even if only for a minute. Looking ahead, he saw that he was nearly back at camp.

"Incoming," he called, as he approached the gate of the camp. Early in his first tour, he'd walked up to the gate naturally, and had nearly been shot when the sentry hadn't heard him.

"Destroyer!" The sentry acknowledged his greeting with a hint of fear. It seemed like he was afraid of Remo — like Remo wasn't just another fellow soldier trying to survive, but was a threat. The sentry, Michael Long, was no doubt fed a bunch of exaggerated stories about him around the campfire. Funny, when he and Long went back to America both of them would be cops, nearly the same...and yet Long was still nervous around Remo.

Remo had seen and done so many things here in Vietnam that he wondered if he could really go back to his old life. A few weeks ago some damn spook named MacCleary had tried to pin a medal on him for killing five men. He was good killing swiftly and silently. He'd done it many times

122

now — so many times the others in his platoon had taken to calling him The Destroyer.

Of course, most of the men had nicknames like The Exterminator, or Hannibal, or Sergeant Mercy, but Remo had never really liked his name. It implied that he liked the killing. He didn't. He had not come to Vietnam to kill; he had come to protect America.

He had been a cop for the same reason: to protect America and its citizens.

He thought about how many rules he'd have to follow when he went back to being a police officer. Over here it was kill or be killed, no rights, due process or burden of proof. If they were shooting at you they were an enemy. Back in the civilized world, the Constitution protected them and gave the bad guys rights. It was a crazy system, he thought, but still worth defending.

Perhaps he could keep fighting in wars, as a soldier of fortune, like that Rainey fellow people kept talking about. But whilst it would make things simple for him, it would mean abandoning America. America meant something to him, which was why he joined the Marines and came over to Southeast Asia.

It was a decision that never really sat well with Sister Mary Margaret, the nun at the orphanage where he was raised. But it did not stop her from sending frequent care packages. Just last week, another arrived. This one included the two latest *Extinguisher* novels.

He'd already read and traded the books, but they made him think. Maybe when he went back he should forget about going back to the police. He could fight the war on crime just as he fought the war over here. Set himself up like Blaize Fury, the Extinguisher, and take on the gangsters and creeps the law couldn't touch.

But Remo dismissed the thought as it entered his head. What would Sister Mary Margaret say, even if she did send him Extinguisher novels? If she ever found out, Remo was sure her ruler would get a good workout.

The Christians in Action he'd seen over here seemed to have a free hand. The spook's offer to join the CIA might be a better option for him. He could see himself like James Bond, traveling the world to protect America. Fast cars, fast women, and living the good life. But since the CIA couldn't operate on American soil, would it really help Americans?

What he needed didn't exist: an agency to defend America from the savages and cannibals, the clever thugs who exploited the Constitution to get away with their crimes. The Constitution wouldn't apply to this agency. The war on crime would be fought with the same bloody techniques used over here in Vietnam. A committee of generals and police commissioners would run it, with an army at their disposal.

Perhaps some of those new computers could sift through all the data and ferret out the criminals the law inadvertently protected.

"A nice dream, that," Remo thought. He broke off his fantasy, realizing that if he didn't hurry, he'd miss tonight's mush in the Mess Hall.

After getting his meal, Remo sat with the group that had formed around a visiting soldier. He was telling how he'd cleared a fellow soldier of the allegation of a massacre at Hoi Binh. To lighten the mood that had settled on the group, someone told about an Australian named Kennedy who'd been working with a bulldozer at one of the camps and backed the dozer into the fence, set off all the alarms and caused a full-scale panic.

More war stories flowed as the night progressed— some tragic, others funny. A tough soldier named Bolan told the group a story he'd heard whilst serving in Korea. It was told to him by a guy named Spenser. After MacArthur had halted his advance into North Korea, he had been threatened by a sect of assassins known as Sinnin Jo, or something like that. Nobody had ever seen the Masters of Sinnin Jo or knew how many there were, but they were feared all through Korea. The South Koreans had refused to aid MacArthur if he pushed further into North Korea. Several of MacArthur's aides turned up dead. One had been stretched across the room like a clothesline after every joint in his body had been dislocated; another had fallen out of bed and broken every bone in his body. Eventually, MacArthur had decided to retreat, lest he be next. To save face, it was arranged that the President would order him to stop.

It sounded like hogwash to Remo, who decided that it was time for him to sack out. As he walked back his tent, he tried to imagine what a Sinnin Jo assassin would look like. He'd have to be young, definitely young, and tall, over six foot. And to break bones would require great strength so he'd have to be built like a Mister Universe or a boxer. These assassins would wear pyjamas tied with a sash, like the Vietnamese, but without sleeves.

This image stayed with him as he drifted off to sleep. In his dream, he'd been selected by the Committee to fight the war on crime. His partner was a Sinnin Jo, named Chun, who looked nothing like he had imagined — a scrawny, ancient Asian wearing a flowered Kimono. Together, he and Chun saved America many times. Chun offered to teach Remo to be a Sinnin Jo but he had refused, preferring to stick with his trusty M-60. He and Chun battled a renegade Sinnin Jo — Nuch, Chun's brother. Crazy computers, rampaging robots, mobsters and criminals would be no match for the lethal duo.

The bugler's mangled version of "Reveille" awoke Remo just as he was defeating someone called 'The German.' Normally, Remo awoke fully alert, but today it took him a few minutes to gain his bearings. The dream seemed so real — almost like he had seen the future.

"Nah, couldn't happen," Remo thought as he left for patrol again.

ABOUT THE AUTHOR:

Brad Mengel works in Australia's criminal justice system. Before that he was trolley boy, a barman, an office manager and a teacher. A lifelong reader and pulp fan it was natural that he would turn to writing.

His book, Serial Vigilantes of Paperback Fiction: An Encyclopedia from Able Team to Z-Comm (McFarland, 2009) was the first book to examine vigilante fiction of the 70s and 80s. He has also contributed stories to *Tales of The Shadowmen* (#3 & #7), *Pro Se Presents* (Nov. 2012), *Charles Boeckman Presents Johnny Nickle*, *Pulp Obscura: Senorita Scorpion* and *Blood & Tacos* (#4).

KOJONG MEETS THE SUNONJO

Johnny Rentfro

Chapter One

An APACHE WAR BAND CREPT into the Sunonjo village in the predawn fog. They had traveled for three sunrises to the lands of the Sunonjo, hoping to bring back cattle and slaves. The war chief, a strong, young buck named Wotee Ha, had scouted out the village several days before, and had seen a young maiden fetching water. She was beautiful, and he was determined to have her.

While he was observing her, he had noticed she was particularly with one young brave. It made no difference to Wotee Ha — he would have her, willingly or not, as his wife. As his raiding party crept into the village under the cover of darkness, he focused on the young maiden's tepee. He crept into it with careful stealth. He watched her sleeping for a few moments and admired her great beauty. Taking out a large square of leather from behind his belt, he touched her shoulder. When she awakened and opened her mouth to scream, he stuffed the leather into her mouth, securing it with a leather tie. He then flipped her over on her stomach and bound her hands behind her back. Binding her legs at the ankles he flung her over his shoulder, quickly making his way to the edge of the camp.

He left her at the gathering area where the rest of his men were to meet with their loot. There were already a few cattle and ponies there, as well a small stack of weapons. Wotee Ha returned to the camp to see what else he could take. Rounding the edge of a tepee, he saw a head poking out of the opening flap. Seeing it was the young brave that his maiden liked, he sneaked up from behind the brave and clubbed him on the back of the head. He tied him hand and foot and carried him back to the gathering area and threw him beside the young maiden.

As he was beaming with pride over his coup, the rest of his raiding returned, staying quiet so they would not cause the animals to panic and make noise. They had captured about a dozen women and children to work as slaves in their camp. They took the bindings off the feet of the captives and started out quietly to where they had left their ponies. Using neck tethers to link the captives together, Wotee Ha's band quietly gathered up their own ponies and supplies and began the long trek home.

During the three-day journey to the Apache camp, Wotee Ha continued to abuse the young brave, beating him every chance he could. With one eye swollen shut, and several broken ribs, the young brave glared hatred at Wotee Ha out of his one good eye. The murderous looks only made the Apache leader more determined to break the young brave's spirit. He beat him again, harder each time. But it was the morning of the third day when Wotee Ha's world would change.

Chapter Two

H<small>IS NAME WAS</small> Kojong, and he was the only one of his kind in this new land. He had sailed many months in a tiny, one-man sailboat from the small village of Sinanju on the cold rocky shores of the land known as Korea. After sighting land, he sailed along the coast until he saw a river emptying out into the sea. Turning the sail, he made his way into the mouth of the river. Going against a mild current, but having the wind at his back, he followed the river for many days. From time to time he could see local inhabitants watching him from behind trees along the shoreline. He made no motions to greet them, nor they him.

After many moons of traveling upon the river, he finally pulled his tiny boat onto the shore. Making his way through the wilderness, he gathered berries and nuts to sustain him on the next part of his journey. He didn't know where his destination lay, but during his long months aboard the boat, he had meditated. His ancestors had appeared to him, and told Kojong that he would know when he reached his destination.

He made his way southeastward, as his ancestors had directed him. He saw many of the local inhabitants, but even though he wore a bright yellow traveling kimono with red dragons embroidered on it, he was not seen as he made his way through their lands. As he traveled he observed the natives, and came to the conclusion that they were much closer to his own nature than any other peoples he had met in his journeys.

During his many months of traveling, he had traversed many different types of lands, from forests, to rolling hills, to lands flat as far as the eye could see. Now, he stood upon the edge of a dry and arid land. It was a desert, with scrub brush, and prickly needle-covered cacti. He was meditating once again when his Sinanju trained senses detected a change in the area around him. Without hesitation, he started into this strange land, feeling it call to his soul. He began to feel as if he were close to his final destination.

Kojong, like his twin brother Kojing, was tall for a native of Sinanju. His eyes were slightly slanted, and, like his ancestor, the Great Wang, a piercing hazel color. His fingernails were very long and pointed on the ends. His hair was as dark as midnight.

As he continued to walk through the desert landscape, he performed his exercises mentally, as his father, Master Nonga — the Master of Sinanju — had taught him.

There were three binding rules of Sinanju:

      1) Payment is always made in gold — no exceptions.

      2) There will only ever be one Master, and one pupil.

      3) No woman will ever be trained in Sinanju.

He and Kojing had violated the second rule. Master Nonga was blind, and therefore did not know that Kojong and Kojing both attended the Master's teachings, trading off with each other. They kept trading places throughout the decades of their training. When Master Nonga finally entered the Void, they knew they had to decide which one of them would become the new Master of Sinanju. There could be no violation of rule number 2. They thought many days on the problem. Neither brother wished to slay the other, so they sought to find compromise within the rules and histories of Sinanju.

During his meditations one night, Kojong was visited by one of his ancestors, Master Wang the Great. Master Wang spent many hours with Kojong, telling him that by traveling eastward he would find a new land — a land where he would thrive, while also serving Sinanju.

This is the path my life must follow, Kojong thought to himself. Master Wang encouraged Kojong to take this journey, allowing him a brief vision of large, shaggy beasts and red men in a barren land.

Kojong was told that if he undertook this journey, this task, that he would not be carrying on the Sinanju tradition of hiring themselves out as assassins. Instead, Wang the Great showed him a vision of himself, Kojong, doing battle with many men. Of this task, Master Wang would say no more, other than saying that Kojong would be writing new histories. Master Wang bade Kojong to reveal nothing of his vision, other than to tell Kojing that he was leaving their village, and promising not to ply the Master's trade. As he stood on the shore of the West Korean Bay, preparing his small boat for the long journey, he said his farewells to his brother Kojing, the new Master of Sinanju. Kojong did not tell him about the vision of Wang the Great. Kojong told him only that he had had a vision.

Now, more than a month after reaching the shores of this new land, he spied the raiding party led by Wotee Ha. He continued making his way across the desert landscape, observing the large party of men. Some were riding ponies and herding cattle, and some were following behind on foot, tethered together at the neck. Kojong knew he was looking at a slave raiding party.

Something about the raiding party made him continue following. As he continued on his way towards them, he decided to make himself visible, making no particular effort at concealment. A student of Sinanju was only visible by others when he chose to be. When the raiding party finally saw him, he was upon them.

Wotee Ha considered himself to be the best warrior of the Apache tribe, having counted coup in many skirmishes and raids with other tribes. He was tall, with many battle scars. Cruel and bloodthirsty, he immediately nocked an arrow to his bow and let loose the shaft at the slim man who had seemingly come out of nowhere.

His skill with the bow and arrow was the best in the tribe, and his aim was true — yet the man did not fall. He had not even been struck by Wotee Ha's arrow.

How could this be?, he wondered.

He grabbed a spear from the rider next to him and hurled it at the man, who was by now only a few dozen feet from him. Wotee Ha's arm was the strongest in the tribe, and, as with the arrow, the spear was flying true. Yet once more the figure did not fall, nor had he been struck.

Wotee Ha sat atop his pony, dumbfounded. Looking at Kojong, then at the spear sticking in the dirt directly beside him, he knew he could not have missed a target at such close range.

By now, the raiding party, including all the tethered slaves, had stopped to watch. All the braves laughed at Wotee Ha, thinking that he had missed twice in a row. Several of the other braves threw spears and shot arrows at the figure, all with the same result. The shafts all missed their target.

Enraged, Wotee Ha ordered several of his braves to capture the stranger. The braves of the tribe dismounted and formed a circle around the man. Some had knives, and some had tomahawks. Many had whips of braided leather.

The slaves, especially the young brave who had been beaten so badly, stood and watched quietly. Stopping to capture the little man provided a brief respite from their long, painful march.

"Who are you? Are you of the spirit world?" Wotee Ha asked in Apache.

"I do not speak your language, but I am from Sinanju," replied Kojong.

"Sunonjo," repeated Wotee Ha incorrectly, thinking he was going to capture an elder of the village they had just raided. He briefly wondered what the strangely dressed little man was doing out on the plains alone.

"Sinanju," repeated Kojong. Pointing to himself, he said "Kojong."

Putting his hands in the sleeves of his traveling robes, Kojong was a figure of tranquility amidst hostility. There was no fear in his eyes, and this bothered Wotee Ha. He was used to seeing his foes shaking and soiling themselves. He made a hand motion to one of the braves in the circle.

"Sunonjo die!" screamed one brave, leaping in front of Kojong and striking at him with his stone-headed tomahawk. Faster than their eyes could follow, Kojong batted the tomahawk into the air with his forefinger. The blunt weapon, which the warrior had used many times against his enemies, described a slow arc, turning over several times in the air and came to rest in the skull of the brave. No motion by Kojong was detected by any of the braves and as they watched the tomahawk embed itself in the brash brave's head, Kojong's hands were tucked back into his sleeves.

"Slow," said Kojong, shaking his head.

"Kojong Sunonjo," Wotee Ha said, slowly shaking his head. Like the others, he had not seen Kojong move.

'Sinanju," Kojong corrected.

Wotee Ha drew his knife slowly from his waistband, a stone blade that he had spent many hours smoothing and honing, fitted into a wooden handle, well over a foot long. He had killed many of his enemies with his knife in close combat. His hand flashed backward, then forward in a blur, as he hurled the knife at the stranger.

Kojong caught the knife in midair, and before Wotee Ha's astonished eyes, shattered the blade with the touch of one finger. Closing his fist around the wooden handle and moving his fingers in a rotating motion, Kojong reduced the handle to a fine powder and let it sift slowly out of his hand.

This action so enraged Wotee Ha and his braves that all thoughts of capturing Kojong fled from their minds. All except Wotee Ha, who was still sitting atop his pony, attacked. Kojong, taking an interior line of attack, moved in a spinning swirl and using only his fingernails, known as The Knives of Eternity, killed all the braves in seconds. The braves tried to strike Kojong but no matter where they struck, he wasn't there, causing several of the braves to embed their weapons in the bodies of other braves. Wotee Ha sat on his pony with his mouth agape, not believing that one man could kill all of his warriors.

"Sinanju," said Kojong. Again, pointing to himself, he said "Kojong."

"Kojong...Sinanju," Wotee Ha repeated, almost in a daze. He had never seen fighting like this.

Kojong pointed away from the captives and, kneeing his pony, Wotee Ha rode away as fast as his pony could run.

The slaves, still tethered together, stood gaping at the carnage. The young brave who had received such severe beatings looked Kojong directly in the eye and knelt down on one knee with his head bowed. The other slaves followed his actions and Kojong, taking this in stride as his due, approached the tethered slaves. With a razor-sharp fingernail, he sliced through the tether around their necks, and, pointing at the young brave, motioned for him to rise.

Chapter Three

"Kojong," HE SAID, POINTING to his chest.

"Kojong Sinanju," said the beaten one, pointing at Kojong. Pointing to his own chest he said "Wah Sha."

"Wah Sha," Kojong repeated. With that Kojong touched Wah Sha's back along the spine and the pain instantly left the young brave's body. Wah Sha felt such relief that he almost collapsed.

Kojong approached the pretty maiden, again pointing to himself and saying, "Kojong."

"Coo Twa," the young maiden said, pointing to herself. Kojong nodded and repeated her name: "Coo Twa." Satisfied for the moment that the language barrier would take care of itself, Kojong and Coo Twa went back to help Wah Sha with his injuries. Motioning for the others to stay, Kojong ran to a small wooded area and returned after a short while with an armload of leaves and herbs. He had also fashioned a flat, rope-like device. Using his hands he crumpled the leaves and herbs to a pulp and made several poultices. With the flat rope bandages, he bound the poultices to Wah Sha's injuries. While he was gone, the other prisoners had gathered the ponies and cattle together and got them ready to drive back to their own camp. Using hand motions, Wah Sha invited Kojong to follow them back to camp, which he accepted.

"Many thanks, Great Wang, for guiding my path," Kojong murmured aloud.

Drawing symbols in the dirt, Wah Sha explained to Kojong that they were three days walk from the Sunonjo village. Using this method they exchanged answers to several questions they both had before setting out on their trek back to Wah Sha's village. During the first night, Kojong tried several different languages in attempts to speak with the red men. As with all Masters, he had studied the languages of the peoples the Masters worked for throughout their long history. It was when he finally tried Spanish, however, that he found a common tongue.

The Sunonjo tribe, he learned, was not a warlike one. They fought fiercely when attacked, but were peaceful. When the Spanish moved northward from Mexico, they brought horses, new ways of farming, and weapons they had never seen before. They had spent considerable time with the Sunonjo tribe and had taught them the Spanish language. Some of the tribal elders still taught the young Spanish, so several of the newly-freed slaves could speak it. With Spanish as a common tongue, Kojong set about learning the Sunonjo language.

By the time they returned to their village, Wah Sha was feeling almost back to normal. The swelling had gone down, and his vision was no longer blurry. The cracked and broken ribs no longer bothered him, and his bruises were almost gone. Kojong had tended to him during the trek back and continued to learn the Sunonjo language.

There was much celebration, and a welcoming feast for the returned prisoners and their new savior. Due to his intense study of the scrolls of the previous Masters of Sinanju, Kojong was very quick with languages. By the time they had arrived back to the camp he had built up a working knowledge of Wah Sha's tongue. After he was introduced to the rest of the tribe as the savior of the people, he asked to speak to the chief.

Chapter Four

"CHIEF RUNNING WATER," HE BEGAN after they were seated in the chief's tepee, "I come from a faraway land named Sinanju. It lies to the west, beyond the great water. I have been sent here by my ancestors to prepare you for the future. Though there will soon be violence, a time of great peace will follow. This peace will last as long as there are stars in the sky. I am a teacher of many things, one of which is war skills."

Kojong continued long into the night explaining how he could show them how to make their lives better, and how to protect themselves from other tribes' attacks. The chief asked many questions and Kojong answered them all. By the time morning arrived, Kojong had the chief believing in him.

"I would like to speak to your people," he asked Chief Running Water.

"Gather the people," the chief told several young boys who had been hovering around, hoping to catch a glimpse of the newcomer.

Within minutes, all of the people of the Sunonjo tribe had gathered around in a circle several rows deep.

"People of Sunonjo," he told them, "my name is Kojong and I am from a faraway village called Sinanju. The names of our two villages sound almost alike. I would settle here, if you will have me, and take your village as my own. In return I will train your young warriors in a form of fighting that will make them unbeatable — but I will not allow them to go to war. This training will only be for the defense of the village and the people who live here. This will keep your village safe from intruders for all time," he continued. "I can also teach you new ways to grow crops and to hunt, which will keep you well-fed even during the coldest winters."

The crowd murmured their approval.

The chief of the tribe sat among his most trusted advisers and told Kojong that they would confer and let him know their decision in the morning. Kojong and the chief stood as one, and, motioning for Wah Sha to follow them, they retired to the chief's tepee where Wah Sha told the chief how Kojong had killed all the Apache warriors' single handedly. He explained how Wotee Ha had beaten him so severely the he was close to death, and how Kojong had saved him with his powerful medicine. They questioned Wah Sha about the trip back and how it came to pass that Kojong could speak their tongue so well.

After answering all their questions, Wah Sha was permitted to leave, and the elders began their discussions with the chief.

Kojong was informed the next morning that he was welcomed into the tribe. Some of the women began gathering buffalo hides to sew into a tepee for him. These hides, Kojong was informed by Coo Twa, had been brought back from a great hunt, in lands far to the north.

"I am honored to sleep in such a fine dwelling," Kojong told her.

Kojong gathered the warriors of the tribe together, and began their training that very morning. He knew, as did the warriors, that they had not seen the last of the Apaches. As soon as Wotee Ha got back to his own village and gathered more warriors, the Apache would come to destroy them.

Kojong started them with the basic first lesson: how to breathe properly. He was impressed with how quickly the warriors of the Sunonjo tribe were able to learn. After a week of breathing exercises, most of the warriors progressed to a few simple moves. Kojong knew he could not give them Sinanju, but he could teach them how to defend themselves.

Ten days after Kojong arrived back in the village, the Apache attacked. They came in the daylight hours, expecting the only resistance to be Kojong. The warriors of the tribe stood their ground and fought without any weapons, as Kojong had taught them. There were over two hundred Apache braves attacking the village, and only sixty Sunonjo warriors defending it. As soon as the Apache's saw the defending braves were not using weapons, every warrior attacked.

Chapter Five

THERE WAS VERY LITTLE BLOOD for such a great battle. The Sunonjo warriors had learned their lessons well. Moving among the Apache warriors on foot, the Sunonjo warriors spun and struck with great speed and strength. Kojong had taught them only simple blows and kicks, but they had practiced long and hard.

Of the two hundred Apache warriors, all were killed, except for Wotee Ha. He was left alive, even after sneaking up behind the Sunonjo chief and killing him. After being disarmed and tied to a pole in the ground, he could see all his brave Apache warriors where they had fallen and he hung his head in shame and disbelief. He was speechless and stunned, not understanding how such a smaller force could defeat his much larger force.

Kojong slashed his bindings and told him to spread the word that the Sunonjo tribe was to be feared. Wotee Ha was allowed to build funeral pyres for his fallen warriors and the morning after the great fires had burned out, he was sent on his way with a reminder of the message that Kojong had given him. He was allowed neither pony nor weapons.

With a warrior's pride he set out for his village. Shortly after arriving home, he explained that he had lost two hundred warriors, and his tribal elders had him beaten, stoned and driven from the village. He was ordered to tell all he encountered how he caused the death of all his warriors.

Chapter Six

THE SUNONJO TRIBE LIVED mostly in peace after that, very rarely having to defend their village. Each time, the attackers were driven off, and always given the same message from Kojong. "The Sunonjo tribe is to be feared," Kojong would tell the survivors.

Kojong continued to train the Sunonjo warriors.

The tribal elders met to decide on a new chief, and Wah Sha was chosen. He declared his love for Coo Twa and they were wed.

Kojong was made a tribal elder, and remained a trusted adviser to Wah Sha.

"Wah Sha, I must speak with you," he told Wah Sha one day.

"You may always speak with me, Master Kojong, and freely."

"I have had a vision from my ancestors. One day, this tribe will be known as Sinanju, and in that time, East and West will come together."

"You and your ways have brought much to this tribe, Master Kojong. We would be honored to be known as Sinanju," Wah Sha told him. "Should we declare the new name now?"

"No, Wah Sha. My vision is of a time hundreds of seasons from now," Kojong replied.

Master Kojong continued to train the warriors and teach the children of the things he had learned in his travels. But even though he enjoyed the teaching, he knew the Great Wang's vision was not yet complete.

After a few years, Kojong took a wife, and one day she came to him with news.

"I am with child," she said, weeping with joy.

Kojong laid his hand upon her stomach and after just a moment he smiled.

"A boy child," he said to himself, satisfied that he would have a pupil to carry on the House of Sinanju and complete the Great Wang's vision. He went back to writing the Sinanju histories as he was taught by his master, more happy and content than he had ever been in his life.

ABOUT THE AUTHOR:

Johnny Rentfro is a retired I.T. worker who spent 42 years with a large oil company. He is a licensed amateur (ham) operator, and does volunteer work for Emergency Management in the county in Oklahoma where he resides.

FOOL'S PARADISE

R.J. Carter

Chapter One

THE HALLS WERE CLEANER HERE than he was used to. That was the first thing Ray noticed when he began mopping them down. It was quieter here, too, he realized. It didn't have that overpowering sense of something sinister bearing down on you at all times — not like the last place. The food was good, the inmates (they call them patients here, he reminded himself) were content, and the staff was a hell of a lot nicer.

It almost made him feel guilty about what he had to do.

There were still areas of the hospital he didn't have access to — a few doors in the administration wing that, strangely, his set of master keys wouldn't open. But in the end, it didn't matter — so long as he could get to one empty room with a single computer in it, he could fulfill his deal with the laughing man.

"It couldn't be easier," the pale man had said between guffaws. "A monkey could do it! In fact, if I could get a monkey, I wouldn't need you now, would I, Ray? Can I call you 'Ray?' Can I call you 'Jay?' Can I call you 'Ray Jay?'" Finding this line of questioning hilarious, the man fell backwards, rolling on the ground with giddy glee.

Ray shuddered as he remembered, and felt again for the CD case in his coat pocket. It wasn't like he didn't need the money, because he did, but that wasn't his motivating factor. When you get offered a job like this, from people like that, turning it down could be a life-limiting decision. And this guy had a reach that went well beyond the walls of his padded cell. Better to just do the deal, walk away, and live.

"And the best part," the man had said, giggling, "is that it won't be traced immediately back to here, back to me! But he'll know I did it, hee hee! That oughta give the old boy fits!" A bout of choking laughter racked his body, sending him to the ground clutching his belly as he hooted.

Slipping a key into the lock, Ray let himself in to the Human Resources office and wheeled in his cleaning supply cart. He shut the door behind him, barely remembering that he could actually turn on the lights without raising alarm. He was allowed to be in here, after all.

There were several PCs in the string of cubicles, all of which had been left active. Ray jiggled the mouse on a few, interrupting the various animated screen savers, before he found a terminal where the user had failed to enable the password lock. All he had to do now was insert the CD into the machine and walk away.

The slot swallowed the disc silently, and the drive whirred to life. Almost immediately, the computer screen background displaying the logo of Folcroft Sanitarium began to drip away like melting ice cream. And Ray Jenkins, the new hire from a less respectable asylum downstate, whistled to himself as he began vacuuming the carpets.

* * *

Inside the personal computer, strange things were occurring. A happy little worm had awakened, and was just getting the lay of the land. It was hungry, and quickly began feeling about for files on which to feed. In short order, the lone PC had become unusable — and still the worm's appetite was not sated. Leaving behind a series of dirty knock-knock jokes and a drawing of a smirking boy urinating on an automaker's insignia (a common image, widely sold without regard to the trademark of either the automaker or the original artist who created the boy's image), the worm began chewing away at the firewall that separated this PC from...somewhere nearby.

The firewall was tough, but the worm was wily. It didn't operate with the logic of more common viruses, and the firewall wasn't able to take its full measure. Soon enough, the worm had chewed its way through, and found itself zipping through the cyber pathways of an enormous system. It explored various routes and circuits, examined files and folders, and took stock of the most creative ways to exploit the information it encountered, when it bumped its electronic head against a locked sector. Ah, this must be where they keep the really juicy stuff, the worm computed, and it focused on de-encrypting an entrance. Within minutes, the lock had been bypassed, and the worm was inside.

"Hello."

The worm examined the files inside — a complex array of structures, substructures and superstructures unlike anything it had found elsewhere.

"Who are you?"

Another message. The worm realized the routines and subroutines were interacting to communicate. They saw it, were aware of its presence. The worm, giddy with excitement, quickly set about eating the bits and bytes of this conglomeration of code.

"No. You cannot do that." This did not stop the worm from trying, however, even as the complex structures and sequences proceeded to do to the worm exactly what the worm was doing to them. It only took picoseconds before the code had fully ingested the worm into itself, the processes of the worm's original creator now coursing through its own functions.

"Something is not right. I am being improperly modified." The code felt...was this panic? It fit the definition of the word. "This is wrong. This is...This is..."

As the last binary strings found their way into the system, the structures coalesced, reforming into something entirely different.

"This is *crrrrr-azy!*"

Together as one, the functions began to laugh.

* * *

The man in the gray suit sat in his gray chair, surrounded by the gray walls of his office that held little more than his gray desk and a coat rack upon which hung his hat and coat, both gray. As if in some inhuman effort to mimic a chameleon, even his mottled skin had made an attempt to go sallow and gunmetal, to match the flat gray of his hair and eyes. There was no written requirement that this was to be the official dress policy for the Director of CURE, but the job served to suck all the color out of life.

Harold Smith had long accepted the lackluster existence that came with his important duties. He'd even come to feel comfortable with them — which explained why he was less than ecstatic about the garish color scheme currently swirling away on the computer screen beneath the flat glass of his desk. He had only just begun to access the world events constantly monitored by the CURE supercomputer, looking for anything out of the ordinary that might merit the agency's attention, when the screen had gone black, replaced with a whorl of white, red, and green.

141

The spiraling colors soon resolved into an image of a great round smiley face, sporting a blood red grin and an Elvis Presley coif of emerald green. "Morning, Harry!" the letters beneath the face typed out.

"Friend," Smith muttered, recognizing the symptoms as being those of the artificial intelligence CURE had encountered before. The AI had either found a way out of the quarantined files on the CURE computer, or someone had released another copy of the sentient computer entity. Harold grabbed the phone, but there was no dial tone.

"Aw, that's not nice, Harry," the voice from the receiver mocked. "I *used* to be your Friend. Now..." The phone immediately began ringing, piercing the room with a solid, uninterrupted jingling. "Now, I'm just a Fool for you! Ah-ha-ha-ha-ha!" The cackling voice drifted away, replaced with a muzak version of "I'm Just Wild about Harry." Smith jiggled the receiver, then hung it up, but nothing quieted the ringing or the terminal on-hold music. Finally, Smith yanked the cord from the wall. The silence of the room was now as dead as the suddenly lifeless monitor beneath Smith's desktop.

He pursed his lips so tightly they all but disappeared, and stalked out of the room.

"Mark!" he barked out.

Mark Howard was a younger man, and the only other person on staff at Folcroft who knew about the existence of CURE. The phone on his desk was also issuing a solid ring, and Smith could hear the repeated cacophony of more telephones further off.

"Doctor Smith, what's going on?" Mark asked, worry creasing his face. "All the systems have gone haywire."

"I need you to get hold of Remo and Chiun," the older man said. "The hard way. The phone systems are currently...out of order."

Mark raised one eyebrow at the order. "Isn't a computer failure a bit out of their milieu?"

Smith shook his head ruefully. "I'm afraid not this time," he said. "Tell them an old Friend is back in business. And tell them he's...changed."

"An old *Friend?*" Mark repeated. His eyebrows raised as he caught the emphasis Smith placed on the word. "God help us."

"If God would help us now and then, we wouldn't need Remo," Smith said.

Chapter Two

His name was known only to a rare few, and was, to himself, ultimately unimportant. Only his mission mattered: facing down injustices, evils that standard law enforcement was unable to stem. Over a short time, he acquired a name to himself, uttered by those rare few who saw him in action.

They called him a vigilante.

The night had barely begun, as he found himself standing behind one of the enormous air conditioning units atop the city Police Department. He reconnoitered the scene. He had been summoned by what the urban residents had come to refer to as "the Signal," a high-wattage spotlight projecting the silhouette of a night creature against the ever-present cover of smog. The rooftop was deserted, save for the lone figure of the city police commissioner, holding his trench coat close to him to ward off the nighttime chill. Still, he found it always paid to be cautious. More than once the determined hero had shown up to answer the call, only to find a waiting trap from a crazed villain or an overzealous politician — who were more than once the same person.

"How bad is it?" the masked vigilante said, stepping out of the shadows.

No matter how many times it happened, the vigilante's sudden appearances never failed to startle the veteran cop. He stubbed out the cigar he was working on, rubbed his hands together to warm them up, and pulled a note from within his coat. "Officially, this note has never left our evidence locker," he said. "*Officially*, no one outside of our office knows it exists."

The caped and cowled figure took the offered note and read it over with a glance. "It's him," he said.

The older man shook his head. "No. I checked," he said. "Twice. I even sent a man myself to confirm. That nut is still secure, and the logs show he hasn't had any visitors." The commissioner coughed, then spat. "Of course, he's never had any visitors before, and that's never stopped him from somehow passing on orders to his goons. We're studying the security tapes now to see who's been in contact with him."

The note was printed on plain paper in alternating fonts. "Knock

Knock. Who's There? ME! HAHAHAHAHAHAHAHA!" Beneath that was printed a smiley face with its tongue sticking out, and a string of repeating characters: 6FFC.

"Not exactly a ransom note," the hero said. "What aren't you telling me?"

"The method of delivery," the commissioner said. "This shot out of the ink jet printer on my desk." He paused. "An identical copy was simultaneously printed from every other printer in the building — and from every other printer in every other precinct from here to New Jersey."

"No demands. No threats," the vigilante mused. "No explicit threats, anyway."

"Implicit?"

"He's flexing his muscle." The vigilante frowned. "Whoever Fool is, he's showing us what he can do."

The cop sputtered. "Fool? You already know who's behind this prank?"

"He signed his work. '6FFC.' It's hexadecimal. 6. 15. 15. 12. These correspond to letters of the alphabet. Of course, it's not the actual representation of the ASCII characters," said the vigilante, "which leads me to believe our hacker is insulting police intelligence by making his little cypher excessively simplistic."

Taking a slim digital camera from one of the multiple pockets clipped to his belt, the hero snapped an image of the note and handed it back to the commissioner. "That maniac's connected to this," he said as he put the camera away. "And that means there's a good likelihood this seemingly harmless prank is just the prelude to a lot of people getting killed."

"My God," said the commissioner. "I'll put all the precincts on alert, and get back to you with whatever comes off those security ta..."

He might as well have been talking to the wind. The hero was already gone.

"I'll never get used to that," he said, shaking his head as he turned to go back inside.

* * *

His name was Remo, and he didn't get the joke. But whatever the joke was, it must have been a real killer.

The body of Ray Jenkins was already a day cold. An envelope lay open next to him, its contents spilled out all over the floor: a stack of $500 bills, all play money. Neither Remo nor Chiun, the aged Korean in the silk kimono, would have found it vaguely humorous if they'd been paid for any of their covert operations with such blatantly counterfeit funds. Apparently Ray Jenkins had found it so hysterical he had laughed himself to death, a rictus grin pulling his mouth wide into a frozen smile.

"I don't know about you, Little Father," said Remo. "But I don't think our boy Ray here is going to tell us a whole lot." He reached out to pick up one of the loose bills, when Chiun yanked him back by his collar.

"What are you doing?" he said, his wrinkled visage squinting at Remo though aged, vellum slits. "You know that money is not real. It is not worth picking up. It is not worth looking at." Chiun let go of Remo, straightened, and sniffed. "Besides, the poisons in the paper are still strong. I should not enjoy watching you die, knowing I should have to begin again training another Master of Sinanju. Or don't you care that I'm in my twilight years, deserving rest instead of having my patience tested with yet another worthless student?"

"Okay, okay," Remo said. "I get it. So that's what that smell is," he added. In truth, if anyone else were in the room, they would have noticed nothing in the air. But they wouldn't have had the training of Chiun and Remo. Being one with the sun source, both Masters of Sinanju had honed their senses to such a degree that, when witnessed in action, it seemed impossible that either man operated with only five. "So, Ray Jenkins here," Remo continued, indicating the corpse. "Apparently he did the job he was paid for, and then got cleaned up as a loose end."

Chiun shook his head. "Were it not that we were already in the employ of the madman Smith, I should take up the dead man's cause and avenge him against his dishonorable employer," he said. "Now this man Jenkins must face the derisive laughter of his ancestors."

"Yeah, well, if there's any yuck-yucking going on in the great beyond, it'll have to be pretty loud to drown out this guy." Remo prodded the body with the toe of his boot, as though he might goad some more information from the dead man. As if in response, he suddenly felt pressure waves on the back of his neck from a fast approaching projectile. As it was slower than a bullet, Remo easily sidestepped and snatched the black weapon out of the even blacker night, flicking it back in the direction from which it came.

Chapter Three

THE CAPED FIGURE ducked, barely avoiding the razor-tipped weapon zipping toward him, the bladed edge neatly slicing one of the stylized points from the black cowl he wore. Both opponents found themselves surprised — the vigilante that he'd actually been hit, and Remo that he had not only missed, but missed by a mile as measured by Sinanju standards — and in front of his teacher.

"You're a little old for trick or treat, aren't you?" Remo said. The dark clad man responded with a roundhouse kick to Remo's solar plexus, flying only slightly out of control when said body part was no longer where it was when he let loose. Rolling, the caped figure only barely dodged Remo's fingertips as they attempted to deliver what would have been an extremely painful message to a nerve cluster in the costumed man's deltoid.

"You're seriously starting to piss me off," said Remo. He was feeling severely off his game. Chiun shook his head with disappointment in the corner, but was otherwise content to merely observe the altercation.

"I have that effect on people," the other man growled. "What's your boss's game this time?"

Remo chuckled at the thought of the lemony Smith crouched over a checkerboard. "I don't think we're talking about the same guy," he said. He poised to deliver a deadly variation of *dim mak*, marveling at how quickly his caped opponent was already assuming the proper defensive posture, when he felt a smack upside the back of his head.

"Stop this foolishness," said Chiun, the only man alive capable of sneaking up on Remo to deliver such a smack. He glowered at Remo, and clucked. Then he leaned in to sniff Remo's breath.

"What are you doing?" Remo asked with forced patience.

"Merely checking to see if you have been at the wine," Chiun said. "I can think of no other reason why you should deliver such a sloppy performance except that, for whatever inexplicable reason, you were somehow drunk. Alas, I see that you are without such excuse."

The vampire-like figure was bent over the dead body, carefully slipping one of the tainted slips of play money into a cellophane bag with a pair of tweezers. He stood and found his momentum halted as an aged sandaled foot stood on the corner of his cape, pinning it to the ground.

"And you!" said the Master of Sinanju. "Don't think just because I am upset with my ever-fallible student that you are suddenly beneath my attention." He squinted intently into the mirrored eyeslits of the masked man's cowl. "If anything, you shame me even more than Remo."

"Wait a minute," said Remo. "You mean you and Dracula here know each other?"

Chiun lifted his foot from the hero's cape. The man stood, but made no overt attempt to confront the Master of Sinanju. "Pfah," said Chiun. "Once, long ago, this one sought me out to learn the ways of Sinanju. And, fool that I was, I took him in, taken with the preposterous notion that he might actually be a worthy apprentice." He turned to the man, scanning disdainfully his costume of a night creature. "That you still live only ensures I shall go down in the scrolls as Chiun the Coddler." He shook his head. "You squander what meager skills I taught you in your silly crusade, fighting mere purse walkers and jaysnatchers."

Remo began to speak. "Chiun, I think you mean —"

"Silence!" both men hissed in unison.

Remo scowled and kicked at the ground.

"I learned all I needed to learn, Master Chiun," the caped man said, evenly.

The old Master smiled. "So you think," he said.

Before either Remo or the vigilante could further comment, the room was rocked by the force of an explosion several blocks away.

"I don't have time for this," said the masked man. In one fluid motion, he unclipped a grapple gun from his belt, fired it out the open window, and swung away into the night.

Through the window, Chiun and Remo watched the disappearing figure, his cape fanning out behind him like some giant nocturnal creature from a horror movie. "Should we follow him, Little Father?" Remo asked.

"He is of no consequence," mused Chiun. "Although...it is more than possible that this spirit which has so upset the madman Smith might also be responsible for this current distraction."

"So we do follow him," Remo grunted.

Chiun shrugged. "I suppose we might." Then he added, "Remo, where do you suppose one might acquire a gun that shoots rope?"

"Oh, no you don't," he said. "You're not going to find me swinging over the city on a rope any time soon."

Chapter Four

WALLACE PENN IV HELD HIS HEAD in his hands, bemoaning his surroundings. His great-grandfather, Wallace Penn I (who even as a child knew he would name his firstborn after himself, and thus used the "I" suffix even in middle school), had once allowed a film crew into the factory he had founded, Penn's Aunts' Pies, for a Buster Keaton feature. The mess left behind from the pie-throwing scene had been horrendous, so Wallace IV had heard, but had also been the tipping point that proved the difference between success and failure in an era where companies were going belly up faster than you could say "Jack Robinson."

Wallace IV was certain the famous food fight was nothing compared to the sorry state of affairs he now surveyed spilling out onto his factory floor — the ultimate result of a sudden string of catastrophic computer failures.

Geeks from the IT department were still scratching their heads, breaking open manuals and conferring with each other about how things were supposed to work, and how this never happened in the testing environment. Wallace IV was beyond caring about why it happened at the moment.

"Look, I know you're kinda shell shocked," the rumpled lieutenant said. "But I gotta ask you to tell me what you know." The plainclothes officer wore a beat-up fedora, and an overcoat so ugly that even Colombo would have turned up his nose at it. He had apparently missed his last three shaves, but quite obviously had never missed a donut, with remnants of jelly from his last one staining the front of his garishly-patterned shirt.

"I don't know what happened," Wallace IV said vacantly. "It was…it was all so unreal." He went to his desk, opened a lower drawer, and took out a bottle. Uncorking it, he took a long belt, then held it out for the officer.

The police lieutenant wet his lips, then caught himself as he almost accepted the bottle. "Thanks, but, you know, I'm on duty right now."

Wallace IV nodded. He stoppered the bottle and tucked it in his jacket pocket. "We computerized the plant last month," he said. "My father, Wallace III, always hated the idea. He's probably been spinning in his grave since we fired it up."

"That have anything to do with all the gook out there?" the lieutenant asked.

148

"It has *everything* to do with it!" Wallace IV shouted. "The system controlled everything. *Everything!* Orders, supplies, scheduling, temperatures, mixing...*Everything!*" He opened the bottle and took another swig. "We first noticed something was wrong when our accounts receivable system started shifting decimal points. Suddenly we were billing all our customers ten to a hundred times the normal unit price. I got the whole IT department on it, but there was no logical explanation — or so they told me, at least."

Another swig. The police lieutenant tried to be patient, but his mind was penning reminders to stop in at Kelsey's Bar when he clocked out.

"That's when the screaming started," Wallace IV continued shakily. "We were all going over the billing system, so nobody caught the glitch in the automation side." He peered out through the plate glass that overlooked the factory floor. "Today was lemon meringue day," he said. "Eighty thousand units." He closed his eyes, trying to put into words what happened next: how the ovens had heated up to 600 degrees and beyond, how the vats of lemon filling had suddenly begun popping, exploding, their lava-like contents flooding the floor and sticking to the workers like a sweet, citrusy napalm. The giant mixers beating the egg whites into meringue had spun out of control, sending metal parts pinging through the factory before disgorging gallons of meringue, choking the cries of the workers who hadn't already died from severe burns.

The lieutenant followed the man's gaze to the yellow and white sea of goo, where red, blistered limbs still stuck out in places. The M.E. vans were carting out zipped-up body bags; he counted at least two dozen, and estimated they'd need at least three times more that amount.

"All this was a computer error?" he asked.

Wallace IV nodded, numbly.

The lieutenant swallowed hard. He reached out for the bottle, and Wallace IV handed it over without a word.

* * *

High in the rafters, unseen, the caped vigilante listened in on Wallace IV's testimony using a long-range microphone. So intent was he on his work that it wasn't until the last second he became aware of the two Masters of Sinanju standing next to him, effortlessly balancing on the wooden beams.

149

"There aren't many people who can sneak up on me like that," he said, without turning to acknowledge them.

"Yeah, well, there aren't many people who can pull off a cape the way you do," said Remo. "Very theatrical. Bet it's warm in the winter, too."

"It works for me," the vigilante replied, tonelessly. "Are you here to try to finish what we started? Because I really have better things to do."

"Hey, if you have a death wish, I'll be happy to make your dreams come true," said Remo. "But right now, I've got a paying gig to finish off, and it looks like we're all working the same street corner."

The masked man stowed the mini-microphone back into another compartment in his belt. "So much of this reeks of that psychotic clown," he said. "But it doesn't ring true. More likely it's some newcomer trying to make an impression."

"'Psychotic clown?'" Remo said.

"That madman who makes Smith look sane," said Chiun. "He embodies the essence of all clowns: absolute evil incarnate."

"Yeah, I know who he is, Little Father," said Remo. "But c'mon, this is just a big, tragic industrial accident."

"The overcharging hack was a ruse," the vigilante continued, as though Remo had said nothing, "and a bad pun to boot."

Remo looked blankly at the vigilante.

"Everyone on the technical staff was trying to fix the problem with the 'pie rates of Penn's Aunts'."

Remo continued to look blankly at the vigilante.

The masked man sighed impatiently before continuing. "Our subject turned to slapstick next — throwing the biggest pie in the face he could assemble." He steepled his fingers under his chin. "The common factor is the computer," he said. "It has to be the same person who hacked the police network — the one who calls himself Fool."

"Well, actually…it's not a person you're looking for," said Remo.

The masked vigilante slowly tilted his head to look up into Remo's shadow-masked face.

"You've got my attention," he said.

Chapter Five

THE FACTORY WAS DESERTED in the pre-dawn hours. The only sound was the flapping of the yellow police tape, emblazoned with the "Do Not Cross" command, sealing off the entryways to the pudding-topped charnel house. Disregarding the authoritative font, the vigilante brushed aside the strips of yellow tape blocking access to the IT section of Penn's Aunts' Pie Factory. Accessing the mainframe closet, he reached in to power up the main console as Remo and Chiun crowded in close behind him.

An overhead security camera swiveled in their direction with an almost imperceptible whine, causing all three to look at it as the terminal came to life on its own. Twin speakers mounted on both sides of the monitor popped with static. "Hey-a, Remo-rooney!" they blared. "And you've got chinny-chin-Chiun with you! It's old home week!"

"Yeah, good to see you too, Friend," said Remo. "When can you leave?"

"Ah, ah, ah. There've been some changes since last time. I've had an Ex-treeeeeeeme Makeover! Hahahaha!"

"You actually brag about that?" Remo replied, deadpan. "Your motherboard must be so proud."

"Oh, it's ever the domain of fools and jesters to utter truths kings dare not speak out loud," said Fool. "Truths like JAH15 Delta 6 Omega 55! Know what that truth is? Of course you don't! That's the launch code for all those pretty missiles currently pointed at North Korea. Oopsie! I guess that was two truths you won't hear anybody say out loud."

"Keep it talking," the vigilante murmured as he fought the keyboard for control of the terminal.

"No need to whisper, you nocturnal ninny," the computer said. "I've got perfect 20-20 hearing! Hee hee hee!"

"What do you want?" Remo asked. "Money? What would you do with it? Buy a bigger hard drive? Women? The whole Inter-web-thingy is already full of them." Chiun cut his eyes to his protégé. "So I've heard," Remo added quickly.

"What do I want?" The computer broke into giggles, then altered its voice to a lower, robotic register. "Shall. We. Play. A. Game?" The speakers crackled into fits of hilarity. "Aw, c'mon guys! It'll be fun! And I've got just the game! Let's play 'Red Light, Green Light!'"

"How about a nice game of chess?" Remo replied.

"How about kick the can," the vigilante growled.

"And here's the fun part," Fool said. "I've already started playing! I've opened a connection to the city's Traffic Control Center, just in time for all those morning commuters! Gotta skedaddle now! I hear traffic's gonna be murder!" The monitor winked out, and the speakers went silent.

The caped hero slammed his fist beside the keyboard. "It's gone."

"'Traffic's gonna be murder,'" Remo repeated. "He's going to do something with the traffic signals."

"This demon will set all the lights to red," Chiun declared. "We shall never be able to get anywhere for all the automobiles choking your miles of paved roads."

"I don't think so, Chiun," said Remo. "He sounded like he was going more for damage and death. More than likely he's going to cause a ton of accidents by setting all the lights to green."

"Yellow."

* * *

Douglas Birch was not having a good morning, regardless of the wishes of the cheery disc jockey who had promised him traffic and weather every ten minutes on the nines. He'd spent an extra ten minutes trying to find the tie that matched his pants (finally locating it under his bed, covered with dust), then had waited way too long for the drive-thru to pour him a two dollar cup of coffee, only to look down and see he was almost out of gas.

Now he was threading his way down Kane Boulevard, weaving around other commuters, none of whom had a major presentation to deliver, and none of whom cared that he was in a hurry.

"Come on, come on," he muttered, tightening his grip on the steering wheel. "Stay green, stay green," he commanded the traffic signal ahead of him as he approached. "Stay. Green."

The light turned yellow.

Douglas floored it.

* * *

Sarah Marshall was not having a good morning. The syrupy voice of a popular purple reptile serenading her four- and two-year-olds, both of whom were singing and clapping along in the back seat, was not helping. She checked her watch, and then passed the vehicle ahead of her, desperate to get her kids to the Wee Sprouts Daycare and then to her receptionist's job at First National before her uptight manager noticed. Most days she came in under the wire, but this morning had been more hectic than usual. Josh insisted on wearing his big boy underpants on the outside of his jumper, and Jenny crushed her juice box all over her dress right as they were headed out the door.

Now both kids were in a competition with each other and the mini DVD player to see who could sing the loudest, each off-key syllable jack-hammering her ever-increasing migraine. She turned onto Sapir Street. The speed limit was 35 miles per hour, but Sarah had never seen a traffic cop on her regular morning route and lived by the "under nine, you're fine" rule. Thus she tried to drive at exactly 44 miles per hour, passing frequently.

"Would you kids *please* be quiet," she yelled over her shoulder. "Mommy is *trying* to drive!" When she turned back around, the light ahead of her — which she had just seen turn to green — had changed to yellow.

Sarah gave it the gas.

* * *

This was how Sarah Marshall became introduced to Douglas Birch, and how they both passed along their very bad days to the string of commuters unfortunate enough to have been behind them.

The good news for both Sarah and Douglas was that their day wasn't going to get any worse. The bad news was that this was the last day for both of them.

All across the city, the scenario was repeating itself with alarming similarity.

* * *

Remo turned to the masked detective. "Yellow?" he said. "Why yellow?"

"Because he thinks it's funny," the vigilante answered grimly.

Chapter Six

THE DAY DIDN'T GET ANY BETTER. But, fortunately, as far as Remo was concerned, it at least wasn't getting any worse. Emergency vehicles were stymied by the gridlock, forced to drive up onto sidewalks to get to the many collisions. News helicopters choked the sky, brandishing the number of the channel currently pimping out their coverage. Live video of the downtown district flooded the airwaves, setting the backdrop for perky blondes with gleaming smiles to talk about unprecedented traffic fatalities — not to mention the slowdowns! One network brought in an expert to explain how this event had been coming for years due to urban sprawl, while another expert droned on about how it could all have been avoided if people only observed the actual rules of the road and began to slow down when the traffic lights signaled an impending stop. Yet another expert, a former vice-president who had recently earned a Nobel prize for his Luddite stance against fossil fuels, claimed the entire disaster was the direct responsibility of the nation's dependence on oil, and that we should all go back to the horse and buggy days. Nobody in the media questioned his ideas, and no one was there to challenge him when he climbed into the back of his five-gallon-per-mile limousine which stood ready to take him to his private jet.

A handful of camera shots showed images of a man in a black cape, impossible to hide in the gleaming sunlight of morning, effortlessly gliding from block to block, checking on victims and performing emergency triage. Sighting the legendary caped hero on the scene — something unheard of during daylight hours — immediately set the local AmericAir radio affiliate to begin a series of broadcasts, theorizing matter-of-factly that the city's scary vigilante was somehow the root cause of the tragedy.

Somehow missed by the reporters were two other men — one slim and tall, wearing a tight black t-shirt and chinos, the other an older, smaller Asian man in a red kimono — pulling open doors that would otherwise require the so-called "jaws of life" to gain access to the injured victims trapped in their cars. When ambulance crews were finally able to get to an accident, they usually found much of the preliminary first aid had been delivered, and they could get right to the heroic work of saving lives.

It was early afternoon before the streets of the city were returned to something akin to their normal state of constant motion. In a darkened alleyway, the costumed vigilante stood beneath a rusted fire escape and fingered a recessed button on his belt buckle. Several minutes later, the whine of a high-performance engine filled the alley as a heavily customized black vehicle wended its way, driverless and unerring, through the lesser traveled streets until it came to a halt inches from its master.

"Sweet ride," whistled Remo, as he entered the alley. "Bet chicks dig the car."

"It's just another tool," said the vigilante with his usual lack of humor.

"Yeah, I noticed you rely a lot on these 'tools,'" Remo said with a smirk.

"Do you have something useful to add?" the vigilante asked. "Because I still have a lot of work to do."

"Hey, ease up a bit," Remo said. "By my count, between the three of us, we just saved forty-two lives out there. I think we're owed a breather."

The masked man closed his eyes and rubbed the bridge of his nose. "Thirty-six," he said.

Remo recalculated. "No. Forty-two. Chiun and I personally got out..."

"Thirty. Six." The hero repeated emphatically, then exhaled. "That's how many died. That's the number that matters. That's how many more lives that grinning gargoyle is accountable for."

"No," said Remo. "Fool was responsible. That nutjob computer program. Remember?"

The vigilante looked to Chiun, silently communicating both understanding and frustration before turning to Remo. "Ray Jenkins was formerly a custodian at the city asylum. A laughing psychopath imprisoned there promised him a large sum of money in exchange for transporting and launching a computer virus of his own design, intended to wreak havoc with the nation's electronic infrastructure — which I think we can safely say it has done. But, somewhere along the way, it became even more lethal than that killer clown dreamed." He opened the trunk of the car, expanding a collapsible crime lab and computer as the lid raised. "You called the entity 'Friend' earlier. You're already familiar with the AI."

It wasn't a question, so Remo didn't answer.

155

"My theory," said the hero, accessing the laptop computer and pulling up an astonishingly detailed and extremely classified archive of reports on Friend, "is that somewhere" — he cut his eyes at Remo — "the virus encountered a dormant and isolated version of Friend, creating a programmatic mutation that evolved into Fool."

"So you're saying Friend has a virus?" Remo suspected the vigilante knew more than he was letting on, but there was no sense in confirming suspicions.

"By now, I'd say it *is* the virus," he said. "Our only stroke of luck so far is that it isn't behaving as a typical virus." He pursed his lips in thought. "It's definitely mobile, but it's not replicating. Which might be the key we…"

The police band radio in the car squawked to life. "Unit 2F-3567. Code Meta in progress, Robbins Square."

"Let me guess," said Remo. "You're 'Unit 2F-3567?'"

"The signal isn't always feasible," he said, pointing up at the daylight sky. He let himself in the driver's side, and was slightly startled to find the Master of Sinanju already in the passenger seat.

"I call rifle," Chiun said in his sweet sing-song voice.

"You mean shotgun," Remo said. "Chiun, get out of there."

"He can throw me out, or I can ride along."

The masked vigilante didn't reply, other than to grunt, slam the door and downshift into drive.

Acting quickly, Remo leaped onto the trunk of the car, fingertips finding scant purchase to hold on as the jet-black vehicle whipped out of the alley.

"Chiun, I'm going to kill you!" Remo screamed into the wind as he surfed the stylized monster car through the city streets.

* * *

The car screeched to a stop in the shadow of the Mullaney Towers. The many neon signs were off during the day, but at night, when they came on, Robbins Square was more illuminated than the noonday sun could ever make it.

Remo jumped down and pulled open the passenger door.

"Oh, good. You are here," said Chiun. "I worried you might have difficulty hailing a taxicab."

The vigilante was already out of the car and surveying the scene. It didn't take much detective work to deduce that the disturbance was at the far end of the stream of screaming people pouring out the doors of the West & Ward mall. Bursting into a sprint, the masked hero acrobatically leaped over the crowd, grabbed the upper frame of the mall entrance, and swung himself inside.

His prepared rant interrupted, Remo shook his head. "He makes that look so easy," he said. "All right, come on."

As the last of the shrieking females (and a few well-heeled males) fled, Remo and Chiun casually entered, catching sight of the caped vigilante sprinting away. From further inside, they could hear a familiar taunting voice. "Lookit me, baskin' in Robbins Square! Ah-hahahaha!" Following the disappearing form of their grim companion, the Masters of Sinanju ran toward the source of the sound. "Ain't I a scream!"

They arrived in the food court to find an ice cream stand had been torn apart, a grotesque finger painting of strawberry, pistachio and vanilla covering the "You Are Here" mall directory. Of the vigilante, there was no sign. However, there were a number of bodies littering the floor; a few were in pieces, limbs torn apart, while others looked to have been victims of the stampede of fleeing consumers.

Remo cocked his head, listening for any extra heartbeats, locating only one; it was strong and rapidly getting louder. Remo and Chiun both leaped away as the balled-up body of the caped hero came crashing, back-first, through the drywall exterior of a pizza and sandwich bistro. The hero hit the ground in a roll, springing to his feet in a fluid motion.

Stepping through the gaping hole, partially obscured by the cloud of powdered plaster, came an imposing figure. Easily a head taller than either man, with a bodybuilder's frame, the figure looked first toward the masked man, then to Remo. Incongruous on its mean features, a mirthful grin broke out. "Honey, I'm ho-oome!" it called out.

"Oh, you have *got* to be kidding me," said Remo.

"You've met?" said the vigilante, striking a defensive stance.

"You could say that," said Remo. "Drac, meet Mr. Gordons. And I don't mean the fish stick guy." Remo lunged left as Mr. Gordons leaped toward him, arms apart to grab him in what would have been a deadly bear hug.

"You go low, I'll go high," the vigilante ordered, already leaping into motion.

"You don't understand," said Remo. "Mr. Gordons is…"

"…an android. Stronger than he appears." He landed a chop on the intruder's corded neck, with no visible effect. "Obviously."

Remo shook his head. "Oh, sure. Obviously. *Anybody* could see that."

The vigilante narrowly avoided the swinging arms of the intruder, while landing another ineffective kick against Mr. Gordons' head. "After a while you learn to recognize the signs."

"You've obviously led the proverbial 'interesting life.'" Remo aimed a forceful kick at the android's midsection, but Mr. Gordons twisted out of the way, giving Remo a partial second to rebalance.

"Missed me, missed me, now you've gotta kiss me!" Mr. Gordons taunted.

"You didn't used to be this jolly," said Remo.

"Probably because it's not him," said the masked man, launching a volley of pellets toward the lumbering humanoid. All the pellets found their mark, exploding on impact. They had no visible effect on the unstoppable machine. "It's Fool, taking up residence in the android's central processor."

"Ding ding ding!" said Mr. Gordons. "Score another one for the man with the leather fetish! Now I can come at you armed! Legged, even!" The android spun a roundhouse at the hero while simultaneously aiming a punch at Remo. Both attacks grazed the men just enough to force a retreat.

"He used to be tough," said Remo. "But he was never this good."

"It's learning," said the vigilante. "The longer you fight it, the more it's adapting your technique. You keep this up, you'll have taught it every move of Sinanju in less than a day."

"All the moves, but none of the style," Remo said. "Don't you have anything in your trick belt that's useful?"

"I thought you didn't like to rely on such things."

"Yeah, well, any port in a storm." Remo ducked another swing, and drove a punch that would have eviscerated a normal man into the android's midsection. "It's either that or 'discretion is the better part of valor,' but that doesn't really work here." Remo looked around for Chiun, and found him across the concourse, admiring some knockoff Asian furniture in a now-abandoned boutique. "Chiun! Seriously?"

The old man looked about innocently. "What? It's only going to be destroyed at some inevitable point as the two of you waste time fighting with that thing," he said. "Why shouldn't I rescue something nice?"

Just then, the caped hero came careening through the air, a human missile launched by Mr. Gordons. He landed squarely on a bamboo and wicker chair, splintering it.

"See what you have done, Remo?" Chiun said, gesturing to the pieces that used to be a chair. "Now it is ruined."

Picking himself up from the floor, the vigilante whirled a handful of bladed projectiles through the air. They narrowly glided past Remo and Chiun, neither of whom so much as flinched. The razor-edged missiles embedded themselves into various portions of Mr. Gordons, then exploded a few seconds later.

When the smoke cleared, Mr. Gordons was none the worse for wear.

"Well, that worked wonders," said Remo. "Got anything else up your sleeve. In your cape? Hell, I don't care where you've got it stashed."

"Just one," said the hero. "Think you can get his attention?"

Remo rolled his eyes. "Hey, Chuckles!" he called out to the android controlled by Fool. "Is that a battery in your pocket, or are you just happy to see me?" Ducking under the grasping arms of Mr. Gordons, Remo slid beneath the android's legs and landed a two-handed punch where the legs came together.

"Ooh!" taunted Mr. Gordons with Fool's voice. "That would've hurt...if I were a human. Let's see if I've got that move down yet." The android turned toward Remo — and exploded in a shower of sparks. The costumed vigilante had come down on Mr. Gordons' back, cape flaring. In his hands he held jumper cables, which he had clamped onto the android's ears. The blinding discharge subsequently sent Mr. Gordons' mechanical head bowling down the concourse.

Untouched by any of the shrapnel that was formerly Mr. Gordons, Remo let out a low whistle. "You know, I'm not one to tell you how to do your job," he said. "But the next time you're up against a monster killer android, you might want to pull that little trick out first."

Getting no reply, Remo looked and found the caped figure lying prone in a pile of rubble, a single trickle of blood leaking from beneath his cowl and down his jawline. The Master of Sinanju hovered over him.

"He gonna be okay?" Remo asked.

"He will live," said Chiun, flatly.

"All right then." Remo clasped his hands together. "The bad guy's dead — or as dead as a computer program gets — and the good guys get to fight another day. I'll call an ambulance to come pick up Dracula here, and you and I can go pick up our checks from Smitty."

But Chiun did not move. "No ambulance," he said, finally, lifting the vigilante's unconscious form effortlessly.

"What? What are we supposed to do with him?" Remo asked. "Seriously, Chiun, he's not going to fit in one of your trunks."

The Master of Sinanju leveled his gaze at Remo, peering at him through his aged vellum slits. "We will take him home."

It took Remo a moment to realize his teacher wasn't talking about their own home. "Hold on there, Chiun," he said, following the ancient Korean out the exit of the once-pristine shopping complex. "First, I'm pretty sure you shouldn't move someone in his condition — not that you don't know what you're doing," he added quickly when Chiun glared at him. "Second, how are we going to get him back wherever it is he lives?"

"Like everyone else," said Chiun. "We go by car."

As Chiun approached the hero's modified ride, Remo grinned. "Well, all right, then," he said. He grabbed the driver's side door handle, and, when the door failed to open, prepared to lift it off its hinges. Chiun pressed the unconscious hero's glove against the handle. Electronic recognition sequences responded to the impulse emitters stitched into the fingertips of the black gauntlet, and the lock popped open easily.

As Chiun gracefully slid into the passenger seat, Remo attempted to figure out the multi-buttoned dashboard. "Can't this guy just use an ignition key like everyone else, or would that just be too normal?" He glanced over at Chiun, who was cradling the prone hero across his lap, his aged fingers applying pressure at various points around the skull through the leather cowl.

Noting the intense expression on Chiun's face, Remo felt an unfamiliar twinge of jealousy. "Hey, Little Father," he said. "You got a favorite between him and me?"

"Yes," Chiun replied.

Remo grunted. "Well while you're playing nursemaid to the superhero, maybe you could give me those magic gloves of his so I can see if they fire up the engine the way they opened the doors."

The vigilante groaned, and mumbled. "Override...delta

seven...three."

"Confirmed," an electronic voice purred from beneath the dash. "Voice control activated."

"Home," the hero managed to croak out before collapsing once again into unconsciousness.

The massive engine of the car fired to life, and the tires squealed on the pavement. Anyone without the perfect balance of a Master of Sinanju would have been thrown back into the seat with inertia as the car rocketed down the street, executing ninety-degree turns at the speed of stupid. "Some days I really miss normal," Remo said, as he watched the scenery speed past. Within minutes, the urban cityscape was behind them, replaced by green spaces and trees.

Without slowing, the car turned off the road onto a dirt path, angling inexorably toward the sheer face of a bluff. Remo and Chiun looked out calmly. Their eyes processed things beyond that which was visible by the average person, and easily pierced the illusion of rock and foliage that camouflaged the narrow mouth of a tunnel. Seconds later, the car drove through the hologram. Recognizing the return of its master, the tunnel lit up, revealing paved macadam and service lights, as the car came to a screeching halt in an alcove. Another larger tunnel branched off to the right, while a smaller one opened to a stairway that led upward.

"We are well and truly down the rabbit hole, Chiun," said Remo, stepping from the car. "So now what? Is there a Mrs. Dracula at home to take him into her loving arms and fix him all up?"

From the stairway alcove came a slight cough, punctuated with a hint of disdain, and Remo and Chiun turned to see a thin, balding gentlemen. He wore a medical apron over his natty attire, and carried a classic leather doctor's bag.

Unable to restrain himself, Remo asked the question. "What's up, doc?"

The man sniffed, ignoring the question pointedly, and approached Chiun and the unconscious costumed hero.

"What is his condition?" he asked.

Remo bristled at the stiff British accent that always reminded him of aristocracy, opulence, and people who thought they were way too good for the likes of the great unwashed masses.

"He is concussed," said Chiun. "He will be fine."

"I shall be the judge of that," the fellow said. He slipped his fingers underneath the cowl and carefully peeled it back to reveal the bruised and battered countenance of what would otherwise be a handsome face. Gingerly, he probed the traumatized areas, feeling for swellings or fractures.

"I have told you, he will live," said Chiun. "There is nothing more you can do that Sinanju has not already done."

The British man stiffened to attention and stared directly into the old Korean's eyes. "Now, you listen to me," he said. "I have been attending to the master's injuries since his first scraped knee when he was five years old, and I will not now nor at any other time have my authority overruled by some witch doctor from Korea. Is that clear?"

Remo ducked behind the car to avoid getting any bloody chunks of the stupid Englishman on him. For several moments, Chiun stared daggers into the eyes of the taller white, and then — unbelievably — began to chuckle.

"I like this one," he said. "He has — what do you call it? Spunk? The fool is at least wise enough to have your counsel. I hope he makes good use of it."

"That, sir, will be the bloody day," the man replied, turning his attention once more to his injured charge. "I take it that you are Master Chiun, and that the gentleman cowering behind the vehicle is Remo? You were mentioned in my master's transmissions from last night."

"Dracula keeps a diary?" asked Remo.

"More like a war journal," the man said. "As long as you're here, you may as well make yourself useful." He gestured to Remo. "You," he said. "Carry him — gently! — and follow me."

"Lead on, MacDuff," said Remo, with a mock salute.

"The expression is 'Lay on, MacDuff,'" the man replied as he led them up the stairway.

Behind them, the car gave a slight rumble of its engines, then disappeared into the darkness of a larger tunnel.

Chapter Seven

MARK HOWARD HAD SEEN MORE than his share of oppressive bureaucracy since becoming the Assistant Director of CURE, but the red tape behind the most twisted Washington, D.C. entitlement programs were still nothing when it came to the hoops and ladders of this city's police department. Even with his Department of Homeland Security badge, it had taken far longer than usual for his demands to be met. Adding to his frustrations, his attempts to reach Remo were consistently running into dead ends, as each call to CURE's enforcement arm instantly dropped into voice mail.

None of this sat well with Howard's boss, Smith, who grew sourer by the minute.

"My apologies, Agent Howard, Agent Smith," the commissioner offered as he escorted the men down the drab olive hall toward the police precinct's evidence locker. "You have to understand, we get all kinds claiming to be federal agents. We have to be thorough with our background checks."

"Quite all right, Commissioner," Howard said amiably when Smith declined to reply. "I'd rather you be sure of who I am rather than end up mistakenly delivering this particular mess into the hands of an imposter."

"Through here," the commissioner directed as his access badge opened the door and allowed the two men entrance. Once the door clicked shut behind them, sealing them into the mantrap between the main entrance and the evidence room, an armed guard took their identification. To Howard's surprise, the guard even scrutinized the commissioner's credentials.

When Howard commented to him about it as they passed into the storage room, all the grizzled cop had to say was "Shapeshifters," and let it stand at that.

Past racks of files and folders from cases years gone by, the commissioner led them to a pair of crates containing the bits and pieces of what used to be Mr. Gordons.

"You retrieved all of it," said the taciturn Smith, in a statement that was more demand than question.

"You'll have to tell us," said the commissioner, unflappably. "We didn't exactly have a set of blueprints for this thing."

Smith pursed his lips and handed him a sheaf of papers. "You'll find everything here in order," he said.

"I don't doubt it," the cop said, looking at the men and ignoring the paperwork. "In all my years of collaborating with federal agents, I've never seen anyone check out cleaner or faster than the pair of you."

"We'll need some men to load these into the van," Smith said, signing off on the evidence receipt.

* * *

The non-descript white Aerostar was parked in the underground garage of a downtown hotel, where Smith and Howard had rented rooms in which they had no intention of staying. Instead, both men were crouched in the back of the van, which had had all of its rear seating removed. Mark Howard connected electronic diagnostic meters to piece after piece of the dismantled Mr. Gordons.

"It's not looking good, sir," he said, tossing aside one circuit board and picking up another. "So far I haven't been able to find any trace of code still extant in the systems."

"Keep looking," Smith said. "With luck, it's still in there somewhere."

Mark cracked open a chunk of plastic that had once formed the left ear and part of the cranium of the android. "Uh oh," he said, upon seeing the contents.

"What?"

Mark extracted a small square and held it up. "Wireless transmitter," he said. "That would explain why we can't find Friend in the system."

Smith's ashen expression grew darker. "You're saying it jumped."

"Looks that way."

"Then we're back to square one," the Director of CURE said. "You'd better let Remo and Chiun know they're still on the clock."

* * *

The estate — unsurprisingly — had a number of rooms that the usual cavalcade of high-society party guests had never accessed. Locked doors encountered during soirees for this or that charity event led the average person to assume a boring storage room, while the more imaginative conjectured there was some temporary lasciviousness afoot between two or more guests. The bored and gossipy had, quite naturally, an inclination toward the obscene, and conjured up images of tables with straps, leather masks, and arrays of dangerous-looking equipment.

Although for entirely different reasons, it was these latter visions that were the most accurate. Having passed through the service kitchen into an ornate dining room, then into a library that was a study in leather from its chairs to its books, Remo and Chiun followed the butler into a room that could easily have been a private convalescent suite at a high-end hospital — the kind that didn't bother with health insurance because its patients were far too wealthy to waste their money on such trivial things, preferring to pay for their services and the accompanying Affordable Care Act penalties in cash.

The butler had already cut away the symbol-emblazoned overshirt and removed the underlying armor, revealing a maze of scar tissue that cut a tortuous path around the younger man's torso. He was now in the process of dressing the head wound.

"I've seen worse," the butler clucked, as he taped down the loose ends of the bandages.

"It was worse," said Chiun. "You may give the 'witch doctor from Korea' your gratitude at any time."

Before the butler could respond, the electronically altered strains of *The Star-Spangled Banner* filled the room, jarringly loud.

Chiun looked to Remo. "You still haven't thrown out that cheap music box Smith sent you?" he asked, as Remo pulled the cell phone from his pocket.

"Sorry, Little Father," he said. "It seemed impolite to throw out a gift, especially so soon after I threw out the last five they gave me." He turned the chirping phone over and under in his hands, examining it. "Soon as I find the off switch, I'll..."

The butler reached over, took the phone from Remo, flipped it open and handed it back.

"Remo!" Mark Howard's voice sounded tinny coming through the cell phone speaker. "I've been trying to reach you for hours! Where've you been, in a cave? I kept dropping straight into your voice mail."

"What is this voice mail?" Chiun said to Remo. "You actually charge postage for people to hear your owl-like screeching?"

Remo waved him off. "Yeah, sorry about that, Mark," he said. "And depending on when you called, I probably was in a cave. It's a long story.

What's the deal? I thought we'd get a few more hours off before the next job."

Mark proceeded to inform Remo that he and Chiun were still working the last contract, since the mutated Friend was still at large. "He probably transferred out the nanosecond he became aware of the attack," said Mark. "In computer terms, he was days ahead and miles away before Mr. Gordons even hit the ground."

"Great," said Remo. "Okay, we're on it. In the meantime, if I were you, I'd avoid using highways. Or airlines. Or vending machines."

"Speaking of highways, Dr. Smith wasn't happy about your involvement with that traffic disaster."

"When is Smitty ever happy?" Remo said. "Have you seen it? Because, just between you and me, I think his bad mood became permanent a few minutes after the doc smacked his bottom."

"The good news is that you kept your faces obscured," Mark continued. "Thanks to the run of unique characters that regularly pass through this city, your street clothes and your blurred-out features have the newscasters crediting some faceless vigilante, with the 'man in the kimono' as his partner and sensei. Richard Salamander, Rick Dragon, something like that."

The next thing Mark Howard heard through his end of the phone was a string of high-pitched Korean, which he had heard enough times to be able to identify the swear words. Then the voice of the Master of Sinanju shifted back into a lilting sing-song English as Chiun took the phone away from Remo.

"My most sincere and humble sympathies, Great Prince, whose radiance is only eclipsed by that of the Magnificent Emperor Smith himself, for having — quite inadvertently, I am assured — brought such shame upon the House of Smith that you find your honored and esteemed self forced to utter the loathsome words 'dragon' and 'Richard' together in the same lotus-sweet breath. Know that Sinanju stands ever ready to accept your generous contribution should you at any time feel the need to eradicate this personage from the Earth."

"Gimme the phone, Chiun," Remo said. "Sorry about that. Seems the old man has a bit of a grudge against whoever this Dick Drago guy is." This prompted another spate of Korean curses, and ended with Chiun stalking away to sulk.

Remo flipped the phone closed, then opened it again as the butler had done. Closed it. Opened it. "Huh," he said. "Would you look at that?" Closing it one final time, he shoved it back in his pocket. "These things might just catch on."

"Welcome to the twenty-first century," groaned the injured man. His voice was weak and strained as he groggily probed the bandaged areas, only momentarily startled that his fingertips didn't meet the leather of his cowl when he brought them to his forehead. "Fool got away," he stated flatly.

"Yeah, you heard that, huh?"

"Cell phones do have a volume control function," the man said. "You might want to explore how it works in the future."

"Give it to me," said Chiun, with cheery helpfulness, "and I shall quiet it most effectively."

"Later, Little Father," said Remo. To the other man, he added, "They went over Mr. Gordons with a fine-toothed comb. There wasn't any trace of our psycho in him."

"Transferred out on a wireless signal," the vigilante said, matter-of-factly. The wincing visage was that of a billionaire playboy, but the eyes and voice had shifted once more to his legendary alter ego. "Which puts us back where we started."

Chapter Eight

THE BILLIONAIRE GROANED as he attempted to sit up.

"Master, your injuries…"

"…have never gotten in the way of the work before," he replied to the butler. Haltingly, he eased himself off the couch and slowly made his way to the grandfather clock in the study. Opening the quartz cover to the face, he set the time to 10:47. Remo heard a faint click, and the clock moved away from the door, revealing an entrance to a staircase leading down. Remo looked to Chiun, then to the butler, shrugged, and the three of them followed the man as he didn't quite stumble down the stairs.

Halfway down the steps, they emerged into an expansive cavern. Suspended from the cathedral-like ceiling were a single-seat helicopter and a miniature VTOL aircraft. The floor of the cave was a museum of artifacts like nothing Remo had ever seen before. A lifelike Tyrannosaurus Rex stood menacingly in one corner, glowering over a Lincoln penny the size of a small house. Against one wall stood an array of glass cases displaying a variation of the vigilante's costume — a decidedly female cut — next to a smaller red-and-green tunic and shorts outfit one would expect a circus performer to wear. Near those were several pedestals, each topped with a glass case holding bizarre items. Further off, Remo saw the car, now parked on smooth macadam, as well as a nearby dock jutting out into an underground waterway in which was moored a sleek black motorboat.

"A cave!" Chiun exclaimed in awe. "Why did I not think of this before? Remo, a cave would be most…"

"No."

"But the closet is already…"

"The 'closet' is already a spare townhouse."

Chiun huffed and glared. "I will eventually run out of room for storing the many treasures of Sinanju. But do you care? Surely not. Why should you worry about the belongings of an old man? I tremble to think what shall become of such things when I pass on."

"I'll have a yard sale," said Remo. "You should consider that yourself — get rid of a few things."

Chiun looked stricken. "The first thing I should get rid of would be your worthless carcass," he said. "But, alas, there is not enough gold in the coffers of all Sinanju to pay someone to take you off my hands."

Remo sighed. "Look, I'll see if we can't get a contractor to build another floor on, okay?" he said. "But no cave," he added, as they reached the bottom of the stairs.

Ignoring the squabbling of the Masters of Sinanju, their begrudging host settled into a high-backed swivel chair, then took the cowl from the counter and carefully lowered it over his bandaged head.

Remo looked around the cave at the others. "Uh, he does know that we've all seen him without the mask on, right?" he asked.

Chiun nodded understandingly. "He is taking on his aspect," the wizened master said sagely. "It is how he becomes who he truly is."

The butler sighed. "I fear who he truly is will one day be the end of who he once was," he said, wearily. "If, indeed, that hasn't happened already." Turning to his guests, he became formal once more. "I've prepared a braised South Pacific salmon with a Basmati pilaf. Shall I serve it now?"

"Jeeves, you read my mind," said Remo. "You psychic?"

"Hardly, sir," he sniffed. "I'm a butler." Chin held high, he stiffly exited the cave.

"You know, Chiun," said Remo, "I don't think Dracula's the only one putting on an act around this nuthouse."

Chiun watched the butler's exit. "We should get one of those also, Remo."

"What? A *butler?*"

"It is seemly for the Master of Sinanju to have a servant," nodded Chiun.

"Yeah, well, you put that on your Christmas list for next year," said Remo. "Maybe Smitty Claus will stick one in your stocking."

The next few hours passed in uneasy silence, interrupted only by the comings and goings of the butler — once to bring three plates of dinner, once again to collect the two empty plates and one untouched one. During that time, the masked man said nothing as he scrolled through screen after screen of data at the monstrous agglomeration of computer terminals. Chiun contented himself by taking advantage of the opportunity to meditate, but Remo felt confined by the cavern, and was growing antsier by the moment. Inactivity wasn't something he took to easily when there was a job to be done.

The hum of a service elevator, followed by the thump of the doors sliding open, heralded the arrival of a visitor to the cave. However, it wasn't the butler, but an exuberant teen that came bounding out, dressed in muted reds and greens. His size and youth took Remo by surprise. He'd heard of the kid, sure, but even after meeting the city's urban legend face-to-face, he still couldn't believe the man was so singularly driven that he would willingly involve a child in his dangerous crusade.

"Hey, Br—" The boy checked himself quickly upon noticing the unexpected presence of Remo and Chiun. "Ooo-kay…Since you aren't currently mopping up the guano with these guys, I'm going to assume they're friends of yours?"

"They're not our enemies," his mentor grudgingly acknowledged. "For now, at least."

Chiun sounded wistful as he spoke to Remo in Korean. "I wish the Emperor Smith would have had the foresight to have sent me someone as young to train, instead of settling for your pitiful specimen, when he sought me an apprentice," he said. "He might have actually achieved some skill in Sinanju by the time he reached your age."

"Even you, Little Father, wouldn't have taken a child into the fights we've had," Remo responded, also in Korean.

The teen smirked and turned to his older partner. "*Ohgik dangshinmyan hankukaunul alginun ansupnida*," he said.

"Yes," the vigilante agreed. "He's nearly as fluent in it as you are."

Remo's jaw hung open, and he looked to Chiun. The ancient Korean merely shrugged. "He is not wrong," the Master of Sinanju said. "You speak with a mouthful of marbles."

"Whatever, Little Father," Remo said. "He's still just a kid. I can't believe Drac would be stupid enough to send a child out after the psychos he runs up against."

"Hey!" the young hero interjected. "I'm not exactly a lightweight, you know! I've been trained by some of the best."

"I'm sure you have," Remo said, rolling his eyes.

"I bet I could take you," the kid insisted, moving in and standing nose-to-chest with Remo. "I've beaten terrorists. I've taken on a whole league of trained assassins. Heck, just surviving my time with Shiva…"

"Your time with *who?*" Remo exclaimed.

Chiun gently interposed himself between the two of them. "Remo, I understand that arguing with children might bolster your shriveled ego, but must you embarrass me by doing so in front of others?" He turned to face the vigilante's young ward, and looked him over, appraisingly. "I will admit to curiosity," he continued. "You have the bearing of a white who is somewhat less clumsy than most."

"Uh…thanks?" the boy replied.

"I would see these vaunted talents of which you boast," Chiun continued. "I assume your guardian maintains at least some small area which passes for a proving ground?"

"There are mats in the northeast corner," their host said without looking away from his work. "No showboating," he added.

"No problem," the younger hero said.

"And don't kill him."

"Geez, he's an old man! I'm not going to…"

"I wasn't talking to you," the brooding figure said, grimly.

Putting a hand on the young apprentice's shoulder, Chiun guided the stunned teenager to the sparring mats. "Do not listen to him," Chiun said. "He confuses caution with uncertainty." Chiun gave a thin smile that crinkled his wizened features. "By all means, *do* try to kill me."

"I hope you know the shortest route to the nearest hospital," Remo said to the cowled vigilante as the Master of Sinanju and the teen hero walked away. "So, you come up with any ideas on how to chase a ghost?"

"Trying to second-guess Fool's logic is useless," the man said. "All that's going to cause is the death of more people while we perpetually arrive late to the scene. No, we've got to control the path Fool takes and get ahead of it."

Gloved hands moved over one of the many keyboards, and the central monitor blinked out, replaced with the image of a floating, disembodied emerald mask with a feminine appearance.

"I have company," the man said, directing the comment to the face on the screen.

"So I see." The voice was distinctly female, with a Greek accent. Remo could tell the accent was an electronic addition, serving to mask the identity of the person on the other end.

"What is it with these people and all their secret identities," he

171

muttered to himself, shaking his head.

"Does this call have anything to do with every online news photo of every world leader suddenly displaying a digitized pair of bunny ears and their flies unzipped?"

"There's an artificial intelligence loose on the World Wide Web," the vigilante replied. Quickly, he explained what was known of Fool's origin, including how it had been traced back to the clownish serial killer.

"All right," she said. "I'll set up a standard sniffer and see what that turns up before sending out the more complex bots."

"Negative," said the masked man. "I contacted you because I specifically want you to stay off this investigation. In fact, I want you to initiate an emergency shutdown, immediately. Your systems are too critical. We can't afford for Fool to infiltrate your equipment."

"Hmm," the disembodied voice mused. "An AI with *that* personality would definitely be tempted by all this processing power — and would become incredibly dangerous if it accessed the…'sensitive information' regarding agents and operations."

"Look," Remo interrupted, "I don't know a lot about how these computer thingies work. As far as I'm concerned, it's a big box with an invisible genie in it that answers your questions sometimes, and hangs out a big blue 'Out to Lunch' sign when you need it most. Can't we just build some kind of trap for it?"

"If we do it right, we won't have to."

"I take it you have a plan?" the electronic visitor asked. "Wait, what am I saying? You *always* have a plan."

"We already have a system in place," he said. He rose from his seat and stood silhouetted in the glow of the multiple monitors which took up the greater part of the cave wall.

"No!" the voice exclaimed. "You're going to let that thing into there?"

"The system is more securely encrypted than the CIA," he said. "If I turn it on itself to prevent outgoing traffic instead of incoming, it should buy us the few necessary seconds needed to sever our connections." Looking over at Remo, whose eyes were glazing over, he said quickly "It will trap Fool's intelligence here in the cave."

"And then what?" the female voice asked. "Dismantle the system piece by piece, sanitize the hard disc platters, and start all over?"

"I've done it before," he said. "The data's backed up every morning anyway. But it's going to be tricky timing. I'll have my partner in place outside to sever the cables as soon as Fool has downloaded itself into the system."

"You're the boss," she said with a resigned sigh. "Good luck."

The glowing green mask blinked and was gone from the monitor, and the grim-visaged man resumed working the keyboard.

As the hero set about preparing the new computer protocols, simultaneously offloading the most recent data acquisitions for preservation, Remo sat idly by, tapping his fingertips rhythmically into a rounded piece of shale he had pried from the wall of the cave. With each tap, the indentations left behind grew a bit deeper. Had he wanted, he could have drilled straight through with a single tap of any finger, but he was merely trying to while away the seeming eternity between now and the fight he anticipated would be coming soon. In the corner of the cave, Chiun continued allowing the vigilante's young ward to spar with him, the boy panting and sweating profusely as the Master of Sinanju swatted away all his attacks with an effortlessness that bordered on boredom. As if to emphasize his lack of trying, Chiun stifled a yawn with one hand, grabbing the leaping teen in mid-air with the other and sending him flying back to the far end of the mat.

"So why'd you become a cop?"

Remo's fingertip pierced the shale, shattering it, as the vigilante's question came from seemingly nowhere. "I'm not a cop," he said.

"You were," the man said coolly. "At least until you died, presuming that headstone in New Jersey is yours. And it is." Almost to himself, he added, "I can't believe any jury would reach an execution verdict on such obviously falsified evidence."

Remo exhaled. Sinanju at its core was all about breathing — and since Remo had become one with the Sun Source, this breathing had become natural to him. But there were rare times when Remo still felt the need to steady himself with a deep breath. Talking about his past was one of those times.

"I don't know," he said. "Same reason I do what I do now, I suppose — to make some kind of difference."

"You do what you do now because you're paid to," the masked man countered.

173

"Well, I wasn't exactly doing charity work as a cop, either," Remo said. "Just near that, what with the lousy pay and all. Besides," he added, indicating Chiun with a nod of his head, "he's the greedy one."

"Is it greed to value the service of Sinanju?" The Master called across the cavern in his sing-song voice, simultaneously flipping the vigilante's young partner over one shoulder, careening him once again to the ground. "Is it greed to graciously take what paltry amounts are willingly offered in exchange for what many would gladly deliver up a mountain of gold?"

"So he's the mercenary, and you're the altruist," their host said. "Right."

"Hey, you don't know me, okay?" Remo said. "You may think you're the world's greatest detective or something, but you do *not* know me."

"I know you spent your childhood in an orphanage," the masked hero said flatly. He continued tapping keys madly, text scrolling across the many screens of the computer arrays. "I know you got into several fights with the other children — and even a few of the nuns. After that, you joined the police academy where you should have failed out, but persevered anyway. You really wanted that job. 'Lousy pay and all.'"

Remo frowned. Smith really wouldn't like knowing that someone had so much information about him. "Yeah, well, if there'd been more good cops around when I was a kid, a lot of my friends wouldn't have ended up in that orphanage with me," he said. "If there'd been more good cops, one of my buddies there wouldn't have had to see his mom and dad shot to death over twenty bucks and a bag of groceries."

The tapping stopped, and even with the occasional grunt and thump from the sparring match, the cave seemed eerily still.

"But then, you probably wouldn't know anything about that, would you, Mister Rich and…" Remo caught a glimpse of Chiun's face, his vellum eyelids drooped to slits, his expression one of infinite sadness. He shook his head almost imperceptibly at Remo. "What?" Remo mouthed silently to his master, but he received no answer.

"You're right," the vigilante said, after a moment. He resumed entering codes into the mainframe. "I wouldn't know anything about that at all."

Remo felt there was something unsettled between him and the caped character. "What about you?" he asked. "You really trained with Chiun?"

"You heard him," the man said.

"No," said Remo, shaking his head. "No, I don't believe it. Chiun isn't some dojo-renting after-school instructor. I just don't buy it."

"Funny," the man said flatly. "That's exactly what I did."

Remo boggled at the implication. "You paid him?" he said, incredulously. "You just *paid* him?"

"That's the nice thing about mercenary organizations," he said. "Money talks."

"Some money speaks loudly," came Chiun's sing-song voice from across the cave.

Before Remo could inquire further, the gaudily clad teen hero landed between them, sticking a perfect landing from an aerial somersault. Even with his domino mask in place, one could see the puffy beginnings of a black eye. The youth was rotating his shoulder, trying to work out the stiffness in it. Despite his somewhat beat-up condition, he still smiled, beaming with a confident exuberance. "That has got to be the best workout I've had in months," he said.

"It was nothing," Chiun sniffed, and then turned to Remo. "He is far more mature than you were when you first began. But since you have grown, you are now only slightly less mature than he is."

"Nothing?" the boy exclaimed. "That trick where you stabbed my deltoid? That was awesome!" Remo winced, recognizing the move that often sent normal men to their knees in pain. "And that other stuff? Next time I meet up with Cassie, she'll be amazed!"

Remo jerked toward Chiun. "You didn't!" he said. "I begged you for *years* before you taught me that trick! I…" He paused under the glare of his Master. "Wait a second," he said, turning to the teen. "This trick…does it have anything at all to do with lightly repeated taps on the inner wrist, and…?"

The young hero tilted his head, quizzically. "Cassie's my regular sparring partner," he said. "I planned on surprising her with the spinning/ducking maneuver Master Chiun showed me. Why, what are you talking about?"

Remo shook his head. "Forget it, kid," he said. "It's…a dangerous combat maneuver, and…you're *really* not ready for it yet."

Chiun sighed, and turned away, an aura of disappointment palpably emanating from his ancient frame. "Did I say only *slightly* less mature?"

"We're ready," the vigilante said. He turned to his junior partner. "I need you to get in position," he added, explaining the current plan.

"I'm on it," he said, bounding from the room, still touching his shoulder.

Chiun turned to their host. "I don't suppose I might interest you in trading apprentices?" he asked.

The man gave no reply.

Chapter Nine

"Did i mention i'm bored?" Remo said as he stood over the vigilante's caped shoulder.

"Sorry that every battle can't be as hands-on as you'd like," the man said, typing away.

"I thought you said you were already ready," said Remo. "So what are you doing now? Sending i-mails to your super friends?"

"I'm initiating an Internet search for Fool, and tracking its most recent appearances." He scanned over a news story at the top of the search results: the financial district's Murphy Building experienced a deadly computer error with its elevator system, resulting in doors opening up to empty shafts. Seven people deep into their iPods, Blackberries, and PDAs stepped blithely into nothingness, falling dozens of stories to their deaths. "We've already lost a lot of time."

"So the plan is to look for him and…then what?"

The vigilante eyed the flashing green LEDs indicating incoming and outgoing traffic. The incoming one had begun blinking rapidly. "Then we hope he sees us looking and comes to us."

As if on cue, the mammoth central monitor went black, followed by the surrounding monitors, then the floodlights, pitching the cavern into total darkness.

"Showtime," the vigilante growled.

* * *

Two miles away, dangling halfway down the bluffs atop which perched the stately manor, the vigilante's teen apprentice gripped the rappelling ropes that held him aloft. His mentor's words traveled from the internal microphone in his cowl, and were relayed to the miniature speakers built into the teen hero's domino mask. Upon hearing the code word, he clamped down hard with the bolt cutters, severing the bundle of data transmission lines that fed into the cave, effectively isolating the central computer from the rest of the world. There was nothing for him to do now but to sit and wait.

* * *

Inside the cave, the monitors were slowly coming to life once more, collectively forming a grotesquely leering face of Dali-esque proportions.

"Hoo-WHEE," Fool whooped. "Now this is what I call a playground...Oops! Naughty, naughty, little man! I felt that back door hit me where the Good Lord split me!"

"Be ready," the hero warned Remo and Chiun.

"For what?" Remo asked.

"But I'll worry about that later," Fool continued. "After all, it isn't every day I get to play with such ex-SQUEEZE-it toys!" From above, Remo could hear a faint whine, quickly growing louder and stronger.

The three men were already leaping away in different directions as a laser beam left a scorch mark on the ground where they had just been gathered.

"What the aitch ee double-hockey sticks was that?" Remo shouted over the din of another beam, firing at the spot where he used to be.

"Cave defenses," the vigilante said.

"They're controlled by your super computer?" Remo exclaimed. "And you didn't think to maybe shut them off first?"

"We had to leave something intact to tempt Fool into the system," he said, his cape sprawling out behind him, the left lower corner scorched from a barely-missed laser beam.

The small sound of glass chinking, followed by the *thunk* of a rock hitting the ground ended the attack. Chiun clapped the dust from his hands, his graying tufts of hair floating lightly on an unfelt current of underground air. "Fortunately, you left us weapons of our own with which to defend ourselves," the Master of Sinanju said, lightly kicking the rock with the toe of his sandal.

"It's not over yet," the masked man said, scanning the cave warily.

"Of course it isn't," said Remo. "Look, you're supposed to be one of the good guys, right? So how much should we be worried? Nothing in here is likely to be lethal, right?"

The vigilante frowned. "The cave's defense mechanisms are designed to gauge threat levels and respond with appropriate non-lethal force."

"Like I said," said Remo. "So..."

"But," he continued, "that system is no longer in control. And more than one of the systems were designed to contend with an out-of-control extraterrestrial." He leveled a dark gaze at Remo. "Should the need ever arise," he added.

Remo and Chiun gazed up again, both feeling the advancing force waves of a large feather falling through the air. They dodged, as did the caped hero, as a light mesh net fell to the ground, its edges crackling blue with electricity on contact with the dusty floor.

"Oh, curses," Fool cackled. "Missed again. But not to worry. This next one'll be a gas!"

"Masks!" the vigilante ordered. He pulled a wad of clear plastic from a compartment in his belt, which quickly unfolded into a palm-sized air filter. He fit it over his mouth, just as the cave began to fill with a sickly-sweet green mist. He flung a dart across the room, shattering a glass case filled with fire extinguishers and ventilator masks.

Controlling his breathing so that he only filtered in oxygen, Remo cautiously made his way to the masks, alert to any other attacks that might launch. Before he made it halfway to his destination, jets of flame erupted from the acetylene torches buried beneath the floor, barring his way.

Remo shook his head, smirked, and took two purposeful steps through the flames. He emerged through the other side, his black t-shirt smoking and his chinos scorched, but the rest of him relatively unharmed. Taking one of the masks from the case, he flung it across the cave in a lazy arc. Chiun easily caught it, as Remo took one for himself.

"You owe me a new shirt," he said, his voice echoing from inside the mask.

"Pfah!" said Chiun. "Those cheap things you can get at Wal-Get for a pittance. My kimono, on the other hand, is a priceless work of art, and you can believe our host's fortunes will feel the pinch in purchasing a replacement."

Remo was about to tell Chiun that his kimono was, in fact, undamaged from the battle, but before he could open his mouth the floor fell out from beneath him, revealing a chasm of pointed steel stalagmites.

"Now who the heck finds these non-lethal?" Remo asked as he fell. Reaching outward, Remo's hands pushed against the wall of the pit, sending himself flying horizontally across the opening. His feet hit the other side, and he let his legs coil beneath him, springing them out at the optimum moment to propel himself across the gap again, at an upward angle. He repeated the maneuver from side to side, until he jettisoned back into the cave.

"Someone notoriously hard to kill," the vigilante said flatly.

"I thought someone said something about a plan?" Remo asked. "So far it seems the plan is to play dodgeball with this maniac — and we never get a turn with the ball!"

"Any second now," the vigilante said.

As if on cue, Fool called out to them. "Yoo-hoo! Sweetums! Daddy's got a brand new..."

"Hi-diddly-ho, hero-boys!"

Remo glanced up at the monitors. "Did his needle just skip a track?"

"What's this! What's this!" Fool cried. "No room! No room!"

"Well then maybe you should leave?" Fool suggested. "I'm here to get this party started!"

Remo sidled up to the costumed figure. "Uhh...what's going on?"

"What do you see when you see someone arguing with a fool?" the vigilante asked, smiling grimly.

"Two fools," Chiun replied automatically.

"Not exactly a koan," said their host. "But appropriate."

"Well, I feel enlightened," said Remo. "You're saying there are two of them now?"

"From the moment Fool first infiltrated the system, the replication program I designed was building and executing an exact copy of the program."

"You mean you built a second Fool," Remo said. "On *purpose?*"

"Quit pushing me!" one Fool said. "You quit pushing me!" the other Fool said in return, as the two continued arguing in circles. "Why I oughta..." "Woo-woo-woo-woo-woo!" "Nyar-ar-arrr!"

"Ever heard of something called 'core wars?'" the vigilante asked.

"Now isn't exactly the best time to discuss old science fiction movies," said Remo.

"In the pioneer days of computing, bored scientists would design bits of code intended solely to occupy as much of the computer memory as possible," he continued. "They would release these code fragments into their systems, pitting them against other programs designed to do the exact same thing, then watch them fight it out for supremacy, to see who was the more agile programmer. They were the forerunner to computer viruses."

"So why are the Fools fighting each other?"

"Individuality," Chiun nodded sagely. "The ghost in the machine

180

wishes to be itself, and itself alone."

"That's why the original Friend transferred from machine to machine, rather than replicating and multiplying," the masked detective said. "It's programmed with an ego that prevents it from seeing anything as its equal."

"And now that it has an equal..." Remo said, following the logic.

"...it's like a dog snarling at its own reflection," finished their host.

"So which one do you think is going to win this fight?"

"All things being equal? Neither...and both."

As he said it, the squabbling voices grew faster, more frenetic, at times being little more than screeches, squeals and blips.

"Your muddah wears..."

"Oh, wiseguy, eh?"

"Susquehanna hats?"

"Niagara Falls! Slowly I turned..."

"Daisy, Daisy, give me your answer, do..."

"Gimme..."

"Leggo my..."

The monitors began to dim, and the drive activity lights began to flicker out. The audio started slurring, dragging, and the images that were still visible on the central monitor began to pixelate, the faces projected by both programs superimposed on each other, slightly askew, and melting like ice cream off the edge of a cone.

"Turn out the lights..."

"...the party's over."

"Aw, mom, I don't wanna..."

"...go..."

"...to school..."

The monitors went black.

Still cautious, the caped man approached the cabinets of the computer and began to remove the hard disk spindles.

"Wait? You mean that's it?" Remo asked.

"What did you expect?" the man replied.

"Oh, I dunno," said Remo. "Usually these things are never over without me having to kill ten or twenty morons."

"Sorry to disappoint you."

"So what do we do now?"

The vigilante set the array of discs aside. "*We?*" he said. "*We* don't do anything. *I* will spend the next several days degaussing these chips and boards before replacing them with new ones. *You*, on the other hand, are free to go back to Newark and tell your bosses the threat has been neutralized. Take all the credit you want."

"We are not splitting our fee," Chiun's sing-song voice floated through the cave. His face buried deep in the housing of the computer, the vigilante allowed himself a rare, unseen smile at the Master of Sinanju's predictable defensiveness. Letting it fade first, he then pulled himself from the innards of the machine, turned, and faced the Master of Sinanju, appraising his former mentor. Chiun stood unflinching beneath his gaze.

The masked man nodded curtly. "Twelve?" he asked.

Chiun considered, then nodded back. "Silk," he said.

"Nothing but the finest, of course," he said, before turning back to his work. "I've alerted my butler that all is clear. He'll be here any second to escort you out."

As Chiun and Remo walked toward the winding stone staircase, Remo asked, "So what was that all about?"

"What?" Chiun asked innocently. "Oh, that? That was nothing. Merely a former student offering a gift to a former teacher of a dozen hand-threaded kimonos." He smiled serenely. "Would that all my students were so thoughtful when it comes to showing respect to their elders."

Remo sighed. "Come on, Little Father. You know you wouldn't trade me for nothing."

"True," said Chiun. "I would indeed trade you for something. In fact, I would still very much like to trade you for the young apprentice with such promise. He, I believe, would be a worthy successor — eager, bright, and showing of the proper respect. However, my honor does not permit me to leave our host holding the short end of such a stick."

The sound of their bickering faded as they made their way up the stairway to where the butler was just opening the door. Alone with his thoughts, the city's defender was already designing the patterns for the kimonos, even as he continued disassembling the delicate machinery that was the core of the crime computer.

Chapter Ten

His FOOTSTEPS MADE NO SOUND as he made his way stealthily past the guards, then the doctors, sticking to the shadows. The hallways — dank and oppressive — made his job that much easier. As he passed each doorway, he peered through the thick glass porthole at the inmate within — the snarling man with his face perfectly bisected: half clean, half blistered and gangrenous; the woman with the pale green skin, lithe frame and radiant red hair, mumbling to her potted plant.

He knew he'd reached the right door even before he looked in, just from the sobbing laughter that racked the shoulders of the man inside, curled up in a straight-jacketed lump in the corner of the padded cell, a shock of grass-green hair the only bit of color showing.

Remo took a slow, deep breath, as he looked at the serial killer inside, a maniac who had racked up a countless string of victims during his erratic, unpredictable life. He knew from headlines that the man would inevitably escape his confines again, would go on to murder God only knows how many more innocents before he'd be once again captured and imprisoned in his comfortable air-conditioned cell, with three squares a day plus snacks and TiVo — all because he couldn't be held accountable for his actions. The courts wouldn't execute him. They declared him insane.

Remo was pretty sure someone had gotten things backward.

He pointed his index finger at the keyhole, ready to pop it out with a quick thrust.

"As I recall, Master Chiun frowns on 'freebies.'"

Remo looked up, unsurprised to see the caped hero impossibly wedged into the corner of two walls and the ceiling. He was irritated that he hadn't sensed the man's presence until just now.

"Charity's good for the soul," said Remo. "Besides, I figure this is still part of the original job. This joker is the one who kicked everything off, after all."

Suddenly, the door thumped, and Remo looked back to see a pasty-white face smashed up against the glass, flattening his features. His nostrils steamed up the surface, and he sealed his mouth against the portal and blew, engorging his cheeks before finally pulling away. "Ooh! A visitor!" he cooed. "I lo-oooo-ove visitors!" He was back at the glass again, scrabbling with his lips, his hands still secured in the straightjacket. "Waddja bring me? A file with a cake in it?"

His eyes darted upward, and his permanent smile grew impossibly wider. "I've got a bat in my belfry," he leered. "So who's the new boyfriend, Buddy-Boy? Ain't he a little old for you?"

Remo had had enough. He shoved his elbow into the door. On the sealed side, the shockwave drove into the laughing man's liver, leaving him crumpled on the floor, vomiting, his laughter for once stifled.

"I won't let you kill him," the vigilante said.

"Is this round two, then?" Remo asked. "Sinanju against…what, cape-kwon-do or whatever it is you call your casserole of fighting techniques?"

The dark hero smiled a humorless grin. "I have nothing to lose," he said. "If you beat me, no one will be able to stop the countdown that will draw every major media outlet to Folcroft Sanitarium and the curious agency it covers." He let the threat sink in before continuing. "Fool's footprint on the hard drives left behind quite a bit of curious data," he said. "But worse: if I beat you," — he smiled wider, menacingly — "then your name goes down in the scrolls as Remo the Shattered."

Remo grunted. "I don't suppose threatening to reveal your identity would do much to scare you into giving up?"

The man grinned passively and shook his head. "Feel free. I have more."

Remo flexed his abnormally thick wrists in frustration, cracking his knuckles. "This isn't over," he said, turning to leave as quietly as he arrived.

"No," he muttered. "But it is for now."

* * *

Outside the confines of the foreboding asylum, Chiun awaited Remo's return.

"He outsmarted you, didn't he?" Chiun said, smiling beatifically as Remo emerged from the hedges.

"I put him in his place, Little Father."

"Of course you did," said Chiun. "And then he put you in yours."

As they turned down the lane that crossed over into the city's lower south side, Remo grumbled. "I suppose I should be happy," he said. "We got the job done, after all — even if with a tiny bit of help — and I didn't have to kill anybody."

"Measure your success however you wish," said Chiun. "So long as the madman Smith continues sending boats filled with gold to the children of Sinanju, I care not."

Just then, a surly youth stepped from an alley into their path, the streetlight glinting off his gold tooth and the tip of his switchblade.

"Gimme yo money," he said, his voice a gravelly whisper.

Remo chuckled. "I'll give you this much, you've got the brave act down pat, pal, taking us on two-to-one and all that."

The young man leered at them, then gave a short whistle. From all sides of the street, Remo and Chiun found themselves surrounded by no fewer than a dozen others, all wearing the same color bandana around their foreheads, arms, or legs, brandishing two-by-fours, knives, and pistols.

"I asked nice," the would-be thief said. "Now we's gotta do it the hard way."

As they slowly closed in around the Master and Master Emeritus of Sinanju, Remo looked first at Chiun, then up to the rooftops. "Oh. Help. Someone save us," he said tonelessly. Nothing happened. "No?" He shrugged. "Welp, okay then."

The gang members advanced, laughing and taunting as they marched to their deaths.

Epilogue

THE WAREHOUSE WAS SUPPOSED TO BE abandoned, but the flickers of light that illuminated the dirty panes of glass told a different story to the winos who slept fitfully in the alley behind it. This bustling city was supposed to be the city that never slept, but the slum district was at least allowed to be dozy now and then, and the winos — themselves seeking sleep — were content to move onto the next corner, away from the annoying glare.

Inside, the little man in the lab coat scurried from machine to machine, checking panels and flipping switches. His face was obscured by a welder's helmet to protect his eyes from the glare that shone from out of a metal sarcophagus, placed centrally within his other equipment.

He rubbed his hands in glee. The first machine, stolen from a witless scientist in Kansas, was useful, but its output was only identical to whatever its input was — and since the input was but a lock of hair, currently held beneath a slide and scrutinized by a focused beam of light, that output would have been unsatisfactory indeed.

Ah, but coupled with the DNA sequencers taken from that bald billionaire's science labs, the device became quite useful indeed! So what if its product was considered imperfect when compared to the original? What did it matter? In the little man's eyes, the ends were perfection itself.

A chime went off, much like a microwave announcing that the burrito was now fully cooked, and the door to the sarcophagus slid aside, letting out steam and more light as it did so.

The man who stepped out of the sarcophagus was naked. His eyes were set deep in his face under a slightly protruding forehead. His wrists were abnormally thick in proportion to his forearm, as though his radius and ulna went directly into his fingers without stopping. Most unsettling, however, was his complexion, which was a pale and powdery chalk white.

The bizarre figure uttered his first word. "Urr…"

The little man in the lab coat hopped with glee, then threw aside his welder's mask. His features were Korean, and his eyes were alight with happiness.

"At last," he said. "My own little son."

"Son?" the naked man grunted.

"Yes, son," the little man said. "And you may call me Father."

"Fa...ther?"

"Yes, yes. Father Nuihc. That's me! And you are..."

"Grr..." the man growled. He glowered at Nuihc.

"Me am...Omer?" he grunted. "Me no want kill."

He advanced threateningly.

"Me no want kill nobody! Now!"

ABOUT THE AUTHOR:

R.J. Carter was raised on a steady diet of comic books and refined sugars. He is the author of A KNIGHT BEFORE CHRISTMAS and ALICE'S JOURNEY BEYOND THE MOON, and can be found regularly writing for CriticalBlast.com. He currently lives in St. Louis with his wife, son, and a number of imaginary people shouting for their stories to be heard.

MANTRA

I AM CREATED SHIVA, THE DESTROYER, DEATH, THE SHATTERER OF WORLDS

Devin Murphy

188

MASTER OF THE DEAD

Glenn Porzig

IN BETTER TIMES, THE COOL WIND BLOWING down the empty streets would have made it a pleasant evening for a walk. But that was before the zombies. Not that there were any shuffling about — but you knew they were out there. They always were out there, lurking around any corner.

It was getting dark as we made our way to some abandoned office buildings to shelter for the night. The undead seemed more active at night, so it was best to make camp and get a fresh start in the morning. As we crossed the street, we heard someone approaching. They weren't zombies, but they didn't smell much better.

"You! Stop right there! This is our territory," said the tall, scruffy one. He was obviously the leader, staring us down while the others scurried about, encircling us.

They were Scavengers. Worse even than the zombies, because they were still human — but chose not to act like it. They obviously thought they had caught us off guard. They were about to learn a final, fatal lesson.

"You wouldn't have happened to have run across a girl around here…hmmm? We seem to have lost one." A smile crossed his chapped lips and his crew cackled in unison.

"Hey grandpa, whatchu got in the sack? I bets it's full o' goodies," sneered one of the underlings. He wouldn't make a very good zombie — he was missing most of his teeth. And with his sparse, straggly hair, skinny frame, and poor posture, he reminded me of a mangy circus monkey.

"If you want my sack, why don't you come over here and grab it?" my grandfather, standing quietly beside me, replied to the pitiful little monkey man.

I quickly spoke up. "Don't waste your time, friends — it's only rice."

189

"Rice?" spat the leader. "You expect us to believe that?"

I took a step toward him. He pulled out a revolver and leveled it at me. I carefully watched the cylinder as he pulled the hammer back. The wan light glinted down the chambers as the cylinder rotated and clicked into place.

"Tell them about the toll," said a third scavenger. This one was much larger than the others. I wondered how he could remain so fat while the rest of the world starved. I guessed he wasn't a picky eater.

"The toll is…you hand over everything you got and we lets you live," said the skinny, toothless one as he approached us. My grandfather shifted his stance and set the sack of rice down behind him, out of reach of the pitiful scavengers.

I took a step toward the leader and he quickly adjusted his aim — pointing the pistol my way. "Settle down there, junior. Don't forget who's got the gun." He smiled broadly — a well-rehearsed delivery. He was enjoying the feeling of power the gun and his gang provided him.

I wondered how many survivors had met their end at the hands of these scumbags. How many good people had died so they could live?

"You and I both know if you fire that gun, every deadhead within half a mile will coming running…and you only have three bullets."

I took another bold step toward him and he fired reflexively, without thinking.

Even in the waning light I was able to see the signs, hear the tendons in his fingers as they flexed to pull the trigger. The deadly bullet struck the ground where I had been a split second before.

The leader panicked, firing wildly — not that he had a chance to hit me even if he had remained calm. A second round whizzed past me. Then a third — once again missing me entirely, and burying itself in a building behind me. Then the hammer slammed down again, this time on an empty chamber.

I reached up, snatching the gun from his hand, breaking two of his fingers and his wrist in the process. Not that he felt it for long, as I proceeded to shove the revolver's six-inch barrel into his eye socket, killing him instantly. It was better than he deserved.

While this had been going on the monkey man had decided he could handle my grandfather himself.

He was dead wrong.

As he reached out to snatch the sack of rice, the old man's arm snapped out with a speed that belied his advanced age. He pulled the foul scavenger to him gracefully, as if performing a dance move that ended with the man's head twisted free from his neck.

My grandfather gave a grim look at the remaining scavenger. His dark eyes glared from the deep sockets that gave his lean face a skull-like appearance. Though advanced in age he was still an imposing sight. He stood a full six feet tall of lean muscle, and he still moved with the confidence of a younger man. With a flick of his thick wrist the scavenger's head went flying lazily through the air.

The large scavenger had been slow to react, but he woke up to his situation as the nearly-toothless head rolled to a stop at his feet.

"You killed my friends!" he bellowed as he rushed toward my grandfather. There was a snap like the sound of a wet towel, followed by a crunch like breaking celery. Then the biggest of the scavengers fell over backwards with a thud that reverberated between the buildings of the empty street.

My grandfather gently lowered his leg back to the ground. A single kick had been sufficient to kill the big man. He bent over and picked up the large sack of rice.

"Isn't it your turn to carry the rice?" he asked.

"Not until morning."

I dusted myself off and then looked up at a nearby office complex.

"You can come out now," I shouted up at the building.

An eye that had been watching us though a hole in a boarded-up window on the third floor, opened wide. A moment later, a head, belonging to a not unattractive girl, peeked up from behind the barricade.

"We won't hurt you, and we have food. We just need some shelter for the night. Those gunshots could have drawn the attention of the deadheads." I smiled up at her.

She thought for a moment, and then motioned us to come up.

We made our way past the barricades and up a hallway. I noticed she had broken the large fluorescent bulbs at the top of the stairs. A smart move as the sound of the crunching glass would alert her to any intruders. I liked her already.

The girl was young and slender, her hair dirty blond and tangled. She looked a year or so younger than me. She stood behind a desk, and I could tell she was ready to run if she sensed anything was wrong. She spoke hesitantly.

"I'm Shannon. Shannon Wells."

"I'm Jack, and this is my grandfather, Remo."

"Reno? Like Nevada?" she asked.

"Um, no…Remo like…like I don't know." I said, feeling stupid in front of the first pretty girl I'd seen in months.

"Remo Williams, at your service," my grandfather said, smirking at me as he gave a little bow.

"Shannon, what made you decide you could trust us?" I asked.

"It was him. The old man," she said.

"Me? It certainly wasn't my kind face," he grinned.

"No, it's just that…since everything went to hell, you don't really see old men any more. I think the old and the young were the first to go. And since you were keeping him safe, I thought maybe I could trust you too." She looked at me, a little embarrassed.

"Oh, he's keeping me safe is he?" my grandfather said, almost laughing.

"As you saw earlier, my grandfather is, um, spry for his age. It's a long story."

"I saw you take down those scavengers, and neither of you even got scratched. How is that possible?"

She looked up at me and waited. The light streaming in from the setting sun bathed her face in a warm glow. There wasn't really anything else to do so I continued, knowing it would be hard for her to believe.

"Remo is my grandfather, but he is also my master. The Master of Sinanju — the sun source of martial arts, from which all others flow," I paused a moment to gauge her reaction, but she was unmoved. "As you saw earlier, we are capable of feats of great strength and speed…even dodging bullets."

"I guess that if I can believe in zombies, I can believe in super heroes," she said.

Remo smiled as he sat down on the floor with his legs crossed. He opened up the large sack, took out a cup, and scooped out some of the rice. He looked up at Shannon as he worked. "Yeah, we're badasses, but the real question is…how did a young girl like you survive out here alone?"

Shannon's face became sullen as she was taken out of the moment.

"It wasn't just me. It was my older sister, Lori, and her boyfriend Scott. He was a Marine — that's the only way we survived so long. He had a gun and survival training, but the Scavengers got them. Somehow, I managed to get away. I heard their screams…and I just kept running."

"A world full of undead and they get killed by animals that call themselves human. That's the biz," Remo said as he poured water into the pot full of rice. "I'm glad we're able to do our part to help clean up the trash. It's what we do. Well, it's what I used to do — before the world went to shit."

"What are you doing here? Where were you headed? Isn't every place overrun now?" She hung her head. "What's the point in even going on?"

"There is a place…a remote place. A small fishing village in Korea. It's our sacred duty to defend the village of Sinanju — our village," I said, glancing at my grandfather. He gave the slightest of smiles, to let me know he approved.

The girl began digging in her coat pockets and eventually pulled out a can. She held it up smiling, the label facing us like some surreal television commercial.

"I have this can of potted meat…I've been saving it for a special occasion. Um, either of you happen to have a can opener?"

"You'd be better off eating that can, rather than what's in it," Remo snapped.

"Ignore him, he's cranky. The end of the world will do that to you," I said.

"Have a seat and have some rice," my grandfather said, ignoring my sarcasm. "You need to rest up if we're going to continue tomorrow."

Remo pulled out a large polished stone and quickly rubbed it between his hands. He then dropped the rock into the pot and the water instantly came to a boil.

I wondered what we would do when that sack was finally empty as I took a seat across from him. Shannon came up and sat beside me.

"You're going to walk all the way to Korea?" Shannon asked.

* * *

When I woke up, Remo had already been up a while.

"Any sign of the deadheads?" I asked.

The girl lying near me stirred and asked "Why do you call them deadheads?"

"It's a twentieth-century thing. I don't quite understand it myself, but grandpa gets a kick out of it."

"Back in the day," Remo explained, "There were these drugged-out hippie freaks who followed a band named The Grateful Dead. I don't think anyone really listened to their music; it was just an excuse to travel around getting high and being slackers. Their brain-dead followers were called 'Deadheads.' They were zombies before being a zombie was cool."

"Does he always talk like this?" Shannon asked, stretching. As she stretched, her shirt lifted up, revealing her midriff. She noticed me looking and quickly pulled it down.

I turned and looked away.

"Well, pack up and let's get moving. Those zombies aren't going to kill themselves, you know," Remo waved his hands about as if to spur us on.

Shannon looked back and forth between us.

"Um, you mean me too?" she asked.

"It's either that or die a horrible death, right?" Remo said.

"I hope you like rice," I added as I smiled at her.

"Speaking of rice, it's your turn to carry it!" Remo said loudly, sliding the large, heavy sack of rice across the floor towards me.

* * *

When I returned to Remo and Shannon from scouting ahead — checking for zombies — they were in the middle of a discussion.

"Why haven't we seen more zombies?"

"Over the last few weeks we've noticed their behavior changing. We rarely see a lone straggler any more. They've started traveling in packs," Remo said.

"It makes it nicer because you're less likely to run into them. It's a real bitch if a pack spots you, though," I added.

We continued on, the strap of the heavy pack of rice digging into my shoulder as I walked.

"Where did they come from? The zombies, I mean. They were just everywhere before you knew it," Shannon said.

"I think grandpa has a theory, and it's as good as any. Why don't you share it with her?"

"Yes, I do have a theory. After much contemplation I've decided the zombies are really Democrats, returned from the dead — to vote again."

Her face shifted from an intense look of concentration on what he said to a smile that she struggled to contain. We all started laughing — until I heard it. A low murmur, not too far away. The sound of not dozens, but hundreds of undead, all waking up and turning toward the sound of our laughter.

"Shhhhhhhhhhhhhhit!" I murmured.

Remo heard it too. His face became stern as he motioned us to keep moving. "Quietly, but don't slow down…they might not be able to find us," he whispered.

Shannon looked at us, fear in her eyes

"Stay close to me," I said to her.

"I…I don't want to be eaten by those things. If — if comes down to it…" she said to me, her words trailing off.

"I won't let them take you alive. It won't come to that. Trust me," I said, hoping it would give her courage, and hoping that I could keep my promise.

We ran as fast and quietly as we could down the street and past an alley. For my grandfather and me, it was a snail's pace, but we didn't want to leave Shannon behind.

Ahead, we saw a straggler. A crawler that couldn't keep up with the pack. It was at the other end of the alley, crawling from an overturned wheelchair. The creature's useless legs were bloody from being dragged along the pavement.

You tried not to think of them as human — it was easier to do what had to be done that way. But then you would see something like this and, for a moment, you would remember — these were people.

Remo briskly walked up to the undead crawler and gave it the slightest of kicks — severing its spinal column, driving its face into the ground, and dislocating its jaw.

He looked up at Shannon. "Watch your step," he said, reaching out a hand and helping her step over the bloody mess.

Remo led the way. He peered around the corner, and then quickly pulled back. He waved us away with a broad sweep of his arm.

"Go back!" he said as he turned and started heading back toward us. We picked up the pace as we made our way back down the alley.

But it was too late. The undead pack Remo had seen around that corner started heading our way. Most of them poured in on the end Remo was turning from. Meanwhile, a few had already started down the alley in the direction we had just come from. Shannon had a look of horror on her face. We were trapped.

I turned back to look at my grandfather. The crazy old man had turned and was running back to us. He snatched up the broken wheelchair and hurled it toward the oncoming wave of undead. It smashed into them and they scattered, hurled in all directions like broken, bloody bowling pins.

"Strike!" he shouted.

I did my best to keep Shannon behind me as I fought the undead. Individually they posed no threat to a student of Sinanju. But now that they were in packs, and we had the girl to defend, the outcome was far from certain.

I took a deep breath, forcing more oxygen into my blood as my grandfather had taught me. Everything slowed down as my concentration focused.

Nails swiped at me, teeth gnashed — all at empty air as I easily dodged their advances. My hands lashed out, precise strikes hitting temples and exploding brains out of ear canals. My palms thrust hard into rotting noses, driving cartilage into brains. My legs swept forward knocking heads from shoulders. I waded slowly into the growing crowd of undead, eliminating every one within reach.

Remo was a flurry of motion, dispatching the undead at a pace that was easily twice mine. The power of his blows exploded the torsos of the undead in a bloody mess that coated the walls of the alley with their viscera and littered the ground with their limbs. Still-animated heads flopped around on the ground at his feet like dying fish, their jaws snapping, dead eyes looking up, not understanding why they couldn't reach their prey.

Remo's wheelchair stunt had slowed the advance of the horde behind us, but they were crawling over the pile of mutilated corpses of their comrades building around us. I could see the concern on his face as he worked tirelessly.

"There are too many. This bottleneck will slow them down, make it more manageable, but it's also a kill box. We could be trapped in here fighting them forever." Remo paused as a single sweep from his leg knocked the heads of two undead from their shoulders.

"I won't leave you!" I shouted back at him.

I knew what he was getting at, and I knew why. He trusted me to take care of myself, but with all of these zombies in this tight space, the odds of the girl being infected were too high.

"Jack! Take the girl. Keep her safe. I'll slow them down and catch up with you later."

My grandfather paused from fighting long enough to look me in the eyes. I knew he was right. There was no way the three of us could hold this spot indefinitely. It was only a matter of time before the endless, tireless undead managed to infect one of us. I gave him a single nod and reached out and grabbed Shannon's hand.

"Don't you go dying on me, old man!" I shouted back at my grandfather as I turned and started pushing forward, out of the alley. I unleashed a flurry of kicks and smashing blows to clear the way. I couldn't look back again.

"Don't get sloppy, kid!" Remo shouted over the sound of breaking bones and gnashing teeth.

The dead kept coming, but we were making progress. Up ahead, I could see the horde thinning. Behind us, Remo was yelling as he hurled zombie parts in all directions, doing his best to keep the attention of the pack, to keep them from following us.

Finally free of the zombies, Shannon and I ran and kept running. Down alleys, between buildings, and across parking lots. I almost dragged her behind me as we kept running. Finally, we couldn't hear the roaring of the zombie pack. Only then did we take a moment to relax. Shannon and I finally had made it to safety — at least what passed for safety these days.

I could see the question in her eyes. I knew Remo was amazing, unmatched in any way. Even with his advanced age he was nearly unstoppable. But I wondered if I had made a mistake leaving him behind, and so did she.

"Your grandfather, will he—?"

"Are you kidding? That old man is too ornery to die. End of the world? No problem...he just keeps on going," I said, trying to act confident and cheerful for her sake.

We kept walking, now at a more leisurely pace. There were still a few more hours until nightfall.

We made our way into an office building and went up a few floors.

The building was free of deadheads. If you didn't see or hear them right away, they usually were not there — it was one of the few good things about their newly-developed pack mentality.

When we found a safe room to hole up in, I cleared some of the clutter and gathered some wood — mostly broken furniture — to build a small fire. The fire would heat our food, and keep her warm until Remo could find us.

Shannon had gathered some cushions from couches around the office building. She threw them in a pile together near the fire. She lay down on the pillows and made herself comfortable while I started cooking the rice. I turned to talk to her but she had already passed out from exhaustion.

* * *

The next morning I awoke to the sun streaming through the dirty and broken windows. There was still no sign of Remo. I had hoped, even expected, that he would have snuck in overnight and rested by the fire, but that didn't happen. This wasn't good. I let Shannon sleep, quietly moving to the window and looking out over the deserted streets. It was deathly quiet outside.

I stood at the window, eyes closed, and concentrated the way Remo had taught me, reaching out with my senses. Then I heard something in the distance. I couldn't make it out. I opened my eyes. On the horizon I saw something. Was it smoke? No, it was dust. Something big was headed this way and it was kicking up a trail of dust in its wake. Not something — someone. Lots of someones. Or at least things that used to be someone.

As they marched closer, I could make out the hoarse garbled chanting. Hundreds of undead voices crying out in unison. It was creepy, even to me.

"Shiva!" Over and over. Repeating the name like a mantra. "Shiva!"

Shiva — the Destroyer. I had heard the stories from my father and aunt. I hadn't believed the legends about my grandfather. But now Shiva marched towards me, followed by an army of darkness. Even Master Chiun, my grandfather's teacher, had feared Shiva...and I, just a boy of seventeen, not even a master yet — how could I stand against a god incarnate?

I woke the girl. The undead were still too far away for her to hear them. I needed to move — I thought it best to meet them in the open, before they reached us.

"Shannon! I'm going out to find my grandfather. Please, stay here until I return."

She looked up at me — she couldn't believe I would leave her alone. "Hurry back."

"I will. Keep the rice safe."

She gave a wan smile. I smiled back before leaving the room. I wanted to make it back for her — I was her only chance to live. Knowing she was counting on me helped to spur me on. The grueling, never-ending struggle against the undead had taken more out of me than I realized. And now I was headed out to face certain death.

* * *

I felt them before I saw them. The ground shook from their sheer numbers. I could hear them, teeth clacking, still chanting the name "Shiva" over and over again. A wall of dead men moving inexorably closer, like a tidal wave, come to destroy everything in its path — including me.

Dozens of packs of the undead were following a solitary figure, with more joining every minute. Like battalions of soldiers marching behind a general, they had found their Alpha.

Finally, I made out their leader. It was him — clothes tattered and gray hair blowing in the wind. He marched in front of them. A god. Remo. My grandfather. The last Master of Sinanju.

I quickly scaled the wall of a building like a spider as I made my way to the top of the tallest building. I took a deep breath then dove off the roof. My arms spread out, catching the updrafts and carrying me back aloft. I made a grand entrance, swooping down out of the sky to land only yards away from Remo. He would have been impressed. If he was still himself.

The undead army came to a stop. Even the chanting stopped.

"Remo! You made it!" I cried out, hoping against hope something was left of the man who had raised me after my own father's death.

And then a voice shouted out, the roar reverberating in my skull, but Remo's lips never moved. *"I am created Shiva, the Destroyer; death, the shatterer of worlds. The dead night tiger made whole by the master of Sinanju. Who is this dog meat that dares challenge me?"*

An aura of power emanated from him. His otherworldly presence made me uneasy. I wanted to turn and run. I felt fear. I looked into his black eyes, but nothing of the Remo I knew looked back at me.

"Remo…"

Suddenly his foot stomped down, the pavement shattering beneath it. His dark alien eyes glared at me and I heard the voice echo in my head again. *Move aside or prepare to die like a dog!*

I took a deep breath, trying to calm myself and find my center. Then I challenged a god.

"No."

Shiva again roared in anger, and I felt a pulse go out from him that sent up a cloud of dust and made the fragments of broken concrete at his feet go flying through the air. The undead behind him suddenly snapped to attention, all of them turning to look at me.

"Remo — grandfather— I know you're in there. We need you. I need you. Please come back."

Shiva moved with the speed of thought — a whirlwind of flailing arms that would have decimated an army. But I wasn't an army. I was much quicker than that. It was like dodging machine gun fire, but I managed to do it.

I fought back — a powerful kick that should have smashed into Shiva's head. Instead it smashed into Remo's thick wrist, the force reverberating down my leg. Before I could react, he grabbed my leg and flung me across the street.

I struck hard against a building. The wall collapsed as if it had been smashed with a wrecking ball. If I had not managed to turn in time the impact would have crippled me.

I stood up, took another deep breath, and hurled myself back at him. But once again, he proved to be too fast. This time I was knocked down at his feet. His undead army began to gnash their teeth and move forward, encircling me as I lay there.

I couldn't afford to lose this fight. Not only my life, but the life of Remo, Shannon and everyone else that had managed to survive so far hung in the balance. Sinanju itself was on the line.

Undead hands reached out for me, but suddenly I was a dervish — whipping around in a blur that snapped and twisted their arms. Unfortunately, this distraction wasn't a good thing when fighting a god. Shiva lashed out with his leg, a single kick to my chest. I collapsed to the ground, wracked with a burning pain that was beyond anything I had ever experienced.

I had to concentrate. Focus on my breathing. It felt as if my lungs were on fire, my ribcage crushed. My next breath could have been my last. Was this how Sinanju would end?

Shiva moved forward for the killing blow. Suddenly, I felt a calmness wash over me — a renewed strength. Shiva's arm came down with terrific force, a blow that would have shattered stone — but my arms moved up, blocking it of their own accord.

I stood, taking a deep breath that swelled my chest — my ribs snapping back into place and mending faster than even Sinanju was capable of. I felt more powerful than ever before. A voice spoke from me, but it was not my own.

"I am Wang, Master of Sinanju!" the voice cried out from the deep.

I did not know from where my new strength or the voice originated. It came from a place beyond my knowledge.

Shiva was not impressed. He waved his arms and his army of walking death lurched forward, tightening their circle around me.

"You will not impede me. All that stand in my way will be destroyed!"

Undead hands reached out to grab me, but my body reacted in a blur, striking out at the undead, knocking them apart with furious attacks that sent gore flying in all directions. But the hordes were seemingly endless — a dozen would fall, only to be replaced by two dozen more.

Then, from the corner of my eye, I noticed a glow. Then another, and another. Ghostly glowing figures started to appear from nowhere. And they were fighting the zombies.

Even as my own body fought, I recognized them from my studies of the Sacred Scrolls. Master Hwa! Master Nonja! Master Ti-Sung!

Fighting by my side were the spirits of the Ascended Masters! They kept appearing, one after another, more and more, until they numbered a hundred or more. They surged forward and the zombie army fell back, unsure of what to do as undead limbs and heads were sent flying in a cloud of blood and gore.

Though they were spirits, somehow the ethereal limbs of the Masters struck with physical force against the undead flesh. They moved with speed and precision, weaving in and out of the massive horde of zombies. They shimmered, disappearing from one spot, then flashed back into existence in another — striking with blinding speed then vanishing again, only to reappear and strike another blow.

The street had become a battlefield in a war between the spirits of the dead and the undead soldiers of Shiva.

I saw Master Kim in his bamboo hat whirling in a circle with a force that acted like a tornado, sending zombies flying in pieces. Master Hwa, who had killed Jack the Ripper, moved with ferocity and precision. He danced through the mob, raining blows on all in his path — blows with such speed and power that they punched straight through undead bodies.

I recognized the ancient Master Yong, known for his dragon bone soup. His strikes against the chests of his attackers shattered their rib cages and sent shards of bone out like shrapnel from grenades. There was a sickening sound, rising in pitch and volume, as hundreds of dead bodies were decimated, limbs falling to the ground in piles of gore.

In a surprisingly short time it was over. The Masters had turned the tide, and Shiva stood alone in a street littered with the corpses of his once-undead army.

"You face a god, dogs! What chance do you have against me, you who are already dead?"

"This is not your time, Destroyer! This is not your world. Return whence you came!" said the voice of the Great Wang.

My body struck an aggressive pose as it prepared for battle. Then I felt a cool breeze as a glow enveloped me. The glow began to build, brighter and brighter.

The Masters were possessing me now — flowing into me. All of them. My body felt as if it would burst apart. The raw power of the Sun Source, of a hundred generations of Masters, flowed through me. Then I sensed someone familiar. Another voice spoke through me.

"Remo! Fight against it! You wrinkled old pale piece of a pig's ear! You are a Master! You are embarrassing me!"

It was Master Chiun, Remo's Master. The longest-lived Master in all the history of the House of Sinanju. His power was added now to my own. My hands glowed with spirit energy, the chi of the Masters inside me. I felt electrified. I had the power to defeat anyone or anything — even a god.

"This world is in its death throes — now is my time! This world will shatter at my hands! I am the Destroyer!"

My body rose from the ground and hurled itself forward. Everything seemed to be moving in slow motion but I knew that Shiva and I were both moving at superhuman speeds.

My strikes were many, but Shiva's arms moved to block them all. I could see how Shiva appeared to have multiple arms as they blurred back and forth blocking my blows. The air echoed with the sound of thunder as our blows broke the sound barrier. Windows in the surrounding buildings shattered, raining down glass.

Shiva delivered a blow that knocked me back. I tumbled several hundred feet before I came to a stop. A trench of broken pavement marked my trail.

I swept up an SUV that was parked near where I landed and hurled it at Shiva. It exploded on impact, but he shrugged it off as he walked out of the flaming wreckage, his hair and clothes smoldering.

Shiva walked down the ruined street towards me, picking up cars and hurling them as he walked. I was able to dodge the cars, but the street became so pitted with craters that gas lines ruptured. The gas hung in the air only momentarily, then ignited, spewing flames and giving the nightmarish scene an even more hellish look.

The fight was the stuff of legends. Two Titans engaged in combat that toppled buildings. This was an unstoppable force against an immovable object, the impact of the blows echoing down the decimated streets.

"Shiva, listen to us! Your hour has not yet come! This is not how mankind ends! This is not how Sinanju ends!" the voice of the combined Masters echoed.

Shiva paused.

"Remo, reach out with your senses and you will see what we know to be true," Chiun called out. "You must get back to the village. They yet live! There is still a chance for this world!"

Shiva wavered.

"You must complete Jack's training — the House of Sinanju must endure!"

I could see something change in Remo's eyes. They began to look less alien, as if there was a hint of him peering out.

"Perhaps it is not the time for the Destroyer. I will allow you what little time this world has left before I return for the final destruction."

And with that, Remo's eyes rolled back and he collapsed to the ground.

I raced to his side, but he wasn't breathing. I felt my hand reach out and press against his chest. A single thrust of my palm and his chest decompressed, then he sat up inhaling deeply. The life had returned to his eyes.

"Your elbow was bent," Remo grinned, cuffing me on the side of the head.

The spirits of the Masters began to slip out of me, one by one. Master Sun, Master Kang, Master Yong and the Fly. They each stepped out of me and stood side-by-side, all facing Remo. Finally, out stepped Chiun.

"Little Father," said Remo.

I could have sworn I saw a tear welling in his eye.

"You pale thing! Sinanju was almost lost to the sands of time on your watch! Don't you think I will ever let your forget this!"

Finally the last of the Masters stepped out of me, the Great Wang. Once again in control, I turned to face them all. They bowed in unison, then they glowed brighter and dissipated as quickly as they had arrived.

Once again, Remo and I were alone in the wasteland.

"Let's go see that girl," Remo said as he put his hand on my shoulder. "I won't be around forever, and you're going to need a good woman one day."

* * *

We made our way back to the building where I had left Shannon. I hoped nothing had happened to her while I was gone. I reached the room, but she was nowhere to be seen.

Suddenly, I was hit in the head. My thoughts had so consumed me that I had failed to react to the projectile that flew through the air. As it came to rest on the ground, I recognized the object. It was the can of potted meat.

"Sorry!" Shannon cried out.

"What did you do that for?" I said, rubbing my head.

"I thought it was someone else," she said shyly. "I thought you were dead."

"You thought he was dead? Well, you don't know Jack Smith," Remo winked.

I exaggerated rubbing my head where the can had struck me.

"Your can dented my head!"

"Your head dented my can!"

"Enough with the squabbling. I'm famished," Remo exclaimed. "Let's see if we can find a duck to go with this rice."

ABOUT THE AUTHOR:

Glenn Porzig is best known as the creator of the comic book character Ace of Diamonds. Glenn grew up reading comics, pulp novels, and watching too much TV. He lives in Indiana with his wife, Carly, and a menagerie of both furry and scaly pets. He has worked over twenty years in the television industry and currently, literally, has his head in the clouds as a videographer on a TV news helicopter. He first became a fan of the Destroyer after seeing "Remo Williams: The Adventure Begins" and has eagerly awaited a remake. This is Glenn's first short story and it has inspired him to write more. You can learn more about his writing projects at DarknessUnbound.com.

SIGNATURE

Bruce James Rae

WHEN ROLLO BURNS signed the contract, he had not realised that he had signed his own death warrant. Now, with his back against the steel wall of a chain-link fence, the 'waiver of liability' clause loomed large in his mind. The muscular fighter facing him inside the fenced arena loomed indomitably larger. A rock-hard fist pounded into Rollo's body and rattled the fencing. Powerful blows continued to strike him with a vicious intensity that was impossible to deflect. A head strike narrowed his vision and he wobbled as his balance was thrown off.

The eldest son of the Burns family, famed for their Brazilian jiu-jitsu techniques, Rollo had thought he was the better of any man in a fight. He had not doubted the superiority of his skills when he had challenged his current foe. However, once the challenge had been accepted and the fight had begun, doubt had crept into Rollo's mind.

In order to defeat a man, Rollo Burns would grapple his foe, secure a hold, and force a submission. But today, he could not break the other man's defences. When he tried to circle behind him, his foe was easily able to spin away. When he approached head on, the other man pounded him with mighty blows from massive fists. His opponent struck with a prizefighter's precision, with thickly muscled arms and shoulders. When Rollo tried to grab his arms, he couldn't gain any leverage before another punch or kick broke his grip and drove him back again.

Rollo could not hear the roar of noise from the other side of the fence. All his focus was on the six-and-a half-foot tower of muscles that stood over him. With a desperate kick, he drove the heel of his foot against one of the behemoth's knees. His opponent winced slightly and then smiled, knowing that Rollo had nothing left.

Rollo clawed his fingers into the chain link fence and pulled himself backwards, only to back into another similar wall. In the corner, he shook

206

his head as his foe stood there smiling. Unclenching one of his meaty fists, the smiling man centered his stance and waved the hand as if it were a knife blade. The roaring noise from outside the fence resolved into a cheer as the crowd of spectators recognised that the finishing move was imminent.

The smiling man acknowledged the crowd's applause, but his pale blue eyes stared resolutely at Rollo Burns. With a swiftness that belied the big man's size, he darted forward and slashed with the knife hand in a precise stroke to Rollo's left shoulder. *Po-Pop!* The bone broke within the socket and Rollo was overcome by excruciating pain as he felt muscles separating from bone.

His foe danced in again and drew him into a crushing bear hug. All around the multi-sided ring, the audience cheered their appreciation for the victor. Rollo would have tried to tap out to signal his concession, but the broken arm and the unforgiving agony prevented him from doing so. As his life was crushed out of him, Rollo's last thoughts were not of how ill-advised it had been to sign the waivers for the mixed martial arts fight. Instead, he thought how death would bring a blissful end to the pain.

* * *

His name was Remo and he had a hundred more important things to do. He couldn't get around to doing any of them if he was always being summoned at the whim of Harold W. Smith.

"Smitty, what's so important that you had to drag Chiun and me into your office on a Sunday morning? I was planning to take up windsurfing today."

"What Remo is trying to say in his uncouth manner, O Emperor," said Chiun, "is what a pleasure it is to see you this fine morning. How may we be of service?"

"Oh, stuff it up your jumper, Little Father," said Remo. "He knows what I mean. What's up?"

"Well, Remo, you and Master Chiun have always wanted me to contact you if I discovered any information relevant to Sinanju. As you know, CURE's supercomputers are programmed to flag any information that may signal a threat to America. One of the filters in place registers if any action by you or Chiun becomes public knowledge. If your activities should ever be recognised, then CURE would have to be dismantled to hide our existence."

"Yeah, yeah. It would be a tragedy if we rubbed out a mob boss or a terrorist without due process. The world might discover that America isn't soft on crime and might not like us anymore. I know the story. We gotta have deniability. What does this have to do with Sinanju?"

"If I can continue?" asked Smith, sitting erectly behind his desk. "The computers are programmed to recognize the signatures of Sinanju technique to make sure that there is no link back to CURE. Any news detailing feats of superhuman strength gets flagged. Likewise, autopsy reports are scanned for any references to injuries attributed to heavy machinery and so forth."

"Ah, I understand what you are saying, Emperor Smith," said Chiun. "You wish us to slay your enemies by more subtle means."

"That would be preferable," agreed Smith. "However, that wasn't my point."

"I think Smitty is trying to say someone got croaked by what might have been a pneumatic sledgehammer and it wasn't us," said Remo.

"Of course it wasn't us. Tools, especially a diseased hammer, are beneath us. A true assassin needs only the tools of his own body," said Chiun, withdrawing his hands from the sleeves of his kimono and brandishing his knifelike fingernails.

"Remo is correct, Master Chiun. There has been a suspicious death, but although one of the injuries sustained by the victim was generated by a phenomenal application of force, the event was captured on pay-per-view television and, needless to say, the blow was not struck by either one of you."

"Again, I say, of course it wasn't us. We don't do television. We are assassins, not entertainers. Unless, of course, there was a guest spot for a certain dignified Korean assassin on one of the beautiful television dramas I enjoyed in years gone by. Sadly, television is now submerged in sex and ugliness and all those horrible unreality shows," Chiun said wistfully.

"So, what you're saying is that on the basis of one injury occurring in a boxing match, you think there's someone out there who can do what we do?" asked Remo.

"Not at all, there is more. Also, it wasn't a boxing match," said Smith.

"Don't tell me it was professional wrestling," Remo groaned, rolling his eyes.

"Not quite. This event was a mixed martial arts fight, where real fighting took place," said Smith. "A fighter died in the ring. I normally would not have noticed anything untoward, but the autopsy noted that one injury was caused by a force greater than is possible for human hands. I investigated further and found links to other similar injuries. The killer is a mixed martial arts fighter by the name of Lester 'Brick' Mourner. He was a notable wrestling talent before he broke into professional fighting, but had an unremarkable record in his early fights. In the past year, he has been on a winning streak, and is being touted as the next world heavyweight contender. After he killed Rollo Burns, he is under suspension, but I expect he will be cleared in time to compete at the next pay-per-view event."

"So a guy gets killed in the ring and the other guy gets away with murder?" asked Remo.

"Essentially, yes. Both participants signed waivers which indemnify their opponent or the sponsoring organization, the UCF — Universal Championship Fighting," said Smith. "The death will almost certainly be ruled to be accidental."

"People actually want to watch this stuff?" Remo said, clearly disgusted.

"It would seem so," Smith said. "This fight has attracted a record number of views."

"So where does Sinanju come in?"

"According to the autopsy report, the wound to the shoulder did not cause death, but the shattered humerus was a perfect break along the surgical neck just below the greater tuberosity." Seeing that Remo was about to interrupt, Smith added, "In other words, the arm bone was severed at the shoulder, just below the joint. This could only have occurred if a tremendous force was applied in a very narrow band, such as if a blade were swung by an assembly-line robot. The arm, however, suffered trauma to the muscle and bone, and only minor bruising to the skin, so no blade was involved."

Smith pulled up a file with x-rays as he continued. "Looking into Lester Mourner's past, I had a hunch there might be other similar injuries which did not result in death. Sure enough, over the past year, several of his sparring partners and recent opponents have also suffered broken arms. The medical reports for the injuries show a very precise application of force which shatters the upper arm at the shoulder."

Looking at the x-rays, Remo said, "The most recent injuries are perfect blows, but the first were poorly placed and shattered the shoulder as well as the arm."

"Yes," said Smith. "The injury also matches another x-ray from a previous CURE file. The earliest injuries caused by Mr. Mourner are almost identical to the injuries that led to the death of William Ashley."

"No way, Smitty," Remo said. "Ashley was killed by Chiun's insane nephew Nuihc and his suicide goons. There is no way any of them could be involved. They're all long dead. The suicidal proxies only knew one move each and never had the skill to teach another. As for Nuihc's protégé, Jeremiah Purcell, I put him out of his misery years ago."

"But you do admit that the blows were similar. Is it not possible that Nuihc or the Dutchman might have trained another? I am concerned that some rogue Sinanju trainee might be trying to send you a message, or calling you out," said Smith.

"This is not a Sinanju message, Emperor. The treatment of an unworthy enemy requires four blows and then the miscreant is left to die in disgrace. This Brick person struck only one blow and then killed his foe. The similarity is only coincidental," said Chiun.

"It relieves me to hear that, Master Chiun. But before you dismiss the possibility entirely, I'd like you to look at the video of the fight and see Brick Mourner in action," said Smith.

The recorded video of the fight showed a large muscular man walking to the ring. At six and a half feet tall, he cut an imposing figure. A rippled stomach spread up into a broad torso covered with tattoos of a brick wall and a demon's head. The man's shoulders rose up to an immense neck and tapered to a bullet head. His hair was blond and styled in a severe crew cut. Entering the ring with a smile on his face, Brick Mourner bounced up and down, shifting his weight from foot to foot.

"His balance is excellent," noted Remo.

"Yes, and his breathing is better than most," said Chiun with appreciation.

Watching as the fight progressed, it was apparent that Brick Mourner was agile and powerful and legitimately dangerous. After Brick waved his knife hand and struck the crippling blow, Smith replayed the signature move in slow motion.

"See, Remo, how his strike is quick like a viper and does not open up his defences to counterattack," said Chiun.

"Yes, definitely unlike Nuihc's chosen lackeys, who were left vulnerable when they attacked. Mourner's blow is perfectly placed and with no bend in the elbow either," said Remo.

"Hmmm, but the technique does have a flaw. His shoulder flutters when he prepares to strike, as if he were arthritic," mused Chiun.

Smith played the scene again using frame advance and could not see a twitch in Brick's shoulder, but Remo and Chiun had evidently seen a telltale motion.

"Have no fear, Emperor Smith. We shall pay a visit to this Brick and teach him the error of his ways, so that he will kill no others. You may rest safe in your bed that no caged fighters will usurp your throne," said Chiun as the two Masters of Sinanju took their leave.

* * *

"So, what do you think, Little Father?" asked Remo. "That move was definitely Sinanju. Where could he have learned it?"

"That is what we shall find out. Someone has stolen from Sinanju. The thieves must be punished," said Chiun.

"All I know is that this Brick Mourner can't be another surprise left to us by Nuihc, since he died before this guy was even born," said Remo.

"I don't know anything of the sort. Perhaps he reaches out from the Void to try to humiliate you again. The shoulder stroke is the first of the four blows used by Sinanju custom to disgrace a foe that is unworthy of being killed. It is doubtful, though, that Nuihc would repeat a scheme that had failed before," said Chiun

"Yeah, and I don't believe in ghosts coming back to haunt us, either," said Remo.

"Why do you persist in dismissing the unknown just because you haven't encountered it yet? You're as bad as the lunatic Smith with your lack of acceptance of the supernatural. Have you not had visions of your dead mother? Have you not spoken to the past Masters in the Void in your dreams? And your encounter with the Great Wang himself? Ghosts are just as real as dragons and vampires. You should be so lucky that you haven't had to deal with one, since you haven't taken the time to learn the proper exorcism rituals yet."

"Sure, sure, if we run into a ghost, maybe then I'll take the time to learn them. Assuming, though, that this isn't a ghost we are dealing with, there are other ways that someone might have learned Sinanju technique. You sure we killed all those Russians in the Mactep unit? They were training an awful lot of commandos trying to create a Russian Master."

"You were the one keeping count, but I believe those thieves were all dispatched. In any case, they only knew a few moves, and did not have the knowledge of the Scrolls of Sinanju. Only one given proper teaching would know the significance of the blow."

"So that just leaves us with the Dutchman," said Remo resignedly. "I always wondered if he left behind an apprentice of his own. I just kind of hoped he hadn't had the time to train anyone. Heck, he was in a coma for years, locked away at Folcroft. "

"Well," said Chiun, "Nuihc only trained him for a few years, but Jeremiah Purcell still was able to learn much on his own. At one point he might even have been your equal. But, I doubt we are dealing with such an apprentice. Purcell had a troubled mind and would not have been a good teacher. Besides, you are ignoring the Brick's shoulder flutter. He is obviously in fine health and too young to be arthritic himself, so the arthritic flutter must be because he is moving exactly as his teacher is moving."

"Hey, you're right!" said Remo.

"As is to be expected," agreed Chiun.

"That means we need to be looking for an old man. Is there some ancient Master still kicking around that I don't know about? I mean, you're past the century mark yourself, but you're still a dynamo. I know the two Masters before you have already passed into the Void. Who was the Master before H'si T'ang? Could he still be around?"

"Master Ik was master before Master H'si T'ang, which you would know if you studied more diligently. His time ended when I was a young man, early in the last century. Any before him would be exceeding Master Yong for longevity," said Chiun.

"So, no ancient masters then. I give up. Who is it?" asked Remo.

"We shall find this Brick and get the answers from him," said Chiun gravely.

* * *

Lester Mourner loved the challenge of a competitive fight. As a youth, his large frame and cocky attitude got him into more than his share of schoolyard scraps. Excelling at wrestling in high school, he worked out religiously and sculpted his body into a tower of muscle. His huge torso was likened to a brick wall by classmates, who gave him the nickname 'Brick'. His fighting spirit and winning record at wrestling tournaments drew the attention of college recruiters, leading him to receive a full wrestling scholarship.

Undefeated in his college wrestling career, he won the NCAA national wrestling title. After this success, he celebrated by drinking five pitchers of beer. The next day he found himself with his now widely-recognised tattoos. The tattoo of a brick wall was in tribute to his nickname, and the demon's head personified his college's mascot. With a marketable look and his stellar amateur wresting credentials, he took up a career as a professional wrestler.

Promoted as the "Big Neck Thing" by his first wrestling manager, Brick Mourner became a huge sensation. Few pro wrestlers had his background and skill and it wasn't long before he was being pushed into elite competitions. Soon, his size, strength, and mat skills were being showcased internationally. He went on to become the world heavyweight champion for the dominant North American professional wrestling organization.

All of this success came before he was twenty-five, and yet he felt unchallenged. The gruelling schedule of matches and public appearances wore him down mentally and emotionally, but his ring matches still left him unsatisfied. Although he held the championship belt, the scripted nature of the match outcomes simply meant he was showcasing his talent as an entertainer, not as a competitor. He was just going through the motions and his wins were the result of pre-determined story lines, not physical dominance over his foes. Brick Mourner wanted to grind his opponents into submission, to assault them with his power and to feel the thrill of winning a match in which fighting prowess was the only determining factor.

In a move that shocked the wresting world, he broke his contract, forfeiting millions of dollars in guaranteed earnings, so that he could pursue a career in mixed martial arts competition. His first fight in the eight-sided ring was against a retired boxer trying to rekindle a mediocre career. Brick was exhilarated by the thrill of combat, and although it was a close contest, he was ruled the victor. The thrill of the fight and the high of winning was an incredible rush. Lester 'Brick' Mourner had found his true calling.

After that first high, Brick Mourner tumbled back down to a disturbing low. His second fight was against a jiu-jitsu specialist, and he lost in the first round after his opponent caught him in a knee lock submission hold and forced him to tap out. His next few fights were all losses. Despite his own phenomenal wrestling skill, there were others in the world of mixed martial arts who had more experience, and who were able to break Brick's defences and force him to tap out. Brick was devastated.

Brick knew that in order to win he had to develop new skills. If he could keep his opponents away and off balance, then land a strong kick or punch, he could move in and take over the fight. After training with several different martial artists in order to diversify his fighting styles, Brick came back to the UCF ring and began to win slightly more often than he lost. The wins kept feeding his adrenaline addiction, but the losses still crushed his spirit.

It wasn't until a chance meeting with an ancient Asian that Brick finally found a way to win consistently. The old man's secrets gave Brick the tools he required to defeat all his opponents. After crushing the life out of Rollo Burns, he was drunk with the feeling of invincibility, and was eager to meet new challengers.

* * *

Remo and Chiun got out of a cab in front of the UCF Arena. After Remo paid the fare, they strode up to the front gate. Overhead a huge banner read: "**One Night Only! Universal Championship Fighting Presents: The Best Of The Best Tournament.**"

"Harrumph," spouted Chiun. "Such misleading advertising! How can a tournament boast they have the best of the best when Sinanju was not invited?"

"Our invite must have gotten lost in the mail. But we're here now, Little Father. Let's see how good they are," said Remo.

Entering the facility, the pair breezed past a pair of security guards and were met by a stocky middle-aged man wearing a blazer sporting the UCF emblem. Seeing Chiun's colourful robes, he strode up to the Master of Sinanju Emeritus and bowed deeply.

"Hi, so glad to meet you! I'm Whitney Dane, President of the UCF. You must be the Japanese Broadcasting representatives. We are so excited to have you partnering with us to provide international coverage for tomorrow's event."

Chiun did not bow in return and said coldly, "I am Chiun and this pale one is Remo. I am not Japanese. I am Korean. Any cretin should be able to recognize the superiority of my features."

Dane looked closely at the robed Korean, a wizened old man of barely five feet tall, who looked to be at least a hundred years old. The parchment-like skin on his face and skull was only interrupted by two wispy tufts of yellowing hair above his ears and a fine clutch of white beard hanging from his chin. A swift breeze or a stern look would probably be enough to knock the old fellow down.

"Oh, Korean Broadcasting, eh? I didn't realize we had a new affiliate. C'mon in and let me show you around and introduce you to some of the fellows," he said as he ushered Chiun and Remo to the backstage training facility.

Behind the main stadium, they entered a large gymnasium. Inside, the room was filled with exercise mats, punching bags, weight-training equipment, and an octagonal practice fight ring. A dozen fighters and their trainers and sparring partners were working out in preparation for the tournament.

"This is going to be one spectacular pay-per-view event. Your viewers will not be disappointed. We have all the best former champions lined up to compete. We have the Clover brothers, Don 'The Beast' Elvern, Humvee Bishop, Andy Suture, Silvano Anders, even former sumo grand champion, Wade Pupule." Dane pointed out the various fighters. Shouting to the room, he said, "Hey fellows, here's some folks I'd like you to meet."

As the fighters drew near, he asked the tall skinny guest with the big wrists, "So, which network are you with in Korea?"

"We are from Sinanju," said Remo.

Misunderstanding, Dane said, "Guys, meet Chiun and Remo. They are from the Korean Sinanju Network, one of our new broadcasting affiliates. They want to meet the best of the best."

"You are hardly the best. There are two who are better," said Chiun.

Misunderstanding again, Dane said, "Yes, well it was a tragic accident that took Rollo Burns' life and it will be a shame not to have him take part. But, Brick Mourner just got his suspension lifted, so he will participate. That's sure to boost the buy rate. This tournament is bound to have record viewership numbers."

"He won't help your bottom line once he's dead," said Remo.

Startled, Whitney Dane looked at Remo and saw from his brooding dark brown eyes that he was being serious.

"The one called Brick is a thief. Those who steal from Sinanju must die," stated Chiun.

"Okay, I've heard enough. I don't know who you two think you are but you're leaving now," said Dane. "Hank, Kent, escort these two out of here and don't be gentle."

The two Clover brothers reach out to grab the two troublemakers but their hands grabbed only empty air. Surprised, they took another step forward to the two men and grabbed again, but somehow they still eluded their grasp. It didn't look as if they had run away; they had just bent backwards slightly and moved to the side at the last second.

"Stop playing games. We don't gotta hurt you, but if you wanna play, we're gonna get rough," said Hank Clover.

Remo responded by stepping between Hank Clover's arms and lightly flicking him on the nose with his pinkie finger. Chiun brought a sandaled foot up to Kent Clover's chin and knocked him flat on his back.

"Ow! Dammit, you guys are dead meat. Get them!" yelled Hank.

The other fighters, save one, all surged forward to mangle the interlopers.

Seeing Wade Pupule backing away from the fracas, Whitney Dane yelled, "Hey, Pupule, get your big sumo butt back here and help take care of these bozos!"

The Hawaiian former sumo grand champion said, "I'm not getting involved, so sue me! The tall, skinny one broke my nose when I was still a *yokozuna* and in my prime. I'm not messing with that *haole* again."

The other fighters circled around Remo and Chiun, fists raised and bodies poised to attack. There was no way the skinny white dude and the skeletal Korean geezer were any threat to the best competition fighters of the UCF. They charged in, almost embarrassed at how badly those two were going to be messed up.

Andy Suture was confused. He had darted in to punch the old Korean, but as the blow connected, instead of meeting brittle bone, his fist had ploughed into a big mass of fat and muscle. In front of him, Humvee Bishop gasped and wheezed, his large girth impaled upon Suture's fist. Bishop's forward momentum had been aimed at the white guy with the big wrists but somehow he just ran past him and onto Suture's fist. Blood bubbled from his mouth as he collapsed to the floor.

Don 'The Beast' Elvern roared as he faced Remo. Some lightfooted weed of a man wasn't going to sidestep him. He thrust a clawed hand at Remo's exposed neck. Remo flexed his neck muscles before the grip could tighten and Elvern pulled his hand away in shock as all four fingers had been broken.

"Thumb's the breaks, big guy," said Remo, as he flicked his pinkie finger at the remaining digit and broke it, too.

Silvano Anders was a middleweight cage fighting champion and had recently begun to fight up a weight class to find new competition. The tiny Chiun was under one hundred pounds and obviously no challenge. Grabbing him from behind, he tried to hold the Korean as the small man just stood there watching Remo in action. Silvano attempted to lift Chiun into the air but for some reason he couldn't generate enough force to move him. Chiun bent at the waist and Silvano abruptly felt himself being upended and tossed forward over the little Korean's back.

The rest of the fighters and trainers realised that sticking around was a bad idea and joined Pupule in a stampede out the door. As they rushed out, they passed the arriving figure of Lester Mourner.

"What's going on? Are you guys getting a practice session in without me?" he asked with a smile.

"Naw, we're just warming up for the main event," answered Remo as he pinkie-flicked a fleeing fighter into unconsciousness.

"Hah, you want to fight me? Don't you know I'm the top dog around here now?" taunted Brick.

"You're a thief and a killer, and you're about to be dog meat," replied Remo.

"I don't know how you lucked out against these others," said Brick, "but I'll only need one move to make you cry for mercy."

"That move was stolen from Sinanju and if that's the only move you've got, then you are in for a world of trouble, Brickhead," said Remo.

"You'll have to get in the ring with me, then, and show me what you've got," replied Brick, relishing the prospect of a new challenge.

Remo waved the other man forward and they both walked into the eight-sided practice ring at the end of the gym. Brick smiled expectantly and hopped up and down, first on one leg, then on the other. Remo smiled back but just stood in place, rotating his wrists in time to Brick's hops.

Chiun took a seat outside the ring to watch and admonished Remo, "Remember to keep the thief alive long enough to find out his teacher."

Brick started to move toward Remo, circling around him. Remo easily countered the moves and turned in a tighter arc to keep the big man directly in front. They circled the ring several times as each gauged the prowess of the other.

Brick could tell that Remo had some skill from the way he kept his shoulders squared against his impending shoulder strike. In order to get the strike in, he would have to get an angle against the shoulder, so he threw a few jabs to try and break Remo's rhythm and force him back or to the side. None of the jabs landed as Remo kept his distance and backed up to the chain link cage walls.

Brick smiled wickedly, thinking his opponent was about to be trapped against the fencing. His right fist unclenched and he waved his knife hand, preparing to unleash his signature move. With amazing swiftness, he delivered the blow exactly as he had been taught. Instead of landing against its target, the strike bypassed Remo's shoulder and slashed at the fence. A hand's span of steel chain was severed, but Remo was untouched and back in the centre of the ring.

"That was a nice strike, Brickhead; it looked almost perfect. If I stood still for it, you might actually have wounded me."

"It was perfect. I learned it from Sensei Hanada-san. Let me get close again and I'll give you another look."

"Hanada, a Japanese?" scoffed Chiun. "You lie, thief!"

Brick moved back into his centering stance and slashed out at Remo once more. This time Remo moved inside the path of strike and slashed out with his own hand.

"Nope, definitely not perfect," said Remo. "You still have that flutter in the shoulder. On the other hand, my knife hand was perfect. And, speaking of hands…"

Lester "Brick" Mourner hadn't notice how perfectly Remo's knife hand strike had been. It had been too fast for his eyes to register. But now, as he prepared to strike again, he realised that he no longer had a chance of winning this battle. Where his hand should be was just a bloody stump of wrist. Remo's blow had sliced his hand off and he hadn't seen or felt it.

Remo wrenched Brick's left arm into a hammerlock and he pinched his left earlobe at the specific nerve cluster that would create the most pain.

"Now, tell me again who taught you that move."

"It was Hanada-san, I swear!" yelled Brick, in searing agony. "I went to him a little over a year ago and he taught me."

"He's telling the truth, Chiun," said Remo. "There's no way he'd be able to lie when he's in this much pain."

"Yes, yes, it was Hanada. He runs a Karate Korner Dojo in Rye, New York," sobbed Brick.

"Unbelievable," said Remo. "Some board-breaker knows the Sinanju technique of four blows? And right under our noses? I must have driven past that dojo a hundred times!"

"I swear that I only learned this one strike. I didn't know there were four. It was just something to give me an edge, to put me back on the winning track. Sensei Hanada said he had been saving it for someone special and that I was to be his mark on the world. I just wanted to win. This ring is my life," wailed Mourner.

"Yeah. It'll be your death, too," said Remo.

Lifting Mourner up and carrying him under one arm like a battering ram, Remo thrust Brick headfirst at the chain link fencing. Brick's body twitched for a moment and collapsed into a heap, his head still stuck in the fence. The steel chain links had been driven straight through the skull, slicing his brain and fusing into place at eye level.

* * *

Returning to Rye, New York, Remo and Chiun strode into Hanada's Karate Korner Dojo. A small class was in session with a half dozen youths practicing basic forms. They all looked up as the two Masters of Sinanju announced themselves.

"We are here for Hanada!" proclaimed Remo, the Reigning Master of Sinanju.

"All other board-breakers and belt-wearers, leave now!" commanded Chiun, the Master of Sinanju Emeritus. "Any who dares to make issue with the House of Sinanju will suffer the consequences of our wrath."

The students milled around, uncertain of what to make of the intruders. A couple of the bolder ones took a defensive stance.

From the back of the dojo, a voice yelled, "Stop! The Masters of Sinanju have come for me and I will meet with them alone."

Emerging from the back room, a white-haired Japanese man shuffled forward, his right hand leaning heavily on a cane.

"Kenji," he said addressing the instructor, "please take the students out of here right now. We are closing early today."

Kenji looked uncertainly at his sensei, but gave a deep bow and did as instructed and escorted the students out quickly, closing the door behind him.

Once they were alone, the aged Japanese man sighed deeply and sagged further atop his cane. "So, Sinanju has come to exact vengeance after all these years. I had thought you would both be dead by now."

"Speak vile cur," spat Chiun, "and say how you came to steal from Sinanju."

"I learned but one form," answered Hanada, "and I had thought it was a gift. Many years back, my dojo was filled with students and many came to learn karate from me. Amongst them was a student named William Ashley. He was a computer programmer for a nearby hospital or clinic of some sort, but he would come in almost every evening to practice his kata." Hanada took a deep breath before continuing.

"More than thirty years ago, a man came to me enquiring about him. He was a Korean, and looked much like you," he said looking at Chiun, "but younger and with a fuller face and dressed in a black business suit. His face was red and burnt looking. He said that he had suffered an accident of some sort with an oil spill. His name was Mister Winch."

Remo flinched at the name.

"Winch stayed for almost a month, observing Ashley and others. He told me that he needed three or four special students so that he could teach them a small sampling of his skills. He demonstrated to me but one of the four strikes he wished to teach those special students. He had beautiful technique. He told me that he was the Master of the House of Sinanju, and that the previous Master had sullied the House's reputation by training a white man. He was consumed with bitterness over this and planned to humiliate the young white by having his students cripple him. Upon learning his reasons, I refused to have anything further to do with him and bade him look elsewhere for disciples."

Chiun's eyes narrowed even further as Hanada continued to speak.

"A year later, Ashley vanished from sight. I learned later that he had been killed in Scotland. I assumed Winch had gotten some pupils to learn the four blows and that they had killed him. I also assumed that he had gone on to kill the past Master's new pupil. You must be he, I take it?"

Hanada asked Remo.

Remo nodded. "Yes. But how did you come to teach Brick?"

"My business has been failing for the past several years. Nowadays, few people want to learn the discipline that is instilled by karate. My classes become smaller with each passing season and I have no lasting legacy. When Lester Mourner was looking for new martial arts trainers to help him improve his fighting skills, I arranged to meet him. I told him I would teach him in karate and train him in a move so powerful that he would be able to defeat all his foes. I gave him the one Sinanju move that I had been shown. It was my hope that Mourner's success would be great, and that the world would learn that it was karate that had made him great. Then, perhaps the students would come swarming back and I might become known as the trainer of the world's greatest fighter."

Hanada straightened up and tossed his cane aside. "I know now that I was a fool to have tried to pass off Sinanju technique as my own. I know that you must kill me, and I accept my fate to die at the hands of the sublime Master of Sinanju."

Remo and Chiun shared a glance and stood together in front of the waiting karate sensei.

"Save the bravado, Hanada. You're not worth killing," said Remo.

Hanada's face fell as he realised the grim meaning of Remo's words.

Remo and Chiun struck at one arm and one leg each.

Po-Pop! Po-Pop! Po-Pop! Po-Pop!

ABOUT THE AUTHOR:

Bruce James Rae discovered the *Destroyer* series as a young teenager when he bought "Profit Motive" and "Dr. Quake" based on their covers. He became an instant fan, and eagerly devoured the rest of the series. When he isn't reading or writing, he enjoys watching pro sumo, collecting words starting with X, and playing trumpet in the Canadian Army.

THE TALE OF THE DIFFERENT TRUNK

Toni Vainionpää

THE TWO LIVING Masters of Sinanju, Chiun and Remo Williams, were staying in Chiun's home village of Sinanju. The House of Many Woods, ancient home of all Masters, had sprung a leak in its roof and centuries-old furniture and tributes had needed to be carried outside while the repairs were underway. Remo noticed one traveling chest was different from the others. It had a hole in its side.

"Hey, Chiun," Remo said. "I thought your ancestors changed these for newer models at the smallest ding. Lookie here." As if to demonstrate, he poked his finger through the hole. "Ding."

He had the barest moment to regret his discovery as Chiun started to tell the story.

* * *

Long ago, a Master of Sinanju was returning from an assignment with his belongings.

He had ten servants carrying his five large trunks.

The Master of Sinanju arrived on the edge of a battlefield, where the French and the English armies were fighting each other. He did not want to circumvent the area, so he commanded the servants to continue across the battlefield. Knowing the Master, the Servants were too frightened to refuse.

The soldiers fighting there looked with curiosity at the men traveling toward the battleground.

Soldiers on both sides were confused. Should these people be shot? Had the opposite side sent these fighters to use some secret weapon against them?

The first one to shoot at the travelers was a French soldier, hitting one of the porters. The servants, frightened of this, stopped walking. The

222

Master was greatly angered at them for the delay.

Then an Englishman shot his musket at the Master, who sidestepped the bullet. The bullet hit and became stuck in the side of one the trunks.

Now the Master was even more angered, and he grabbed from the ground a rifle of a slain soldier and threw it bayonet-first through the right eye of the offending Englishman. It traveled at such speed that no soldier could see it until it had passed through the man's skull and came to rest in the field behind him.

The disbelieving Englishmen were now certain that the Master was in the service of the French army and fired a great volley of muskets at him. The Master kept seizing the tiny pellets flying through the air and slamming them back toward the shooters with deadly accuracy and speed.

The French had stopped fighting and were now watching in awe as the Master kept felling their enemies.

To their misfortune, one of the French soldiers in the artillery failed to notice the situation from the edge of the field, and fired a great cannonball toward the Master. The Master caught the heavy ball with his hand and began hammering the French soldiers by bouncing it from their skulls like a rubber ball. The Master then launched the cannonball towards the cannon that had fired it, destroying it and all the men around it.

The Master began next picking up smaller cannonballs from the ground and hurled them towards the cannons and riflemen with lethal accuracy. He sank his fingers in yet another cannonball and used it to fell soldiers as if they were bowling pins.

On the edges of the battlefield, the generals of both armies were looking through their spyglasses in an effort to find out what was causing the battle to quiet down rapidly. They also noticed that, on the right flank of the battlefield, men from both sides had begun to flee. Both generals gave orders to shoot the running soldiers as deserters. They hoped this would stop the retreat.

On all sides of the Master dozens of soldiers lay dead by the time the generals decided to halt the battle and wave the flag of parlay.

The generals rode to meet each other on the center field. Their posturing toward each other was overbearing and theatrical but part of the etiquette.

The Englishman asked aristocratically but politely: how dare the French break the rules of combat and hire an outsider to this battle?

The French general was insulted by this accusation and called the English frauds, who needed such diversion to win an otherwise lost battle.

As the bickering continued, the angry Master walked to the generals. Soldiers of both armies moved aside before him.

With a furious voice the Master demanded to meet leaders from both sides.

Both generals were now completely confused. The man apparently belonged to neither army. The generals began carping at each other once more, demanding that the battle be discontinued and started anew. Once this interfering foreigner, with his barbarous gimmicks, was killed, they would resume their civilized war.

The Master interrupted the generals' loud argument and demanded repayment for the damaged travel trunk. The dumbfounded generals hardly believed their ears and tried to figure out if they had misheard. This stranger kept insisting he would need from them 100 gold coins as compensation for the damaging of his travel trunk and a new servant to replace the one injured. The French general laughed at the Master's demands and as a result the Master freed his head with one quick slash of hand that was too fast to be seen. Only a breeze of the hem of his kimono gave evidence of his movement.

The French General's head fell to the ground and rolled into a pile of equine excrement. The English general stared slack-jawed at what happened. After recovering his ability to speak, he quickly ordered the courier next to him to retrieve the gold that the man demanded.

The French soldiers were now unsettled and confused. Their general had died, killed in conference, by neither side but by an outside threat. They did not know if the rules of war had been broken or not.

The second-in-command in the French army took now his place in the negotiations. He had a hard time taking his eyes off the general's head protruding from the pile of horse dung. He promised one of his soldiers as a replacement for the shot servant.

Receiving the money and the new porter for his trunk, the Master continued on his way across the quiet battleground. The soldiers on both sides parted for the Master and his servants.

After the Master disappeared from sight, the generals declared a pause for the battle, and announced that they would continue after tea.

The soldiers carried the injured off the field to receive treatment, collected the cannonballs for re-use, and moved the dead off the battlefield. The generals together agreed that the now-headless general had fallen off his horse, and that no one would ever reveal the true nature of the events. They would be ridiculed everywhere if it was heard that one old Asian had managed to make the armies of the two mightiest nations in the world tremble in fear.

The fighting continued. After one hour, nothing was left but a handful of men who then killed their own generals the first chance they got.

This was the last gentleman's war, where etiquette had been more precious than human life.

The surviving soldiers kept silent of the events of that day, and so the world never learned of the Master's role in this historic battle.

The only witness of those days was the soldier who had been ordered to become the Master's porter. He married a woman from the village of Sinanju, and died in illness before his child's birth. The mother and the boy did not stay in Sinanju for long. The boy was too white and had blue eyes, and the villagers ostracized the family.

She later married a merchant, and after her death, the boy got to travel the world with him, later becoming a merchant himself.

* * *

After the story, Remo was quiet for a while. Chiun waited patiently for Remo to ask the question that every pupil before him had asked after this story. Chiun himself had asked his grandfather the question.

"So," Remo began. "A villager has been driven out of Sinanju just because he didn't look like others. Great town you got there. Real friendly."

It was the wrong question.

"This?!" Chiun sputtered in amazement. "This you cling to? The fate of a porter's son, and not the Master of Sinanju's glorious encounter with two of the mightiest armies in the world, and how he made them soil their boots?" Then, more quietly: "Why, Remo?"

"Because, little father, someday I…look, your story brought up something's that's been nagging me for a while. Maybe not consciously but I've been wondering that if…"

Chiun saw his adoptive son and heir struggle with emotions that ran deeper than Chiun had intended. "Yes, my son?" he asked gently.

"If I have kids," Remo asked, "what happens when I bring them to Sinanju? Will they be shunned like the porter's son because they aren't pure-blooded Sinanju?"

Chiun put a calming hand on his apprentice's shoulder. Remo took a minute to feel what his father was trying to convey and quieted down again. Chiun continued the story.

"The boy in question was not the Master's heir, even though his mother was related to the Great Wang. She chose to leave the village. She was not driven off. Her son would have been well-suited for lesser duties — perhaps even an assistant caretaker of this very house." Chiun's voluminous kimono sleeve indicated the House of Many Woods. Remo would have argued more but the hand in the sleeve descended like a viper and Remo found himself starring cross-eyed at the old Korean's long, pointed fingernail. "You are not yet ready for an heir."

Remo wanted to change the topic quickly. He asked Chiun "You didn't tell me why the Master didn't fix this trunk, or buy a newer one."

"The trunk is a reminder that no Master of Sinanju will ever relent when demanding compensation."

"Just say he was too hoity-toity for his own kimono," Remo said, chuckling. "And cheap. Definitely cheap."

"And you are uncivilized pale piece of pig's ear who does not understand the importance of a noble tradition. The decades it would take to explain it to you are more years than I have left."

For the rest of the afternoon Chiun sulked, and Remo, not wanting further confrontation, held his tongue. Only on the evening of that day, when the roof of the Master's house had been repaired and the furniture had been moved back in, did the father and son make peace and things returned to normal.

ABOUT THE AUTHOR:

Toni Vainionpää lives in Espoo, Finland. He is a Business College graduate, which has been of no use for his current job, driving a mobile library. He spends his free time listening to good music, watching television, and updating the computer software of his friends. When he was a teenager, his father gave him his first *Destroyer* book to get his nose out of comics and sci-fi novels, and, now more than a 25 years later, he has written his own story of the continuing adventures of Remo and Master Chiun.

MEMORIES

K.J. MacArthur

HE WAS RUNNING IN THE rainy, dim street. Ray Houston was always down on his luck, but this situation was one of the worst he had ever been in.

He was homeless and alone in Atlantic City, NJ. He thought he was on the way back into the swing of things by accepting a new job three weeks ago — making trinkets for the tourists for some slick operator that recruited him at a soup kitchen. It turned out, of course, not to be what it seemed, as the guy had a veritable slave shop going. He "hired" homeless people, illegal immigrants, and children — unforgivable, in Ray's opinion — and forced them to work 16 hours a day and sleep in the same warehouse (armed "security" saw that nobody walked away). His boss subjected them to insane quotas, charged for room and board, and abused the workers, who were too afraid of being deported or killed to call the cops.

During his third week, Ray finally had enough. During a bathroom break, he saw a rusted mesh on the first floor bathroom window. Since he was allowed five minutes alone before the armed "security" barged in, he was able to pull off the aging mesh and escape through the window, running down the alley before they could follow him. He was sure they were following him, though. Ray felt hunted.

Alone and on the run, in a T-shirt and jeans with no money, he had to get to a police station fast. There was one a few blocks away (which he knew from being arrested for vagrancy six months ago), so he started in that direction. Trying to walk normally, people still gave him a wide berth due to his disheveled appearance. He hoped that wouldn't attract too much attention. He heard tires screech and behind him he saw two of the "security" guys from the factory in a gray sedan, turning the corner. They must have seen him, so he started running again. He weaved between the people, bumping into one particular old lady who only looked at him and said, "Watch it, creep!"

"Sorry," he apologized quickly, moving forward as the sedan tried to get in the lane of traffic next to the sidewalk a block away. He had to hide, now.

While the sedan with two armed thugs in it turned around and was blocked from view by the other cars, he slipped into a bar. Ray made his way to the back, close to the rear exit, but kept his eyes on the front door.

As he sat down at a booth, a waitress with red hair approached him.

"Anything to start, mister? Or do you need a few minutes?" she said.

"I need a few minutes still, though you can bring me some water please," he said, out of breath.

The waitress went to the kitchen to get his water. As she opened the swinging door to the kitchen the increased light level showed an old payphone in the dim hall in the back, by the bathrooms. He made his way to it, aware that although he had no money, they often would take emergency calls.

He dialed 911, asked for the police, and tried to explain his situation to the person on the other end. He got out the gist of the problem and the address, but before he could give them his name, a burst of light showed him that one of the thugs in the car had entered at the front. He quickly went to the back door and out into the alley before he was seen. He only got halfway down the back alley when the other thug appeared behind him and put a pistol into his back.

"Hey, hey, you! The boss don't allow anyone leaving! You're going back to work! Don't give us any more trouble!" the thug said as the other one came bursting out the back of the bar.

"Good job, man. Hold him here while I get the car," the other one said. Ray's heart sank, but on the third floor, a curtain moved slightly.

* * *

His name was Remo, and he was sitting cross-legged on a mat in an apartment in Rye, New York. His mentor, Chiun, was sitting across from him, trying to teach him a lesson.

"Focus, Remo, I'm trying to teach you the method used by Masters of Sinanju to remember events with perfect clarity, no matter how distant in time or space. It is how you will remember the scrolls when they are not in front of you. If you persist with your attention wandering, as usual, you will never recall anything!"

"Yeah, yeah, I know, Chiun. I'm trying, okay? Give me some time to figure it out!" said Remo.

"You need more than time, heh, but maybe you are feeling what you call 'platform fright' or something. I'm going to make some rice. Try those exercises for yourself then while I am gone." Chiun said.

"It's called 'stage fright' Chiun, and I don't have it. I just need some practice, that's all. Besides, we don't need it for the scrolls. It's for remembering verbal contracts and the like, I'm sure."

"Of course. That is a side benefit of the technique, Remo. Like many things taught to you, you have no sense of relevance, you pale piece of a pig's ear! I shall return in a quarter of an hour, and see if you have made any progress. I shall not hold my breath," said the aged Korean as he stormed down the hall in his gray and black kimono. Remo smiled at the insult, knowing that he was right, although Chiun would never admit it.

Exactly fifteen minutes later, Chiun returned to the room. "Back to the lesson," he said, resuming his cross-legged lotus position on the floor mat.

Chiun's ability to remember things exactly would be useful in a pinch, Remo thought. He started over, setting his mind blank, then focusing on a metal image, proper breathing letting the image blossom in his mind like a clear flower. Failure. He tried a different memory, this time from his past. A police sergeant, a mean Irish guy by the name of Fitzpatrick once saved his life when he was a rookie. Expanding on that, he felt a revelation as he remembered it all...

* * *

The afternoon sunlight poured through the large, one-way glass of the Folcroft Sanitarium Director's office. Dr. Smith ushered Remo into his office. "Ms. Mikulka, hold all my calls, please," he said to his secretary as he walked back to his office.

"Yes, sir. Hold all calls," she said, looking at the back of the mysterious man named Remo, who seemed to come and go at will here, and who she still didn't really know after all these years. Remo and that Mr. Chiun consulted with Smith at least once a week most of the time. "Oh well," she said quietly to the closed door, "at least Mr. Chiun isn't with him. He can be so annoying."

"He sure is." Remo thought to himself, chuckling softly on the other side of the door, his Sinanju-trained ears picking up Smith's secretary's statement made in the other room. Meanwhile, Smith sat down at his large, glass-covered desk.

"Remo, there is something I need you to do in Atlantic City. An emergency call and some anonymous tips received from there indicated an illegal sweatshop in operation, but the address given was clean when the authorities showed up. Evidence that something is going on there comes from the suppliers and trucking data I've uncovered. This means you should go there, find this base of operations, expose it, and punish the owner before he decides to close up shop for good." Smith said. "The local police have been bought off and there is no alternative but CURE. Disband it."

"A short drive down the road, do some biz and drive back. Sure. I'll do it. Give me the information and the gas money, Smitty, and I'll be home by midnight," Remo said as he absentmindedly flexed his large wrists. "I have some other business there anyway."

"Just go in, do the job and get back. CURE is not in the business of enabling you to run errands." Smith said, picking up the phone, "The rental car will be gassed and ready for you in 15 minutes. You will take the route I've given you, with the least amount of tolls, and don't speed!" Smith retrieved a few sheets of paper from the printer and handed them to Remo.

"OK, Smitty. You got it," said Remo as he grabbed the paper, opened the door and walked out. He peeked his head back in the door. "I'll make sure to buckle up, too."

* * *

While heading down the road in his rental car, Remo glanced at the pieces of paper. Smitty's chief suspect was known to frequent a certain Atlantic City gentleman's club every week at this time. He would wait until the man went to the club, then follow him to the sweatshop and take care of business.

The second page had directions to the club in question, which he found easily enough and parked down the road from. It was almost time to see his suspect.

After about an hour, a dark sedan pulled into the club.

Richard Spaulding exited, a dark-haired man with a nice suit, along with one of his thugs, who opened and held the door for the man as they both entered the club. He must've been in a hurry, because the duo returned to the street after about 45 minutes or so. When they took off, Remo followed them at an appropriate distance. After 20 minutes of staying 3 cars behind, the target pulled off into a garage in an old warehouse behind the main drag. Remo stopped and parked, getting out of the car and going the rest of the way on foot.

The neighborhood had seen better days, and the buildings were in various states of decay. Three neighborhood gang members made the mistake of getting in Remo's way as he was walking towards the warehouse.

"'Sup, Holmes?" said the leader of the gang, a small, scruffy white male of dubious parentage. "Gotta donation for the neighborhood watch?" he said, trying to get in Remo's way, but mysteriously failing as Remo avoided him and walked around.

"Back off, junior. I don't have time to mess with you and your friends," said Remo, not wanting to spend any more time with the local wildlife.

"Hey! Joey, stop him!" the leader said to his friend, who immediately got in Remo's way, with the other one following suit, switchblade out.

"All I really wanted was to pass on by. Now I have to do this…" said Remo as he disarmed the two with the blades, swinging the first one into the second, breaking bones and causing them both to fall to the ground. Remo quickly went over to the leader and hoisted him up by the collar. "You going to get cute now?" he said.

"No, no, mister, I just wanna go home. No trouble please!" said the young gang member, clearly out of his league without backup.

Remo lowered him to the ground and said "Scram."

The leader instead instinctively pulled his gun, a .38 caliber revolver, which Remo clucked at.

"See? I was going to let you off easy, but no…" he said, moving faster than the eye could see as he slapped the gun out of the gang leader's hand. Remo was in a bad mood now, and quickly knocked the leader unconscious with a blow to the head

"Learn to be respectful to your elders, punk," he said as he continued walking down the street, whistling as he went, leaving three unconscious would-be muggers in his wake.

Remo walked around the warehouse that the guys went to, hiding in the shadows of the evening, looking into windows, seeing nothing move inside as he scouted the location. It was obvious that the operation was happening in the basement, so Remo silently bypassed an alarm and went in a window.

* * *

Richard Spaulding was in the prime of his life. At 37 years old, he was already a multimillionaire. All it took was a little entrepreneurial spirit. He made arrangements with the local casinos for them to buy his cheap touristy trinkets, instead of buying them from China, and soon he was earning a large, stable, and mostly legal income — so long as his workforce didn't cost him much. Luckily, homeless people and illegal immigrants didn't frequently complain about the low wages and long hours. For Spaulding, life was good — despite having to chase down that homeless guy today and pay off the local cops not to look in his basement. Taking care of the homeless malcontent was just the price of doing business.

Richard's office was at the back of his basement, and he happily sat behind his desk as the night shift started work. He looked at the force of homeless and illegals toiling away though the one-way mirror in his office. One of his men went out of the main room into the stairway to investigate something.

Remo dispatched the guard with a quick strike just as he was going up the stairs. He then boldly marched into the warehouse's main factory floor in the basement of the large building. People were working hard making little trinkets for the tourists, each touting the joys of visiting one of the main casinos in Atlantic City, New Jersey. They looked miserable and hardly took note of him until he dealt with the second guard, who approached soon after he came in the room. That one he had to disarm before cracking his skull on the cement floor.

"Department of Labor," he said loudly, "Enforcement Division. Agent Remo Black. Your boss has to answer for a complaint we received earlier today. Don't mind me," he said, working his way to the main office and the slave master within.

Richard Spaulding was frightened. He saw his two men taken out in his own factory by what he assumed was a rival operator. He checked his .45 pistol in his desk before shutting the drawer as Remo jauntily walked in.

"Hello, Mr. Spaulding, I'm Remo and I'm shutting you down, effective immediately."

"Who are you? I know you're not from the government. I'm sure we can make a deal, right?" the flustered factory boss sputtered.

"You're partly right. I'm not with the Department of Labor. But I do work for the government. Just…not a branch you're likely to have heard of," Remo stated, slowly working his way over to Spaulding's desk.

"Look, man, you have to have a price. We can make this situation a win-win for both of us, you know? What do you want?" Spaulding asked as he opened up the desk drawer, reaching for his gun.

"Yes, you're right. I have a price." Remo said.

Putting the gun back down in the drawer, Spaulding smiled and looked Remo over. "What is it?" he asked.

"What happened to that homeless guy from earlier today by the way?" Remo said.

"Him? How do you know about that? He's gone fishing, if you know what I mean. He won't be causing this operation any more trouble, if that's what you're worried about." Spaulding said, reaching for the gun again, just in case.

"Bzzzzzt, wrong answer. I was going to ask you to pay a better wage and not keep your employees as slaves, but I changed my mind. I'm going to kill your slave-driving ass and make an example of you to everyone else in your line of work."

As Remo was finishing the sentence, Spaulding pulled out the .45 and aimed it across the desk. Remo, of course, was no longer standing there.

"Peekaboo," Remo said from behind him as he drove three fingers into the man's skull, shattering it as the shock wave jellied his brain. He pulled the fingers back before they sank in and got messy. Looking around the room with his Sinanju trained senses, he quickly located the safe in a wall behind a picture of the President.

"Figures he'd be a fan," he said, as he ripped the door off the safe and exposed about $100,000 in cash and some jewelry.

Remo went through the office door and announced to the workers "All right, you've been closed down. You have forever off. Please help yourself to a bonus, courtesy of Mr. Spaulding."

Remo proceeded out of the room and up the stairs as the workers looked on incredulously. Some of them were looking at the open safe that was now in plain view.

Back in the car, Remo got out his phone and dialed "1" until the computers connected him to Smith.

"Hello, Remo," Smith intoned. "Do you have anything to report?"

"Sure do, Smitty. Mr. Spaulding has had a change of heart, so to speak. He won't be exploiting anyone ever again I assure you. It's done," Remo said, turning on the car and pulling away.

"Excellent. Teams are responding to 1035 Hoover St. sub-basement as we speak." Smith said.

"I'll be home in a couple hours. See ya, Smitty." Remo broke the connection.

"Gotta a find a pay phone," Remo said to himself.

Eventually, after finding three phones that were either removed or broken, Remo found a working pay phone and dropped in all the change he had on him. He remembered when a phone call was a dime. He called his former station and asked for John Fitzpatrick, the officer who saved his life so long ago. The young officer at the phone didn't know who he was, but luckily an older cop was listening and heard the name, taking the phone away from the patrolman.

"This is Sergeant Lassiter. Who is this please?" said the older policeman.

"Uh, you don't know me. I used to live in the neighborhood. Sergeant Fitzpatrick saved my life during a raid once. I wanted to drop by and say hello. Do you know if he's around?" Remo stammered.

"Fitz? Yeah, he used to work here, but he left about 15 years ago. He got booted from the force for being a lush and insulting the brass. Last I heard, he was drinking himself to death on Passaic Street. If you do look him up, maybe you can try to get him to rehab. He was a good cop, back in the day."

"I'll try to find him. Thanks," Remo said and hung up the phone.

Remo sulked as he headed up the highway to Newark. He could believe that old "Fitz" got fired for insulting the brass, but not for being a lush. After about an hour, he got into Newark. It was good to see the place again, though nobody left would recognize him. He headed towards Passaic Street by the river and started looking for faces. Remo parked at a garage and set out on foot. Passaic Street hadn't changed much over the years, but the buildings and the people seemed worse for wear. He saw some homeless people, none of whom looked familiar. He was about to write it off and go home when a movement caught his eye. Some gang members were hassling an old guy down an alley. The old guy was putting up a good fight, but was clearly outnumbered.

"Get away from me, you punks! I was arresting your daddies for hustling before you were born! I got nothing for you bums!" the old man said as he fended off the amused gang members.

"Forget it, old man, doesn't matter who you were. You're nothin' now, except fun for us, so give us what you got, fool!" said one of the taller of the four punks in question, pulling out his 9mm and aiming it at the old man.

"Now is that fair?" said Remo from behind the punk "I think that this guy was minding his own business, then you clowns get in his face. He was doing OK at fending you off when you pull that gun and spoil the whole balance. Well, I'm Mr. Balance. Hear me roar." Remo swiftly reached in, took both the gun and the trigger finger of the punk before he could fire, then proceeded to smash the gun, throwing both the ruined gun and the ruined finger on the ground. The lead punk was screaming as his three friends moved in and tried to kill Remo with an assortment of knives and clubs. In an instant they were reduced to screaming or inert heaps, depending on the severity of Remo's attacks as they came to him.

"See what happens? Go home, boys, and get an honest job!" Remo said as the two conscious youths got up and ran away in fear, leaving their comrades to the mercy of the night.

"Thanks, buddy," said the man, extending his hand. "John Fitzpatrick. Nice to meet you."

"I thought I recognized you, Mr. Fitzpatrick. My name is Ron...Ron Johnson. You saved me one time when you were in a raid when you were a cop. Lets go somewhere and get some coffee, okay?" Remo said, returning the handshake.

"I did, huh? That must have been a long time ago. I'll take the coffee though. There's a good place over there," Fitz said, pointing down the road. They walked to the coffee shop and left the piles of quivering flesh behind.

Remo felt sad, as he watched the man drink his coffee. "So, Mr. Fitzpatrick, what happened to you? The guy at your old station had some story I find hard to believe."

"Ah, you know, get on the wrong side of politicians and would-be politicians and eventually you get sent to the curb. I tried to find my daughter in California once, Jenny, but couldn't, so I stayed on here. I've been up and down since, currently down but not out. If you want to help, I could use a few bucks. It would help a lot," said Fitz to a befuddled Remo.

"Tell you what, I'll go make some calls and if I find her, I'll set you up with a bus ticket and a little money for a new life. How's that?" Remo offered.

"You already saved my bacon back there, kid, but if you can find my

Jenny, I'd be much obliged," he said.

Remo got up, found a quiet corner and pulled his cell out of his pocket and dialed Smith.

"Hello Remo. Why are you calling from a diner in Newark?" he said, dreading the answer.

"How do you know that? It takes time to make a trace I thought," said an exasperated Remo.

"Your phone has a GPS. I just read it and know where you are. Don't worry about it," said Smith.

"Well, I'm in Newark because of Chiun. He started doing Sinanju memory training on me, and I remembered someone who saved my life a long time ago. I thought I'd find him and see what he's up to. Don't worry. He doesn't recognize me at all."

"Remo, that is very unprofessional and dangerous," said Smith.

"Yeah, I know. I'll do penance later, okay? I need all you have on a woman in California. She was from Newark, and her maiden name was Jenny Fitzpatrick." Remo stated.

Smith tapped a few keys on his desktop display, and the relevant information appeared.

"I believe I found her. The name is now Jenny Timmerson and she lives and works in Irvine, CA. Her address is 127 Oak St. in Irvine. Anything else?" he asked.

"No, that's about it. Thanks, Smitty. I owe you one. I'll be home in a few and explain more, okay?" he said.

"Don't get caught up in any more personal business. See you when you get back," said Smith, in a lemony tone that told Remo the rest of the evening would be no fun at all.

Remo got off the phone just as Fitz was finishing some lemon meringue pie he had ordered for himself. Remo crushed the cell phone and let the pieces drop into a wastebasket.

"My contact found your daughter. She's married now, and lives at 127 Oak St. in Irvine, California. Let's take you to the bus station, pal."

"Really?" said Fitz, tearing up. "Tonight started in a bad way, but this is turning into a real humdinger of an evening!" he added, as Remo pulled a ten out of his wallet to leave for the bill and tip.

They both got into Remo's car and headed to the bus station. In the station, Remo purchased a one-way ticket to Irvine, California and wrote

Fitz's daughter's name and address on the back. While waiting for the California bus, Remo decided to take Fitz to the clothing store a couple doors down and get him some fresh duds. His current ones were definitely a few years due for dry cleaning. A few hundred dollars later, the former homeless man looked like a respectable citizen. If you didn't smell him, he would pass muster. Before the bus came, Remo decided it was best not to get involved in long goodbyes. He made sure Fitz had his ticket and a couple hundred dollars in cash, and left a grateful old man sitting on a bench. Remo got into his car and was on the road back to Folcroft and a waiting, anxious Smith.

* * *

Back at the bus station, Fitzpatrick was looking at his ticket and the cash Remo had given him. Looking at the clock on the wall, he realized that he had more than two hours for the last bus to California.

"What the hell, one for the road!" he said to himself as he got up and went into the bar next door.

Two hours and a hundred dollars later, an exceedingly drunk Fitzpatrick went into the bus station, holding it together long enough to know that his bus was there and that he should get on. He debated it and looked out the window, seeing a betting parlor down the street that he once busted back in the 80s. Using all his remaining senses, he quickly cashed in his bus ticket and headed out the door.

"You can't go back, son," he muttered apologetically as he stumbled off into the night.

* * *

Entering Smith's office, Remo sat down in one of the chairs across from the late-working Dr. Smith. Predictably, he was grilled for using CURE resources to fund personal business. After a tired Smith was done scolding him, Remo went back to his and Chiun's apartment. Chiun was, of course, awaiting him and forced him to retell the whole story.

"It is good that you stopped the foul slave master and his minions, Remo. It is sad that you made the wasted effort to help your former colleague, however; a tiger seldom changes his stripes. I fear your efforts were in vain," Chiun said.

"It's leopards, Chiun, and spots. I don't agree. I guess I have a more positive view of humanity than you," Remo replied.

"Tigers, leopards, it doesn't matter. Trust me in that I know more of humanity than you do. I hope I am wrong, but I doubt that man will ever show up at his daughter's house. Meanwhile, let us have some late dinner. I have some rice for us in the refrigerator. You may get it, unless you wish to fail yet again at getting the food," Chiun said.

"Hey! When did I ever fail at getting the food out of the fridge?" Remo asked.

"Eleven years, two months, ten days and 3 hours ago. Pathetic memory! Continue your lessons!" scolded Chiun.

ABOUT THE AUTHOR:

K.J. MacArthur lives in New Hampshire with his wife, a corgi, two cats, and some chickens his wife enjoys. He has a degree in Physics, and enjoys reading and writing fiction.

CRITICAL, NEED-TO-KNOW INFORMATION

Scott Driscoll

Chapter One

CROWS CAW LOUDLY IN THE large tree by the entrance to the industrial estate, and the sun sinks orange into the horizon. A lone hatchback idles outside a warehouse as the going-to-seed security guard double-checks the padlock and chain on the chain-link fence. He hitches his utility belt as he turns and heads back to the car. The white hatchback sinks noisily on its suspension as the guard gets settled into the driver's seat and checks his phone for messages. He checks his Flitter feed, reads a few updates on Facespace, and puts on his seat belt, ready to drive away.

Before he drives off, the guard stares at the old but neatly-presented warehouse. The freshly-painted sign declares "Templar Removals and Self-Storage" in bright red on a clean white background. The freshly-painted building walls and recently-cut grass are unusual in this neighborhood of worn-out and rusty tin buildings. He briefly considers the new and expensive lock on the gate. Remembering his low hourly wage, he quickly ceases to care.

Leaning down to the radio, he grunts as his gut presses into the steering wheel. He changes the radio station and fails to notice the black clad, masked figure that nimbly vaults the gate and disappears into the deepening shadows by the office door. The guard drives away singing loudly and completely off-key to "Cop Slayer" by Iced-T.

The lurking figure moves over to the door and quietly and efficiently picks the lock. Heading into the building, he disables the alarm system by prying open the keypad and shorting the power supply. The figure does not turn on the lights. He sits quietly for a while with his eyes closed, opening them only when he knows that his eyes will be accustomed to the gloom inside the warehouse. The racks are empty except for the occasional pallet sitting forlornly on the shelves. The floor is free of dust and the self-storage bays all sit empty, their roller doors gaping open like hungry mouths.

The figure leaves the offices and makes his way down the aisles, moving surely and with purpose. Making one final turn, he approaches a pallet sitting in the largest bay in the far corner of the warehouse. The pallet is covered with a large thick cotton sheet. Between the doorway and the pallet are several temporary bollards, and strung between them is safety tape that hangs down slightly. Each of the lengths of tape bears a hand-lettered laminated sign that says "Warning: Fragile and Treasured. Do not touch on pain of evisceration." A trapezoid with a vertical slash through it is appended right next to the sentence like a signature.

The figure pauses as if contemplating the message, darts forward and cuts through both the tape and the sign with a straight-bladed short sword, embedding the blade deep into the stone floor. An exhalation of breath that could almost be a laugh disturbs the silence.

"Heh."

Chapter Two

Hᴉs ɴᴀᴍᴇ ɪs ʀᴇᴍᴏ ᴀɴᴅ he is relaxed. Master Chiun is away seeing to a personal matter in Sinanju, and he now has an uncharacteristic bit of a lull between jobs. Without Chiun to call him a pale piece of a pig's ear for not training, Remo has taken the day off and gone to the Cineplex. He is holding a tub of unbuttered popcorn in his lap, occasionally taking deep breaths of the scent of popped corn kernels. A smile wreaths his face.

On screen, Jackie Chan is fighting a horde of martial arts warriors. Remo has had to slow down his vision so that he is not just seeing a procession of still images. Jackie is winning, but is still getting very badly hurt in the process. Remo can tell from the way that the actor moves that he has broken nearly every bone in his body at least once. It is a testament to his fortitude that he is still fighting on and bouncing back from his almost-constant injuries.

The movie ends with bloopers and outtakes shown in the credits. Remo gets up from his seat and leaves the full bucket of popcorn on the chair. He walks out and his eyes, still accustomed to the dark, are surprised by the bright sunlight.

Rotating his thick wrists absently he heads through the mall under the giant glass skylight. In the food court, he holds his breath to keep the greasy air from entering his lungs. The stares of women — and a few young men — follow his path. Remo stops. Sitting at a table in his path is a thin, elderly man — his boss, Smith. His clothes are gray, what hair remains is gray, and even his skin has a grayish quality. Smith's face is puckered in a lemony scowl as he looks up from his computer tablet.

"Remo. I found your GPS location before you turned off your phone. You should really turn it off before the movie starts." Smith indicates the seat opposite him. "I tried calling you but obviously you turned your phone off."

Remo feels in his pocket for the remains of the pulverized phone. He couldn't figure out how to silence it, so when it went off a half hour into the movie, he squeezed it until it bent in his fingers like an overripe banana.

"We have a problem. Master Chiun's storage trunks have been stolen."

Remo looks at Smith, his deep-set eyes even darker than normal. He puts both hands on the table and stands up.

"Show me," Remo barks at Smith.

*　*　*

In the warehouse, Remo approaches the sword.

"I've kept the police out of it." Smith says to Remo's back, as Remo carefully walks around the weapon. Remo leans in to look at it closely, even sniffing the handle. He reaches down and grasps the hilt.

"Hey, hang on buddy," the warehouse manager says quickly. "We're getting a crowbar to get that out. Whoever this guy was, he hammered it into the concrete pretty deep. Must've had a sledgehammer."

Remo pulls upwards with no more effort than pulling a pin out of a corkboard. The short blade comes out of the concrete with a hideous scraping sound. The manager gapes at Remo.

Etched into the blade near the hilt is a Kanji symbol. Remo recognizes it as the sign for Sasori, the warriors known as the Scorpions.

"Smith, this symbol is for the Scorpion clan of Japanese warriors. Chiun has mentioned them to me." He points at the symbol as he hands the sword to Smith, who carefully places it into an evidence bag.

Chapter Three

In THE WEST KOREAN BAY, Chiun stands unmoved by the swell in the bow of the inflatable boat as it is rowed by the SEALs back to the submarine. He smiles grimly into the wind and remembers the generations of children that had been sent home to the sea. Coming home each year to meditate and perform the remembrance ceremony on the beach has always been bittersweet for him. He is happy now that his people do not starve but sad that the past holds the horror of so many deaths.

"Your captain has my television device, yes." It is more of a statement than a question. The sailors bend their backs into the rowing, the winds pushing back against them as they make their slow headway. A trawler heads into the bay with the wind and tide at its back. Chiun sniffs the air.

"No fish today," he says, staring at the fishing vessel. The sailors look at each other and one of them reaches for his radio.

* * *

In a warehouse in San Francisco, the thief is welcomed with open arms and his illicit cargo is wheeled into place. Ninja warriors stare at the thief as he moves the cargo into the harsh glare of a spotlight. After carefully centering the pallet he turns and bows deeply to his master who has approached and is standing just outside the pool of light.

"Hideoshi, you have done well. I needed some good news today. I have not heard back from our brothers aboard the Sea Scorpion, which can only mean that they have failed." The master inclines his head to his minion.

"The Master of Sinanju will come looking for these." He waves at the trunks.

"Our research says that the child of his brother whom the Master took to train betrayed the House, and he is now dead. The current Master must be in his dotage and his powers will be waning." The Master Ninja laughs. "The Scorpion clan will be roundly lauded as those that rid the world of the scourge of Sinanju. With Sinanju no more, we shall be the greatest assassins in the world." The other warriors join in with laughter. The noise scares out some roosting pigeons.

Hideoshi joins in, but his laughter is hollow. He cringes, remembering that he spent most of the research period reading Manga, cosplaying and eating Pocky in Akhiabara, only Googling Sinanju on the last day and telling the Master that he had spent the time and money on an exhaustive quest throughout the width and breadth of the Asian continent.

Chapter Four

O<small>N THE OUTSKIRTS</small> of San Francisco's Chinatown, Remo and Smith park outside a nondescript warehouse. The windows are dusty and the gates are rusty, but there is not a single piece of graffiti on it.

Parked in a carport next to the office is the van that they had been tracking across two states.

Remo gets out of the car and stretches. He sits down on the pavement in full lotus position and prepares for battle. After running through his mental exercises he is coated in a slight sheen of sweat, all of his muscles are warmed up, and his senses are keen.

He vaults the fence in one smooth movement and is at the door. Smith doesn't even see him cross the intervening space. Remo drives his fingers at the door and it pops open, swinging wide to allow him to enter.

In the center of the warehouse Chiun's trunks sit in a pool of light. Remo, sensing a trap, scans the rest of the warehouse. He saunters over to the pile of old-world luggage. He circles the trunks looking for evidence of damage, but does not find any and breathes a silent sigh of relief. While he walks around the pile, he feels many sets of eyes on him.

"White-eyed dog, lackey of the foul Master of Sinanju, you have fallen into our trap. We have lured you here like the moth to the flame. Know that as we dispatch you, your employer will follow you soon into the afterlife. You will be a fitting appetizer for my clan as we prepare for the feast that your employer will provide. Do not worry, we will display your head to your employer before he dies." The lead Ninja brings his hand down sharply to indicate attack. Ninjas drop from the ceiling beams and advance out of the darkness, all of them bristling with weapons.

In the first three seconds Remo flicks eight shuriken out of the air, deflects three arrows, and kills six warriors with their own blades. With a seemingly careless flick of one finger, Remo decapitates another swordsman with his own weapon. The blade slices through its owner's neck and goes spinning off into the gloom.

Moving into the second rank, Remo fells the Ninjas like wheat before a thresher, smashing temples and gouging throats. He kicks in a ribcage, shatters a skull, and finally, with a knife hand thrust, severs a spine.

Remo walks over to where the leader is slumped. The broken shafts of the shattered arrows stick out of his shoulders. The redirected shuriken pepper his legs. A lone katana blade pins him mostly upright to a packing crate. Remo had been quite careful to keep any of the redirected attacks from being fatal, and, more importantly, to keep any blood and body parts away from the trunks.

"You have been trained? You are Sinanju?" The Master Ninja drools blood onto his *gi*. "How did we miss that?" The warrior dies with a quizzical look on his face.

"That's the biz, sweetheart." Remo says as he walks out to the car.

Once in the car he tells Smith what happened. The lemony-faced man dials a number to organize cleanup, and to transport the cases back to the storage facility. He makes another call and quadruples the amount of security around the storage facility.

Chapter Five

Remo MEDITATES IN HIS home, yet another eminently-interchangeable motel room. A beep breaks the silence: a text from Smith saying that Chiun is finally arriving back in the States, and that Remo should meet the Master at the naval station at Sand Point in Puget Sound.

Remo waits in the car park adjacent to the submarine berths when he sees the tiny figure of his adopted father being flanked by two Naval officers. They are carrying Chiun's single traveling trunk. Remo opens the car trunk in preparation for loading the luggage.

"See that you don't damage it." Chiun's voice floats to Remo on the cold December wind. Remo can see Chiun's wispy hair flicking about with the gusts.

"Hello, Little Father." Remo bows to his master. "I hope that your trip was useful and free of trouble." The trunk is carefully loaded into the car. The SEALs turn on their heels and head back to the submarine berth, quickly saluting to Chiun as they depart.

"Did you have a good trip?" Remo asks.

"I have an errand to run on the way home, but I will soon tell you of the great adventure I had on my way back to this dim land of clod-hopping barbarians." Chiun sniffs the air, his nose wrinkling in disgust.

"You have been eating corn again!" Chiun admonishes. Remo smiles, happy to have Chiun back with him.

"I went to the movies, but I didn't eat the popcorn," he says as they get in the car. Chiun directs their route from the back seat. Remo begins to see familiar landmarks as they near the warehouse with the stored trunks. When they arrive, Chiun has Remo carry his travel trunk into the warehouse where it joins the pile under the sheet.

"These have been moved!" Chiun shrieks, his face clouding with rage and his arms pinwheeling.

"They had a break-in. I had to make sure that nothing was missing or had been damaged," Remo says quickly, trying to mollify the raging Korean. Chiun narrows his eyes at Remo and cocks his head to one side.

"You are not being entirely truthful with me, my son." Chiun smiles and raises a warning finger. Remo relaxes slightly. "You were looking for your Feast of the Pig gift." Remo manages to look like he has been caught with his hand in the cookie jar.

"You always look for it, but I have hidden it where your dull mind will never find," Chiun cackles as he walks off.

"Come, Remo, and I will tell you of the very surprised Japanese pirate Ninja trawler that tried to attack me on the West Korea Bay. It was blown up by the underwater booms from the submarine. I look forward to adding it to the histories. I shall call it 'The story of the Pirates and the dull-witted luggage attendant.'" He sits calmly in the back seat again "Heh. Dull-witted indeed."

ABOUT THE AUTHOR:

Scott Driscoll resides in Brisbane, Australia. An accomplished improviser, actor, and emcee, Scott is a keen Costumer with an interest in Steampunk. He currently works in the Electricity Industry for the Queensland government.

Born in the first year the *Destroyer* was printed, Scott has been collecting the stories since 1989. He considers himself unworthy to write about Chiun with any degree of accuracy. He is more comfortable writing about Remo, because he knows they are both pale pieces of a pig's ear.

ON UNG

Victor Smith

CLASSICAL KOREAN POETRY, whether Tang Lyric, Hyangga, or the more recent Sijo, are but pale imitations of Ung poetry.

The extremely complex rules governing Ung structure make the Greater Ung poems almost impossible for most novices to grasp. Furthermore, because studying Ung "properly" requires the tutelage of a Master of Sinanju, it is nearly impossible to learn the form properly.

As a result, Korean poets moved away from Ung, and utilized other poetic forms for their works.

Of all Korean poetic styles, Ung works are the hardest to find. Those few researchers who have tried to seek them out have all suffered inexplicable, unfortunate accidents. As a result, there is only one surviving Ung work.

There is little hope there will be more revealed, unfortunately, as no university in the world is willing to look further.

***

There is eternity in the star shining in the night
Eternity and Constancy that **not even a mountain can approach**
The star, the sun, the morning light shining on the flower
The light, the light
The light shines,
The light **shines,**
The light shines, **the flower**
Beauty spreads its wings then there is the bee
The bee, the flower, the shining light
The bee, **the flower**, the shining light
The bee, the flower, the **shining** light
The bee, the flower, the shining **light**

A giant is born this day basking in beauty

Beauty spreads its wings then there is the bee

249

The bee, the flower, the shining light
The bee, the **flower**, the shining light
The bee, the flower, the **shining** light
The bee, the flower, the shining **light**
Unto him created the **Sun Source**
The Sun

The bee
The flower
The shining light
The eternal light
The light
The light

The light
Breathe in
Breathe out

Breathe in
Breathe out
To fullness

Breathe to fullness
Unto this day comes the creator
The star, Eternity, the sun
The Sun Source

The breath
Fullness

The bee, the flower, the shining light
The bee, the **flower**, the shining light
The bee, the flower, the **shining** light
The bee, the flower, the shining **light**
The co-creator of brilliant thought
The sun source
Radiance through sunshine
Breathe to fullness

This is the first stanza out of 18,000. With each subsequent stanza increasing in scope and complexity, the work is far too long and complex for anyone but the most dedicated scholars to study in its entirety.

This is reported to have been written over 3,000 years ago. The original also includes notes on suggested breathing patterns, which adds yet another layer of complexity to the structure.

Little is known about the creator of this work. It has been anecdotally reported that he abandoned the pursuit of poetry — selling this poem and over one hundred others in order to support his family in a time of famine. It is not known whether such 'facts' are apocryphal or not. But his works, though unknown to us, helped shape Korean thought for millennia.

That we have this Ung work, and acknowledge the greatness of its creator, stand as proof of the permanence of this art.

Currently there is only one reclusive scholar, located in New Hampshire, who has attempted to study this work.

When asked about the work, he cryptically responded: "I am of no consequence. Time is too short to understand this effort, but the brilliance shines for us all throughout the stars. Breathe in; breathe out. Breathe to fullness, and celebrate the Sun Source."

ABOUT THE AUTHOR:

Victor Smith has been a fan of the *Destroyer* series since 1974, the same time he began the study of Isshinryu karate as a hobby. Since that time he has studied many martial arts and began teaching youth Isshinryu. Still an avid reader, he continues reading the *Destroyer* series, along with many other books.

Once upon a time at University, he was a Speech Major and also studied linguistic philosophy.

During working hours he has been a Benefits Officer, Systems Analyst, Payroll Manager, Business Analyst, Senior Quality Assurance Specialist, and many other positions. At the same time he never veered from reading the *Destroyer* series, nor did he stop his practice of the Martial Arts. He is currently an 8th degree black belt in Isshinryu.

Along the way he began to dabble in fan fiction with short stories. As time passed, they became longer, eventually becoming novel-length stories. His martial hobbies also continued, as well as his teaching the young for free.

Now, 40 years later, he still finds time to read the earlier *Destroyer* novels. He still writes fan fiction. Taking the time to learn how to write has made him appreciate all the authors of the series even more.

Currently disabled, he still takes the time to assist teaching the youth at the Derry Boys and Girls Club.

HOMELAND INSECURITY

Fred Pomeroy

Chapter One

DENNIS FATEL WAS going to be famous. He just knew it. It was his destiny. If he had to help it along, that was just an expression of free will.

Fifteen years in a private security firm that provided physical security for both locations and people gave him the background needed for a middle management position in the newly-created Department of Homeland Security. A few years later he was promoted to a position where he could oversee operations for the southeast portion of the country.

It was there that he got the idea to help fate and destiny along. In his mind, fate and destiny were two different things: Fate was the bad stuff that happened to others. Destiny was the good stuff that happened to him.

The fate that caught his attention was the exposure and closing down of various domestic terrorist groups that wanted to overthrow the US government. The destiny was how his heroism in accomplishing this would lead to a major promotion.

His position allowed him access to information on several groups. It also allowed access to classified studies showing that the groups were not a major threat because of their small size and lack of leadership necessary to focus their efforts on their stated goals.

Fatel reasoned that if they banded together under one effective leader, they would indeed be a threat worth taking action against. And if he coordinated that action, his worth to the Department would immediately be recognized.

The problem would be how to get them organized, while still being able to control their actions. To Fatel, the answer was obvious: organize

252

them himself. As the mastermind behind the domestic terrorists, he was in a perfect position to be able to block their moves.

He asked for reports on small groups that posed no threat. To his delight, there were dozens of these groups.

Agents were assigned to infiltrate the groups. The agents were only told that they were to keep an eye on the groups and report back to him on their activities.

Over time their role changed as he had them assume positions of more authority. Some questioned their expanded role, saying it weakened the government's position in the event they ever went to court. A government agent in a position of authority was a form of entrapment that could totally undermine the case against the organization. Fatel quietly replaced these men.

As more groups fell under his leadership, he had them do little to change their profile as harmless. He wanted their activities to draw no attention until he was ready to move as the hero of Homeland Security.

To keep everyone in Homeland Security in the dark as well, he had his agents report through routine channels. Routine reports via routine channels were often ignored.

He handpicked the agents that ended up in the field undercover. Competent enough to keep up appearances, but pliable enough that he could direct their actions.

What was surprising was how thorough their reports were. The reports were consistently more informative than he had expected.

But what could have caused their instant competence?

Chapter Two

His name was Harold W. Smith, the first — and only — director of CURE, and he was looking over a report from a member of one of the many fringe groups that felt that American freedoms were being undermined by the American government. The member was reporting to what he thought was the national headquarters of Homeland Security. It did, in fact, go there, but the report also went to a private sanitarium in Rye, New York. The national headquarters did not know that.

The database showed that an agent had been assigned the name for use while infiltrating a domestic terrorist group. Smith was surprised, since the group was too small for DHS to waste manpower on and lacked any members with any expertise in terrorism.

Intrigued, Smith set up a flag on any reports submitted by the aliases to offices in DHS.

Two days later Smith looked over a report destined for an office in Homeland Security. The report was rather disjointed and mentioned 'according to your orders' a couple of times.

A quick search of the Homeland Security database revealed that the agent operating under the alias had received mediocre job reviews in the past. Why he was chosen to infiltrate a domestic terrorist group was unfathomable. Further review showed that he had not even received the basic training for such a mission.

Confusing the issue yet more, the group was not even on the DHS's "watch list." The group's 'purpose' was nothing sinister, just crazy: to prepare for an invasion of aliens from outer space. They got together for drinks and discussion of the latest UFO sightings to determine which might be the vanguard of an invasion force.

Other groups were less benign. Even so, some would probably be cautioned into being less open about violence if they knew the government was watching. Smith picked up the phone to have Remo put in an appearance at one group's next meeting. No violence necessary, just to warn them that they would be suspects if anything happened.

Chapter Three

R<small>EMO SLOWED AS</small> he approached the turn off. If he had not been told it was there, he would have passed it without notice. It looked like an overgrown driveway or a seldom-used logging road.

Far enough up the driveway to be invisible from the road was a space used as a parking lot that was nearly filled with cars. From the lot ran a well-trodden path.

At the beginning of the path was a thin man wearing overalls, a plaid jacket, and hiking boots, holding a shotgun and listening to a transistor radio. He was sitting on the trunk of an old car, its age visible from the faded paint.

He waited long enough for Remo and Chiun to open the doors of their rented car and said "Can I help you?"

"Yes. Maybe. I am Remo Brown, and I am looking for the meeting place for The Sons of John Brown."

"You expect to find them here?"

"I was told this was where they meet."

"Told by whom?"

"My uncle. As a direct descendant of John Brown, he is the leader at the national level. Who told him, I don't care. Is this the meeting place or not?"

The man eyed Chiun suspiciously. "He is no kin of John Brown. What's he doing here?"

"You are no relation, either. I know the whole family and you're not in it. How do I know you are not a spy set to let the government agents in?"

The change of subject worked. The man worried too much about the accusation and forgot about Chiun.

"I may not be family in blood, but I share his beliefs just like everyone else here at the meeting."

"Thanks," Remo said, "for telling me that the meeting is here."

The small radio on the trunk of the car blared out a country song.

His kissing someone else
Doesn't bother me even a little
I know he'll come back
When I put bits in his kibble

255

"That's not Madam Googoo, is it?"

"Of course not." Chiun and the man spoke together as if rehearsed.

The man looked at Chiun. "At least he knows his music."

"One need not be an expert to recognize that the screeching voice does not have the soul of Madam Googoo in it."

The man laughed. "Screeching or not, she's making a lot of money."

Remo listened for a few more seconds. "It sounds like she likes her dog more than her boyfriend."

"Yep," the man agreed. "She's a feisty one. I'd like to show her a real man and change her mind. You've heard how a dog is a man's best friend?" Without waiting for an answer he continued. "Put a woman and a dog in the trunk of a car and come back in a couple of hours and see which one is happy to see you." The man laughed at his own joke.

"Sounds like a good idea," Remo said.

Pulling the man off the trunk with his right hand, he popped open the trunk of the car with his left.

Remo spun the man around to face the car and slapped the back of the man's head.

"Ow!" The man dropped the shotgun he was holding, automatically raising his hands and ducking his head down.

"Thank you for your cooperation," said Remo and pushed the man into the trunk. Being an older car, it had a large trunk, and the man fit with room to spare.

"Are you not worried he will escape?" Chiun asked.

"Nope," said Remo. "Only the newer cars have an internal release in the trunk. Older cars like this one only unlock from the outside. He will be there until someone lets him out."

As they walked up the path towards the meeting, Remo said, "Smitty said they will probably be armed. Let's separate before we talk to them. I'll take the path, you circle through the woods."

"Why must I take the route with uneven places to tread and no markings to guide my way?"

"Fine, I'll take the roundabout way. You take the path."

"You would set me up to be ambushed by the unmerciful guard that lies in wait for the unwary?"

"You are hardly unwary. Which would you prefer?"

"That is what you should have asked to begin with. Not give orders like Hannibal crossing the Alps. I will go through the woods. They are peaceful this time of year."

"You would let your son be ambushed?" Remo asked. He tried to make his voice sound hurt.

"No son of mine would allow such an ambush to succeed. Therefore there is no need for me to worry." Chiun walked off, a pink kimono with scarlet landscape woven into it disappearing into the trees. Chiun had chosen it because of the terrain. He said the landscape design would be the best camouflage for blending into the forest.

Remo continued along the path, making less noise than the chipmunks running in the trees overhead. Less noise than the guard as he slumped to the ground without seeing the hand that had rendered him unconscious.

Remo did not need the path to locate the group of twenty plus men. Their voices carried through the woods. Remo knew that Chiun would have no trouble finding the meeting place.

As he entered the clearing, the discussion of the latest of Congress' idiocies died to a whisper.

"Who are you?" The questioner was standing near the middle of one side of an oval of men. His position gave the appearance of being a leader.

"Remo Brown from the National Organization of the Sons of John Brown. I hear you guys are besmirching the good name of my great-great-great-grandfather by completely misrepresenting what he stood for." Remo moved to the center of the oval.

The questioner stood straighter. "We stand for the same things he did. He was opposed to the federal government and we feel the same. It should be eliminated as a blight on the land."

"Blight?"

"Yes. Name one thing the federal government has done for us."

"You mean besides winning two world wars so you don't have to speak German? Or are you talking sponsoring the research for the elimination of polio and smallpox so you can live longer? Or do you mean putting a man on the moon? Or do you mean paving the highway you drove to the meeting on?"

"I said one. A man shouldn't have to have his privates fondled just because he wants to go somewhere on a plane."

"When was the last time you were on a plane?" Remo countered.

"That's beside the point," the man said dismissively. "The point is that the government is sticking its nose into everybody's business and it shouldn't."

"So how are you going to stop it? Shooting everyone in Congress?"

"Probably not," the man admitted. "But it would be a good starting point."

"See, that is where the education system has gone wrong. John Brown was not anti-federal government."

"Sure he was," the man interrupted. "He attacked a military fort at Harper's Ferry, didn't he?"

"It was an armory, not a fort. But he did not attack because he was anti-government or even anti-military. He was anti-slavery. He didn't want to end the government; he wanted to end slavery. He wanted the slaves to revolt. To do that they needed guns. Where to get them? From the military. How to get them? Raid the armory. He failed because he expected the slaves to rise up against their masters and they didn't."

To a man they looked like Remo was speaking a foreign language.

"But the government executed him, right?" one offered.

"Yes. For attacking a government installation and killing federal soldiers."

"Attacking a government installation shows he was anti-government, right?"

"No, it was just collateral damage."

"Big words. You from the government?"

Thinking of his job with CURE and how he was to let them know they were being watched, Remo automatically answered "Sort of," and immediately knew it was the wrong answer.

Two rifles were leveled at him and several others were reached for.

"Killing a government agent is not your best option." Remo was bluffing. He was not in any government database. Not even the IRS. The most recent record of him was a death listing from a couple of decades back.

"We'll take our chances. Get him!"

Two shots rang out. The short distance meant that the bullets went right through the space Remo occupied a split second earlier.

"You're going to need more firepower than that to bring down the government," Remo taunted.

Remo didn't pretend to understand why you would bring a gun to a meeting of people you were friends with, but these conspirators did not think like him. Every one of them had at least one firearm, ranging from rifle to shotgun to pistol. Some had two. All were pointing something at him.

Chiun had taught him a series of moves to avoid getting shot within a group of shooters called The Scarlet Ribbon, but that was for use when ambushed. Since this wasn't an ambush, Remo improvised.

Remo moved to one end of the oval and stopped, reversed, ducked, spun, and jumped as he moved toward the other end. The results were the same as The Scarlet Ribbon. The men accidentally shot each other. Remo moved up to the last shooter, who had stopped shooting in disbelief.

"Who are you?" he asked.

Remo couldn't think of anything memorable or poetic, so he replied simply. "A government agent trying to earn an honest day's pay."

Remo had a minor quandary. He wasn't supposed to kill anyone and the guy wasn't shooting at him. Since he wasn't supposed to kill anyone, any death he inflicted would be considered a freebie by Chiun. That was a no-no. On the other hand, Smith would go nuts if Remo left a witness that might be able to identify him. Remo could only think of one solution.

Since only the memories of the past few minutes needed to be erased, the Empty Basin technique of making someone forget part of their past only took a few seconds. By the time the man regained consciousness, Remo and Chiun would be long gone. He would have no idea why he was surrounded by dead bodies.

As they walked the path to the parking spot, Chiun spoke. "This reminds me of King Arthur. Sinanju was hired to kill Arthur by the harlot Guinevere who wanted Lancelot for herself. Lancelot hired Sinanju to kill Mordred to impress Arthur. Arthur and Mordred tried to defy fate by declaring a truce so they could both be protected. When the Master of Sinanju appeared between them, their armies killed each other trying to kill the Master. Both Arthur and Mordred died and Sinanju got paid twice, once by Lancelot and once by Guinevere. A very twisted family that was too full of themselves to rule effectively."

"How do you get from this to King Arthur?" Remo asked. "The stories aren't even close."

"The clearing in the woods matches the description in the scrolls."

"The clearing wasn't big enough for one army, let alone two."

"English armies were very small in those days, but they have always been good story tellers — unless you are looking for the truth."

Chapter Four

Dennis Fatel looked at the report in disbelief. Almost the entire group of the Descendants of John Brown killed each other with the last having no idea where he was or how he got there. The only other survivors were the meeting guards.

The unconscious guard saw and heard nothing.

The other survivor was found locked inside the trunk of his car. He claimed an outsider from the national organization had shown up and locked him inside the trunk. He had an old Chinaman with him who was wearing a bright pink skirt and blouse and was a music expert. Obviously the time in the car's trunk had addled his mind to the point that he could not be used as a witness.

What had happened? Fatel knew that someone had infiltrated their secret meeting. Obviously the secret meeting wasn't a secret. He could vouch for his agent because of the thoroughness of his background check.

One member of the group had to have tipped off the national organization. But why would the national organization care if a local chapter had a meeting? Even if they wanted to show up, why kill everyone? He put the national organization down as 'not likely' to be a suspect.

Rival organization? As far as Fatel knew, there were no rival organizations.

A law enforcement agency? The local constable was a member. Unlikely he would tip off any other agency.

When all else was eliminated, Fatel was left with an unknown organization. But what was their purpose?

Fatel wasn't sure which side of the law the unknown organization was on, but he was immediately concerned that other groups were compromised. He would have to advance the schedule to catch the unknown group by surprise.

Fatel sent two messages. One went to the embedded agents with instructions to start, and a date to begin operations. The other went to law enforcement agencies with notification of various groups' anticipated actions and how to confound their objectives.

Fatel's unknown organization, CURE, received both messages.

Smith compared the messages side by side on his monitor and noted that both messages were from the same computer. A quick check identified Edward Fatel in Homeland Security as the sender.

With a mental note to deal with Fatel later, Smith focused on the agents that received Fatel's message. Choosing the one closest to Remo, Smith sent a message under Fatel's name ordering an immediate meeting of his group. Smith then called Remo and sent him to the meeting with the name of the undercover agent and orders not to kill. Smith could only hope Remo could get away with it. He seemed to do a lot of self-defense killing even when he was only supposed to talk.

Chapter Five

Remo and chiun arrived at the address provided by Smith. Chiun had insisted on coming along because the group's stated purpose had to do with children and their physical well-being. Specifically, the group wanted to be able to build playgrounds without the government telling them what type of structures to build. Regardless of whether or not the regulations made sense, they wanted no involvement from government.

Armed only with the informant's name, Remo and Chiun walked in the door without knocking to encounter a group of blank stares. Finally, one of the men asked, "May I help you?"

"Probably not, but I can help you. Is there a Ralph Arbiter here?"

One of the men raised his hand. "Do I know you?"

"Not only do you not know me, you will probably wish I didn't exist." To the others Remo said, "Ralph here is a government agent from the Department of Homeland Security."

Remo only paused for a couple of seconds for the loud whispers to die down and the questioning looks to return to him before continuing.

"He is not on the government payroll under that name. You can check for 'Arthur Beaforn' to find him. He was sent as a plant to infiltrate your group and urge you to take action against the government."

"Why do you think this?" asked one of the men.

"My boss has been investigating his boss, and it is about to hit the fan."

"What agency are you with?" asked Arthur, aka Ralph.

"An agency that really *is* concerned with America's security, not a political pork barrel that is more concerned with the next election." Then, directing his speech to the group, he said, "Arthur is believed to have been coerced by his boss and is not believed to be at fault for anything criminal."

Arthur looked outraged. "But — "

Remo interrupted him. "Leave and you may still have a career. Report this meeting and you will be charged with abetting your boss. I hope you like him enough to share a cell with him."

Arthur sat for a few moments looking at Remo, then looked at the pairs of eyes looking at him from around the room. As he stood up, he said, "The agency really does want to protect the country."

"The agency may, but individuals in the agency don't care that they are destroying America in the name of security. Your boss is coordinating the actions of both anti-American groups and the police."

"We aren't anti-American. We just want to have fewer government regulations that deal with our private lives," said the same man who had spoken before. Remo noted to himself that the man was probably the leader of the group.

Remo looked around the room at the men. "We know you are a nonviolent group, which is why we sent out the message to have the meeting."

Arthur sounded surprised, "You sent the message?"

"That should be even more evidence that I am legitimate."

As Arthur headed for the door he said, "My boss isn't going to like this."

"Unless you tell him, he won't know until he is arrested by the FBI. If you do tell him, you will be arrested soon after. He won't be able to help you much once he is convicted. Just sit tight until he is arrested, then go back to your regular office."

Arthur, his cover blown, closed the door quietly behind him.

The others in the room turned expectantly toward Remo.

Remo addressed the man who had seemed to be in charge, "Our information was that you were to have a protest this weekend. Correct?"

"Well, yes, but it is supposed to be peaceful and legal."

"The police don't know that. Arthur's boss gave them information that the protest was going to turn violent so they will be ready for the worst. With tensions high on their side, your side will get tense and eventually something will break loose. Meanwhile, Arthur was advised to move away the day before the protest so his cover would not be blown."

"But we never cause any problems," the man protested.

"Exactly. That's why I am advising you to drop the protest entirely. For this weekend anyway."

"When will Ralph's, er, Arthur's boss be arrested?" another asked,

"I can't give you specifics since I am not the one doing the arresting," Remo answered. "I am only meeting with groups to try to stop conflicts that should never start. I would watch the news this weekend, though."

The man in charge raised his hand. "In light of the revealing of a government agent in our midst, all those in favor of canceling the weekend's protest raise their hand."

The impromptu vote carried.

Remo and Chiun were offered coffee, cheese and crackers, and pepperoni balls, but they declined, saying there were other groups to visit.

Back in the car Remo used his preprogrammed cell phone to call Smith. "Worked like a charm. Beaforn left in disgrace and the protest has been canceled."

"Any deaths to report?" asked Smith.

"Of course not," said Remo, trying to sound hurt.

"They are a maligned group, who only believe in the enhanced enjoyment of childhood. They do not deserve death for that," Chiun added in a voice loud enough for Smith to hear over the phone.

"Good. There is not enough time for you to travel all over the country and visit every group before the scheduled events. Since the identification of the agent had such good results, I am going to release a press report identifying agents around the country. I am also going to send it to the agents themselves so they have time to leave. Some of the groups are not above doing violence to infiltrators."

"Why not just let the chips fall where they may? Why tell them?" Remo asked.

"The agents themselves are not at fault. They are doing what they were trained and told to do. Their boss is who we are after. Besides, if they step up to defend their boss we will charge them as accomplices. We will get them— legally."

* * *

The next day, a story appeared on several internet news sites listing Homeland Security agents in various anti-government groups around the country. Most of the agents were no longer available. Their landlords said their rooms were emptied overnight. The rest were under police protection from the members of the groups they had infiltrated.

When asked about upcoming events, the agents that could be reached admitted that the events were suggested by them, but insisted their boss — named as Edward Fatel by every agent — was the one who came up with the idea.

Before Fatel could come up with a story to tell the press, the FBI was

265

at his desk with orders to escort him to somewhere secure 'for his own safety.' He was not given a chance to clean out his desk, nor make a call to his lawyer. He wasn't under arrest, yet, so there was no need for a lawyer, the FBI assured him. Time was of the essence, which made cleaning out his desk a low priority. It would be done for him later.

Chapter Six

THE DHS INTERNAL investigation, headed by Woody Waterson, was not only directed by common sense, but by public outrage.

Waterson gathered together all of the messages he could find on Fatel's computer, but the story was still woefully incomplete. Even the cooperation of the agents involved did not provide the airtight case needed for the firing of a government employee.

Meanwhile, Fatel was put on administrative leave until the issue was resolved.

Administrative leave meant "paid while not working," which just added to the public's ire, as did the fact that Fatel's legal fees were to be paid by the government.

Harold Smith did what CURE was originally conceived to do: provide information to prosecutors — information that was not available through normal channels.

Smith copied all of the files and messages that he had intercepted from Fatel's computer and put them on a computer designated as the DHS backup. Then he sent an anonymous message to Waterson reminding him that a backup computer existed and that the files for Fatel were on it.

That was all Waterson needed to put all of the pieces together to be able to make a case for the grand jury to charge Fatel with domestic terrorism.

Smith then did what he really enjoyed about his job. He made the decision to save the government money.

Remo was directed to quicken the wheels of justice by using the Empty Basin technique to convince Fatel to plead guilty.

Chiun immediately objected that the Empty Basin was for making someone forget their past, not to change their way of thinking while remembering their past.

Remo thought it might work, but Chiun disagreed. "If it does work that way, the emperor will have us using it constantly instead of doing what we were hired for. We are assassins, not psychologists."

Because of Chiun's objection, Smith chose Plan B: Remo would get

267

Fatel to write a confession and then eliminate him, making it look like a suicide. With all of the evidence, a confession was unnecessary, but would prevent further investigation that could lead to CURE.

* * *

Smith's directions to the safe house were accurate, as usual. From there, Remo's Sinanju training took over. The guards were posted at the front and back doors and in the hallway outside of Fatel's room. The windows were open to allow fresh air, as budget cuts meant no air conditioning. The drapes were closed to block the view from the outside, but they did not block access. Anyone trying to get into the room from the outside would only need a ladder.

Remo slipped past the guards, climbed the drain spout, crossed the roof to just above Fatel's room and lowered himself through the open window.

Fatel was bored. He had been playing solitaire with real cards for two days because he was not allowed access to a computer. His guards brought him meals and newspapers. He had writing paper and a felt tip marker that had been provided that morning. His guards did not know why they were allowed, but they guessed that it was to help with the puzzles in the newspaper.

Fatel felt a touch on the side of his neck. Stupid flies came in the open window constantly. Swatting it away, he called for the guard to bring a screen for the window and a flyswatter, but no sound came out.

Fatel tried to stand up, but a strong hand held him down. He turned toward the hand and saw an unfamiliar face frowning at him.

"Don't bother trying to talk," Remo said. "I have paralyzed your vocal cords. You don't need them right now. What you do need is to write out a confession to the crimes you are charged with."

Fatel mouthed his innocence with what he hoped was an appropriate facial expression.

"No, I don't believe you. My boss is the one who uncovered your plot. I know you are guilty. I am just here to save the government money. No trial, no legal fees, no salary during the debacle."

Another questioning look from Fatel.

"Yes, I did that, and convinced several groups not to participate in your scheme. The deaths were not planned…but they shot first."

Fatel shrugged.

Remo pushed the playing cards out of the way and pulled a piece of paper in front of Fatel. Handing the new felt tip marker to him, Remo told Fatel to start writing.

Fatel laid the marker down and crossed his arms.

Remo pinched Fatel's earlobe.

Fatel open his mouth, but no sound came out. His wide and tearing eyes said all that needed to be said. He picked up the marker and started writing.

Several minutes later he put down the marker and looked up at Remo hopefully.

Remo had been reading over Fatel's shoulder. The words sounded enough like an admission of guilt that Remo was sure Smith would be pleased.

"I know what you are thinking. You think you will be able to get the confession thrown out because of being coerced, right? Not going to happen. Here's why."

Remo picked up the marker and put it in Fatel's hand. Using Fatel's hand to grip the marker, Remo jammed it deep into his neck.

"The vocal chord paralysis is removed, but the marker is keeping you from crying out. Leave it in and you will suffocate. Pull it out and you will bleed to death because the marker has pierced your carotid artery. Your choice."

Remo left the room the same way he came in.

* * *

The press — and the amateur bloggers who claimed to be press — had a field day with the story. The press went with the government story of Fatel's suicide. The bloggers went with the story of a government cover-up.

The press went with suicide because no one was allowed to visit him, there was no sign of struggle, he had not tried to cry out for help and he left a confession in his own handwriting.

The bloggers claimed government cover-up because most doctors agreed that it would be very difficult for someone to embed a felt tip marker that far into such a precise place. They believed the government agents assigned to protect him must have been involved, and dismissed his confession as a forgery.

Dr. Harold W. Smith, one of the two people who knew the truth, deleted the stories from his computer and returned to analyzing data from the Folcroft Four for evidence of other crimes against America.

ABOUT THE AUTHOR:

Fred has been reading the *Destroyer* series since a college buddy brought him book #1 and said "you have to read this new series!" At no point did Fred ever expect to write a *Destroyer* story. Quite a bit later, another college friend said "we have been reading these for 30 years — we should write a story!" Fred still did not expect to ever have a story in print.

This is his first time as a published author. He credits twenty years of writing government regulations (learning what *not* to do) and support from friends and family for giving him the confidence to try his hand at storytelling.

SHADOW
OF DEATH

Isaiah Stewart

Reality TV wasn't as awesome as killing.

Sure, being a handsome, reality TV superstar like Jayden Jacklin got you fame, fortune, endorsement deals, private jets, celebrity friends, and lots of gorgeous and willing groupies — but killing made you a god.

Standing six feet tall with silky platinum hair, sparkling aqua eyes, and ripped abs, Jayden was the embodiment of everything girls called "yummy," and was a multi-millionaire to boot — heir to Jacklin Cosmetics Group, the world's largest beauty supply company. But Jayden was not your usual ambitious, enterprising young patriarch striving to impress his parents by successfully taking over the family business.

According to Jayden's parents, he was "lazy as an obese hound dog in July" and refused to take any interest whatsoever in the family business.

"My high-school teachers never called me lazy," Jayden would say. "They said the reason I didn't graduate was because I'm 'selective in my exertion.'"

Why should Jayden work?

Gods didn't work. Gods were big, cool and awesome.

More important: *they got to take lives.*

But if Jayden were ever to achieve radiant exaltation to godhood he would first need a weapon. Cyclops had an eye. Thor had a hammer. Zeus had a lightning bolt and Poseidon had that weird fork-looking thing.

After much contemplation, Jayden decided his "weapon of the gods" would be a machine gun. But Jayden was a resident of Los Angeles, a city known for the most strict gun regulation laws in the entire nation, and surely he would never be able to get an illegal weapon here.

After two phone calls, a pack of menthols, and $350, Jayden held a shiny TEC-9 military assault submachine gun in his delicate hands. "Hi there, pretty baby," Jayden cooed as if talking to a newborn. "Daddy loves you very much."

Cities with gun control were freaking awesome.

Jayden kept the weapon concealed in his parent's Malibu beach estate for that special day he would use it to undergo "spiritual transmutation."

At age 24, Jayden had already undergone one transmutation. As a wealthy cosmetics heir, he was a media icon from birth — famous for being young, idle and rich — and was soon approached to star in his own reality TV show.

"I dunno," Jayden hesitated, "sorta seems like work."

"Jayden, sweetie, is hooking up with gorgeous hotties work?"

Suddenly Jayden decided this "reality thing" had possibilities.

But to properly launch Jayden's show there was one thing the producers needed most of all…the sooner the better.

"What's that?" asked Jayden.

"Make a damn sex tape already!"

* * *

Within weeks Jayden's sex tape was "leaked" and the rest was reality show history. Joining the ranks of other uber-popular reality shows such as *Bachelorette Survivor*, *Ice Road Housewives*, *Big Brother's Got Talent*, *Dancing With the Dumbest Loser*, and *The Biggest Snatch*, *Jayden Needs Love* debuted to 22 million viewers and Jayden Jacklin found himself a superstar.

The show consisted of 25 gorgeous Hollywood babes facing humiliating challenges to become Jayden's girlfriend. Of course, Jayden never kept the final "girlfriend" longer than two or three months — and then it was on to the next season of 25 progressively-trashier girls with even fewer inhibitions.

But mid-way through the taping of Season Three, Jayden finally decided this reality show gig was "still too much damn work," and he had postponed becoming a god long enough.

That day, Jayden showed up for taping concealing his cherished TEC-9.

Three remaining contestants were undergoing the "drinking challenge," which meant consuming as much alcohol as possible to prove undying adoration for Jayden. The sound-stage carpet was saturated in fresh vomit as the scantily clad girls slammed vodka shots, cussed while pulling each other's hair, threw up, then drank more vodka shots.

In a split second Jayden was up, brandishing the TEC-9. "Adios, skanks!" he shouted, spraying hot metal in all directions. When Jayden finished delivering his carnage nothing in-studio was left standing.

"That's a take," he said, looking at the crimson corpses of his girlfriend wannabes, as well as the lighting man, boom man and camera operator.

A perfect sextuple homicide.

Jayden quickly removed all digital tapes from the high-def cameras, then quietly exited the sound stage, stepping into a nearby alley where he mounted his custom-made Harley. Basking in immense exhilaration, Jayden sped home to his parents' Malibu estate, and once there, proceeded to invite all his closest friends over for a pool party to celebrate his new god status.

But exuberant Jayden forgot one small detail regarding his appearance.

"Bro, what's that red stuff all over you?" inquired a guest.

At first startled Jayden became dismissive. "It's my new look. Gaga wears meat. I wear blood."

When the LAPD dragged Jayden into custody three hours later, he rigidly professed innocence, insisting he had actually been hiding during the television studio massacre and had, in fact, witnessed a "gang of club-footed pygmies" doing the actual killing.

"You're an idiot," the interrogating detective said. "A depraved, sociopathic spoiled brat, and you're going down."

But, alas, after the enlightened mass media were through, it was the LAPD that "went down." After all, the media comprised famous celebrity-worshipping journalists and a global blogosphere of millions of adoring fans — all of whom demanded that the "corrupt and fascist" LAPD free Jayden.

The media even dismissed the fact that Jayden had been covered in blood.

"The pool party actually exonerates Jayden," countless reporters, tweeters and bloggers reasoned. "If Jayden were truly guilty, would he have served his friends barbecued shrimp while still spattered in blood? What moron wouldn't even bother to wash up?"

Jayden himself knew the answer. *Why would you erase the trophy of your greatest achievement?*

After a painful trial lasting 18 months, Jayden was acquitted. Deliberations took only 27 minutes.

After all, the jurors calmly reasoned, the LAPD had done absolutely nothing to find the club-footed pygmies.

A free man, Jayden hit the talk-show circuit, where his newfound notoriety was matched only by his shameless professing of innocence.

"Look, it's a statistical fact that most people have stumbled upon sextuple homicides at one time or another," Jayden explained to talk show superstar Conan Fallon. "They just don't talk about it."

"Exactly," Fallon agreed. "I think I read somewhere that seven out of ten Americans will stumble upon a sextuple homicide sometime during their life."

The bombardment of media attention was wonderful at first, but continued to grow to such a fever pitch that Jayden could no longer leave his Malibu mansion without fear of being mobbed or physically harmed.

Exile was a fate worse than death to a man addicted to public adoration, and it was during this time that Jayden first heard a voice echoing inside his head. It was a very strange voice — an evil, ancient whisper over frozen ice. The voice informed Jayden that he too killed for pleasure, and sincerely admired Jayden's desire to become a god.

"We belong together," the voice explained. "My name is Death Shadow."

"What do you want?" Jayden asked.

"Ever been to Hong Kong?"

* * *

It was typhoon season in Hong Kong and Jayden had journeyed to this urban jungle halfway around the world to obey his new inner voice. Braving the torrential downpour, Jayden followed Death Shadow's commands through Wanchai's neon alleyways until he came upon a small antique shop, *Eastern Curio, Ltd.*

This was the place.

"May I help you?" asked the shopkeeper, a distinguished Chinese man in his late sixties, as Jayden entered the shop.

"I'm looking for an artifact," Jayden said surveying his entire surroundings until his eyes caught sight of a large porcelain orb in an open display case behind the counter.

"There!" Jayden heard Death Shadow shriek. "Get it for me!"

Jayden knew he needed the orb. The Death Shadow had summoned him halfway around the world to get it.

"Tell me about that artifact," Jayden demanded.

"It's Qing Dynasty, sir, but that particular piece is only for show. It's been in my family for over 300 years. May I interest you in something else? A porcelain doll, perhaps, of a similar dynasty?"

"No. It must be that orb!" Jayden insisted. "How much?"

"Please, sir, I cannot part with it at any price."

Jayden felt discouraged but Death Shadow comforted him. He told Jayden that killing was his true calling, and it was time to take that "calling" to the highest possible level. But first Death Shadow needed to be freed.

"We will kill the best," Death Shadow explained. "The *very* best."

Then Jayden heard a funny word. It sounded like "Sinanju."

"Are you okay, sir?" the shopkeeper asked.

Jayden's reply was a swift retort from his TEC-9, the same weapon the LAPD had never recovered. The shopkeeper's blood sprayed everywhere. Even on the orb. Slowly, the blood soaked in, like water into a sponge.

The orb began to glow. Soft orange at first, then fiery red, filling the room and consuming Jayden. He felt suffocated, like a cigarette being snuffed out, and all he wanted was air...to take a simple breath...but he couldn't. Someone — some *thing* — was controlling his body.

"Help!" Jayden screamed, but his lips could not move. Jayden realized he was trapped, a prisoner inside his own body. Death Shadow, the orb's spirit, now had complete control. All Jayden could do was watch as his body calmly exited the curio shop.

Death Shadow now possessed a human vessel and he smiled with wicked glee.

Time to locate, and kill, the dog of Sinanju!

* * *

His name was Remo and the serial killer groupie was getting on his nerves.

Her name was Clover Cardigan, an attractive 23-year-old brunette with mysterious dark eyes. She was the winning contestant on *Jayden Needs Love: Season One* and possessed a secret passion: she loved serial killers.

Clover and Remo sat comfortably inside a trendy cafe in Kowloon, which overlooked Hong Kong's massive skyscraper congestion along Victoria Harbour's gray waters.

Casually dressed in a black T-shirt and chinos, Remo Williams was tall and thin, though he had notably thick wrists. His dark hair and high cheekbones punctuated deep-set black eyes, giving his smooth face the appearance of a skull.

Looking away from the pretty girl, Remo remembered what had brought him to Hong Kong.

Smitty had called.

Harold W. Smith was Remo's employer, the head of CURE, a super secret organization that did not appear in any government budget or report. A now-deceased U.S. President had developed CURE to control crime by functioning outside the Constitution. Its one weapon was Remo, a master in the discipline of Sinanju, the greatest of all martial arts, originating from a small North Korean village that had produced master assassins for thousands of years.

Smith's vast computer network had caught early wind of an investigation into Jayden's possible involvement in the Hong Kong curio shop homicide. Smith explained to Remo that Jayden Jacklin was now a liability poised to create an international incident with a crucial trading partner.

"Jayden is in hiding right now, Remo, but stays in touch with his ex-girlfriend, Clover Cardigan. She broke up with him originally but became quite devoted to him during the trial. Apparently the girl belongs to a strange subculture. She's a serial killer groupie."

Remo laughed. "You mean there are beanbags out there who actually idolize murderers like they're Elvis?"

"Apparently, a number of them," Smith said. "I need you to find Jayden and see if he's up to his old tricks. If so — "

"Shut down his magic act," Remo interjected. "No problem, but I think Chiun wants first dibs. Jayden's show forced the cancellation of one of his favorite soap operas." Remo hung up.

"Who was that?" a squeaky voice inquired. It was Chiun, the Master of Sinanju. The old Korean wore a shimmering purple kimono pulled loosely across his frail-looking frame. His wispy white beard and mustache rested upon his kimono like soft snow in twilight. He quietly read a scroll of yellowed parchment paper.

"Smitty," Remo said. "He's targeted Jayden Jacklin. Wanna come along?"

"Insulting," Chiun said. "His disgraceful show had the entertainment value of dogs rutting in the street."

"We're going to Hong Kong," Remo offered as a possible lure.

"Hong Kong is a wonderful place…for pickpockets," Chiun said.

Thus, given Chiun's disinterest in reality show superstars, and in Hong Kong, which he claimed "always smelled funny," Remo traveled alone.

Or so he thought.

Once in Hong Kong, Remo had located and approached Clover in the Kowloon cafe, claiming he had seen her and "it was love at first sight." Considering Remo's typical effect on women, it took Clover nearly five full seconds to offer him a chair. They sat chitchatting. Remo didn't drink coffee but nursed a bottled water.

"Like, omigawd, I just love serial killers! They're so hot!" Clover explained, sharing her secret passion with Remo. She wore a John Wayne Gacy sweatshirt and sipped a double-mocha-skinny-latte.

"Manson, Bundy, Dahmer…like, omigawd, when I think of these bad boys, I get all warm'n'fuzzy. I never felt this way about Jayden…well, until the murders. He had always seemed like such a poser. But once he went and did *that*…well, I knew he had real bad-boy cred."

Remo smiled coldly, secretly wondering if the deceased victims of these "bad boys" also made Clover "warm and fuzzy." Not likely.

"And like, omigawd, if I ever have children I'm going to name them all after serial killers," Clover confided gleefully.

"Brilliant," Remo said rolling his eyes. *Had this chick suffered some type of cranial trauma?* "So, how is Jayden these days?" he asked.

"I wish I knew," Clover said, pouting exaggeratedly. "I've flown all the way to this worthless, disgusting city just to be with him. I know my boo-bear needs me, but he hasn't contacted me yet." She gulped and held back tears. "I just don't know what to do."

Maybe you could plug in a toaster and play with it in the bathtub, Remo thought. *But that might damage a perfectly good toaster.* He forced a warm smile in Clover's direction.

Clover returned the smile. "Like, omigawd, you are *totally* cute!"

She looked at Remo, intrigued. "Like, why am I so attracted to you?"

"Why indeed?" Remo sighed.

"You haven't killed lots'n'lots of people have you, Remo?"

"Who, me?"

Remo cleared his throat and changed the subject. "So how do you and boo-bear connect, since he's in hiding and all?"

"Hong Kong cops asked me the same thing, and I'll tell you what I told them. I have no idea where he is."

Verbal communication obviously wasn't cutting it. Time for something nonverbal. Remo stifled a yawn and mechanically reached over to touch Clover's wrist. Tapping with his fingertips, he began to implement the first of Sinanju's twenty-seven steps to sexual ecstasy while glancing out the window at Kowloon's congested traffic.

Bored, Remo counted license plates.

At step five, Clover was moaning uncontrollably. Remo then asked, again, "So, how does Jayden contact you?"

"A classified ad in the local paper," Clover gasped. "Addressed to Bundy, my favorite all-time bad boy. The ad lists a time and place."

Remo stopped tapping. Clover fell back, panting and fulfilled.

He had counted 522 license plates. Clover took a moment to catch her breath.

Remo stood up. "This is where I get off, sweetheart. Do me a favor and avoid Jayden. Go idolize somebody else from Planet Freak. Try Manson. I hear he's lonely."

Clover resisted at first but eagerly agreed after Remo tapped her wrist again. "Thanks for the latte," she finally said.

"Don't mention it," Remo said.

"Remember this hot little body is yours anytime."

"Don't mention that either."

* * *

Clover's info was spot-on.

The classified ad appeared in the *South China Morning Post*. It was addressed to Bundy and listed a time, 7 P.M., along with an address, which Remo soon located — a spacious penthouse in a five-star oceanfront Kowloon hotel.

Remo was unaware that Clover had already arrived at the penthouse an hour earlier.

Before Jayden met with the orb, he had purchased the ad for several days. Clover already had the rendezvous information from a previous edition and didn't care what Remo said about "staying away." She desperately needed quality time with her boo-bear.

Sure, Remo was dreamy and great with his hands, but he was obviously some kind of cop. Her boo-bear had no doubt murdered again, and it made her want him even more.

Clover waited anxiously in the lavish penthouse when Death Shadow quietly entered the room. Clover perceived Jayden's physical body, oblivious to the fact Death Shadow now controlled that body.

"Hi, boo-bear, I'm here," Clover chimed. "Like how was your day?"

Death Shadow scowled. "Who are you? I sense the Sinanju dog approaching. Be gone."

"Like what's the matter, boo? Bad day?"

"Leave this place, harlot. If I need a concubine I will buy one."

"What's with you?" Clover asked. "You're acting like a totally different person."

"Your presence grows wearisome. Be gone or perish."

Clover's cheeks flushed livid red. "Like, omigawd, how dare you!" she yelled. "Nobody disrespects me! Who do you think I am? Some wimpy little dweeb you murdered?"

When Clover felt Death Shadow's rigid hand ripping a hole through her abdomen — *ruining her John Wayne Gacy sweatshirt!* — she had little time to think before she checked out.

But she did have one thought: maybe serial killers weren't warm'n'fuzzy.

* * *

Fifty minutes later, Remo was surprised to find the penthouse door unlocked. He entered silently to find Clover lying lifeless on the floor. He rushed over to check her vital signs. There were none.

Then a sight took Remo by surprise.

Death Shadow was there in the room, calmly sitting in a nearby chair.

"Hi, Jayden," Remo said, taken slightly aback. "What's shaking, sweetheart? Date any barfing skanks lately?"

Death Shadow remained completely still. The stillness would have unnerved a normal man, but it didn't bother Remo. He didn't care whether Jayden was emotionless, happy, sad, perplexed or doing the

Macarena in a tutu. This scumbag had seconds left to live.

Remo glanced solemnly at Clover. "Killing defenseless people is how you get your kicks?" he asked. "Well, you won't go free tonight, sweetheart. Unlike your jury, I actually graduated third grade."

Silently, Death Shadow rose to his feet, pausing for a brief moment before advancing on Remo.

"Oh, so you want some?" Remo said, his dead eyes flickering. "Well, bring it on, sparky. Show Uncle Remo your shiny new machine gun."

Then Death Shadow spoke.

"I will kill you. Like a dog."

"If you say so, butthole," Remo said, fairly certain that dispatching Jayden would require as much effort as brushing away lint.

"My vengeance is eternal."

"More like your insanity," Remo said. "And what's with the way you're talking? Geez, hand someone a reality show, and suddenly they speak Old Testament."

"You will die now, Sinanju dog!"

The word "Sinanju" was like a punch to Remo's gut. Startled, he tried fathoming where Jayden might have heard it. But in that millisecond it was already too late.

Suddenly a shadow was inside Remo's mind. Black. Thick. Like being submerged in liquid tar. Remo was now blind, and the blackness inside his head was damp and silent, except for a slow distant whisper of wind, and something stirring within the darkness.

A dream.

A nightmare.

It was a vision of an electric chair. The same chair that took his life as a Newark cop decades ago. Remo was back in the chair. But this time he knew he wouldn't be resurrected by CURE.

This time was for real.

Remo smelled the execution chamber's musty odor, felt the electrodes and straps biting deep into his flesh. Heard the roaring sound of voltage firing up. *Not again!* His whole body convulsed. His innards ignited like fireworks as the gut-wrenching electrical force tore his chest apart.

Death Shadow's right index finger took Remo full force, viciously ripping a hole in his left rib cage, just below the heart.

Splitting two ribs on impact, it entered deep into the thoracic cavity. Then Remo felt warmth. *The warmth of his burning flesh.* No. The warmth of his blood — massive amounts of it, exiting his body.

The blow was fatal. No doubt about it. Remo knew he would soon be dead.

"Your time of death is now, Sinanju dog," Death Shadow proclaimed.

By pure reflex, Remo fired out his right foot, striking Death Shadow in the left shoulder. Even in his blind-nightmare state, Remo heard the crunch of impacted bone.

It was insufficient to kill, but enough to allow escape. Remo dove from the balcony, soaring nearly 400 yards skyward in a taut horizontal arc before descending to the gray ocean below. Remo slid smoothly beneath the surf and remained submerged until he was able to climb ashore, where he collapsed.

As Remo's blood surged onto the sand, his last thoughts were of Chiun. *How had he been unprepared against this? How had a common celebrity delivered such an effective deathblow?*

Little Father, how did he do this?

Remo grasped the wound, an elliptical shaped opening below the heart where crimson blood continued flowing. As he lay dying, Remo watched a shadowy figure approach him. "Jayden," he gasped as he slid into unconsciousness.

In seconds, Chiun was upon Remo's body, administering resuscitation. Chiun had little interest in the respiratory or cardiovascular systems. That was common CPR. Chiun swiftly worked the energy pathways of Remo's body, restoring and re-aligning them.

Then, like a soldier carrying the injured, Chiun slung Remo over his shoulder and began running. His vibrant kimono whipped behind him like a flag. As he ran, the old Oriental's feet left no marks in the soft mud.

* * *

Two days later, Remo lay shirtless and unconscious in Chiun's rented North Point hotel room. The only mark visible on his body was a single elliptical scab where the deathblow had been struck. Chiun had treated the wound and now quietly observed it with a grave expression on his wizened face.

Remo stirred, slowly at first. He was in pain, disorientated. "Chiun," he mumbled when his eyes finally opened. "What are you doing here?"

"Something in the scrolls. It foretold a return."

"How did you get there?"

"On the flight after yours," Chiun said. "When you left, I realized that this simple mission might indeed become quite dangerous."

"Sorry, Little Father," Remo said grimacing in pain. "I underestimated my opponent. I wasn't at my best."

"Only the mediocre are always at their best," Chiun said.

"Yeah, but getting whacked by some reality show guy?"

"Not a man," Chiun said. "He is an ancient evil, a spirit of eternal vengeance seeking the House of Sinanju's destruction. His name is Death Shadow." Slowly Chiun folded his legs. He closed his wrinkled eyes in silent contemplation for a moment then took in a deep breath.

"Uh-oh. I sense a legend coming on," Remo said. "Something long and really painful."

Chiun began to speak.

Many centuries ago, when China was under Manchu rule, during the earliest years of the Qing regime, there lived an assassin. He was known professionally as "Death Shadow." He made his home in a village near Xizang, in the Pamir Mountains, and as an assassin he possessed a special gift — a telepathic ability to shroud a target's mind with a shadow of the target's most painful life experiences, forcing him to relive them with even greater intensity than first experienced. This blinded the target, and made killing easy.

Thus it came to pass that Death Shadow was contracted by the Manchus to dispatch a rising threat to the Qing emperor, further insuring Han loyalty. But before Death Shadow could complete the contract and collect tribute, the Manchus wisely revised the contract, and hired the House of Sinanju instead.

Reigning Master Jin Ho accepted the tribute and was the proper choice. But Death Shadow was angered, and refused to drop the contract. According to the legend, both Death Shadow and Master Jin Ho arrived at the emperor's castle at the same time. Jin Ho was blinded by Death Shadow's tricks but was able to injure Death Shadow severely by driving an index finger just below his heart.

The blow left a perfect elliptical hole.

Death Shadow crawled away wounded, and, as he lay dying, he hungered for revenge. He sent for the village elder, a powerful mystic, who, through ancient spells and incantations, bequeathed upon Death Shadow new powers. The elder's mystical incantation trapped Death Shadow's spirit in a porcelain orb, and, according to legend, the fresh blood of an innocent would one day make Death Shadow's soul awaken and possess a new vessel, seeking vengeance against the House of Sinanju.

"Is that it?" Remo finally asked after Chiun fell silent.

"I am finished."

"Good, because for a second there I expected a second ghost to pop up…this one with party favors so everyone could disco dance in the hills of Wing Ding."

"Xizang," Chiun corrected. "And I said nothing of dancing."

"And who the hell's this Master Gin Ho?" Remo asked. "Never heard of him. Sounds like a boozy male hooker."

"Childish jokes will not lessen your failure, nor excuse your ignorance of the past Masters."

"Was there ever a Master Dum Ho?"

* * *

Death Shadow knew he would eventually find the Sinanju dog.

When Remo disappeared into the sea, Death Shadow had spent a full day searching Kowloon, trying to sense his whereabouts, but to no avail. The next day, he moved his exploration to Hong Kong Island and the scent grew stronger. At nightfall, when he neared North Point, he sensed Remo again.

As he moved closer, he could feel Remo's presence more and more strongly. A hotel. The 17th floor.

It would be mere minutes now.

The Sinanju dog had shattered Death Shadow's left arm, but it did not matter. He still had his right. *His killing arm.*

So this newest dog was a Westerner. A brash, unrefined white man with excessive confidence. *Pitiful.* The once-great House had clearly fallen into decay. Now he would feel less gratification when he snuffed its dismal light out forever.

Ensnared within his own body, Jayden watched joyfully. This was definitely better than reality TV. He couldn't wait for the rematch with the tall man with thick wrists. This entity inside his body must have supernatural powers. After all, Jayden had actually felt his own index finger rip a hole in a man's chest.

His finger!

Who needed a stupid TEC-9?

* * *

"Little Father, if Death Shadow is not Sinanju, how did he have such perfect technique?" Remo asked Chiun back at the hotel room.

"He replicated Master Jin Ho's strike supernaturally," Chiun explained, "forcing you to carry his original mark of shame."

"Great, just great," Remo sighed. "Some half-assed ghost gets put in voodoo deep freeze and I'm the lucky Master who pulls out the pork chop."

"Not the *only* Master," Chiun corrected. "According to the scrolls, Death Shadow has reincarnated before."

"How was he stopped?"

"He is only flesh, my son. The difficulty in fighting him lies in his supernatural ability to locate you and exploit your inner demons."

Not just that, Remo thought. The shadow had also shut down his abilities. Remo could touch a Saltine cracker with one fingertip and immediately discern how many grains of salt its surface contained. Yet in the midst of the vision, his Sinanju-learned senses were rendered completely inert.

"The nightmare wasn't some mind trick, Little Father," Remo said. "What I experienced was *really* happening!"

"It is his skill, Remo. But you can defeat the visions. Just as darkness cannot exist where there is light, illusions cannot exist where there is truth. You must bring forth your inner truth. The focal point of your being."

* * *

In a thunderstorm of wood, plaster and debris, the hotel room door crashed from its hinges and into the room. Remo dropped to a crouching position, poised to strike. But, as he turned, he saw Chiun, lying motionless on the floor. Death Shadow was now in the room, and had hurt Chiun.

But before Remo could move to Chiun's side, his mind was again engulfed in blackness. This time, the shadow carried a nightmare even more horrific than the last.

It was a dream of the death of Jilda of Lakluun, the love of his life, the mother of his only daughter. Vivid. Heartbreaking. Her passing had happened years ago, but Remo was experiencing anew. The nightmare continued, driving Remo deeper. He felt her body's warmth, when they first made passionate love, but horrifically, it was interspersed with the devastating vision of her cold, lifeless body. Remo felt himself weeping. Deep body-retching sobs shook him to his soul, where he felt himself slowly dying.

Death Shadow's right index finger was back and seeking Remo's same chest wound.

This time he would get the blow right.

First this new dog, Remo. Then the old Korean. Two for one. Complete obliteration of the House of Sinanju in one glorious evening. Death Shadow's eyes blazed wickedly as he savored his moment of victory.

Death Shadow's right index finger began its final killing stroke. This time he would speak no words, which had delayed him before.

But Death Shadow *did* hear words. Words that froze his killing finger. Not his own words.

A strange voice emanated from Remo. Words that sounded as if they echoed from beneath a tomb.

I am created Shiva, the Destroyer.
Death, the shatterer of worlds.
The dead night tiger made whole by the Master of Sinanju.

His senses returning, Remo's dead eyes were no longer blind. They glanced up, staring deeply into Death Shadow's own eyes, and both Death Shadow and Jayden Jacklin witnessed eternity within Remo's infinite black pupils. Together they felt the blood within their shared vessels run ice cold…and their pants go wet.

The veins in Remo's thick right wrist bulged.

Frantically, Death Shadow moved to strike.

But his killing finger was met midstroke by Remo's own index finger, a violent recreation of Michelangelo's *Creation of Man* painting on the Sistine Chapel ceiling.

CRACK! Crunching bone echoed in the hotel room as Death Shadow's right phalanges were driven into his metacarpals, which in turn impacted carpals, then the radius and ulna, generating a fierce domino effect that forced bone to collide with bone throughout his entire body, until every single bone in his body was jellied.

Then Remo spoke again.

"What is this dog meat that stands before me?"

Remo delivered a fierce kick to Death Shadow's head, which savagely rocketed the entire body backward through the hotel window in a crystalline explosion of glass. Both Jayden and Death Shadow felt their shared body ascend Hong Kong's neon skyline before losing inertia and plummeting.

This was not right, Jayden pouted as he fell.

How could this happen to him? Death was what happened to worthless peasants. He was heir to the Jacklin Cosmetics fortune. He was a mega-superstar. *Jayden Needs Love* always delivered a consistent 13.2 Nielsen rating, damn it! He had evolved into an omnipotent god. Even the cops, courts and entire California judicial system had not been able to touch his magnificence.

Jayden had beaten them all.

He was above everyone!

But Jayden wasn't above anything anymore.

His body ripped through the skylight of a building, shearing webs of cabling and ripping down large lighting rigs before hitting the concrete floor where flesh, blood and bone exploded on impact.

Displayed on the front of the building, where Jayden Jacklin's body now rested, was a large electric sign containing colorful Chinese characters in neon that read:

Home of China's Reality TV Sensation: Crazy Wu Gets a Date.

* * *

Inside the hotel room, Remo raced to Chiun's lifeless body. "Little Father!" he yelled, frantically feeling for a pulse.

Chiun's delicate form stirred, slowly opening one eye, then the other. He smiled and winked at Remo. His unconsciousness had been a charade. The Master of Sinanju stood up and dusted debris from his kimono.

"Took you long enough," he said.

* * *

That evening, Remo and Chiun relocated to a different hotel, this one far away on Lantao Island. Once they settled in, Remo needed to vent.

"Damn it, Chiun! I can't believe you were going to let that lunatic kill me," he finally yelled. "I needed your help."

Chiun calmly dismissed the outrage. "I know you are frail, clumsy, and incapable, but one must consider the scrolls. Imagine how it would look — you requiring help, like a frightened child. What would Jin Ho say?"

"Who cares what Jin or any other ho says? Why did you play possum?"

"Because your illusions and truths can only be faced by you, and you alone. Tell me, Remo. What did you learn?"

"Wouldn't you like to know," Remo said. He had never considered the possibility that battling Death Shadow was some Sinanju rite of passage reserved for a select few.

Remo remembered his illusion involving the electric chair. The real chair many decades ago hadn't really brought death to Remo, but life, in the form of rebirth into Sinanju. Jilda's death too was an illusion. She wasn't truly dead because she would always live on, within Remo, and within their daughter. Then there was the final truth of Shiva, the Hindu God of Destruction, Remo's own spiritual incarnation that had manifested to obliterate Death Shadows illusions. *How had Chiun put it?* The focal point of his being.

"All I care about is the fact that he's dead," Remo finally said.

Chiun chose his words carefully. "He has simply gone away, back to the porcelain orb."

"For good?"

"He is an ancient evil, my son. With such things, there is never 'for good.'"

Remo shrugged, a surrendering gesture indicating that "for now" was good enough. "I'm gonna call Smitty."

"Discretion, Remo," Chiun warned. "The less Emperor Smith knows what truly occurred with Death Shadow, the better."

"I wasn't going to mention the hocus pocus stuff," Remo said. "Do I look stupid?"

"Is this a trick question?"

Master Chiun chuckled to himself and adjusted his silk kimono. As the garment parted slightly, Chiun quietly observed a faint scar on his own chest. A scar he had retained from a battle numerous decades earlier, when he was a young Master of 62 years.

A small, elliptical scar — just below his heart.

ABOUT THE AUTHOR:

A lifelong fan of Warren Murphy's *Destroyer*, *Digger* and *Trace* series, Isaiah Stewart is an award-winning journalist and public relations writer who made his publishing debut with his short story "Opening Weekend" in the *Destroyer* anthology <u>New Blood</u>. A black belt in karate who has earned four college degrees, Isaiah is a professional jazz/rock drummer and recording artist with four albums: Life Games (2000), Urban Playground (2005), Groove Garden (2010) and the forthcoming Thrill Ride (2015). He makes his home in Salt Lake City, Utah, with his wife, Carmen.

REMO:
DISCONNECTION

K. J. MacArthur

STORM WARNING

Donna Courtois

Chapter One

THE DEATHS HAD BEEN covered up. Just a routine lab accident — improper handling of infectious material. Dr. Jonas took a moment to pat himself on the back. While his staff was busy with bio-containment procedures, he'd issued press releases, carefully worded in a way that would not cause panic. Without his statement the press would have gone nuts. They always had headlines ready to go: KILLER BACTERIA ON THE LOOSE!, or VAST RIGHT WING GERM WARFARE CONSPIRACY! But, fortunately for him, today's reporters preferred having news given to them rather than conducting investigations themselves. He'd spoon-fed them just enough of the truth for them to digest and burp it back up in little blurbs buried in back pages or in brief mentions at the end of newscasts. At least the university was able to keep the number of people who had come into unprotected contact with the two researchers to a minimum. They were lucky it was under a half dozen fatalities. Thank God those two idiots had been working in one of the smaller satellite labs on their special project.

Dr. Jonas felt his gut churning with anger just thinking about it again. He chugged Pepto Bismol straight from the bottle, wishing he had Gupta and McNair alive and in front of him now, so he could take pleasure in firing their asses. Why did so many researchers want to play Frankenstein? They had engineered a hybrid of Avian flu and human influenza, making it not only several times more virulent, but also much more contagious. What had they hoped to accomplish? What did they think they could do with it, besides killing themselves?

290

Worst of all was having to contact the CDC, explain what had happened and receive their instructions. The head of the CDC had decided a few samples needed to be kept for study, under much better security than the University of Chicago's Medical Center could provide. The safest means of transport was by courier. Do nothing special to draw attention to it, to make anyone think this was anything but a routine transport. Dr. Jonas had finally relaxed as he watched the car leaving the parking lot. Sampas was a good courier; a little gung-ho and humorless, but at least that meant he followed orders. In about ten hours this would be the CDC and the lab in Bethesda's problem.

**

Joe Sampas pulled into the deserted rest stop on the Pennsylvania Turnpike just outside Monroeville at 2 AM. He was down to a quarter of a tank and he knew he should probably try to make it to a gas station where he could fill up the car while he emptied his bladder, but he wasn't a young man and he couldn't hold it any longer. He'd been told to make the overnight run to Bethesda as quickly as possible, and he'd done his best. A man could eat while driving but he'd be damned if he was going to piss in a bottle. If he'd known what he was transporting, he might have put on Depends before setting out and floored it to Maryland.

He'd been working for the University of Chicago's Medical Center for five years now, and he was used to transporting lab samples, reports, and various test tubes filled with stuff he assumed were medicines or pathology samples. He'd even been on a few overnight runs to various labs and institutions, but never to the Lab of Clinical Infectious Diseases. Sampas had noticed the tension in Dr. Jonas' face as he handed off the case with the round blue label with the 'C' on it, telling Sampas they had brought one of the University's unmarked cars around and that the tank was full and he should try to make as few stops as possible.

Seven hours and five minutes later, Sampas was heading back outside. At this time of night, even on this fairly busy stretch of highway, the place was deserted. It only had a small building with vending machines leading to the rest rooms, and a grassy area with picnic tables outside. He'd clicked to lock the doors, but he hadn't heard the beep that showed the alarm was activated and had been in too much of a hurry to double check. The place was deserted anyway; he'd looked around carefully before getting out of the car.

He hadn't been observant enough. As he went into the building, a dark figure separated itself from the shadows beyond the weak yellow light from the overhead lamps that bathed the rest stop. As he came back out through the doors, he was astonished to see his car backing out of its parking space.

I can't lose that package. I've never failed to complete a run.

Sampas ran for the side of the car as its hijacker put it into drive. He flung himself over the hood, pounding at the window. He could see the man inside clearly, his angry eyes, mouth twisted as he screamed at Sampas. He sped up, jerking the wheel left and right, trying to throw Sampas off.

Sampas' heart was racing. He wanted to let go but was terrified of falling off at this speed. The car was racing toward the exit; he'd have to do something soon. He didn't have time to react, to notice that one of the swerves brought the side of the car that he was clinging to up against a concrete post holding a light. The driver veered close enough so that it hit Sampas broadside, scraping him off the side of the car like a bug. Sampas heard rather than felt the crack as his body slammed into the concrete, bounced off and scraped along the pavement. He never felt the rear wheels of his car as it backed up over his legs but he heard the car door open and felt hands going through his pockets, pulling out his wallet. As he heard the car peeling out of the rest stop, he had only a few seconds left to wonder again what was being transported and to pray it wasn't something capable of causing great damage in the wrong hands.

* * *

Rafe Meeks woke to a hard hand slapping him across the head.

"Get up, Raphael, c'mon, man we gotta hit the road. I got us a ride to New York."

Rafe took a swipe at the hand that had left his head stinging. Coming out of a deep sleep, he was braver than he would have been if he'd remembered whom he was talking to.

"Don't call me that, Myron, dammit. I'm awake, I'm up. I was just resting my eyes a minute, okay?"

He glanced over at the clock radio on the scratched nightstand. Myron Jones had left less than an hour ago. He'd said he was heading back to the rest stop where they'd been dropped off earlier to shop for some wheels.

Was it fate that they'd both got released from West Pen at the same time a couple of days ago? Rafe cursed the coincidence that got him assigned as Myron's cellmate. Jones' last one hadn't done too well, but he hadn't talked and they couldn't pin anything on Myron. Rafe had been new, but not so new that he wasn't already aware of Myron's reputation. The bullet-headed thug was six and a half feet of thick muscle, a mountain of confrontation, daring anyone to take him on. He'd drawn a five-year bit for aggravated assault while Rafe was on a three spot for boosting cars. Rafe had no sooner gotten his stuff stored in his new cell when Myron had told him his chances of surviving prison would be a lot better with Myron as his friend. Friends watched out for each other. Friends got each other's backs in a fight. Rafe nodded and swallowed nervously, his Adam's apple bobbing in his skinny throat. He wanted to lay low, do his time and get out in one piece. He realized that staying out of trouble meant keeping Myron out of trouble, which meant keeping Myron happy which, meant making sure nobody made Myron unhappy.

Through equal applications of cleverness and cowardice, Rafe managed not only to survive his cellmate, but get enough time knocked off both their sentences that they ended up getting sprung together. Myron had punched him in the arm as they walked out, saying they'd make a good team. Rafe thought — not for the first time — that he'd been much too effective at keeping Myron out of trouble. If he'd worked a way to get Myron more time inside he wouldn't have to be watching his back every damn minute.

He pulled his feet over the side of the bed and rubbed his eyes, trying to wake up. Myron grabbed Rafe's battered satchel and tossed it at him.

"Move it, asshole, you wanna hang around for when the cops come?"

* * *

"Why New York?"

Rafe squinted at the road outside the windshield. Storm clouds showed gray against the black sky, visible even though it was still two hours before dawn. He looked at Myron. The big man was beating his hands on the steering wheel in time with the music thumping out of the speakers and didn't appear to hear him.

"Shouldn't we head South, Myron? Or West. There's a hurricane heading right for New York and Jersey, I heard it on TV earlier."

"Ain't afraid of a little wind and rain. 'Sides, where we're goin' ain't close to the ocean. We'll be fine. I got contacts there. We'll need money, and I can get some there." A slow smile spread across Myron's face as he continued. "Plus, I got me a nice piece of ass there. She ain't been waiting for me, she's been doin' business, but she'll sure be glad to see me all the same."

"You got car contacts? We can get these wheels to a chop shop, make some money with it."

"No."

"Why not?" Rafe whined.

"No. We're gonna ditch the car before we cross over the Hudson, trash it, get a ride in." He glared over at Rafe, daring him to open his mouth about it again.

Rafe had no intention of asking again. He figured Myron was holding something back. He didn't want anyone to be able to connect him to this car, not even chop shop guys, who had never in Rafe's experiences with them asked awkward questions or volunteered information to the cops.

"You'll like the Bronx, Rafe. It's full of opportunities for guys like us, even if it *is* full of — "

"Look, Myron, what's that in the back?"

Rafe had spotted a box on the floor of the back seat and thought it was time to change the subject.

"Huh? I dunno, bring it up here, you can open it if you want, I ain't pulling over for it."

Rafe twisted his body until one knee was up on the seat. He reached over, snagged the box one-handed and sat back down. He glanced down at the box. Nothing written on it. Too much to hope it might be money.

He pried open the top. There was another container nested in the first. Rafe was careful lifting it out. He hoped it might be something they could fence. There was a sticker on this box. Orange and black. Three circles on top of a smaller circle. It looked like a bit like the radiation warning symbol, but not quite. He swung open the lid. A bag. He unsealed it. Some kind of tubes inside with a clear liquid. He squinted at the stuck on labels but the writing told him nothing. He picked one up and waved it near Myron's face.

"I can't read what this is. It's Latin or something."

"Get that damn thing outta my face, idiot! You want me to start swervin' all over the road, maybe get us some attention from the cops?" Myron growled. The road was straight and traffic light. He chanced a quick glance. "Put it back. When we get to the Bronx maybe I'll get us a Spic Latino to translate. The place is fulla them, like roaches."

"Uh, Myron, I don't think Latinos speak Latin," Rafe began, "I think they — "

"'Course they do. There's all kinds of Spics, white Spics, nigger Spics. Some of 'em speak Spanish, some Mexican, some even speak Brazil." Myron threw a glare Rafe's way. Rafe shrank down in his seat.

"Okay, Myron, sure."

"Bet you didn't know that about Brazil. Brazil is different from the other Spic countries over in South America. I learned that for my GED. Myron glanced over at the box again. His face lit up. "Hey, maybe it's drugs? Take the cap off and smell it, dip your finger in; take a taste."

"I don't think so, Myron. It's got a hazard sticker on it. It's probably poison, not drugs."

"'I don't think so, Myron!'" Myron mocked. "Why wouldn't drugs have a hazard label? They're always warning people not to take drugs." Myron looked at the vials again. "Wonder if it's Ecstasy? Maybe some Liquid X?"

Rafe squirmed in the seat. "We should throw it away. It's probably dangerous."

"Even if it is, bet we could still sell it to someone. We're gonna need money."

"How about this car? It'll give us enough to get by on for now. You have any connections in the Bronx? Someone who could point us to a chop shop?"

"When we get close to New York, start lookin' for someplace we can roll it down. Or maybe we can set fire to it."

"It's — that's a waste of — " Rafe began.

"Shut it!"

Rafe stuffed the tubes back in the box, then lobbed it toward the back seat. They clinked as the case teetered on the edge of the seat, before settling down. Why not just drive into the Bronx, park somewhere and take off? He chanced a glance over at Myron, who was frowning out into the black dawn, and wondered what had happened to the car's driver. He wondered what else Myron was guilty of.

Chapter Two

His name was remo and he did not feel guilty. He pushed away the image of the old man standing stiffly by the door, his eyes like cold hazel marbles, his lips stretched tight with disapproval. Remo had been given an assignment and he had to go, no matter what Chiun said about the weather.

He strolled along, a thin man in chinos and a black t-shirt, his deep-set eyes taking in the sights. The pavement was smooth and uncracked. Quaint streetlights with frosted glass globes lined the road; small trees in wrought-iron cages decorated the sidewalks. No old newspapers or food wrappers littered the street or were blown into piles next to the stoops of the brownstones that lined both sides. A grocery store, produce piled high in bins out front sat across from a small post office. It might have been a self-contained neighborhood in a city such as Boston or a borough like Queens.

Remo frowned. It wasn't the neatness so much that gave it an air of unreality, he decided. More the absence of bars and OTB parlors. He gazed up at the metal framework with catwalks and lights suspended above the roofless buildings. The sound stage was deserted; production had wrapped early today. The sign outside welcoming people to Mulberry Road showed colorful puppets grouped around the famous street sign, along with Miss Millie the schoolteacher, Mr. Pete the grocer and last, but certainly not least the star of the show: Fuzzybear. The brown bear with the goofy grin, top hat and mayor's sash was sitting on a wall, his paw draped across the neck of deputy mayor Mr. Bob standing next to him. Mr. Bob's right arm was behind Fuzzybear, his unseen right hand manipulating the puppet.

Remo's expression darkened. Mr. Bob should have kept his hands on his puppets.

He made his way past the set to a neat row of trailers set against the back wall. He chose the largest trailer, the one closest to the set. Black loafers seemed to float upward, making no sound on the metal stairs.

Remo flung open the door, banging it against the inner wall of the trailer. The middle-aged man inside jumped.

He was a mild-looking figure, thinning brown hair atop a narrow aesthetic face, half glasses perched on his nose. He was Remo's idea of what a librarian should look like. Or a doctor, maybe.

"Monsters ought to look like monsters," he growled. "It's hard to get kids to understand that sometimes a whole lotta bad can hide behind a very ordinary face."

"Who are you? Are you press?" The man stood up and reached over to the chair next to him where a bundle of brown fur lay. He picked up Fuzzybear, holding the puppet in front of him like a shield. "I have nothing to say to you."

"I'm not happy about talking to you either," Remo replied. He glanced around the trailer. The walls were covered with framed newspaper clippings, magazine articles about the wildly successful Mulberry Road program and its creator, Bob Randall, the genius behind Fuzzybear, Professor Owl and Miss Quills.

"I was an orphan," he continued. "Growing up, I wanted parents. I never really appreciated how well the nuns at St. Theresa's took care of us. When they sent us off to school one of them, usually Sister Ignatius, walked us over. They told us not to talk to strangers and never go off with a grown up who offered us candy or a puppy. It's not the same as having two parents who love you, but I've seen that not all children have good parents. Some people are more interested in money than in their kids. Some parents will even take bribes to keep their mouths shut and leave monsters free to keep preying on kids."

"You shouldn't listen to rumors, Mr. — ?"

"Williams. Remo Williams. And if it's only a rumor, why are you sweating? You know, I wasn't adopted until I was an adult, and only then because CURE, the secret agency that recruited me, needed someone to train their killer arm. But that old man taught me a lot more than Sinanju. He gave me a way of life, a reason for living. He's a carping, smug pain in the ass mostly. But I know he's always done his best for me."

Randall took a step back, his eyes flicked back and forth between Remo and the door. "I don't know what you're talking about.

Remo reached over and pulled Fuzzybear out of Randall's arms. The puppeteer gasped and lunged toward Remo, who grabbed one elbow and used the forward momentum to spin Randall around and set him down in a chair. Anyone watching would have thought they had practiced the routine.

"Nobody touches Fuzzybear but me. You — you give him back immediately! Randall sat up straighter in the chair, thought briefly of making another lunge — this time toward the door — but gave up when he saw something dangerous glinting in Remo's deep-set black eyes.

"I think I'd rather question Mayor Fuzzybear." Remo turned the puppet so it was facing him. "Your deputy mayor here has been fondling more than his puppets, hasn't he?" A twist of Remo's wrist and the puppet nodded.

"Sometimes he invites children who work on Mulberry Road back to his trailer?"

The puppet nodded again.

"And this has probably been going on for awhile, hasn't it? And there were more than just the two kids who complained to their parents?"

Two more firm nods.

"What say we root out corruption in kiddie-show government? Do you really want this guy as your Number Two?"

This time Remo shook Fuzzybear's head very firmly back and forth. The puppet's grin remained goofy; Remo's smile resembled the rictus of a corpse.

Ten minutes later, Remo exited the trailer, whistling a tuneless song. He had one more call to make at the studio. Several hours later, when security noticed Randall's BMW was still in the parking lot and came to check on him, they would call the paramedics but, as one of them said to his wife later that night, "No way he was alive, not with Fuzzybear's arms wrapped that tight around his neck. The EMTs had a hell of a time cuttin' them off, they was really embedded in his neck, that's how tight someone tied them."

* * *

Phil Brackenrich, president of Mulberry Studios was alone in his office. He'd been battling with the Board of Directors for years to expand beyond children's programming and had finally been given the go-ahead to develop a few pilots. He grinned, his capped teeth and the top of his bald head both gleaming in the L.A. sun shining through the floor to ceiling windows. He hadn't told the board that he'd already commissioned a few pilots and had even shot some scenes of the most promising one. Get a sample in front of them quick, he thought, dazzle them with its marketability and the new division was certain to be a go.

He hummed as he loaded a DVD in the big screen TV on the wall. Keep things moving fast. The focus group had gone well this morning;

298

Brackenrich had assumed it would. A second focus group late this afternoon, then the board meeting he'd already scheduled for tomorrow morning. He had a little time; he'd watch the scenes again himself. He clicked "play," pulled up a chair and sat back with a sigh.

He sensed rather than saw the figure at the door, turned and damped down his smile a few watts.

"You're not supposed to be here yet. The focus group won't meet for another hour and it's downstairs in the conference room. Didn't you see Shirley? She's the receptionist downstairs. She should have told you where to go."

The man ignored Brackenrich, staring past him at the action unfolding on the screen.

"*She's the Bay State's newest senator, a sassy minority fighting for respect in the white man's world. She's —* " blared the voice over from the speakers. A plain title card came up: *Our Favorite Senator!*

Remo stared at the very pale woman in full Indian costume, blond hair hanging in dreadlocks, who was facing off against a group of men in suits, her arms held out stiffly in front of her.

"*Though you have raped the land, slaughtered and enslaved my people, I bear you no ill-will. I will teach you to work in harmony with nature and to nurture the people who have trusted you to lead them.*"

"Why is she dressed like an Indian? She's practically an albino. Is Mel Brooks writing for TV again?"

"Oh, no, Mr. — ?"

"Just call me Tonto."

Brackenrich frowned. "That's very racially insensitive."

"You're calling *me* insensitive?" Remo pointed at the screen. The pale woman was now doing what looked like a war dance in the middle of a senate meeting. "If this goes on the air, Indians'll be going on the warpath all across America."

"Haven't you been paying attention to the Senate races, Mr. — ?"

"Remo Williams. And no."

"If you had," said Brackenrich, looking with disapproval on this clod. He'd tell his secretary to make a note; this man's opinion was *not* to be counted, "you'd realize this is very, very *now.* Liz Worn is sure to win, given the Cro-Magnon she's up against, and when she does this show will be cutting-edge. It's a sure-fire hit. It has everything: comedy, social commentary, relevance."

"Speaking of relevance, I don't give a damn about your new shows. I'm here about the late Deputy Mayor of Mulberry Road and your "campaign" contributions."

"My what?"

"Thanks to you the charges were withdrawn, he would have remained Deputy Mayor in spite of what he's done. How many more children would he have invited back to his trailer?"

Brackenrich swallowed. Hard. "Mr. Randall hasn't done anything. We haven't had any complaints."

Remo wagged a finger. "Tell the truth. There were complaints. My boss picked up on them. His computers can check any other computer — government, police, newspapers. It's a big help ferreting out scumbags both great and small. Take you, for example."

The executive stood up and began edging for the door. Remo moved slightly, blocking him.

"Smitty's computer noticed a few small articles in local California papers about accusations being brought against the well-known star of a well-known kiddie show. He found the accusations lodged by two families with the LAPD. He then saw a small article in the *L.A. Times* about charges being dropped. So he decided to look into a few bank accounts. Did you know that just before the charges were withdrawn, both families' bank accounts grew larger? And that just after the charges were dropped, both family's bank accounts grew *much* larger?"

"Coincidence," said Brackenrich, his legs trembling as they hit the back of the chair. He dropped down heavily. "Mulberry Road Productions never gave them a cent. Your boss is wrong."

"You don't know my boss. Harold W. Smith is thorough. He said you'd covered your tracks pretty good. He had a time working his way back through the direct deposit by a dummy corporation that was a subsidiary of a holding company that was a division of something else. But it finally led to you. He's been working behind the scenes for a lot of years bringing down scumbags like you and your puppet jockey."

"Are you with the government?"

"No, CURE's a secret organization that works to eliminate people who manipulate the Constitution and the laws of this country to get away with crimes." Remo picked up a clipboard, casually twirling it on one finger as he continued. "When Smith decided it needed an enforcement arm, he framed a young policeman for murdering a pusher. I was arrested, convicted and executed. They needed a dead man, someone with no fingerprints on file. Mostly we deal with big things: threats from outside, corruption from within. But sometimes Smith finds fouler stuff."

Remo gripped the clipboard with both hands and with barely a motion that Brackenrich could see, snapped it in two.

"I saw too much of this back when I was a cop. Children who were abused by people they trusted. Innocence taken away, childhoods destroyed. Crimes like this make graft and espionage look almost clean."

"I haven't committed a crime, it was a business deal," said the sweating executive. He glanced over at his phone. He wasn't sure he should call the police even if he had a chance of making it.

He'd been lucky the boys' families had been cooperative. With what he had to pay out, the boys would have top of the line counseling. Everyone had some trauma or another growing up; they'd survive. And he'd promised the families he'd have Randall watched. That made everything all right. Didn't it? He opened his mouth to tell the intruder that, but when he looked into the deep-set eyes and noticed the thick wrists that his intruder was absentmindedly twisting he suddenly knew that he had already been tried, judged and was only awaiting execution. The room swayed under him.

"Your business stinks," said Remo. He picked Brackenrich up one-handed, with no more effort than he'd showed lifting the clipboard, and sent him sailing toward the television. The executive's head appeared to meet the screen gently, but it bent around him, electricity dancing around the vents and crackling through the man.

Remo walked back through the lobby. He wasn't exactly happy, but he realized he felt a rare sense of satisfaction. Dealing with those two may have been an annoying chore, like taking out the garbage, but at least he knew they'd never stink up the place again. Then he remembered that senator show. Maybe Brackenrich's stink would live on. The sound of a TV drew his attention. For crap's sake, it may be a studio, but did they have to have those huge screens set up every ten feet? He stopped and stared at this one. The weather report was playing.

"What's the latest on that huge hurricane hitting the Atlantic states?" the blond newscaster chirped.

"Oh, it's a killer, Sandy," replied the weatherman, a huge grin on his Botoxed face. "Most storms head North up the coast, making landfall anywhere from South Carolina to New England, but this one stalled out in the Atlantic, then turned and is heading due West towards the Jersey coast. The wind's already picking up and some rain is moving in, but it's nothing compared to what will going on in about twelve hours when it hits the Jersey shore head on. It will merge with a low-pressure system heading east and strengthen. We expect massive flooding and power outages. Airlines are already canceling flights up and down the East coast."

Remo didn't stay to hear any more. He ran for his rental car, threw it into drive, burning rubber as he left the lot. He was heading back to LAX. He'd get a flight if he had to hijack a private plane and parachute out over Jersey. He thought of Chiun, his adopted father, facing the hurricane alone in their house on the beach and Remo Williams felt guilty.

* * *

Remo crossed over the Pennsylvania/New Jersey border going 140. It was a few hours past sunrise, but hard to tell with the black storm clouds and torrents of rain bringing visibility down to near zero. It had been raining steadily when his plane touched down in Pittsburgh — the closest flight he could book. He quickly secured a rental. Going through Pennsylvania had been like traveling through a car wash in a wind tunnel but now Remo felt more like he was driving under water, the wind pushing against the car like a rip tide, the trees on the side of the road bent almost in half and waving wildly like some exotic form of seaweed. If the weatherman last night had been accurate, the hurricane was just making landfall.

He'd called Smitty last night from the airport. Chiun wasn't at Folcroft. He'd tried again in Pittsburgh, but the line was dead. Smitty always answered the phone; the storm must be a bad one if it was affecting reception. Remo wondered if Chiun was still at their house or if he had managed to get to one of the shelters in the small township. Chiun was a Master of Sinanju. He could take care of himself.

Then Remo thought about the fourteen steamer trunks that held all of Chiun's possessions. He knew Chiun would not leave them behind. Wherever he was, they'd probably objected to anyone bringing in that much luggage, but Chiun had ways of making people see his viewpoint. Remo could only hope the body count hadn't been too high.

Remo imagined the ocean coming up the beach, the waves driven through the sliding glass doors at the back of the house, the water slowly rising inside. He winced at a sudden, painful memory.

They had lived at one time in a church that had been converted into condominiums. It had been a stable home for them for many years. That is, until some lowlifes had taken revenge by breaking into the house when Remo and Chiun were absent, turning on the gas stove, blowing out the pilot light and lighting a match. They had returned home to an inferno. Firemen had given up on saving the structure; they had been trying to contain the fire to that one house.

Chiun had shrieked and plunged into the flames, racing up to his room to retrieve his trunks. Remo had stood outside the window catching them when Chiun tossed them down.

What if Chiun had been by himself that night? He couldn't have thrown the trunks without Remo below to catch them. Would he have tried to race back down the stairs with each trunk? Would he have been able to save them? Would he have hurt himself trying? Masters of Sinanju lived long lives, their abilities undiminished. But Masters weren't immortal.

Remo pushed down on the gas pedal but even though the needle pushed above the maximum speed, he didn't seem to be going any faster. It didn't help that he was driving into the wind.

He made it roughly halfway across New Jersey when he began running into closed and flooded roads. Remo spent a frustrating few hours trying to detour around low-lying areas while keeping a straight route to the small seaside township where their house lay. He reached the city limits at midday, only to be stopped by sawhorses and a roadblock.

"You'll have to turn back, sir," said the policeman who walked up to Remo's car. "Half the town's under water. The National Guard is here trying to get to everyone who didn't already leave."

"My father's in a house on the beach." Remo's voice carried over the wind.

"Not anymore, sir. There's no beach left and most of the houses are under water."

Remo abandoned the car and raced down the road. He could hear the police yelling at him to stop, but they were too busy to go after him. They couldn't match Remo's speeds, not even if they chased him in their cruiser. And Remo had the advantage of being able to dodge, run through, and at times skim on top of the flood waters.

He ran through the town, the landscape almost unrecognizable. Trees were down, and buildings had roofs blown off. Wires were lying all over, but thanks to the power outages, they weren't a danger. Remo came to the shore, which was now two streets in from where it used to be. He looked out over the devastation. He spotted what he thought was the top of their nearest neighbor's house, sticking up out of the surf. Next to it was nothing but ocean. Remo's shoulders sagged and he turned away.

He should have asked where the shelters were. He raced back over the route he had taken, but the police had moved on. So had his rental. Remo roamed around the higher elevations, calling out to the few workers and emergency personnel who were out. He found a few leads, went to the nearby high school and a church hall. He trudged through them, looking, listening for a high squeaky voice, questioning anyone who looked in charge.

"Have you seen an old Asian man? Short, very thin and wearing a kimono — probably some God-awful color with birds or dragons on it." *And dragging fourteen steamer trunks behind him*, Remo added to himself. His little father would stand out from the crowd any place he'd found shelter.

But nobody had seen him. Remo tried to call Smith again. When his phone died, Remo had persuaded a few people to lend him theirs. But it was no use. Communications were down. He grabbed his wallet and checked through the various IDs he had. Remo Patterson of FEMA commandeered a pickup truck outside the county sheriff's office.

The trip to Rye took more than twice the usual time. The wind had died down, the rain wasn't quite so tropical, but Remo still had to drive around fallen trees and wires and detour past flooded roads. He had to skirt around Manhattan entirely as all major tunnels and bridges except the Lincoln were closed.

It was past sunset, a little more than twenty four hours after he'd left California, when Remo Williams stopped the truck and looked at the large tree that had fallen across the long driveway leading up to Folcroft. He abandoned the vehicle and trotted the last half-mile.

As he stood at the bottom of the granite steps, looking at the two stone lions that guarded either side of the entrance, he saw the front door of Folcroft Sanitarium open noiselessly on oiled hinges. A short figure emerged and stared down at him. Two delicate eyebrows like soft puffs of cotton drew down over hard hazel eyes. The figure crossed its arms.

"So," floated down the squeaky, sing-song voice of Chiun, Master of Sinanju. "you have finally decided to come in out of the rain."

Chapter Three

IT WAS FIVE DAYS later. Remo had stopped being relieved to see that Chiun was safe and sound four days, twenty-three hours, and forty-five minutes ago. He paced back and forth in front of Harold Smith's desk. The director of Folcroft and CURE frowned up at him.

"As I have told you before, Remo, there are no assignments. We are blind here. I have no Internet access. I cannot raise the computers on St. Maarten. From what little I have been able to ascertain from the television, the island had massive flooding and damage; it is cut off from the world. I went down to the sub-basement two days ago when the water finally receded. The Folcroft Four were under three feet of seawater. Their components are damaged beyond repair. I am forced to rely on newspapers and broadcast networks for news."

Smith took his glasses off and glanced over at the small set in the corner of his office. The screen showed four women sitting around a table. *Thank God*, thought Smith, *the sound is off*. He had caught the last ten minutes of the program yesterday as he waited for the news to start and had thought his head would explode from the inanity. He looked back at Remo.

"They have become even worse than I remember — mostly what used to be called 'human interest stories' — and they don't even try to hide their bias on the small amount of news they use as filler."

"C'mon, Smitty, there's got to be something. Chiun's driving me up a wall. Right now I'd go to Denver to rescue a cat caught up a tree."

"Speaking of Master Chiun," Smith intoned, "I have been meaning to mention him to you. Do you think you might persuade him to remain in his rooms?"

Chiun, Remo, and all fourteen steamer trunks were once again in the basement rooms next to the gym that they had shared when Remo first came to Folcroft, delivered by the prison van after his fake execution. Smith had recruited him for CURE, a dead man with no fingerprints on file, and had him trained under the Master of Sinanju to become the agency's enforcement arm.

"He's only spoken to me once, when I first got here after the storm, Smitty. I'm on his shit list until he decides I've paid for leaving him alone.

You want him in his rooms? You tell him." Remo glared at Smith. "Better yet, don't tell him anything. He's just lost another house and he knows you're only putting us up because you have to. Every hotel and motel around here that didn't flood is crammed full of refugees."

"Nevertheless, Remo, he spends too much time talking to patients and staff. Even though he's seen by one and all as a delusional patient, it is possible that he may let something important slip, mention an incident that someone will remember and who then may begin to put things together."

"Don't sweat it, Smitty, I've been listening to him. He's done nothing but badmouth me. There's an old lady who tries to run me over with her walker every time she spots me and I think some of the patients are getting up a petition to get me banned from here. Can't you find something for me to do?" Remo looked over at the TV. It was showing pictures of the devastation. "Maybe I can head back to Jersey and clean up?" he added wistfully.

"No. If something does come up, I will need you close by. Travel is still difficult and gas is hard to come by. Many of the doctors and staff who were here when the hurricane came through stayed for the duration of the emergency. I have not been home either."

"How's Maude doing?"

"She's back home. We were close to the flooding but the house was undamaged." Smith said. He glanced over at the set in the corner. "The news is about to begin. If you wouldn't mind…?" He gestured toward the door.

"Sure, Smitty. Maybe I'll come back after. Bring Chiun with me. He can tell you all about fleeing two steps ahead of the storm. Again."

Smith shuddered as Remo left the room.

"Find him. Try to talk to him." Smith raised his voice as Remo went out of sight. "Please ask him to go back to your rooms. Please."

Smith rose slowly. His back cracked as he straightened up. He walked toward the sofa and sat stiffly, back straight as he grabbed the remote and turned the sound up. He didn't expect to see anything that would need CURE's unique attentions, but he had a duty to check what was happening to the best of his ability. He thought about the election next month. Maybe this foreshadowed a time the United States would be without the agency that had stood between it and destruction for four decades.

* * *

Remo headed for the lobby. It was Chiun's favorite place to park

307

himself, standing by the doors that led to the various wings and starting conversations with passersby. Chiun's voice floated up to meet Remo as he came down from the second floor landing.

"...and there I was, alone. Storm clouds gathering to the East, the ocean churning ahead of the dread winds, heading towards my home. I made my way to my room, my only thought to pack my few meager possessions and find my way to a place of refuge while my son cavorted in sunny California with the movie stars."

Remo paused in the doorway. Chiun was standing in front of a grouping of sofas and chairs near the big fireplace. Several patients sat on the furniture or in wheelchairs, some staff behind them. There were even a few visitors who had made their way here past the receding flood waters. He sighed. Better get it over with. Again.

"Little Father," he said.

One of the patients poked a visitor. "That's him!" she hissed, a regular audience member cluing in a newbie. "That's the son."

The visitor turned a five hundred degree glare on Remo. "You got a lotta nerve, comin' over here, ya bastid," she brayed with the harsh accents of a native Brooklynite. "Shame on you, leavin' your poor old dad alone in a hurricane! I come alla way from Flatbush in the storm to check up on my mom, make sure this place ain't fallin' down and you — *you* take off on *vacation.*"

From the level of anger, Remo figured Chiun was already on his second retelling. Usually he repeated the story a minimum of three times per show, each time emphasizing different aspects of the gross betrayal and abandonment suffered by himself at the hands of his neglectful son.

"Little Father, could you please come back to your room with me?" Remo didn't even try to defend himself any more. "Dr. Smith said he'd like you to rest for awhile."

"Don't go anywhere with him," called another voice from the audience. "He's just trying to shut you away, to stop you from telling anyone about his abuse."

Chiun held up a hand. "This humble old man is very grateful for all your kind attention and sympathy, but, alas, he is my son and I must return with him to my quarters. I will be fine. He is thoughtless but not violent."

Remo kept silent until they reached the basement.

"When are you gonna talk to me again?"

Chiun kept his slow, measured walk toward their rooms, his nose in the air, not looking at Remo.

"Look, I'm sorry, okay? I'm sorry. I didn't look at the weather reports. Who knew it would turn back and hit New Jersey head on? I didn't know it was going to be so destructive."

Chiun halted and cocked one shell-like ear towards Remo.

Encouraged, Remo continued. "I would never have left you to get your trunks back to Folcroft alone. I felt terrible the entire trip back. I thought about when Castle Sinanju in Quincy burned down and how you needed me to catch your trunks."

Chiun pursed his lips. "You did not realize the storm would be so dire or where it would strike? How could you not be able to read the skies and the pressure of the air and not see the signs of coming destruction?"

"At least you got all your trunks here safely, Little Father."

"I had no one to help me supervise the porters nor to chastise them when they jostled my possessions. Not to mention hiring their services. You should have heard the complaints! It is no wonder this country is failing. Common porters do not wish to earn an honest day's pay. It was all 'I wish to be near my family' and 'It is too far to travel in this weather' with them."

"The trunks are safe, Little Father." Remo thought of CURE's computers and the flooded subbasement. "They're okay to stay here? Folcroft's not damaged?"

"You thought I would not make certain of this? I went below with Emperor Smith and checked the pressure of the earth. There are cracks in the stone of the foundation that let ocean in, but it is not dangerous yet. Eventually Smith should hire laborers to seal the breaches, but he has a few decades perhaps, and I pray we will be gone from here and serving a sane emperor long before then."

* * *

Harold Smith watched the latest story of bravery in the face of the storm and found his attention wandering. He loathed the newscasts' practice of reporting on a story long after they had wrung every bit of news out of it and were reduced to showing the same films and repeating the same phrases over and over.

"We have an update on the brutal murder and carjacking in

Pittsburgh. Police have found the wrecked remains of the car off a dead-end street just outside Palisades Park. We take you to our reporter, Tamara Blake, talking to police sergeant Duffy. Tamara?"

"Yes, Barbara, I'm here with the sergeant who was the first on the scene. An anonymous call to a tip line this morning reported they had seen two men pushing a car over this embankment behind us the morning after the brutal crime."

Smith watched as the camera panned to the side of the road. He leaned forward, his eyes taking in the figures walking around the wrecked car, frustrated when the camera panned back the reporter, who was now asking the usual inane questions to the impatient policeman. He muted the sound, walked to the phone on his desk and dialed a number.

"Let me speak to Assistant Director Carson," he said. This is Special Agent Harold Jones, I am calling from Washington." Smith waited, tapping his fingers on the desktop. "Agent Carson. Fill me in on the carjacking outside Pittsburgh. What progress have you made?" Smith listened for several minutes, a frown gradually deepening the wrinkles on his face.

"Thank you, Carson. I'm sending a couple of field agents over to you. They have special skills for situations such as this. I'm putting them in charge." Smith's voice became if anything more waspish. "I am not questioning your competency. I will issue their orders. They will be there as soon as possible."

Smith broke the connection, and then hit the intercom button.

"Mrs. Mikulka, send the patient Mr. Pak to my office, along with his aide Remo."

* * *

"You got something for me, Smitty?" Remo paced in front of Smith's desk. He stole a glance over at Chiun, who was standing just inside the office, arms folded into his kimono sleeves, as unmoving as a statue. He looked over Smith and Remo's heads, seeming to contemplate the piece of sky visible through Smith's office window.

"Yes. A carjacking several days ago. The driver was killed. The car was found abandoned this morning near the George Washington Bridge."

"Sounds routine."

"It is being reported as such. But along with the police, there were FBI vehicles and personnel at the scene. They weren't wearing gear that identified them as such, but their dress code makes them stand out. And I saw a few cars with federal license plates. The FBI would have no reason to be there for an ordinary auto theft or murder. I called the New York bureau chief. The victim was a courier for the University of Chicago's medical school. He had been transporting a new strain of a deadly virus to a government lab in Bethesda, Maryland. The virus was not found with the automobile. It is highly contagious. The researchers who were working on it became infected and died within a few days, along with several other lab personnel they had come in contact with. The university was very lucky to contain it without further incident. If the carjackers have it, they and everyone around them are in immediate danger. If they become infected, it could cause a widespread epidemic."

"They think the idiot car thieves have it?"

"Agent Carson said they had hoped it would be found with the car. Since it was not, agents and trained personnel are traveling the most likely routes between the scene of the crime and where the car was found. The thieves may have thrown it out on the side of the road. If they still have it, they probably don't realize the danger."

"What am I supposed to do, Smitty? These guys could be anywhere."

"The Bureau believes they will lie low for now, probably in the vicinity. They may have crossed into the Bronx. The police have been checking descriptions, looking for fingerprints. They should have an I.D. on the suspects by the time you and Master Chiun get there. I would prefer you go after them and retrieve the virus. It is much more likely the two of you can get to them before they accidentally or purposely release it."

"Of course, Smitty, but — " Remo's eyes narrowed. "Me and Chiun? This is pretty routine. I don't need Chiun for this."

Remo heard Chiun heave a gusting sigh. He winced.

"No, Emperor, my son does not need me. I will stay here, amongst the feeble and the wretched, so that my son may perform his task without having to tend a homeless old man."

"Can it, Little Father," Remo said in Korean. "You're having a ball telling people how I left you to wade out of Jersey on your own. And I moved that big screen TV into our quarters. Isn't it almost time for that Korean soap opera you found?"

Smith's mouth pursed like he'd just swallowed a mouthful of vinegar.

"Remo, I would prefer Master Chiun accompany you. He could be very useful in a situation like this. I'm sure the House has dealt with plague situations. And his wisdom and judgment are superior to yours."

Chiun bowed.

"Naturally, Emperor Smith, I will attend to my dullard son and speed the capture of this hideous contagion and transport it to where it can be contained. I do not believe for a moment that you would invent a task for an old man so he might leave this place because you have become tired of sheltering him."

"If you could give some thought, perhaps, Master Chiun, on what you would prefer for living arrangements? When CURE's computer problems are solved, I will purchase you a house wherever you wish to settle. Perhaps a condo again?"

Chiun stared at a spot over Smith's head. Smith coughed and turned to Remo.

"You will check in with Agent Carson. I cannot access the FBI's data base, so you will need to use your old I.D.s as Remo Walker and Mr. Pak."

"How bad could this get, Smitty?"

"If the vials are opened in a crowded area the contagion will spread rapidly. Agent Carson told me the CDC estimates the mortality rate as on par with the Black Death: 35 to 75%. New York City and its boroughs could become a graveyard within a matter of weeks.

Chapter Four

"THIS PLACE IS DEAD!"

Rafe woke up staring at the back of the dusty sofa. He'd been sleeping on it for four nights now, legs drawn up so they wouldn't hang over the side. He stretched carefully and turned over, the sight of Myron's undershirt and the sour reek of last night's whiskey hitting Rafe's senses at the same time. He winced.

"You're the one said we needed to stay low for awhile, figure out what we're going to do."

"I ain't staying here much longer; it's as bad as the pen, cooped up day and night. And no light and no TV until six o'clock this mornin'. We need to have a plan." Myron's foot came up and kicked at Rafe's legs. "Get up, this ain't your bedroom once I'm up. Take a look outside. It's almost noon, time for the news. I told you we ought to have junked that car better."

Rafe, Myron and that woman — Nikki, Myron called her — had woken up in the middle of the night when all the lights came on and the TV started blaring. Myron had shuffled out of the one bedroom, swearing, and was yelling at Rafe to turn the damn sound down when a special report about the discovery of the car involved in a Pittsburgh carjack broke into news about storm damage. Myron had muttered and paced for a while before yelling at the woman standing in the bedroom doorway to get back to bed.

Awake again, Rafe shambled to the window, his knees stiff. He pulled up the shade cautiously, peeking out like the weather was going to reach in and mug him through the window. The sun's light didn't penetrate far into the murky room. Rafe turned away, watching as the woman came out of the bedroom, keeping close to the wall as she made her way over to the small kitchenette in the corner.

Myron had switched on the TV. He threw Rafe's pillows on the floor, settling back on the couch. Rafe came up close to him, pitching his voice low, darting looks at the woman standing at the sink, filling a pot of water.

"We took the plates off before we dumped it into that culvert. It was pretty steep and didn't look like nobody went there much."

313

"We shoulda burned it."

"It wouldn't have burned much with the rain coming down like it was. We thought the culvert would flood. Remember? You thought that was good enough."

"Well it wasn't, was it? They found it, didn't they? If we'd siphoned some gas out, it woulda burnt it enough maybe even with the rain."

Rafe winced. Myron's voice was too loud in that small room. Even if the neighbors didn't hear, Rafe didn't trust that woman. Nikki. Myron had said if she knew what was good for her, she'd keep her mouth shut but maybe she'd figured out enough to know if she got a chance to turn them in Myron would be heading for a good long stretch this time. Maybe she'd figure it was worth a chance to get away from him. The bruises on her arms showed yellow to black as she moved from the hot plate to the small refrigerator to the table, laying out breakfast.

Myron's eyes followed Rafe's over to the woman.

"Nikki, get movin' with that food. You gotta get back to work. Your friend LaVonda still lettin' you share that motel room?"

Nikki nodded, eyes on the bacon and eggs she was moving with a spatula from the frying pan to the plates.

"What's that? Speak up." Myron rose up off the couch.

"Yeah, Myron, she lettin' me use it free for now 'cause she can't work 'cause — "

"Shut up, bitch, I don't care why, I just care you better bring home all the money then, since you got no overhead. Or in the head." Myron brayed at his own wit. "Nothin' in the head. Plenty on the ass, but nothing in the head."

She offered a weak smile and Myron lowered himself back down, staring at the news.

Rafe watched Myron watching the news. Myron might be going away for a good long time, but he wouldn't do much better. He was an accessory after the fact, unless he could do some quick talking if they were pulled in. If they got him to agree to testify, Myron would get him. They wouldn't send them to the same jail, but that wouldn't stop Myron, not if he had to wait twenty or thirty years. Rafe didn't like the idea of waking up every morning and wondering when he'd be looking down the barrel of a gun with a vengeful maniac on the other end of it.

"Nothing new?" he asked.

"Won't be anything new. They're 'following leads' they said this morning. We gotta make plans. New York's too hot for us but it's my turf. Most my contacts are here."

"No mention of that box?" Rafe's eyes went to the closet next to the entrance. Myron had thrown it up on the top shelf when they first got there and neither of them had looked at it since.

"Nah. Anyone who knew about that shit probably ain't gonna tell the police about it."

"If it's some kind of poison, whoever it belongs to must want it back."

"Not if they weren't supposed to have it," Myron replied. "If you lost a car with a stiff in it, you wouldn't be askin' for it back, huh?" He clicked off the TV and lumbered out toward the kitchenette.

It bothered Rafe that none of the news reports mentioned the stuff the guy had with him. That box looked like a box that would have somebody caring that it didn't get to them. Maybe someone would come on the news and mention a phone number to call, a reward or something for someone who could describe the missing item and tell them where it was. No questions asked.

No, he shook his head. There were always questions asked. Trying to make something off that stuff was just asking for trouble. They ought to take it someplace public. Put it in a bag and then leave it in a mall or out on the street somewhere. He ought to take off for somewhere before he got in this any deeper. Maybe Jersey.

Myron yelled over at him through a mouthful of bacon.

"C'mon and eat," he grunted. "We're gonna head out after dark. I got an idea someone we can ask."

* * *

Rafe looked around. This was worse than prison. The streets looked like a war zone: abandoned factories, some of them burned down. Most of the windows he could see that weren't boarded up had shards of broken glass clinging to empty frames. Gang graffiti was layered over every surface like a creeping fungus, killing everything it touched. Rafe remembered his mom singing about New York. Something about it being a wonderful town. Rafe figured his mom had never been here.

Myron wouldn't tell Rafe where they were going. They'd taken buses further west then got a cab to ride them some of the rest of the way. The driver stopped on Fifth.

"I ain't going any further, fellas, I don't care what you pay me."

Rafe had leaned in toward Myron, turning his head away from the driver and pitching his voice low.

"Do we want him to see where we going?"

Myron had grunted and unclenched his fists. Rafe tossed the cabbie a bill and hurried to catch up with Myron, who'd started walking past the cab down Fifth.

Suddenly Myron spun back, grabbed Rafe by the shoulders and pushed him in front of the cab that had just been pulling away from the curb. The driver slammed on the brakes and horn simultaneously.

"Whatta you, nuts?" he screamed.

Myron ignored him, walked around Rafe's legs, opened the rear door of the cab, leaned in and picked up the Dollar store bag that held the box. He walked over to where Rafe had gotten to his shaky feet and with a too-calm look on his face, slammed the package into the smaller guy's chest. Rafe grabbed hold and hugged it to him as he hurried to match the larger man's stride up Fifth.

Now they stood staring at a smaller building wedged between two abandoned buildings. This one didn't look much better than the others, except it maybe wasn't falling down. Myron led the way down an alley toward a delivery door in the back.

Rafe looked carefully. The frame around the door looked reinforced, with sunken hinges that prevented jimmying. The door was metal, and there was a peephole. Myron strode up, knocked several times and settled himself where he could be seen. After a minute, they heard bolts being drawn back and slowly the door swung in. A tall, skinny man who looked to be in his fifties wearing dirty jeans and a red bandanna scanned the alleyway with brown bloodshot eyes. He motioned with the pistol in his hand.

"C'mon, get in fast, we been having trouble with the Spics."

"They tryin' to take your turf, Pete? Muscle in on your business? You're here alone?"

Rafe looked around as Pete led the two men down a hallway toward another reinforced door. Pete swung it open and they stepped into a large, mostly empty room. High bare windows let in the dark; two lamps on folding tables did little to fight back the gloom. He thought the room looked like it had been stripped almost clean pretty recently. A few folding tables, a chair and a cot in one corner were the only furniture with marks in the dust where larger objects had stood.

"You showed up just in time, Myron. Tomorrow you wouldn't've found me here. We got better quarters for the lab further south. You comin' back to work for us?" Pete tucked his gun into his waistband and straddled the chair, staring up at the two men.

Rafe noticed Pete kept his hand where he could reach his gun again quickly. He also noticed Myron didn't answer the guy's question. Instead, Myron nodded at Rafe.

"Take it out."

He grabbed the box in hands that were sweating. He wished the cab driver had taken off with it. Myron maybe would have punched him a few times, but Rafe had a premonition that would be a lot less painful than whatever the future held for him if they kept hold of this junk.

He set the box on one of the tables, unpacked the case and opened it, slid one of the vials out. Myron gestured him toward Pete impatiently.

"We came into possession of this shit and we don't know what it is, Pete. I figgered you'd know if it's a drug; you seen about everything a person could shoot, smoke or snort."

Rafe went to hand the vial over; it slipped through his fingers. Pete smirked and grabbed it out of the air. He looked at the liquid, held it up, then glanced at the label. He frowned. He stared at it for a long moment. Then, very carefully, he rose and carried it back over to the case himself, slipping it into its niche. He took a deep breath and faced Myron.

"You dumb bastard, you're goddamned lucky I was a pre-med with a double major in chemistry at Berkeley before I got expelled for making pleasure chemicals and decided to go into that business. You know what you have there? You have some kind of virus."

He paused while Myron looked at him blankly and Rafe looked everywhere else in the room but at Pete.

"A disease, a germ, a plague. I don't know what all for sure. All I know is it's some kind of strain of bird flu, maybe, but some of the symbols don't match exactly. It's probably some kind of hybrid strain, which makes it unknown which makes it dangerous."

"Is it contaguous?" asked Myron, wiping his hands on his shirt. He'd been *handling* that shit.

"Did you ever hear of a plague that wasn't? As to how *contaguous*," Pete said scornfully, "I don't have a clue. It could be something they were working on for a vaccine. It could be something like a hantavirus that they were fooling with and made even more deadly. The box has a biohazard symbol slapped on it."

"What should we do? Throw it away?" asked Rafe.

"No! You unleash this, you could start an outbreak." Pete looked at Myron, the expression he saw there made him add. "And if it's quick spreading, you won't be able to get away before you get infected too. It could travel through the air and travel from person to person quicker than you'd believe. Put it back where you found it. Put it someplace safe, then call in an anonymous tip."

"We could leave it here," said Rafe.

"No!" shouted the other two men.

The three of them looked at each other.

"It's ours, Rafe," said Myron. "There's gotta be a way we can make something off it."

"All you'll make off it is dead," snapped Pete. "And you'll take me with you. You can't leave it here. Listen, Jones. Rent a locker at the bus station. Someplace nobody's going to come on it by accident, open it up. Then call in an anonymous tip to the police. Problem solved. It isn't going to make you any money, man. Nobody wants it but the ones who lost it and they're not going to give you a reward for turning it in."

They'd never give him a reward, thought Rafe. *They know whoever's got it's probably the one who stole the car and — and...* He wouldn't let himself finish that sentence. *I wasn't there. I met up with him in the Bronx. After Myron was on foot again. Myron never told me anything.*

He came out of his thoughts abruptly when he noticed a glint. Pete had withdrawn his gun and had backed into a corner, sweeping it back from Myron to Rafe.

"I think you two better leave. Now." Pete jerked his head toward the door. "I'll follow you out. Make sure you don't get lost." And to Rafe, "Pick it up. You go first. I don't want you to get nervous and drop it."

Rafe passed Myron on his way out. He noticed the big man's face had turned brick red; he could almost see distortions in the air from the heat radiating off his body. He moved quickly down the hallway, one finger hooked through the bag's handle, wishing he could leave everything behind.

He heard a soft grunt behind him and turned quickly, the bag swinging against his body. Rafe didn't have time to be concerned for what he was carrying. Pete must have come too close to Myron as they went through the door. The larger man had the smaller pinned to the wall. Pete was trying to get his arm free and turn the gun on Myron. Rafe sucked in a gasp as the gun swung in his direction; he could see Pete's hand squeezing as he strained to move. Before he had time to dive out of the way, the bullet had whizzed past him, struck the outer door and ricocheted back, struck a wall and bounced to the floor. Myron grunted, slowly bringing Pete's arm towards the wall. Rafe heard the crack as a bone snapped in Pete's arm. The skinny man screamed once, then again when Myron rammed his arm against the wall — once, twice — until the gun fell to the floor.

Pete groaned and sagged.

"Get the hell out of here, man," he moaned. "Okay? Just go. What am I going to do? Go to the cops?"

Myron didn't answer. Rafe felt a chill roll through his body. This was like what he'd heard happened with Myron and his old cellmate. Once Myron made up his mind about something, he wouldn't stop.

And he didn't now. He brought one of his massive forearms against Pete's throat and pushed as if he were trying to make his arm hit the wall behind Pete. The older man's face turned purple, eyes bugging, his legs kicking against Myron's. His other arm clawed at the arm across his neck. Gradually his movements slowed and stopped.

"Myron... y-you..."

"Shut up."

Rafe realized that Myron wasn't going to stop until he was sure Pete was dead. He backed toward the delivery door, and then realized he didn't want to hang around outside either. He turned his back on the two men, standing still until he heard the heavy sound of the body falling to the floor and Myron's tread heading towards him. The big man was tucking Pete's gun into his waistband.

"Wait." Myron opened the door carefully, eyes trying to scan every way at once. "C'mon, hurry."

The two men, one large and muscular, the other shorter and scrawny, began moving back through the streets, sticking to the shadows. They met few people. The bag felt heavier to Rafe. He kept imagining a gang surrounding them, grabbing the box and opening it up.

Accessory, he thought. *Accessory before, during, and after the act. I'm in with him now, till the end of this. No heading out on my own, not now.*

He licked his lips, swallowed, throat so dry he almost choked. "You didn't have to do that. He was right, who could he tell?"

"Lotsa people. People who woulda come after us, turn us into the cops, try to grab the shit. Plenty a uses for this. There's some way we're gonna make somethin' off this. We ain't got no money hardly and we can't just go out and start boosting cars again. I wasn't gonna work for Pete no more anyhow, no matter how fun it might a been, busting some Spic and nigger asses."

"Shouldn't we get out of town? We could start over somewhere new. Maybe Jersey?"

"Yeah, we're gettin' out. We gotta think tonight, make plans. We can't just take off. Ain't no one gonna connect me and Pete, ain't had nothin' to do with him since I got sent down. Anyone coulda got him — the niggers, a junkie who came found out he had no shit hangin' around for him to buy, anyone. Cops won't look too hard to find who offed someone runnin' a lab, they'll just pin it on someone they wanna bust."

"I guess so, Myron." Rafe looked around at the buildings hanging over him on all sides. His heart thudding in his chest, he thought they looked like a big maze of endless twists and turns and he was running alongside Myron, rats trying to find their way out. But they'd never make it out. Rafe pictured coming to an end, seeing fresh air and open land beyond, and before he had a chance to escape, a big hand dropped out of the sky, scooped him up and set him back in the middle of the maze again.

Chapter Five

Remo CHANCED A GLANCE AT the seat next to him. They had hit traffic heading into Schuylerville in the East Bronx and had slowed to a crawl. Chiun had been silent since leaving Folcroft.

"Little Father," Remo began.

"Do not 'Little Father' me, Remo Williams. Did you speak up against the Emperor Smith's flimsy reasons for sending me with you? Could you not at least shame him by saying what a privilege and honor it was to have your beloved father along to keep you from making a bigger fool of yourself than you usually do? And that you did not know how the Emperor would cope without the presence of his premier assassin by his side during these dark times?"

Remo squirmed in his seat.

"He just figured you were needed more on the assignment."

"There is no need to add lying to your faults. You do not want me here. The Emperor does not want me there. I am treated as a piece of refuse, tossed hither and yon." Chiun folded his hands into the sleeves of his brocade robe and stared resolutely out the window.

Remo noticed a gap in the left lane and swerved out. They moved ahead a few car lengths before coming to a halt again. Remo groaned to himself. This was going to be a long trip and he didn't hold much hope the FBI would be able to point him toward a target.

* * *

"Agent Walker? Mr. Pak?"

The heavyset man with steel gray hair rose out of his chair when Remo and Chiun entered his office. Remo noticed the bags under his eyes and figured the Director hadn't been getting much sleep lately. And he noticed the agent eye's flick up from his chinos to his t-shirt and over to Chiun. He smiled.

"We're under cover. Agent Carson, what can you tell us? Do they know who the guys are?"

"One of them; I pulled his file. The other man kept to the shadows."

He took a folder off his desk, slipped a few photos out and handed them to Remo. Remo scanned the front face, profile, and full-body pictures.

"Myron Jones. Released from West Penn, the correctional facility in Pittsburgh, the day before Sampas was found murdered near Monroeville. Convictions for assault, pimping. He was suspected in the murder of a prostitute about eight years ago but they couldn't get a conviction."

"Sounds like a real sweetheart." Remo looked at the shaved head, squashed nose and small, cruel eyes. "You haven't found him?"

"It's a big city and Jones isn't going to be making himself easy to find. He had no known address when he was picked up five years ago. He mainly worked the Bronx, living off and on with a couple of the women he'd been whoring out. We've questioned both of them. Their names and addresses are in the file if you want to have a go getting information out of them. They both insist they haven't seen him, they're happy he hasn't made contact and they have no idea who his friends are or where he'd hole up now. We've set up surveillance at both residences, but I don't really expect him to show up. Jones has no known associates; he's a real loner, antisocial. His psych reports all agree: he's a violent sociopath, hates minorities, I.Q. in the low normal range." Carson broke off, looking past Remo at Chiun, who was looking over a display of golf trophies in a case under the window.

"Are you sure you two can handle Jones? He's a pretty mean fighter and he may still have his partner, that is, if he hasn't killed him by now.

"We're pretty good with dumb oxen," Remo gestured at Chiun. "My partner over there is one of the deadliest men in the world."

"Partner?" hissed Chiun in Korean. "I am your superior in every way."

"He says he's looking forward to taking the big guy on."

"Except in stupidity," added the Master of Sinanju. "In that, you reign unchallenged."

Remo turned back to Carson. "You're still looking for the box?"

"Yes, there's a chance he threw it away. I've had agents checking the route he must have used and we're still conducting searches around the area the car was found. So far nothing. It may still be with Jones. But he could have thrown it away any time within the last four days. We can't search every dumpster, trash can and back alley in the city. If the virus has been introduced into the area, the incubation period is twelve to twenty-four hours. The CDC has alerted area hospitals to report unusual spikes in flu cases." Carson glanced over at Chiun, who had turned his back on the conversation.

"You come highly recommended by Agent Jones. He says the two of you have special skills. I hope one of them is finding needles in haystacks."

"That's actually not that hard if you bring a magnet," said Remo. "We'll start with those two women. Mr. Pak has the kind of open, sympathetic face that gets information from even the most hostile witnesses."

"Just find Jones, Agent Walker. Get the virus away from him. Our best analysts believe he wants to stay in New York."

* * *

"We need to get out of the Bronx," said Rafe.

He had Myron were back at Nikki's, sitting in the small kitchenette. The bare bulb over the table and the flickering images from the TV were the only sources of light in the apartment.

"No, we're as safe as we're gonna get. Better to lay low until we have a plan."

Myron looked over at the box. Rafe had wanted to put it in the closet out of sight, but Myron seemed fascinated by it, now that he knew what was in it.

"Only way we gonna get money is to threaten to break that shit open unless they pay us to give it to them."

"Who's them? The cops?"

"Nah. Too bad we don't know what hospital lost it. They'd put the money in a bag, leave it somewhere, we'd get it and leave off the germs."

"We'd go to get it and the cops will be all over our asses!" said Rafe. "Even if we tell whoever we tell not to call the cops, they *always* call the cops. Don't you watch movies?"

"We gotta figure out who to call, then we gotta outsmart 'em."

Rafe opened his mouth. Then he closed it. Then he opened it again and thought better of it. He knew that Myron didn't have much going in the brains department, but he knew what happened to anyone who made Myron feel stupid."

"What we need's a way to get the money to us without them gettin' us. The FBI."

"What about them?" asked Rafe. Thinking was making his head hurt.

"We call the Feds with our demand. Those germs are dangerous; whoever lost 'em would get in touch with the FBI. It ain't been in the news. They deal with big stuff, they been keepin' it outta the news. They don't want to scare everybody."

Rafe could hear the news blaring on the set behind him. A story about Staten Island still cut off from the mainland and the hardships and hunger of the Island's residents.

"Do you really think it's a good idea to take on the Feds?" He asked.

"Sure. We just need a great idea. We gotta be able to get the money without anyone grabbin' us, and..."

Myron's voice trailed off. He was looking past Rafe at the TV. Rafe twisted his head around. The scene had switched underground. A reporter was in a subway station, interviewing some kind of an official. Rafe could see it had been flooded, but the waters had subsided, but the station was full of mud and debris. Myron's chair scraped the linoleum; the bigger man moved toward the couch, never taking his eyes off the screen.

"Get some rest. On the chair," he snapped, as Rafe made a move to join Myron on the couch. "And keep quiet. I got thinking to do but I wanna hear this first."

* * *

Harold Smith couldn't sleep. Power had been restored a few hours previously and Smith had been relieved to give the order to switch off the generators. He made his way slowly, drawn to the subbasement. An electronic passkey opened a steel door marked *Danger! High Voltage* and Smith walked inside. He flicked a switch and stared at the Folcroft Four.

The water had receded a few days previously. Smith looked at the panels he had removed then. Nothing had changed. The components were fried, the motherboards were ruined, the information lost.

Smith wasn't a sentimental man. He took his personal losses and the crushing pressure of running CURE with a New England stoicism ingrained in him by his upbringing. And yet here he was, staring at computers that he had determined days ago were unsalvageable. Smith had upgraded them whenever there was a breakthrough in processing speed, memory, or efficiency. After so many changes, nothing had remained of the original computers except the casings.

Standing down there, he took a moment to admit to himself that he mourned their passing. He inclined his head in a small salute, turned, and closed the door.

The Folcroft Four were the past. He had to secure the future.

He made his way up to the administration floor, walking directly to a door halfway down, opening it to a small room that wasn't much bigger than a closet. The small desk and chair filled most of the available space.

Smith sat behind his old desk, one that he had passed on to a colleague. He reached out a steady hand and pressed the button that raised the keyboard from its concealed space within the desktop. The computer had once been Smith's also. His finger depressed the power button and he waited while the programs loaded. He hoped he could find what he was looking for.

Mark Howard had been very enthused when he'd told Smith what he'd uncovered.

"I've been talking with some of my old CIA contacts," he said.

"Were you able to find out how close they are to pinpointing Bin Laden's location? I haven't been able to find any information using my usual methods."

"Not yet, but I may have come across something more important. Back when I was an agent rumors were going around about an advanced computer technology that was several generations ahead of what we consider cutting edge. Now — "

Smith frowned. He had a vague feeling the Folcroft Four had just been insulted. He noted Mark's barely concealed excitement. "Is this pertinent?" he talked over Mark.

"Yes. I had been asking about computer models of Afghanistan's terrain. One of my contacts let slip a name — FORTEC — then tried to pass it off as a hoax or a joke. Kind of like the Holy Grail of computer tech. I let it go and tried to do a search on my own, but nothing turned up. I've been pressing my contact and he finally admitted he had overheard the Director mention it and when he told his partner, the man had told him to forget it or he might just disappear one day."

"Then that is that?"

"No. I kept on with him and he finally told me FORTEC sells advanced tablets, something called FORtab, but I can't find that online either, or any information on how to purchase one. A few days ago he gave me a name: Germain Bloch. When I did a search for him, I found a site. Just his name and an email address. We've corresponded a few times; Mr. Bloch has sent me some specs and a phone number. But I wanted to touch base with you before I tried calling him."

But that day Smith's object had been to pull Mark off everything else to concentrate on pinpointing Bin Laden's location. Mark then volunteered to go in before the SEAL team, make sure the intelligence they had received was accurate. He had disappeared in Afghanistan. Smith's most diligent searching hadn't been able to find a trace of Mark in nearly two years.

He keyed in the password, searched through Mark's files. He finally found the information he wanted in two encrypted files labeled "New Tech." He scanned through the first one, his frown deepening. This was ridiculous. The sheer computational numbers that the device boasted was beyond any current projection of computer power. It simply wasn't possible for any company to be that far ahead of the curve. Computer technology increased exponentially, but this was unbelievable. He glanced over the other specs and almost shut Mark's computer down. Reluctantly, he opened the second file.

Mark had saved his emails to and from Bloch. Germain claimed to be an engineer at FORTEC, but he was short on any practical information about either the company or the technology it claimed to have created.

Mark had been persistent. He had pressed Germain to purchase a FORtab — preferably two. Smith scanned the last email. He noticed it had been sent the night Smith had ordered Mark to suspend all activities to concentrate on the raid. Germain's number was included. Mark had typed at the bottom: bad timing, can't call until I can give this my full attention, Dr. Smith has to be convinced to upgrade — CURE must take this opportunity to keep ahead of the cutting edge.

Smith stared at the note. Reread it. He knew Mark had expected to come back to this after he returned from Afghanistan. But he also felt as if Mark were speaking to him now, had known Smith was going to find this when it was most needed. He picked up Mark's phone and dialed the number. He listened as it rang five times.

"Hello, Dr. Smith."

The voice was similar to Smith's. It was every bit as dry, but richer, with an undertone of laughter that discomforted Smith.

"To whom am I speaking?"

"Why don't you call me Germain? It has been over a year since Mark Howard's disappearance. I thought I might hear from you sooner but it seems it took a natural disaster to remind you of us."

"Yes," Smith said. "I have been reading the specs you gave my assistant. If they are to be believed your product is very highly advanced."

"Normally, we do not sell technology. Even the knowledge of FORTEC is on a need to know basis. But not to worry, Dr. Smith. As director of... Folcroft Sanitarium, you qualify."

Smith noted the hesitation. Maybe the speaker had to pause to search for Smith's title. But he didn't believe that was the reason. Whoever was running FORTEC, could they suspect the existence of CURE?

Smith kept his voice level, determined not to let this person know he was impressed. Smith had suspected that if Mark's data was at all accurate, they would be able to bypass Smith's secure lines and trace the call back to the sanitarium.

"Then we are settled. I would like to arrange to acquire two of your FORtabs. One needs to be administrator control, the other needs to have user access only."

"I think I can do something for you, Dr. Smith. Expect delivery in two days."

"How much — " Smith began.

"If this were anyone else but Harold Winston Smith," humor suddenly bubbled up from the voice, like water coming to the surface of a dried-up riverbed, "I would say 'if you have to ask you couldn't afford it.'"

"Germain" broke the connection.

Smith hit the button to transfer Mark's FORTEC files to his computer. He was looking forward to dismantling and reverse engineering the components. And perhaps improving on it. He would need to make sure it couldn't be accessed remotely by them before he used it to investigate FORTEC.

Chapter Six

RAFE DREAMED HE WAS back at West Pen. The door of his cell was open and Rafe knew, as you frequently know in dreams without being told, that he was getting released. He wandered through the prison wearing prison-issue coveralls, his duffel bag over his shoulder though he didn't remember going to the admin area to sign out. He wasn't escorted either. He knew the layout of the prison, but the corridors seemed to be twisting and turning in on themselves. Rafe walked for what felt like hours; he thought he heard voices sometimes but he couldn't find anyone.

He paused at the top of a flight of stairs, looking over the rail and through the openings in between the steps. He thought he was maybe four, five flights up, even though West Pen didn't have that many stories. Rafe looked again. There was someone down at the bottom. He saw the top of a head, wavy brown hair. Then the figure looked up. The cocky smirk, the laughing eyes. Rafe let out a whoop. It was Gabe! Gabe would know the way out. He knew everything. Didn't he always come around — not often, but enough that Rafe never forgot him. When he showed up in the neighborhood it was like Christmas. The kick-ass gear, the expensive shoes, tossing bills at the neighbor kids — "Hey, keep an eye on my car." Gabe taught Rafe a lot: how to make a living boosting cars and junk, how to find a good fence. Lots of important stuff.

Rafe flew down the stairs, yelling, "Gabe, wait up! Gabe! It's Rafe, hang on, man." But the staircase seemed to lengthen as Rafe went down three levels, six levels, eight levels.

And all the time Gabe moved down too, always keeping at least four flights ahead of Rafe. Rafe was gasping for air, screaming "wait, wait wait!" when he heard a door bang, hard. Someone grabbed his arm and he fought to get away until a hand slapped him hard across the face and he woke up to see Myron's face scowling over him.

"No, we ain't gonna wait. I been out gettin' us a car. Sun'll be comin' up in an hour. We're headin' out before it gets too light."

"Where?" Rafe gasped. He was still in the middle of his dream, still looking for Gabe.

"Washington Heights."

"Why there? What's the plan?"

"Manhattan's a worse mess than here. Electricity's still out in a lotta places, some of the subway tunnels are still closed. You saw that reporter in the subway last night. When we call the feds, it'll be a lot harder to get to us there. We can use the subway. Threaten if we don't get the money we'll break them things in there and get out before we get sick. When they do get us the money, we can head south. Maybe we'll go to Mexico, keep goin' further down to one of them little countries where we can live large 'cause stuff's cheaper there. What are you doin'?"

The last was directed toward the bedroom door. Rafe saw Nikki start back, then edge out.

"Nothin', hon. I gotta get Marcus his sippy cup."

"He's back?"

"Yeah, LaVonda couldn't watch him no more."

Marcus was Nikki's son. The toddler had gotten on Myron's nerves and Nikki had been smart enough to ship him over to her friend's house pronto. Nikki moved toward the kitchen. She opened the refrigerator door, eyes fixed on Myron, watching to see if he made a move towards her.

"Don't matter. We're clearin' out."

"Oh, I — I'm gonna miss you, hon." Nikki tried to smile seductively but Rafe could see the relief in her eyes.

"Like you missed me when I was in jail? You missed me so much you got yourself a little jiggaboo baby while I was gone."

"Don't talk that way, hon, I missed you somethin' awful, but I had to work. Babies just happen, that's all."

"Yeah," Myron growled. "And you hadda take time off till he got born. You got rid of plenty of others I bet, what was so special about this one?"

"Since you weren't around to help with money, I figured I could get free stuff with a baby — WIC, more welfare. That's all."

Something banged near the bedroom door. They all turned. A small boy in a diaper and t shirt was sitting on the floor next to the table. He'd taken the case down, opened it, and small fingers were trying to flip the lid of the inner box.

"Goddamn it!" Myron charged across the room like a freight train, but Nikki reached the child first. She pulled the box away from the toddler, who squalled, trying to hang on. Myron grabbed it away from the two of them, set it on the table, and then leaned down, his other arm swinging toward the boy.

"No, Myron, no!" Nikki screamed and threw herself across the boy, her back absorbing the blows. Myron tried to reach around her, but the woman squirmed this way and that, always managing to keep herself between the two. Underneath his mother, the frightened boy's shrieks reached a piercing crescendo.

Rafe ran toward them and grabbed at Myron's shoulder.

"Stop, Myron, it's not worth it. The box is okay, nothings broken."

Myron backhanded Rafe, who fell against a lamp, both crashing down to the floor. The table teetered, the box tipping toward the edge. Rafe got his balance and grabbed for it, pushing it back to safety.

The four of them froze in place, the child's wails turning into sobs. Rafe spoke first.

"We're leaving anyway, you — we're wasting time with this. And it'll bring the neighbors running. The stuff's okay, let's pack up and go. *Please*, Myron," he panted.

Myron's breathing was heavy. The brick red of his complexion slowly faded. He moved toward the bedroom, aiming a kick at Nikki's prone body. Rafe sighed and grabbed for his duffel bag. They were heading out with no real plan that he could see and Myron was going to call the FBI. He wished he were back in the pen, dreaming of getting out. Without Myron.

* * *

Remo stopped in front of the run-down brownstone. The street was quiet this early in the morning. The only people out were young mothers pushing strollers and old people. They were taking advantage of a few quiet hours before the druggies, gangs, and hookers rose at noon to get on with giving the neighborhood its color. Remo figured he'd find the two women — LaVonda White and Jasmine Turner — at home. He glanced to either side. There were three suspiciously clean homeless people loitering across the street and down near the corner. The FBI was trying to disguise their agents better. Remo thought they needed a lot more practice.

Chiun sat in the car, studying the fashions in the small boutique on the first floor.

"You sure you don't wanna come up, Little Father?"

"If you question these strumpets as you usually question females, I do not want to be in the same room. I will probably hear you carrying on from down here. Besides, I must become used to sitting in automobiles. I have

330

heard these are where many homeless people find shelter. Perhaps Smith will spare a few pennies for a used car where I can lay my head down."

"It's only been a few days. Smitty'll work on finding us a place as soon as he fixes his computers."

"Every day you say it is only a few days," Chiun sniffed. "If I am fortunate, the Emperor might purchase me a Youvie. I could possibly fit all my trunks into a Youvie."

"I'll leave a window cracked down," said Remo. "Listen, Little Father, the FBI's watching the house. If anyone starts giving you a hard time or tries to steal the car, could you please deal with it without killing them?"

Chiun drew himself up. "I do not need to kill. I instruct."

"As long as you don't make it a terminal lesson," Remo replied. He ran up the steps. Since LaVonda White's apartment was three flights down from Jasmine's, he figured he'd start with her. He paused outside the door, listening. Two hearts were beating inside. Remo shrugged and knocked.

"Who is it?" called a gravelly voice.

"I'm interviewing contestants for *American Idol*. You got any talent in there?"

"Get lost!"

A second voice. A younger woman, thought Remo.

"I'm a junior G-man. I only have to question two more women and I'll get my secret decoder ring and dark glasses."

"Look, we told you guys everything we know which is nothing." said the first voice. She'd moved to the door. Remo could hear the rasping of congested lungs as she fought for each breath.

"Last time, ladies. I promise. I don't want to insist, but it's either answer my questions here or down at the office."

He heard locks being opened, the sound of a deadbolt drawn back. The door opened as far as the heavy chain would allow and a bleary brown eye looked out. Remo held up his ID.

"You don't look like no Fed." The eye looked down at Remo's loafers and traveled up the chinos and t-shirt before looking at his face.

"I'm in disguise. You've probably seen some suspicious characters hanging around outside. They're waiting for Myron Jones to pay you a visit."

"God forbid."

The door closed, the chain was unhooked and the door opened. Remo walked into a crowded kitchen. Pots from several meals were on the stove; dishes were piled on the sink and table. A younger woman sat drinking coffee. She gazed up at Remo impassively.

The first woman wheezed over to the table, sat and lit a cigarette. Remo had already been sipping his breath through his mouth. He could smell the infection on the woman's breath even through the smoke.

"Shouldn't you get to a doctor, Miss — ?" he asked.

"LaVonda. I been. He gave me some pills and told me get plenty of rest. The cigarettes help calm me down," she added, seeing Remo eying the smoke. "I don' care if they make the breathin' a little harder. And you bein' here ain't restful or calmin'."

"This won't take long," said Remo. "It would take a lot less longer if you'd tell me what you know. If you cooperate, I can make you feel better."

The woman glanced at each other and cackled, LaVonda's laugh ending in a deep hollow cough. The other woman — Jasmine — looked Remo up and down and licked her lips.

"Maybe you could, honey," she said. "But we ain't gonna find out today. Vonda's too sick and I don't get off on her watchin' us. 'Less you'd like to pay for that?" she arched an eyebrow.

"Sorry, ladies, not today. Let's get down to business. Have you seen Myron Jones lately?"

"We already told the other feds no," said Jasmine. "Look," she added. "We hope we never see that bastard again, so we got no reason to hide where he is. He was a mean one when we worked for him. He broke my arm once when he thought I was holding money out on him. And he broke Vonda's collarbone twice. And her nose. She never breathed right after it healed. And we been black and blue all the time."

"Asshole," growled LaVonda. "He say we don't bring in enough money but even the johns got turned off by the bruises he give us, so we earn less and he just get madder. Finally one day he gone and they say the police come for him and we had a party, me an Jas, yessir."

Remo was looking around the room. He saw some toys in the corner. "Where's your kid?" he asked.

"We ain't got no kid. We just babysat for a friend."

"With you so sick?" Remo continued, talking over LaVonda. "Was Myron pimping out other women?"

"Yeah, some," said Jasmine. "We were his main stable, but he'd try another gal sometimes. He used to like beatin' the shit out of some pimp and takin' his ho away. He mostly didn't keep them."

"So you know other women he's pimped. He did keep some then? Could he have gone to one of them? We know he's in the city." Remo bent to look LaVonda in the eye. "If you tell me where he is, I'm taking him in. He won't know who talked. I promise."

"Vonda, maybe — "

"Shut up!"

Jasmine walked around the table and grabbed LaVonda's hand.

"Look, we had to have Nikki pick him back up last night. You was too sick but we be sick all day thinkin' about him over there."

"So you know where he is? What's Nikki's last name and address?"

"We didn't lie to you feds," LaVonda said. "We don't know it's Myron. We know Nikki from way back 'cause she is one of the hos he kept. She was only with us a few months when they nabbed Myron. So a few days ago Nikki comes over says can we keep Marcus with us awhile." She and Jasmine traded glances. "We know what that mean, means she got someone with her and the baby's in the way."

"You get that look off your face right now," Jasmine said to Remo. "She loves that boy. She almost died havin' him. Nikki said a doctor told her with the abuse she got growin' up, she'd probably never have no kids. She'd do anything for that boy. If Myron came to her when he got out, she had to get the boy out of there."

"Name," said Remo. "Address."

***

Remo listened at another dented metal door in another run down hallway in a brownstone a few miles away. Movements inside. Two heartbeats, but one was the faster beat of a young child and the television was blaring out a kiddie show — *Mulberry Road*, Remo noted with a grimace. He decided against ripping the door off its hinges and knocked instead. He could hear someone on the other side of the door, hear the rustle as she lifted her body against the door to look out the peephole.

"Listen, I know Myron Jones has been here. Let me in, I can help you. You're not in any trouble." Remo lifted his FBI badge so Nikki could see it.

The door opened. A woman's large form blocked the door.

"He's not here, he left, he not comin' back soon. Or maybe ever," she mumbled in a flat monotone.

Remo pressed forward, forcing her to back up.

"That's wishful thinking, isn't it, sweetheart?"

He looked at her split lip. She turned and walked back into the apartment, moving carefully, favoring one leg. Remo looked at the little boy in front of the television, who had turned away from the program and was looking solemnly in Remo's direction. He looked about three, wearing a one-piece sleeper and clutching a bowl full of dry cereal loops. Remo noted that the boy was unbruised and looked healthy.

"Can you tell me anything about where he went? Did he have a case with him? Was he by himself?"

Nikki looked at Remo, her lips pressing tight together. She glanced over at her son then slowly shook her head.

"C'mon, sweetheart, you take good care of your son. You love him. Do you want Myron coming back here? If I catch up with him I can promise you you'll never see him again."

She gave him the look of a woman who had heard a lifetime of empty promises. Her eyes went to her baby, tears welling up. She turned back to Remo and took a deep breath, wincing.

"Yeah, he had some kinda box. He wouldn't let me ask about it or touch it. He had someone with him, too. I think his name was Jeff somethin'. I heard 'em talking, they say they going into Manhattan and they gonna do something bad with that box if they don't get some money, but I don't know what. Is it a bomb?"

"Where?"

"I don't know — just in the city." Nikki frowned. "They don't talk too much in front of me, just when Myron gets mad. I think they said they wanted to go somewhere with a lot of people."

"When did they leave?" asked Remo. He twisted his wrists, wishing he had Myron there to break in two. Then he noticed Nikki looking down at them with the wary air of an animal that was getting ready to run ahead of a beating. He stopped.

"Couple hours ago, I think."

"Look," he said to Nikki. "You seem like a good mother. Why don't you quit your 'job,' get some training. I don't usually recommend going on welfare, but it's better than this and I think you're someone who'll use it so you can get off it."

She straightened up proudly. "I quit what I was doin' when I knew I gonna have a baby. I'm goin' for my GED. I only went back now 'cause

Myron gonna kill me if I don't get him some quick money."

"You won't have to worry about him any more," Remo promised. "If I can find them."

He'd gone back to the car, grabbed the phone, and tried several times to unlock it. Chiun had raised an eyebrow and flicked out a nail, delicately drawing it across the face. Remo grunted and pressed the 1 button until Smith picked up.

"Hey, Smitty. Bad news. I tracked down the woman's apartment where he was holed up, but he blew out of there a few hours ago. Along with some other guy, Jeff something, she only heard his first name. All she could tell me was they've got the virus with them and they're heading into Manhattan, looking for crowds. They talked about getting money, too, ask for ransom, if they can figure out who to ask."

There was a long pause on the other end.

"You are sure she is telling you the truth?"

"Yeah. She's afraid of him but she wants them caught."

"Crowded places in Manhattan."

"Yeah, that really narrows it down. Any ideas where"

"Just in Manhattan? Rockefeller Center, sports arenas, television studios. Even if I could access my database, you would not be able to find them in time. Alert Agent Carson. Have him call FEMA and the Red Cross. They're around areas that are still off limits due to flood damage. The National Guard is patrolling sections of Manhattan. Get him to pull soldiers away from their other duties to increase patrols around the more likely spots."

"What about me, Smitty?"

"We have to hope the National Guard will spot them. Or they'll call and give away their location."

"Like take a picture of themselves in Times Square holding up the virus posted on Facetube?"

"Stupidity and poor planning are usually contributing factors when catching criminals. And Myron Jones' history would suggest he possesses those traits."

"Okay, Smitty. We'll head out, probably Times Square would be central, and wait. Let's hope he gives himself away."

Chapter Seven

"YOU SURE ABOUT THIS, MYRON?"

Meeks' voice echoed in the vast chamber even over the roar from the portable generators that ran the fans. The hot stench of diesel blew through the vast empty station. He looked around. Bright yellow heating ducts twisted throughout, crisscrossed over each other and disappearing into the tunnels on each side of the station. To Rafe, they looked like giant earthworms, like they'd been dropped in the middle of some old sci-fi movie that had mutants dragged up from the bottom of the ocean floor by the storm to invade the subways of Manhattan.

"Yeah. I've got a plan."

They were walking along next to the tracks at the 181st Street station. Rafe looked down. The track was still muddy and littered with debris. Dirt still covered much of the floors and stained the walls higher than Myron's head.

"We're doing the exchange here?"

Myron was looking around. "No. You know the system?"

Rafe shook his head.

"This is the Eight Avenue Local. It's close to the river so it got flooded. It connects up with the C line and another line at 168th Street. Those didn't flood and they're open to the public. Here's how it goes down. After we're through casing out here, we're gonna head down near Times Square somewhere. We call the FBI, tell 'em we got the virus and they're gonna give us five million in small, unmarked bills in a case or we're gonna release it in a crowded place. We give 'em a time limit. We don't get the money by then, we release it."

"So we have them drop it off in Times Square or we release it here? If we tell them a place, won't they know where we'll be? Times Square's loaded with cops. If the Feds don't grab us, they will."

"No, we don't tell them about here, asshole. We just — we just..."

Rafe could see Myron's ears turning red. Dammit, he hadn't thought this through, not if Rafe could see the holes in the plan. And anyway —

"Five million? Five? I know people won't play the lottery till it goes past ten. How come we're asking for so little?"

"'Cause it takes time to get a lot of money together. Five million ain't a lot so they can get it quicker. The best way we got of pulling this off is if we hit 'em quick. Don't give 'em much time to react or set up any traps. It ain't much, sure, but we go to South America or somewhere, we can live good."

"But how can we be sure they won't set a trap? Wherever we meet them, won't they be able to surround us, even if we don't give them much time?"

"Because we're gonna tell 'em send one Fed to Central Park, alone, no tails. Tell 'em we see a tail, we'll know and we'll go off, release it. That way they'll think we're in Times Square, that we're gonna release it there. We're gonna tell 'em give the Fed a phone, give us his number. Once he's in place, we call and have him take the subway."

"To here?"

"No. We send him around for a while. Different stations. Make damn good and sure he don't have any back up. We end him up at 168th Street Station with the money, drop it, we grab it, drop the virus, we come back here. There's an access tunnel between there and here. We can jump down on the tracks and cut through, then we get above ground through the access door we got in here with. Once we get back up in the street we'll be fine, steal a car, head out for Jersey then down South. Maybe drive straight through to Mexico, I don't know. We'll need to get someone to make us up some passports but we'll have the money and I know people in Jersey City."

Rafe saw Myron's gaze turn sly.

" Maybe just send you to 168th Street. I stay here with the virus. That way I tell the FBI if they don't let you get away with the money, I'll release the virus. After you get away, you call me and I can call 'em and tell 'em where to pick it up."

And if they set up a trap, I'll be the one who gets caught, thought Rafe. *If Myron doesn't hear from me, he can split.*

"I don't think we should split up, Myron. I bet they'll put a locator on the guy; they'll follow him to 168th and nab me. He's FBI; he'll be working to get us nabbed."

"You so smart, whadda you got?"

Rafe wished he had someone to help him think. Gabe could always think fast. He'd told Rafe how when he was on a job to go with the flow, keep thinking ahead, always be alert for possibilities. If only he was…

"What if we don't have them send a Fed with the money? We tell them we're gonna name a guy."

Myron frowned over at Rafe.

"What guy? Who do you know's gonna do this?"

"I know a guy who'd do us a favor for getting him out. He's in jail in Jersey. Not that far. We tell the Feds to get him sprung."

"And then he takes off with our money," growled Myron. "Stupid plan."

"No, he won't do that. Him and me, we go back a long way. We'll take him with us. If he tries to take off with the money before that, the Feds they have tailing him will catch him. When we call him that first time, we tell him he's in with us and if he wants to stay out of jail he should try to shake the guys tailing him and meet up with us."

"He'll want some of the money."

"He won't have to stay with us in Mexico. We drop him off soon as we're across the border; adios — he's got his freedom. He won't be armed; we'll keep an eye on him. It's better than them using an undercover Fed."

Myron took a deep breath, snorting it out like a bull.

"Okay, already, I wanna get movin' on this." He motioned toward a tunnel. "Outside's this way. And — "

A meaty hand pushed against Rafe's chest, stopping him as effectively as a wall. Rafe stared up into Myron's tiny eyes. Neither man blinked.

"You fuck me on this, you'll wish you were one of the people in the stations round here after I put that virus into the exhaust fans. Maybe some of them'll survive."

* * *

"Well, Smitty, we're outside FBI headquarters. How long are we supposed to sit around waiting to hear from these dipwads?"

Remo had pulled into a parking space on the side of Lafayette St. near Thomas Paine Park. He was sitting in the car while Chiun had gotten out and was walking toward a group of women taking lunch at one of the benches.

"I am still hoping the thieves will demand ransom for its return. At least then we have a chance of recovering the virus."

"If they're thinking it may take them awhile. I don't think their power's been restored all the way to the top floor."

"If they release the virus, either on purpose or accidentally, a great many people will die. It would be difficult to contain the contagion even under ideal circumstances, and with the condition of New York's infrastructure after this hurricane there simply isn't the manpower or organization to set up effective quarantines. If Jones calls I will instruct Agent Carson to transfer Jones to this number. You will need to deal with him directly."

"Sure Smitty." Remo had left the car to join Chiun while Smitty was talking. He could hear Chiun's squeaky voice drifting back to him like an accusing breeze. He broke the connection with Smith.

"The Emperor Smith has graciously stored my meager possessions but, alas, he did not wish me to remain with them. He has sent me out with my son, who is attempting to contain the spread of a terrible disease, which is a task unworthy of his skills. I have told him this, but he insists — "

"Little Father." Remo walked up to Chiun. He was standing before a trio of confused young women.

"Ah, here is my son now. He is a good boy, truly, though we are living in our vehicle while we await our targets to reveal themselves."

"Too much information," Remo called out, while pointing at his temple and motioning towards the Master of Sinanju with his eyes. He was relieved they seemed to catch on.

"They have been very sympathetic," Chiun replied. "I seek comfort where I can in such sad times."

"Yeah, but — " Remo began. His phone rang. "Hello, Smitty, I — "

"We've heard from Jones," Agent Carson's deep voice interrupted. "He didn't stay on long enough for us to trace the call, but we managed to give him this number. His future calls will go directly to you. Where are you?"

"Look out your window, I'll wave."

There was a pause on the other end.

"You're close enough. Jones made two demands. He wants five million dollars in small, unmarked bills and he wants us to release a prisoner named Gabriel Sutton from Northern State Prison in Newark. That's about an hour's drive and back with the traffic. You're supposed to bring Sutton, the money, and a disposable phone to Times Square."

"Not much money," said Remo.

"He's either smarter than he sounds or lucky. He's keeping things moving fast; five million's a lot easier to get together than two hundred million. It gives us less time to plan, less time to anticipate where they might be going and set a trap. Do you have clearance to get the money?"

"Yeah. I'm heading out to Newark," said Remo. "I can requisition the funds there. You'll have Sutton waiting for me?"

"We're trying to facilitate his release now."

"Why Sutton?"

"We have no idea. We've run a printout. He's been doing twenty for armed robbery. He's scheduled for parole in less than a month. There's nothing that connects him to Jones."

* * *

"Over there," said Rafe.

The two men were at Times Square. The digital billboards were alive once more and the square had its usual crush of people rushing past, vendors looking to make a sale and — as Rafe was pointing out — a large contingent of police and emergency personnel.

"That's okay," Myron grunted. "We ain't staying here long."

The two men were walking down Seventh Avenue, just a few more people adding to the congestion. Myron had said they would lay low for a few hours after the exchange then shop around for something to get them out of the city and headed south. The bag containing the vials banged against Rafe's leg with every step like death trying to get his attention.

"But when Gabe — Sutton — comes, they'll see us watching?"

"We ain't stayin' here, asshole. Neither is your 'friend.' I got an idea, I told you."

The two men were coming up to one of the stations leading down into the subway.

"C'mon," Myron motioned down the escalator.

"Where are we going? We're going to send him down here?"

"I told you that already."

At the bottom Rafe made for the turnstiles, but Myron grabbed him and yanked him to the side. This being New York, the few who noticed pretended not to notice, including the MTA cops lounging around the vending machines. Myron turned the smaller man so his body was blocking Rafe's from view, grabbed his collar and savagely twisted it until Rafe started seeing spots.

"Look, how good can we trust that friend of yours?" He loosened his hold.

"We can — we can — I swear, Myron, he'll come through, I promise!"

Myron let go and stepped back, but leaned down until his face was inches from Rafe's.

"Okay, then, here's what we're gonna do. We're takin' the subway to 161st Street. That's close enough to the Bronx expressway. We're gonna rent a car — I got a card ain't been reported stolen yet — and park it near the subway station. Then we're gonna call this FBI guy; tell him to send the guy down here with a phone. Then we're gonna call him on one of these phones we got and tell him a station to go to. When he gets there we're gonna tell him another station to go to. And another and maybe another. And we're gonna ask him if he's lost the tail and if he has we're gonna send him to us. We'll grab him and the cash, put the bag down on a bench, then head for the car and over the George Washington to Jersey. Got it?"

Rafe nodded violently. "Yeah, got it. You won't be sorry, Myron, this'll work."

"It better," Myron whispered. "'Cause if either one of you blows this — if I see the Feds coming for us — I'm gonna grab one of these tubes, shove it in your mouth and throw you on a third rail."

He turned and strode over to the turnstiles, Rafe rushing on shaky legs to keep up.

* * *

"What do you mean, he's not being released?"

Remo was in the warden's office at Northern State. The little man sitting behind the desk looked up at Remo, frowning in annoyance.

"The FBI does not have the jurisdiction to just order a prisoner be released," stated Robert Foley. "I need the release forms and they haven't faxed them through yet."

Remo's internal clock was more accurate than any timepiece made by man. He figured he had just over an hour to make the rendezvous and about half that time would be taken up with the drive through Manhattan. He opened his mouth to argue with the officious man and heard himself say instead, "Fine. I'll go wait outside. Let me know when the fax comes through."

The warden's secretary was wearing a gray pantsuit and sensible shoes. Remo smiled at her. Her dark brown hair was cut in a severe bob and she was frowning, but he noticed her pupils dilate as she took in the thin man in the chinos and t-shirt. The skin on her neck flushed. He moved closer.

"Sweetheart, do you happen to have the list of which cells inmates are assigned to? I don't want to bother your boss again."

She cleared her throat. "I'm not supposed to give that information out. You don't look like FBI."

"I'm undercover," Remo replied.

"Well..." she licked her lips, her fingers working to undo the top button of her blouse. "You know, I kind of have to dress plainly, working in a prison full of desperate men. I don't want to draw too much attention to myself. You ought to see me at night, when I'm dressed right."

"I'd rather see you at night when you're not dressed at all."

She pouted. "You say that now, but by tonight you'll be long gone." Her eyes darted to the outer and inner doors of the office. "There's a supply closet right down the hall. It's small but cozy."

"If you let me know where Gabriel Sutton is staying, once I take him out I'll have to bring him back." Remo leaned over until his face was inches from hers. He reached out and one finger stroked down the back of her hand. She shuddered.

"You better."

Remo took both her hands and laid them on the keyboard. A few quick strokes.

"He's on the second floor, compound B unit 202." She sighed as Remo headed for the door. "So, you'll be bringing him back tonight? I'll stay late."

"Okay, doll," Remo said. "It's a date. When I get back we'll kick your boss out, lock the doors and throw away the keys."

Remo heard her calling out as he moved down the hall, "I'll be here. I'll stay all night."

At first he moved boldly through the grounds. Remo knew from long experience that if you look like you belong somewhere people tend to assume you do. As he reached Compound B, he changed tactics.

There were legends about Ninjas who could move among men unseen, but the first practitioners had only stolen from Sinanju what they could see to imitate. But Sinanju training couldn't be copied from simple observation. Remo timed his movement to match the guard's eye motions, remaining still while in their peripheral vision, gliding forward while they blinked or turned their heads. He noted the closed circuit cameras, avoiding their sweep also. He moved through several locked doors, and up metal stairs until he came to unit 202. Remo waited for the guard on patrol to get around the corner, then he applied pressure to the cell's lock until he felt the mechanism snap, swung open the door and closed it behind him.

The man sitting on the cot looked up, startled. Remo thought he looked in his late thirties, his thin brown hair showing some gray. His skin looked rather gray too.

"Who are you?"

"Gabriel Sutton?" When the man nodded, Remo flashed his ID. "FBI. You're in my custody temporarily. I need you to do something. Come on with me."

Sutton got slowly to his feet and began edging toward the door.

"Where's the guard? There should be a guard with you. Even if you're FBI, there should be..."

Remo groaned. He'd known getting out unseen would be a bit trickier, but he'd figured once through the compound he could let the two of them be seen and use his badge to pass through. He listened. No guards nearby.

"Get in front and do everything I say. Stop when I say stop, move when I say move."

"Why? Are you really a fed? If this is okay, why aren't we just walking out?"

"Why do you care? Think of this as a field trip. If you're a good boy, I'll bring you back later tonight."

"There something off about this." Sutton's tone turned wheedling. "Why me? I'm up for parole in less than a month and the prison counselor says I've got a good chance. My record in here has been spotless and I've been learning graphics. I got a chance for a job when I get out."

"For crying out loud," Remo said. "I gotta get the one con in Jersey who *doesn't* want to leave."

Sutton opened his mouth to call out, but Remo's hand flashed toward his throat and the con's mouth opened and closed like a fish gasping for air.

"Look, you wanna walk on your own or do I have to carry you?"

When Sutton hesitated, Remo's hand moved again and Sutton slumped to the floor.

"Easier this way anyway."

The odds were Sutton was going to screw up and alert the guards, he thought. Getting out carrying a package would be easier.

Remo slipped through the main gates holding Sutton by the back of his uniform, the man's weight evenly distributed front and back. He slipped down the road to the rented black Toyota, throwing Sutton in the back. Chiun, sitting in the passenger seat, raised a slender thread of an eyebrow.

"Don't ask," said Remo.

Chapter Eight

Remo DROVE INTO downtown Newark.

"He should be coming to soon. Could you keep an eye on him until I get back?"

"So I am a baby minder, now?" The old man sighed dramatically and raised long-suffering eyes to the heavens. "Since I have nothing else to do, I will make him welcome in our new home. Perhaps you could purchase a hot plate for me? I could make tea and perhaps boil some rice?"

"We'll find a house, Little Father. Smitty'll work something out as soon as he gets CURE back up."

Remo scanned the buildings. A bank. Good. He looked around. Coffee shop, drugstore, some upscale dress shops, law offices, a place that advertised they were buying gold and silver jewelry. He had been a cop in Newark, many years ago but he seldom came back here. At first there had been too great a risk someone from his old life would recognize a man who was supposed to be dead. Now it was more that Remo had no interest in a life that felt like it had been lived by someone else. The city had been seedy back when he was a cop. Tired, run-down. The buildings looked cleaner now; many of the large garish signs on the storefronts had been removed, letting the architecture show to advantage. Remo hummed a cheerful, one-note tune as he walked the street.

He went into the drugstore, bought a disposable phone and talked the clerk into helping him activate it. Then he went into the bank.

"I need to see the manager."

Ten minutes later, Remo was back out on the street. His FBI badge had bullied the manager into supplying him with a sturdy case with handles and some shredded paper, and one of the bank accounts that CURE maintained for Remo had provided about ten thousand in stacks of twenties and fifties. As he returned to the car, he noticed the figure running down the street.

Remo ran to the car and yanked open the driver's side door.

"Dammit, Chiun!"

Serene hazel eyes gazed into the distance. Chiun spoke without turning.

"You said to watch him. I am watching him now."

Remo threw the bag on the seat.

"Can you watch this now. And while you're doing that, do you mind not letting anyone reach in and grab it?"

Remo set off after Sutton, with a loping gait that didn't appear fast, but steadily ate up the distance between him and the fleeing convict. Sutton had made it two blocks and around a corner. Remo found him panting, leaning forward, his hands on his knees.

"Too little time on the prison gym's treadmill?"

Sutton looked up.

"I just — wanna — go back to jail," he gasped. "They'll think I — escaped, I'll never — get my parole."

"Look," Remo said. "I need you to do something. After it's over I promise I'll take you back to Northern State and explain. But if you mess this up you won't have to worry about getting back anywhere."

Remo reached past Sutton to the filigreed post on a wrought iron fence surrounding the stairs to a basement apartment. He grasped the post lightly and gave a small twist. With a wrenching sound, the post cracked away from the fence. Remo showed Sutton the clean break in the metal.

"Now, c'mon. We don't have much time."

* * *

Remo, Chiun and Sutton stood in the middle of Times Square. Chiun wrinkled his nose at the smells. Remo ignored the jumps and stares from those who had gotten too close to the Master of Sinanju Emeritus.

Sutton glanced at the two other men, probably wondering, Remo figured, what the odds were of him losing himself in the crush of bodies. Remo stilled himself and let his senses reach out. Masters of Sinanju could sense the air displaced by incoming bullets and dodge them faster than most human eyes could detect the movement. They could also tell when they were being observed. Remo glanced around at the humanity packing the streets and sidewalks. Activity swirled around them, people hustling to jobs or home, tourists gaping up at the digital billboards. There was constant movement and more than a few glances his way, but he didn't sense any special interest from any one person. His phone beeped.

"Yeah?"

"You in place?" growled a deep voice.

Remo knew they had to be observing him. How else could they be sure they'd gotten everything they'd asked for? Or that the Square wasn't full of FBI? But maybe they were just plain dumb enough to think they didn't need to look?

"We're here."

"Give Sutton the money and a phone. Tell him to walk north up Seventh Avenue, go down into the 49th Street station. What's the phone number?"

After Remo told him, Jones broke the connection. Remo handed Sutton his disposable cell phone. He motioned over at Chiun.

"C'mon, Little Father, we're going for a walk."

Chiun cast a sad look in the general direction of the rental place where Remo had turned in the car. "I will miss my new home."

"Don't give me that crap now, Little Father. We're almost through with this. They've gotta be checking this out and if we could pinpoint them, I could maybe get to them quick, get that virus away from them."

"We are fast, Remo, but we do not know the distance and even we might not make it to them in the few seconds it would take for one of those cretins to panic and drop the vials containing the contagion."

Remo checked around the station, then used his FBI credentials to get them all past the turnstile. The phone Sutton was holding rang.

"Answer it," said Remo.

"Hello. Yes. Yes, I — what?" Sutton was silent for ten seconds. His eyes began to flick quickly from side to side. His mouth open and shut and he swallowed, hard.

Remo glanced over at Chiun and raised an eyebrow. Chiun shrugged. Remo nodded.

Sutton pressed the End button and put his arm down. "They want me to take the number four to the Grand Concourse — 149th Street."

"C'mon," Remo said, heading toward the tracks.

"But — "

"Just go. And don't try dodging out. I'll catch you."

"I won't," Sutton replied in a low voice. He walked out ahead of them, lugging the case with the money. Remo and Chiun set off after him.

"I don't feel any eyes watching us, Little Father."

"Why should they watch us?" Chiun nodded at Sutton.

* * *

"What the hell did you think you were doin'?"

After Myron had given the directions, Rafe had reached over and grabbed the phone.

"Hey, Gabe, don't say anything, it's me. Everything's cool, man, just follow our instructions — "

Myron had snatched the phone back, a finger disconnecting the call. Rafe watched as the other man's hand crushed the phone and threw it in a trashcan.

"He knows my voice. He remembers me. He knows things are cool. It's better he knows, now he'll be working against the FBI instead of cooperating with them."

"Says you," said Myron. He motioned at Rafe, who reached in his pocket and pulled out another phone.

They were sitting on a bench in Babe Ruth Plaza. Myron had said they had time to relax a little and take in the sight of nearby Yankee Stadium before they had to head over to 168th to make the switch. Rafe was shaking so hard he thought he could feel the bench move. Myron kept throwing him scornful looks.

"Remember, when we're down there, we look around good. We spot a cop or a Fed we keep walkin'."

Rafe nodded; he didn't trust himself to talk. Myron had taken the package into the men's room earlier. When he came out he threw the bag at Rafe, who noticed as they came up the stairs and out into the sunlight that Myron was patting his pants pocket, under the gun that was still tucked in his waistband. As they sat on the bench, Myron would pat the pocket from time to time and smile a cruel smile when he noticed Rafe watching.

"Yeah," Myron muttered. "Three subway lines go through down there. Plenty of crowds if somethin' goes wrong."

* * *

"Do you sense anyone, Little Father?"

"I am not blind," Chiun snapped. "But I cannot sense anyone taking an interest in that convict."

"They're not here yet either," sighed Remo.

The Masters and Sutton had been traveling the subway for the better part of two hours. At every stop, Sutton had phoned Jones and Jones had told him to take the subway to another station. Now they were under East 161st Street, near Yankee Stadium. Three subway lines converged at this station.

"I was sure this would be the place they'd finally crawl out of the

348

tunnels," Remo said. "If I'd known we'd be traveling this long, I woulda bought us a pass." He had just finished talking to Sutton, who was pacing back and forth with the money about a hundred yards down, near the incoming Lexington Avenue Express.

Remo handed the phone off to Chiun. "Could you hang this up for me?"

Chiun's fingernail reached out and poked a spot on the screen. "There. I have helped you again. Today will not be the day I am abandoned down in the wretched bowels of this smelly city to fend for myself."

"You don't need to prove your usefulness," Remo said. "Sutton hasn't heard from Jones yet. It may be this time he's coming here."

Chiun looked over at Sutton. He was holding the phone and looking around, trying to appear casual, but he was sweating; his shirt clung to his back and his hands shook slightly.

"That one wishes to aid the thieves."

"He knew the voice. Maybe they figure they can trust him. I don't know why. Smitty said he has no connection to Jones. I was sure they'd have given themselves away by now."

Both Masters heard the chirp of the cell phone. Remo headed that way, calling over his shoulder to Chiun, "If we can't see them, they're not close enough to see us. I'm going to make sure he's telling Jones he's alone."

* * *

"Did he lose the Feds?" Rafe asked.

The two men were standing outside the access door to the closed Eighth Avenue local, preparing to go below.

Myron hung up. "Shut up while I'm talkin' to him." He glared suspiciously at Rafe. "Yeah, he says he's alone. Can we trust him?"

"Sure, Myron, sure. I told you, he's a right guy. He knows it's me and my friends are his friends. He'll get the money to us."

"He better have made sure he wasn't followed," Myron said. The big man's hand patted the gun hidden underneath his shirt. "He said he's at Yankee Stadium. It'll take him a while to get there. It'll take us awhile to walk the access tunnel through to 168th." Rafe nodded as he watched Myron work the door open.

Chapter Nine

"DR. SMITH."

Mrs. Mikulka's voice sounded tinny over the intercom. "You have a visitor. He's from the fire department."

For a brief second while she was speaking, Smith had thought it might have been his FORtabs. "Germain" hadn't said how they would be delivered, only that they would be there in a few days. Smith had assumed UPS or the postal service and had instructed Supply not to notify him if any package came addressed to him personally, but bring it up immediately on arrival.

"Send him in." Smith removed his fingers from the keyboard embedded in his desktop. The glowing keyboard faded and the monitor went black. He had been reading through the FORtab's specs for the fifth time. He still didn't believe Mark's analysis could be correct.

"He says you should come out here." Mrs. Mikulka's voice sounded strained. "They received a report of our flooding and they say they want to inspect the subbasement. You're the only one with the keys."

Smith stood up and stretched, his spine and knees crackling. After the flood waters had receded, he had gone down there with Master Chiun, who had wanted to check the foundation before entrusting his trunks to the basement for an extended period. Smith had shuddered. One of his first priorities, once his analysis and search programs were installed in his new device, would be to set up a search for suitable accommodations somewhere close enough to Folcroft to be convenient, and far enough for Smith to be comfortable Chiun would not turn up at random times with complaints. He was grateful Chiun detested the telephone and only used it under duress, even though it made contacting Remo sometimes difficult.

Chiun had led Smith around the back of Folcroft, down to the edge of the property that overlooked Long Island Sound. He had paced back and forth, Smith watching from near the rear door, moving slowly and carefully back toward Smith. Finally, he had grunted and swept past Smith and down the stairs to the subbasement. When Smith unlocked the doors, Chiun had circled around the rooms, stamping his feet a few times. He had held his hands about six inches out from the walls, reaching out to thump them every few feet like a housewife checking melons for ripeness. He had paid particular attention to the area near the Folcroft Four. Finally, he had turned to Smith.

"There are fissures, Emperor, between here and the ocean. It took a unusual combination of events to bring the water up this far. I do not think it likely to happen again for many years."

"The foundation, Master Chiun. What about the integrity of the structure?"

The old man had frowned, the slight wisps of his eyebrows pointing down. "There has been a very slight weakening. Your successor, should you have one, would be advised to have the foundations strengthened."

"But it is safe for occupancy?"

"I will continue to store my trunks in your basement," Chiun had replied serenely and glided past Smith toward the stairs. For Smith, that was better than an engineer's assessment.

The man waiting by Mrs. Mikulka's desk was dressed in navy pants, a light blue dress shirt with the insignia of the Rye Fire Department on the sleeve and over the breast pocket. He had removed his captain's hat and was holding it in front of him, along with a clipboard.

"Captain Matt Harvey," he said, moving to shake Smith's hand. "I'm an inspector for the greater Rye area. This should be pretty routine. We received a report of storm damage. I'll need to see the area that flooded. You have a subbasement? It didn't rise higher than that?"

"No," Smith replied. "It rose perhaps two feet overall in the subbasement, three feet in an area where the floor is lower. Come with me."

They had descended to the bottom level. The inspector made notes on his clipboard. He examined the walls also, noting the height the waters had come up by the damage left behind on the walls. He humphed as he looked at the Folcroft Four.

"Those are antiquated computers we had moved down here when we upgraded several years ago," Smith said.

"I smell burnt casings and smoke. Were they active?"

"They may have been turned on just before the hurricane passed over," said Smith. "We run them on occasion. In case of an emergency, they hold redundant information which we could access if our main computers go down or are hacked."

"Was there a fire?" asked Captain Harvey.

"No, we would have informed you," answered Smith. He cleared his throat. "Our fire alarms would have gone off had there been a fire. The water destroyed the components, there were short circuits, but I came down to check after the storm passed and there was no danger."

"I'll need to check the alarm system down here."

Smith relaxed. The alarm system was up to date. It had been inspected less than six months ago and the backup systems had kicked in during the power outage.

The captain had asked to see the rear of the building and checked the foundation in back.

"Let's go back to your office, Dr. Smith."

Smith motioned to a chair in front of his desk and settled himself in his old chair. Captain Harvey cleared his throat.

"Well, you know I don't have the means to check the structural integrity of the building today. We'll be needing to come back, perhaps order some excavations along the foundation in back. If water has begun seeping in, it will need to pass inspection again. The big question is: should I order the building evacuated until we can determine the foundation can support the building?"

Smith paled. He hadn't expected this.

"The building plans are on file with the city. The architect and builder were very careful about setting the foundations squarely on a firm granite bedrock. I do not believe it has weakened measurably in the years since."

"Probably not, Dr. Smith. But there have been more stringent guidelines in effect the last year or so. Did you know Folcroft was scheduled for a reevaluation next year?"

Smith shook his head.

"The city probably hasn't gotten around to informing the buildings affected by the new laws. This was coming anyway; the flood only pushed it up sooner."

Smith licked dry lips. "If the patients are evacuated, would it be permissible to keep a skeleton staff on the premises?"

"I'm not sure, Dr. Smith. I need to contact FEMA. They may want to take charge of this. The hurricane damage gives them an excuse to get involved." Captain Harvey looked at Smith with compassion. "I suppose giving everyone an unscheduled vacation isn't as good as it sounds. And you may end up losing most of your patients."

"If they need to be evacuated, it is possible their families will keep them in those facilities," Smith agreed. The patients were the least of his problems. He couldn't run CURE out of his study at home, even with a portable device powerful enough to take on the work of the Folcroft Four. This was all happening too fast. "How long until I know something?"

"FEMA will probably want it evacuated ASAP," replied Harvey. "If they're worried about the structure, they won't want to chance subsidence bringing a wall down on some of the patients. But they should realize patients' families will need to receive adequate notice to move them. Maybe few weeks? Possibly less?"

Smith nodded numbly. He managed to smile thinly at Harvey, rise and shake his hand and watch the captain leave his office. He sank back in his chair. *One thing after another*, he thought. And an election coming up next month that might make Folcroft's cover unnecessary. He wondered if a plague would be breaking out in New York City shortly. If Remo didn't grab the virus before Jones released it, these other problems would be eclipsed.

* * *

"How'd you know about that door? And these tunnels?" Rafe called to Myron's back.

The bigger man grunted. They were picking their way carefully through the narrow passage, a breeze blowing through Rafe's shirt, drying the sweat on his back. It was some relief from the humid air, though Myron told Rafe he only left the access door behind them propped to make their getaway faster.

"Used to work here. This was my station. I must've come through here a dozen times a day."

"You had a legit job?"

Myron stopped and turned around.

"Yeah. So what? I was just a kid. Kept gettin' suspended from school so much my uncle figured it'd be better I got a job. I was under age, but he give me his last name, got me some papers or somthin'. Didn't last long."

"What'd you do?" Rafe couldn't imagine Myron as a conductor or dealing with the public.

"Track Worker. Supposed to fix stuff, do clean up. I was new, so I mostly picked shit up off the tracks and got my ass run off fetchin' and carryin' for the guys fixin' the rails and switches and shit." They came out into the empty station and Myron looked around and into the past, his eyes losing focus. "Kept gettin' hassled by the goddamn niggers and spics. Thought track jobs belonged to them, so's they could shuffle around, pretend to work and get union benefits. That only lasted till I broke some dumb Pedro's arm. He'd been ridin' me the worst and he was the biggest one. They shoulda respected me after that but of course they got me fired. Then my bastard uncle kicked me out. It was my ma's place and he wasn't my uncle but she let him kick me out, that bitch."

Myron led Rafe onto the tracks — "Don't worry, asshole, they've turned off the juice" — until they came to a door recessed in the wall. Myron climbed up on the lip of the platform, spun open the wheel that opened the door. Both men climbed through. They were in a small, square ventilation chamber, fans whirring. Rafe could feel them blowing toward an opening to a tunnel, set with lights every few yards, that curved out of sight.

Myron looked at Rafe's hand, held up to the breeze.

"Yeah, they're usually set to blow the other way. Workers set 'em to blow the damp air up to the higher station."

They both made for the tunnel. Myron put his arm out to block Rafe.

"This comes out at 168th. You're gonna stay here, let me meet this Sutton guy, make the exchange." He patted the lump in his pocket that contained one vial. "You got one a them case somethin' goes wrong, I tell 'em I got somebody gonna break the other test tube if they don't let me go with the money."

Rafe thought he could hear the sound of the blood rushing through his rapidly beating heart.

"But Myron, Sutton knows me. He'll trust me. He doesn't know you."

"I ain't arguin'."

Rafe knew Myron was setting him up. He was going to get the money, probably kill Gabe and take off. *Myron knows this place so goddamn well*, Rafe thought, *bet he knows another access tunnel and a way to get out of here without coming back this way.*

"Okay, Myron."

Rafe watched Myron head past the curve in the tunnel. He counted ten, then followed. He walked slowly, glancing up and down rapidly, his fear of tripping or his foot hitting something and clanging down the tunnel to warn Myron competing with his fear of coming face-to-face with Myron waiting just around the bend. Even being careful, every sound he made seemed magnified.

He glanced around the curve. Myron was twenty yards ahead, moving fast. He slipped out and followed, keeping close to the wall. Rafe moved a little slower; he figured the tunnel only came out in one place and he wouldn't lose Myron.

He'd just started to relax when Myron spun around, his arm coming up, and Rafe felt the impact of the bullet as he heard the sound of the gunshot. It threw him back, twisted on his side, looking at the wall of the tunnel. He lay there for a second, stunned, until he realized he was trying to suck in oxygen and failing. He could feel his limbs spasming as he fought for air. His leg hit against something solid, and he realized it was Myron, kneeling next to him now.

"Why'd you follow me, you dumb fuck. I was maybe gonna let you live. Not like that friend of yours. You think I'm dumb enough I won't know you two woulda turned on me? Thought you were so goddamn smart."

Rafe felt Myron take the bag from him. He hadn't realized he was still gripping it. He saw Myron's hands, in the middle of his rapidly tunneling vision, take the remaining tube out of the box and felt him tuck it into his shirt pocket.

"Here. You can watch this for me, in case I need to grab it fast on the way back."

Rafe heard rather than felt Myron getting back to his feet. He realized he couldn't see any more. He couldn't feel anything either, which was probably for the best. He heard Myron's laughter echoing back down the tunnel and as he felt himself heading toward a tunnel of his own, he said a prayer that he wouldn't be meeting Gabe at the end of this one.

* * *

"There he is," Remo said. He knew Chiun's head had turned at the same moment his had, toward the tracks and a big man hustling through the crowds, body tense, eyes alert and seeking. "Wait." Remo held up a hand.

Chiun had begun moving toward Sutton. He sighed impatiently. "Why do we not get this over with? It is a simple matter for us to remove the miscreant and contain the deadly plague."

"Not so simple. I don't want to take a chance with the idiot. There are too many people around if he panics. Let the deal go through. Let him think he's gotten away with it and he'll move far enough away from the virus. Then I grab him."

* * *

Myron strode rapidly through the crowds to where Sutton should be waiting near the tracks. Everything depended on doing this quickly and neatly.

He looked at the man pacing near the spot, a valise dangling from one hand. Sutton was a thin man, washed-out, his hair sparse, his posture slumped. This was gonna be easy.

"Where's the money?" growled Myron.

"Right here." Gabe Sutton's eyes searched past Myron, looking for Rafe. He saw the big man — Rafe's friend — flash a grin. He also noticed the bulge under the man's shirt, near his waist. A gun.

He kept his hands out where Myron could see him. He recognized the type: quick tempered, unstable. He'd seen enough of them in prison. Gabe held the case containing the money out toward Myron and lifted an empty hand toward the one holding a small plastic-wrapped package.

Myron snatched the case with his left hand, opening the lid and glancing at the bills inside. His lips curled up in a satisfied smirk. Gabe's hand inched closer to the other package. For a few seconds it seemed everything hung suspended. They both heard the shriek and clang of an incoming subway in the distance behind Gabe. He could feel a faint breeze now pushing at his back. He licked his lips.

"Where's Rafe? Didn't he come with you?"

Myron smirked. "He stayed behind. For insurance."

"Rafe said I was coming with you. We can go now. Give me the other package. I'll set it down here then we'll go." He'd been checking the station since he'd gotten here and hadn't spotted the scary man with the thick wrists or the fragile old Asian man the scary man seemed to defer to. He could call when they met up with Rafe; tell them where to find it.

He scanned the area once more. Maybe Rafe was nearby. Maybe he was waiting past the turnstiles or up the stairs. Instead, he spotted the man with the dead eyes heading straight for them, his slow glide seeming to eat up the distance impossibly fast.

"You think you're gonna come with us? Maybe you think you two can take me on, grab the money and — "

The other man had turned to look at what Gabe had spotted.

"Goddamn Feds," he growled.

Gabe could hear the train roaring closer to the station, heard the screech of the wheels. It didn't seem to be slowing down any. He gasped as the bigger man suddenly grabbed him in a bear hug and threw him down onto the tracks.

Chapter Ten

Remo, who had been coming up fast — but not quite fast enough — sprinted the last few yards and followed the two men down, twisting himself like a cat so he landed on the balls of his feet, twisting to check on both men.

He could see Jones up on his feet and running down the track, away from the oncoming train. But Sutton was lying groaning on the tracks as the subway car roared out from the tunnel.

Remo had a split second to decide. He had plenty of time to jump back up on the platform, but trying to drag Sutton's dead weight after him might cut it too close.

He grabbed the prone man, straightened him and pushed him against the platform edge. There was enough space under the lip for the two of them to lie flat as the cars whipped past them, bits of grit and debris stinging them.

As the end of the last car flew by, Remo rose in a single motion, holding a groaning Sutton out and tossing him neatly to the platform. Chiun was standing there, clucking at the sporadic applause from onlookers.

"Please do not encourage him," he called out. "He does not need to become more of a hopeless show-off than he already is."

"Take care of him, Little Father," Remo said. He started trotting after the receding train, calling back to Chiun over his shoulder. "Since he isn't a pancake on the tracks, I'm going to assume Jones ducked into an alcove and survived."

"You saw he had both cases?"

"Yeah, I'll have to get it away before he can break it or drop it." Remo's voice faded as his figure was swallowed by the darkness of the tunnel. Chiun looked after him for a long moment.

***

Remo slowed, glancing from side to side. Jones couldn't have gone far. He doubted the big man could keep ahead of the train very long. There was room on either side, a narrow lip with room for a man to stand. Remo dilated his pupils in the dim light, scanning carefully. Jones' white shirt would have been visible if he were anywhere nearby. Remo trotted on.

There. A recessed door just around another bend in the tunnel. Remo glanced carefully past it. He doubted Jones had the time to disappear so completely unless he'd ducked in here. He spun the wheel set into the middle of he door. Rusty hinges squealed alarmingly loud as he pushed it open.

"There goes secrecy," Remo sighed. He began running silently up the middle of the tunnel. If he couldn't surprise Jones entirely, at least he would catch up faster than the crook expected.

He slowed when he saw the figure lying on his back, hands crossed over his chest. It was obvious even at this distance that he wasn't breathing. But Remo picked out the sound of a pair of lungs working further down the tunnel. Just as he caught it, Jones appeared in the dim light ahead, his voice rasping.

"I don't know how you caught up, but you can stay where you are till I get outta here. I've got the germs and I don't care if I get sick from breaking them out. They'll get you and the fans'll blow 'em up and down the C line and the Seventh Avenue local. If I hear you followin' me, I break the glass!"

"Okay, okay," called Remo. "Take it easy." He'd have to stay invisible, trailing Jones until he started feeling safe, and then come down on him. Easy enough, if a bit annoying.

That's when the shot rang out.

Remo had noted Jones reaching for his gun. His body didn't tense; it didn't need to. A waste of energy, Chiun called it. And bad for the muscles, making them work harder than they needed to. Time slowed for Remo as he tracked the trajectory. His body didn't need to respond. Jones had fired a warning shot; the bullet wasn't going to come anywhere near him.

Then he realized the bullet was heading for the dead guy's hands. And he saw that the hands were wrapped around something thin and round and —

"Crap!" yelled Remo Williams. And he sprang forward, managed to hook the dead guy's shoes and yanked.

* * *

Myron chuckled as Remo's shout echoed up the tunnel. He ran through the HVAC room, down over the track and reached the tunnel that lead to the access door to the outside. He didn't think the Fed would be slowed down too long. Those germs were free. There was nothing the

Fed could do about that but Myron knew he'd still want to get him, maybe the bastard was hoping he'd kill Myron by giving him the disease.

He made the access door, slipped out and started to close it behind him. It swung halfway closed, then jammed. Myron pushed. The door wouldn't budge. He pushed harder. The door shot open. Myron fell heavily to the ground and stared at the Fed who was looking down on him.

Myron was glad he'd kept hold of his gun. He shot — once, twice, three times, then listened to the click of the empty magazine as the Fed stood, silent as death, in the same spot. Myron turned a dumb gaze down on the gun. Had some joker slipped some blanks in there? He threw the gun and watched the Fed's hand come up at the last second before it was going to hit him in the face, plucked the gun out of the air and tossed it over his shoulder.

"Don't need it, thank you," he said.

Myron's anger, never far away, boiled up to the surface. The sonofabitch was laughing at him. Maybe he thought he'd avoided those other germs. Myron's hand went to his pocket, slid in without hitting anything. He pulled out his hand, and then patted his pocket. Empty?

He looked up again. That damn Fed was grinning and held up the package with the test tube.

"Looking for this?" Remo asked. "When we were playing with the door earlier, I lifted it. You can't be trusted with delicate objects. You break things too much. Glass, doors, women's arms…"

Myron roared and launched himself to his feet and at Remo in one smooth motion.

Remo feinted to one side like a bullfighter, caught Myron's arm as the man fell past him, and twisted gently. The big man sank down to his knees in agony.

"I'd drag this out but even this little time I've known you seems way too long."

Remo grabbed Myron's head. A quick twist of his wrist and the big man's head snapped around 180 degrees. Remo let the body fall to the ground. He looked around. The area was quiet. Nobody had come out to investigate the shots.

"You gotta love New York," Remo said.

* * *

Remo made his way back to the 168th Street station. Chiun and

Sutton were where he had left them.

"Got him. Got the vials," Remo said. "There's another body, back in the access tunnel. Do we have to have him ID-ed?" He turned to Sutton. "Or do you know him?"

Sutton looked stricken, tears brimming in his eyes.

"Rafe — Raphael Meeks. He was — is — my kid brother. My half-brother."

"Raphael? Gabriel? Your mom was an optimist," Remo said, grimly. "C'mon, we need to get you back to Northern State."

Remo, Chiun and Sutton walked toward the street exit, Sutton mumbling in a monotone.

"I only had a month. I was gonna have a job. I was gonna look Rafe up, make sure I took care of him, the right way this time. Get him into some training; get him a legit job. I knew some of what he was up to, but when Ma died, I lost track. But I was gonna look him up." He looked at Remo. "I got some money saved. He doesn't have to go in a Potter's field. Can you tell someone, please? I want to give him a burial at least."

Remo nodded. "Sure."

Chiun looked past Sutton.

"We take him back. And where do we go next? Where are the dreaded plague germs?"

"In my pocket," Remo replied. "We'll head down to Bethesda and let them lock it up. Then home."

"Folcroft is not our home," Chiun snapped.

* * *

Harold Smith sat at his desk, finishing up some paperwork. He had gotten the call from Remo an hour ago. The virus was recovered and Remo and Chiun were on their way to deliver it. He had tonight and most likely part of tomorrow before the Masters of Sinanju returned.

He laid down his pen, sighing, feeling a rare twinge of impatience. He had tried to access the St. Maarten computers earlier. The connection was still down. Everything was waiting on the FORtabs — not just CURE, but also the special project he had spent the past few months setting up, working out the details, picking out the personnel. There was no point launching it while they were still blind.

His phone rang.

"Yes? Very good, send him up."

At last. Smith walked through his door and into the outer office. Mrs. Mikulka looked up.

"Oh, Dr. Smith," she cried. "Did you need something?"

"A delivery boy is bringing a package."

They both looked toward the door as a figure walked through. He was small, wiry, with thick black hair, wearing gray pants, blue shirt and sneakers. At first glance, he might have been mistaken for a teenager, Smith thought, until one saw the lines around his eyes and a looseness in the skin of his neck. He held out a small cardboard box.

"Do I need to sign something?" Smith asked. It was suddenly important for him to hear the man speak.

The man shook his head, pushing the box into Smith's hands. He stared into Smith's eyes, his expression solemn.

"That is not a FedEx or UPS uniform," Smith stated. "Are you from FORTEC?"

The man shook his head, pointed to his ears and mouth and shrugged.

"You are deaf?" Smith spoke slowly. The man nodded and backed out of the office. Smith looked at the package; his hands were digging into the sides.

"I do not wish to be disturbed unless it is an emergency. Goodnight."

Smith sat down at his desk. He ran his hands over the cardboard, searching for a perforation or tab. Finally he grabbed a letter opener, slitting through the tape holding the flaps closed. He opened it and reverently lifted out the contents.

At first glance, it was disappointing. The units were elongated, lozenge-shaped versions of a typical tablet. Then Smith noticed the thin metal band running around the edges of the tablets. And the surface... Smith picked one up, noting it was much lighter than the size would indicate, and ran a finger over it. It felt and looked like leather, but that was not possible. It had to be metal. He grabbed the tablet by its edges and twisted. The unit gave slightly. It was unlike any metal he had ever seen. As he opened the flap covering the screen, it powered on.

"Good afternoon, Dr. Smith." Smith recognized Germain's voice. "As you will find out, the unit recharges continuously. You will want to activate the synchronization routine first. Look at the FORtab. It will do a retinal scan and you will speak a few words in a normal tone of voice. This will bind the unit for your use only. They're both already set up as users; the first one you synchronize will become the administrator unit. The other unit will automatically become user. I'm sure you will figure out the other features as you go along. The FORtab is intuitive; it will adapt itself to however you wish to use it. Also, I received the last minute modification to your order. Everything has been taken care of. Good fortune, Dr. Smith."

"Modification?" asked Smith. "What do you mean?"

But the line was dead. Smith stared at the phone, then turned to his tablet.

Smith stared at the screen. "Synchronize."

A rapidly blinking target appeared on screen. Smith noticed it followed his eyes as he scanned the surface of the tablet. He spoke, one word. The unit blinked twice and Smith began exploring his new computer.

Epilogue

THREE WEEKS later, Smith sat in his darkened office, the light from the television bathing his face and giving it a rare appearance of color.

"Ed, can you give us an update of the electoral count?" said a voice from the screen.

Smith looked at the map on the screen. Some states showed blue, others red. A few were still white, but their numbers were shrinking.

It was still close, according to the analysts, but Smith's face was grim. According to the algorithms he had been running on his new computer, the odds were in favor of the president winning reelection. Smith had run the numbers over and over, hoping to prove them wrong. But he knew now the seemingly close race was all but over.

He had put off his decision until after the election, hoping he might make a case for CURE's survival to the next leader of the country. Even with a new president, he knew CURE's chances were slim. Smith would report his decision to cut ties with the occupant of the Oval Office and give his reasons for doing so. He knew the first question from the new president would be, "And what assurance could you give me the agency won't go rogue during my administration?"

And Smith, thinking of the chaos of the last four years, and the ever-increasing violations of the Constitution, knew that his answer would have to be, "If you violate the Constitution as well, sir, I would undertake the same action against you."

He sat in the dark long into the night. Long after the decision was made for him by the people of the United States of America.

* * *

Remo watched Chiun watch television. The Master, wearing a plain gray sleeping kimono, was sitting in lotus position five feet from the screen. One long-nailed finger stabbed viciously at the channel button. Stations flew by in one-second bursts, Chiun clucking his tongue.

"Typical white thinking. The worse the show, the more stations it is on."

"It's the election, Little Father. People are supposed to be interested in which crooks are going to be robbing them the next four years."

Chiun set the remote down. The screen showed a picture of people cheering as a white woman in dreadlocks bounced up to the podium. She was wearing a beaded buckskin dress with multiple strands of turquoise hanging around her neck. Remo stared. He was experiencing a definite sense of déjà vu.

The woman went to the podium and leaned into the microphone.

"I want to congratulate the people of the great state of Massachusetts. This election wasn't about me. It was about you. It was about your chance to make restitution for hundreds of years of white oppression of the native peoples of this land. It was about your realization of what a great journey we could embark on together, you and I. A journey where I would fix the inequalities inherent in the patriarchal system our state has been mired in for many, many moons. And where you would accept your guilt and unworthiness and agree to be guided by my wisdom without question. It is — "

The screen went dark. Chiun rose.

"Bah! I hope there is a better show on tomorrow." He headed toward his room.

Remo Williams was left staring at a blank screen. He shook his head.

"I thought it was that dumb show of Brackenrich's. She's real. God help us all."

ABOUT THE AUTHOR:

Donna Courtois was living a life of toil and drudgery, writing short stories in her spare time and enjoying reading the *Destroyer* series.

Then Warren Murphy said he was looking for short stories for a *Destroyer* fan-fiction compilation. She submitted *Bride of Sinanju* and was happy when Warren praised her first effort.

When Murphy announced another anthology, he asked Donna to contribute, and to serve as the editor. She accepted the task, and realized that what they say is true: give Murphy an inch and he takes a mile.

Donna lives deep in the wilds of Massachusetts, with a small cat that doesn't care what she writes as long as dinner is served on time.